A CASTLE TO KEEP

A Militess & Mage Novel

MONICA ENDERLE PIERCE

GOLDEN
FLOWER

STORIES THAT STAY WITH YOU

Copyright © 2017 Monica Enderle Pierce
Cover Illustration Copyright © 2017 Qistina Khalidah
Title Page Illustration Copyright © 2016 Qistina Khalidah
Developmental Editor Maia Driver
Copy Editor Mel Sanders
Cover Design by Scott Pierce
Book Design by Monica Enderle Pierce
Created with Vellum
Ebook ISBN-13: 978-0-9859761-6-3
Print ISBN-13: 978-0-9859761-7-0

A CASTLE TO KEEP

GOLDEN FLOWER

STORIES THAT STAY WITH YOU

SEATTLE, WA

MONICAENDERLEPIERCE.COM

DEDICATION

For Scott, always.

KALIX
NORTHERN WASTES
Kholodson Sea
TELEYANSK
SCHORVALA
Yasan Khot
Lake Boorsook
Chono Khot
Lake Jera
Garrison
Ballard River
Beach Camp
The Thumb
North Selga River
Floria
Tatlis
URSINUM
Drevya
The Fist
THE GREAT GREEN OCEAN
NALVIKA
The Choker
Lake Tatlis
Khara
Tatlis
Kharaton
Ayestra
The Silver Sea
Ystwyth
Ostendra
BESERA
Fayet Desert
Eskis
South Selga River
Fayet
OR-HALEE
Or-Halee Cid
Vala
Selt

"Our perceptions shape our reality." Halina's father, Ursinum's King Vernard, liked to say that after he'd lied through his smiles to bend the world to his will. But that was kings for you, always creating their own history and rewriting everyone else's. Unlike her father, Militess Halina Persinna, Margrave of Khara, favored the truth, even when it came with sharp, bloody teeth. Something it possessed in abundance lately.

She sat in a hard, high-backed seat and considered Sokos's cramped worship hall and the lies she'd been telling from one end of her holding to the other for the past month. She turned the black band on her right ring finger around and around, and contemplated how the truth was likely to bite her, sooner rather than later, right on her saddle-sore arse. She hated this game of half-truths, hated making up stories to calm frightened villagers.

Dim and smoky, the worship hall felt older than the dirt its baked bricks and trampled floor were made of. It was a gathering place dedicated to Quoregna's triad of gods — Khotyr,

Skiron, and their daughter Semele. It held relics and symbols representing birth, death, and life. The cycle, a circle, like the ring she turned on her finger. It soothed her, that warm, smooth ring. A gift from her lover. A talisman to keep her safe, made from magic and proof of his power, proof of their love. She turned it around and around.

Many citizens waited to speak to their margrave, their eager and anxious faces turning toward her, their voices rising and falling like the Silver Sea's waves breaking on Kharaton's rocky harbor walls. Her nose stung with the stench of the closed, dark hall — a miasma of sweat, grease, and wood smoke that rivaled the stink of Kharaton Castle's barracks on a summer afternoon. There was another odor in the mix, something acrid, nauseating. Fear. It oozed from pores, seeped from armpits, stank like plague and could spread just as fast. Fear was the enemy Halina had fought all across Khara.

She looked up. Skulls — human and otherwise — hung from the rafters, turned slowly, clicked and clattered, a rattling reminder of death. Thin strips of bright red ribbon fluttered between them, some holding fresh and dried flowers, pungent and sweet. Along the large room's perimeter, red baskets held bones and more flowers. Skulls for Skiron who ruled death, red for Khotyr who bled to birth the world and everything in it, and Semele's flowers to remind everyone of the beauty and sweetness of their fleet lives.

Halina felt the weight of the gods' presence in that hall, their judgment, their expectations, and the weight of their disappointment.

Or maybe that was her own.

She turned the warm, smooth, black ring.

To her right, Earl Sokos surveyed the hall. She was more than twice Halina's age and considered the gathering with pale green eyes and the bland expression of a farmer watching a flock of squabbling hens. The earl glanced at her ruler, Halina nodded, and the woman pounded the floor with a wooden staff. "Silence! All of you. Give Her Ladyship your attention." Her booming, husky voice filled the room.

Halina stood and the crowd quieted. She fought the urge to groan. Her back ached after a month spent in the saddle and in strange beds, or no bed, as she'd visited even the most remote corners of her holding. "Khara is muddy, miserable, and starving. Her citizens are dead or displaced by the spring's relentless floods. But Sokos and its neighboring villages were spared the worst of the destruction. Because of that, I've told Earl Sokos that the task falls to Kharaton and to all of you to harvest three times the normal yield this year."

Both grumbles and agreement met her statement. Halina's voice rose to silence them again. "You already have refugees. More are coming. We saw them on the roads, traveling from as far as Northu." She swept the hall with her gaze. "Feed them. House them. Put them to work in the fields. Help them forget their losses and their heartache. Aid them and aid me.

"As your margrave, it's my responsibility to help my tenants rebuild, replant, survive. I've seen such suffering during my month of travel." She looked down. Her hands were tight fists, the white bones of her knuckles pressing against her scarred skin. "Blood and bones! The destruction. Villages gone, the land scoured of all life so that not even seedlings will take." She looked up, around. "I ask for your aid. I need it. Khara needs it. This holding is mine on paper, but the land belongs to the people who farm it, the water to those who fish it."

That met with more grumbling, more nodding, more heads shaking. They weren't buying her brave face. Khara was hurting and they looked to their margrave to ease the pain.

She was trying; the gods knew she was. But there was no quick fix for her march's suffering.

The earl stood. "Sokos will help. Our soil is rich and our people are strong. We'll do as you ask, Margrave Khara, because you've always come to our aid when we've needed you."

"And I always will." Halina offered her hands. Earl Sokos clasped them, her grip's strength belying the woman's wrinkled face. "Thank you," Halina said.

"Where's the aid Tatlis promised us?" a man shouted and others repeated the question.

"King Vernard," she said, her voice rising above them, the voice of a field commander who knew how to be heard over the clash and screams of war, "*our* king, has sent his soldiers elsewhere, but his money has paid for food, fodder, tools, clothes." It was a lie. Tatlis had sent nothing and Halina had emptied Kharaton's treasury to cover her struggling people's needs, as well as ill-timed, long-overdue renovations to her castle. "But, more importantly, Khara cares for her own. We always have. We always will."

"Because we don't matter to the fat, lazy arsehole ruling Ursinum," someone else said, perhaps a bit louder than he'd intended.

The moment that followed was filled with nervous feet shuffling, throats clearing, the gentle creak of the bones hanging overhead, the crackle and pop of damp wood on the fire.

Halina knew who said it, the big, blond man with the growing space around him. She waved him forward. A smile tugged at her lips as her head slowly tilted to the side. The man stepped up. At least he had the bollocks not to cower and hide. "You know that fat, lazy arsehole is my father, right?" she said.

He folded muscled arms over a barrel chest. "Yes, Your Ladyship, and not half the leader you are." Voices raised in agreement.

Halina fought the urge to gut the loyal idiot. Ambivalent as she felt about her father-king, and she'd first tried to kill him when she was only a child, she couldn't let such a statement pass unaddressed. That kind of sentiment got people, like her, executed for treason. "Can't say I agree with you, having followed him into many battles. He's a good king, neither fat nor lazy. But, yes, bit of an arsehole." That got a few laughs and a spreading grin from the fellow until she leaned forward and said, "But only I'm allowed to say that." His smile failed. "The king owns the march and everything you see. He charged me with protecting it. I, in turn, tasked you with enriching it. We work together. And we *never forget* who rules us all."

The earl's staff snapped up, caught the fellow's chin, and sent him sprawling. "We don't insult the man who lets us live here," she snarled. At her nod, soldiers dragged him from the hall. "A night in the stocks should help him remember respect." She remained standing, glaring, challenging her villagers as Halina sat. "Anyone else want to insult King Vernard?" When no one came forward, Earl Sokos lowered her staff and returned her attention to Halina.

"I've come not just to ask for your help, but to offer my assistance. What grievances have you to place in my hands?" she asked the peasants, traditional words she'd spoken year after year, in village after village since she'd become Khara's margrave.

A man and woman approached the dais. He held his

yellow knit cap in shaking hands and she stared at Halina with haunted eyes.

"How can your margrave be of service to you?" Halina asked. What fresh misery would they drop in her lap?

"Our children are dead," the man replied.

She cringed inwardly but let no emotion show on her face. Khara's people needed strength and reassurance from their margrave, not tears. "I'm grieved to hear that. It's a terrible sorrow to lose a child. What aid may I offer to your family in this matter?"

He shook his head. "Not just my family, Your Ladyship." With his cap he indicated the men and women crowding the hall. "All our children."

Halina's blue gaze swept the crowd. They were too numerous to have come from the same village. "All of you have lost children?" The majority nodded in unison with murmured assent. "But Sokos was spared the worst of the flooding." She looked to the silver-haired earl for confirmation.

"That's correct, Margrave," Earl Sokos said. Her thin brows furrowed into a straight line, her knuckles showed hard and white on the hand that gripped her staff. "This is the first I'm hearing of these deaths." Halina heard worry in the woman's voice.

From all quarters of the hall a single, chilling whisper spread. "Shrikers."

Halina raised her hands to quiet the crowd. "Was there illness?"

"No, Your Ladyship," answered the man.

"What about among the livestock, the fowl, the wild animals? Any unexplained deaths?"

Heads shook all around.

Once again, the whisper spread. "Shrikers."

"Shrikers took their souls," a woman shouted from the back of the room and, as if she'd broken some unspoken taboo, calls of confirmation echoed in the great hall.

"Yes! Shrikers."

"It was Skiron's beasts, all right, Your Ladyship."

"Damnable shrikers and the necromancer that brought them."

This was the plague of fear that Halina sought to curtail, one as virulent as the unrest the man's complaints about the king would've sown.

She leaned forward. "Why do you blame creatures so rare they're almost myth?"

"I heard dogs outside the house that night," the man's wife replied.

"Me, too, Your Ladyship."

More agreement echoed through the hall.

Halina said, "A group of dogs isn't the same as Skiron's soul collectors. Perhaps there's a roaming pack of feral curs."

"No!"

"It's shrikers!"

"They weren't normal dogs, Margrave Khara," the woman called over the shouts. "Skiron's punishing us."

"My husband was taken too," another woman added. "He tried to stop it from stealing my daughter's soul. The beast tore him apart but left Garia's body untouched."

"My mother always said if you heard one of Skiron's dogs that meant his necromancer was nearby and you'd soon be dead."

Halina suppressed a sigh. "The god's necromancer *is* nearby." She pointed eastward and added, "He's been your neighbor for two decades. But I assure you, he didn't raise Skiron's beasts to take your children."

"How do you know?" an old man shouted.

Halina kept her voice steady as she replied, "Because the Sun Mage hasn't done it before. Why would he do so now?"

"Necromancers can't be trusted!"

"He wants us dead!"

"Whose children will be next?"

Halina stood at that last question. Her chair tipped back and thudded against the raised wooden dais. Silence smothered the crowd and she stepped down from the platform. The man and his wife who'd raised the issue shrank from her as she approached, but their peers hemmed them in. She stopped before them. She looked to the husband, who swallowed and twisted his cap tighter. She looked to his wife. The woman met her gaze, eyes wide and fearful, lower lip trapped between her yellowed teeth.

Halina gripped his shoulder and took her hand. She spoke to them, but her words were for all her people. "I don't know what's befallen your children. Had I been there the night of the attack I would've fought to my death to protect them." Her voice grew louder until it filled the hall. "Now, I will do all that I can to discover who or what is causing these deaths and stop it."

"Even if your lover was the one who killed them?" a man called from the anonymity of the crowd.

So. News of her affair with Gethen had traveled fast and far.

A rising mutter filled the room in the wake of that fleet piece of gossip.

She turned and caught the earl's eye. The woman thudded her wooden staff and called for quiet again as Halina retook the dais. She remained standing until silence muffled the crowd.

No point hiding the truth; it had a way of always making itself known.

"I will cut down anyone who threatens Khara's children." She scanned the faces from one end of the hall to the other, front to back and across the middle. Halina lifted her chin as her hand gripped her sword hilt. "*Anyone*. Without hesitation."

As that reply was absorbed, she turned toward the corner of the dais and the brawny, fair-haired soldier scowling there. "Captain Thaksin, I'm charging you with recording the circumstances of these attacks and gathering evidence of any illness among livestock or wild animals." She faced her citizens. "You know and trust the captain of my guard. Furnish him with all the particulars of your loved ones' deaths, no matter how insignificant they may seem. The smallest detail may hold the very clue that's needed to solve this mystery."

The captain of her guard bowed. "We'll hunt down the beasts, Your Ladyship. I promise you that." He pointed toward the doors. "Proceed back to the bailey. I'll join you shortly to record your complaints."

As the people shuffled toward the great hall's double doors, Halina gestured for him to approach. "What do you think?"

"It's some illness making dogs vicious."

She nodded. Beside her, Earl Sokos said, "I agree."

Halina turned to the woman. "Send soldiers to the villages in and around Sokos. Impress upon them the importance of the details and clear information. And make certain that at least one in each group can write. I'll take the information back to Kharaton and will ask the Sun Mage to review it."

Earl Sokos didn't even blink at that. "Whatever you require, Your Ladyship." If she had an opinion — favorable or not — of

Halina's relationship with Gethen of Ranith, she was smart enough to keep it behind her teeth.

Thaksin, however, was not. "I can handle this investigation without that mage's aid, Your Ladyship."

"Gethen knows the ways of Skiron. You don't." Halina's steely tone brooked no argument. "Unless you're a necromancer unbeknownst to me, Captain."

"But—"

Halina leaned forward, her voice a quiet snarl. "Don't let jealousy compromise your position."

He scowled, jaw working like he was chewing a curse and dark green eyes angry, then he jerked a nod, stepped back, and summoned two pages. A few words exchanged and the youngsters scurried off for parchment, quills, and ink as Thaksin stalked through the hastily parting crowd toward the hall doors.

Halina swallowed a few choice words of her own rather than hurl them at his back and ignored her earl's keen gaze. A sizeable crowd remained in the hall and she closed her eyes. She had many more decisions to render and only two days to do so. She was more tired than she remembered being in the seven years since the War of the Winds ended. Thak's jealousy wasn't helping.

Over the past eight months, Khara had been laid to waste by dark magic and none of her strength or skill with a sword could undo the destruction of a bitter winter and a brutal spring. Yet she'd sold that lie in each village on this trip — that she, as Khara's margrave, the daughter of King Vernard, and the Red Blade of Or-Halee, could fix her citizens' problems and ease their woes. In truth, she was as impotent as a puppet. And the unexpected news of deaths in Sokos hinted at more evils.

At that moment, more than anything, Halina wanted to be home. But she was dutiful, Gethen said to a fault. She opened her eyes. Considering the number of villagers still waiting to speak with their margrave and the relentless ache in her back and arse, he might be right.

"Your Ladyship?"

Halina looked up into the earl's careworn face. "Forgive me. I was distracted by the tragedy of so many lost children."

Earl Sokos inclined her head. "Of course, Margrave. The news weighs heavily upon us all." Indeed, it weighed down the older woman's voice and shoulders in a way Halina didn't recall seeing before. A woman of great strength, Jocasta Sokos had wrested the earldom from her incompetent brother when she was only twenty-one. Thirty-three years later, she still garnered solemn respect from Khara's lords, ladies, and the margrave most of all.

Halina gripped the woman's hand. "Thank you for supporting me. It holds more import to me than you know, Jocasta."

The earl squeezed her fingers. "You will always have my support and respect, Your Ladyship."

Halina nodded, drew herself up, and gazed out at the crowd, her spine straight, her expression schooled. "Who speaks next?"

Fluffy clouds scudded across the blue sky. A gentle breeze swayed the trees all around. It carried a mixture of scents: fresh-turned earth, rotting vegetation, stagnant water, burning corpses. Green grass shoots pushed through mud and debris on either side of the road. Halina and her soldiers were heading home. The sun was high and hot. Sweat trickled down her back and between her breasts. She wore gray leather, chain mail, and plate armor. Leather creaked, metal clanked, the horses snorted, and Khara's gold-and-blue banners snapped at the front and rear of their line. Riding alone yet surrounded by a dozen devoted militairs, Halina's thoughts were on Gethen, and on more than a dozen dead children as she contemplated rumors, death, and their implications for her future.

She peered up at the blazing sun. What had happened to Sokos's children? Shrikers were an impossibility. She was damned sure she'd have noticed if the God of Death had come knocking on Khara's door. Gethen was the only necromancer in Quoregna's four kingdoms powerful enough to summon and control such beasts. Halina was certain that he wouldn't, he hadn't, and he had no reason to do so.

"Blood and bones," she muttered. The rumors and news would reach Tatlis. The Sun Mage already engendered suspicion. He was a Beseran necromancer in Ursinum — a stranger in their kingdom, a man in service to Skiron who'd refused to give fealty to King Vernard. This would be one more reason, on a list of many, for her father to block her marriage to Gethen. The gods knew he could afford to prevent their union. He'd thrown her into every bargain he'd made since she was knee-high to a weed.

I love you. She mouthed the words. They still felt strange on her tongue, like a foreign language she'd heard but never spoken yet was beginning to understand. Gethen's devotion reminded her that she was more than a soldier, a servant, a sword for her king. He challenged her to be greater, to question, and to refuse. "Bollocky bollocks." She'd sworn to her people that she'd kill him if he'd brought the shrikers. Khotyr take her if the king held her to that. Gods forbid she be forced to choose between her lover and her king.

She was pulled from her troubled thoughts as Thaksin reined his horse back until he rode beside her, so close his left leg brushed hers in the right stirrup. Ahead was the crossroad that would take him and two Sokosian soldiers to a cluster of outlying fishing villages. The other road took Halina and the rest of her militairs home.

"So. Shrikers." He looked askance at her, blond brows arching over forest green eyes and a rugged, scarred face. Thaksin was twice her age and well below her rank, but he was a powerful ally, on the battlefield and off.

"What about them?" She wiped sweat from her brow, scanning the northwest road and the Valmerian Plain. Farms dotted the countryside, some intact, many in ruins being rebuilt, their people struggling to clear gravel, boulders, and the splinters of obliterated villages from their fields. Fertile soil lay buried beneath many feet of flood debris.

"Why do you think the deaths are attributed to them?"

"That's obvious. The people want an explanation for their suffering. The offerings to the gods aren't working. They need something to blame and necromancy is a convenient whipping boy." Halina frowned at her unfortunate metaphor and added, "Which worries me."

"You told them it wasn't the mage's doing." Thaksin glanced over his shoulder, suspicion in his narrowed eyes. Magod, Gethen's groundsman, rode in line behind Halina; she was training the younger man to fight.

"We both know what I say and what others think are two different things." She considered her captain, certain he was thinking it, too. Thinking that Gethen of Ranith was Skiron's servant and all of Khara's problems stemmed from his battle with the Rime Witch eight months prior.

"With good reason," he muttered.

"Not that horseshit about Gethen again, Thak. I won't entertain your paranoid theories."

"You'll keep hearing them from me until they finally get through your thick skull, Halina. What man murders the woman he claims to love?" He grabbed her arm. "One who lies. One who's using you."

She pulled free and said through clenched teeth, "You heard the full story." This was a too-familiar argument.

"And I still say that's horseshit. He brought you back from the edge of death to buy your trust."

Halina urged her horse ahead and, for a few moments, rode with only her irritation for company.

But soon Thaksin was beside her again. "Will you inform King Vernard?"

"Of what?" she snapped.

"The children's deaths, Margrave."

She scowled as mud splattered her horse's chest and hit her cheek. "No." She wiped it with an equally muddy sleeve. The track was alternately muck, gravel, and baked clay; rutted, ruined, and slow-going.

"But your people—"

"Must provide evidence if they want me to tell the king that children's souls are being stolen by enormous, maggot-infested, undead dogs."

Thaksin sucked his teeth. "Rumors travel fast and make their own road unless you direct them."

"Which is why I won't direct this one into my father's face." This conversation was going exactly where she didn't want it to go.

"Speaking as your captain and a man who *truly* loves you, be careful, Halina. If the shrikers really are killing again that necromancer's head will be the first removed by His Majesty's blade."

She didn't appreciate his emphasis on truly. "Gethen's guilty of nothing and there are no shrikers."

"No? Just like he *accidentally* gutted you last winter?" He touched her thigh, an intimacy she once would've welcomed. "How can you be sure those beasts aren't back?"

She couldn't and he knew it. She smacked the captain's too-friendly fingers away. Her warhorse Abelard tossed his head as she pulled him to a stop, her hand heavy on the bit. She immediately eased off on the reins.

Thaksin dropped his chin and looked at her from beneath his brows. "I don't want to see you made guilty by association."

"Are you speaking as my captain? Or as my ex-lover?"

His next question turned the heads of the soldiers around them. "Are you asking as my margrave or the Sun Mage's plaything?"

He didn't try to dodge her gauntleted fist. It smashed his mouth and Thaksin's head whipped to the side. He recovered and leaned over, spat blood in the dirt then faced his liege.

Halina pulled the misericord she kept in a sheath upon her left vambrace. She stuck it under his chin and said loudly enough for all to hear, "Your only concern is discovering the real cause of these deaths as quickly as possible. I don't need my king or my villagers calling for the Sun Mage's blood. And I won't have you spreading disloyalty because I don't spread my legs for you anymore. Make me doubt you, Captain, and you'll be eating your bollocks for breakfast. Do you understand?"

His swelling lips stretched into a bloody smile. "Of course, Your Ladyship." He nudged his horse forward to join the

Sokosians waiting at the crossroads. With a grudging glance and a sharp nod for her, he took the path toward the sea while the remainder of the Kharaton contingent turned northwest.

Halina contemplated Thaksin's wide, armored back and his suspicions as he rode away. Like many of her soldiers, he'd often enjoyed her affections before she'd taken Gethen as her only lover. But Thak's resentment at being barred from her bed lingered. Halina sighed. He was a fine man and an outstanding captain. They'd always had an easy, honest relationship, which she hoped to continue. But only if he yanked the stick out of his arse and accepted that the man she planned to make her husband wasn't him.

Gethen was the former crown prince of Besera and Quoregna's most powerful mage. But more than being her peer, he was her equal. Thaksin was not; he was the son of a pikeman and as loyal a soldier as she could hope for, but not a husband for a margrave. And not a man whose love she'd ever returned. There'd been a time when he'd understood that.

Magod pulled his horse abreast of hers as she nudged Abelard forward. "Still doesn't trust my master?" he asked, his clipped Ayestran dialect making her smile.

"No." She leaned a little closer and lowered her voice. "Steer clear of him when he returns to Kharaton. You shouldn't receive the brunt of his jealousy as a proxy for Gethen, but Thak's a volatile man."

Magod nodded. "Don't want to be on the captain's bad side."

"It's a dangerous place." She returned her attention to the ragged landscape, the unexplained deaths, and that laden sentence: *I love you.* Who knew three small words could so utterly change how she saw her world and everyone in it?

CHAPTER 2

"Margrave Khara approaches the Northeast Gate!" The shout traveled from guard to guard stationed atop the wall that protected the village of Kharaton, an echo gaining volume as it approached Kharaton Castle.

Gethen's gaze followed the wall, but he couldn't see the riders from his position on the castle's ramparts. As he strode toward the North Tower for a better vantage, furtive glances and whispers followed him. With his dark hair close-cropped on the sides and left longer on the top in the style of his homeland's men, he stood out among Ursinum's fair- and fiery-haired populace. Though he was a sorcerer and once trained to be a king, Gethen eschewed the traditional robes and ostentation of his peers for dark trouzes, a light, hooded tunic, and a leather travel brigandine.

Masons, carpenters, and soldiers vied for space atop the castle. The keep's blue-shingled roof was open to the sky and workers, moving with the confidence of rats in walls, clambered across wooden scaffolding erected inside and outside the building. They were doubling the height of the four-story central tower and reinforcing the crumbling foundation and walls of its long barracks.

"The margrave approaches!" echoed the lookout in the narrow stone tower atop the castle's guardhouse.

Rectangular with round, four-story towers at each corner, Kharaton Castle was Ursinum's easternmost stronghold. The large bailey accommodated gardens, a stockyard, and two wells. The building's massive stone taluses sloped away from the tops of the outer walls to plunge into Kharaton's deep harbor, moss-slick and topped with machicolations and murder holes.

"Raise the gates!" Soldiers relayed the message along the curtain walls that fronted the castle, a first set of defenses.

An adolescent apprentice glanced up as Gethen's long shadow fell across her. The girl's eyes widened and she offered a hasty curtsy then scuttled from his path, a mouse caught in a hawk's gaze. She yelped as her wooden bucket, filled with broken masonry, barked her shins.

He scowled. Shadows winked across his path. The sun was lowering and black-and-white sea crows circled to land upon the west-facing Captain's Tower. He returned to scanning the walled village for the movement of riders.

"Look lively and mind your posts!"

The long bailey below him became a hive of activity as servants rushed to prepare for their lady's homecoming.

"Lower the bridges!"

Beyond Kharaton was the vast Valmerian Plain, a sea of waving green grass and brownish-black swaths of mud and flood debris. Past the plains, the distant spires of the Valmerian Mountains dominated the skyline — green on their flanks and frosted white year-round at their peaks. Surmount the mountain passes and he'd reach Tatlis, the great city that was the capital of Ursinum and the seat of the Persinna family — Halina's family.

"Prepare to welcome Margrave Khara!"

To Gethen's back, ships bobbed on the tide within the shelter of Kharaton Harbor's stone seawalls, their white sails flapping and slapping with the late afternoon breeze. Beyond them was the open expanse of the Silver Sea, and on the distant opposite shore rose the purple towering mountains of his homeland Besera.

He continued to scan the village and was rewarded with a flash of sunlight on metal, then gold and blue, and a glimpse of auburn hair that quickened his pulse. His lips curved into a smile that Halina surely would've labeled wolfish.

"Raise the portcullises!"

The iron lattice gates that protected the castle from intruders rattled and squealed as soldiers cranked them upward. There were two portcullises, one mid-span within the footbridge barbican and the second within the shadows of the castle's guardhouse.

"Lower the bridges!" The two wooden drawbridges rattled and thudded into place between the portcullises, connecting Kharaton Castle to the village.

"Welcome home, Lady Khara!"

Gethen lengthened his stride as soldiers up and down the parapets repeated the message, a rolling wave of excitement.

Hooves clattered and metal jangled as Militess Halina and her company of soldiers rode across the wooden drawbridges. Her auburn hair caught the sun and drew Gethen's eye. She wore leather and armor. But even from the castle's ramparts, mud was obvious on her trouzes and boots and on her buckskin gelding's tan belly and flanks. Their travels hadn't been easy.

He strode across a covered parapet toward the guardhouse. Soldiers bowed their heads as he passed, but he felt the dagger prick of their gazes between his shoulder blades. Their fear was a sure path to conflict.

He'd only traveled to Kharaton Castle from his Ranith Citadel that afternoon in anticipation of Halina's return. When she was away, he made sure he was too, preferring his hermitic life to the suspicion and temptation that came with being among Kharaton's populace.

"Welcome home, my love," he murmured. His reunion with Halina would be more than just sweet. Already with the sight of her, warmth suffused his chest and spread outward to reach his limbs and invigorate him. Within her presence laughter sounded lighter to his ears, mead tasted sweeter on his tongue, and the sun warmed his skin and shed more light into the dark corners of his world. Halina had become vital to Gethen, a presence he craved, a relief he sought. She eased the yearning he felt for the power of souls, the itch to murder the men around him and steal the spark that animated them, a spark that could push him to dizzying heights of necromantic power. It was an urge he'd easily kept at bay as the Shadow Mage but now, as the Sun Mage, found increasingly insistent.

He reached the flat roof of the guardhouse as her horse Abelard cleared the barbican's shadows and emerged into the open space of the north bailey. A stable hand captured the gelding's black bridle and Halina dismounted. Around her, the other soldiers and Magod followed suit. Conspicuously absent was Captain Thaksin, much to Gethen's pleasure. The man was a pillock, a fiercely loyal, fiercely jealous pillock who'd made the mistake of falling in love with his margrave.

Eugen, the steward of her castle and lands, emerged from the central keep. "Welcome home, Margrave," he called as he wove around the masons and carpenters plying their trade within the bailey. Trim and hard as an ax head, he joined His Ladyship, his bald pate reflecting the late afternoon light. He was young to have lost his hair, a reminder of the demands that came with his position over Kharaton Castle's daily operations; demands he fulfilled with quiet authority and absolute loyalty.

"It's good to be home, Eugen." She pressed her thumbs against her lower back, underneath the edge of her plate armor, as she surveyed the bailey.

Gethen rested his arms on the stone battlement and leaned forward to gaze down on her. "Looking for something, Militess?"

Halina's gaze traveled up to meet his. "Ah, yes, the freeloading mage. Have you delivered the imperial tokay you promised me?"

"Two barrels, Margrave Khara."

"Only two?" she scoffed.

Gethen smirked. She knew his mead was a slow brew — slower now that Magod was training with Kharaton's soldiers — and this hadn't been a good year for honey. "Forgive me for disappointing you, Your Ladyship."

A page took Halina's demi-gauntlets and gloves as she stripped them off, then received her sword and scabbard. "My forgiveness will be earned with the quality of your mead, Sun Mage." She turned and crossed the crowded bailey toward the keep with Eugen at her side. As her soldiers and the stable hands led the horses into the stockyard, the steward pointed out finished stonework and wooden beams piled around the castle, the men making mortar beneath a canopy, tile makers carefully stacking hundreds of newly-fired blue roof tiles.

A smile tugged at Gethen's lips. He nodded as Magod

raised his hand in greeting, then he turned from the battlement and continued his stroll along the rampart, into the northern watchtower, and down its stone spiral staircase to the stockyard. From there he entered the warmth and noise of the kitchen. He paused to sniff, appreciating the delicious aroma of the crusty brown bread a servant was smearing with pale yellow butter and the sweet tang of fresh sunberries. But Gethen turned away from the spits that sizzled and popped with fat dripping from two plucked chickens. He ate neither meat nor fish.

He wove around the cook and her staff, ignoring her complaints.

"Go on! Get those dishes up to the Margrave's room, nimwits." She ladled soup into a deep bowl and added, "You'd think you'd never seen Lord Rhyshis before with the way you gawk."

Only Halina's cook and her steward called him Lord Rhyshis. Most of the servants called him Master Gethen or Master Sorcerer. Or *that necromancer* when they thought he wasn't listening.

He descended into the undercroft, which had been carved from Kharaton Castle's bedrock foundation and housed the cold storage and the treasury. Abutting the storage areas were the crypt and the dungeon, their locked doors a dark reminder of the parts of the castle that no one wanted to visit. Cool year-round, the only light came from heavily barred windows set high into the pale stone walls. There were wall-mounts for torches, but the amber ball of mage fire that Gethen summoned to float just above his head was lighting enough.

"Careful with those placements," a man said, his voice echoing off the stone.

"I am, I am, Trefor. I'm not a dolt."

A group of construction workers labored around one of the massive stone columns that underpinned the castle. They'd erected wooden stanchions around the supports and had brought in stone to widen all of them, reinforcement to handle the increased weight of the heightened keep.

"No, but you are an idiot," one of the men replied and the group's laughter was lost to the knock and thud of hammers, the ring of steel on stone.

They were doing much the same kind of work beneath the gallery stretching from the South Tower to the western Captain's Tower. The wing faced the village and offered quick access to the castle's gatehouse, barbicans, and curtain walls. It housed Halina's officers and soldiers, but the outer wall was unstable, the floor joists rotten. During reconstruction, all the castle's militairs and soldiers temporarily occupied tents outside the curtain walls in a causeway usually reserved for spillover from the village market.

Gethen reached the wine cellar unseen. He didn't have a key, but that rarely stopped him. A brief murmured incantation and a touch had the door unlocked and open. He decanted two bottles of the honey wine Halina had requested, closed and locked the door, and ascended to the servant passage — a hallway that bisected the length of the castle, permitting the staff quick access to the central keep and various private rooms in the outer perimeter, including Halina's spacious eastern apartment.

Maids and servants scuttled past him bearing food and table settings, many buckets of steaming, sloshing water for Her Ladyship's bath, and kindling for the hearths in her bedchamber, bathing room, parlor, and study.

The militess's return suffused the castle with the pulse of her blood magic. The quiet indolence that had filled the vacuum created by her absence had ended with the return of the woman who was Kharaton's heart. Like bees growing warm with the sun, Halina's servants and staff had recalled their purpose and launched from their hive in service to their ruler.

Gethen reached the dark, narrow stairs that led from the lower passage to the fourth floor landing. Halina's private apartment occupied the top floor between the North Tower and the Weather Tower and overlooked the harbor and the Silver Sea. He paused at the first floor as her throaty voice carried to him from within the keep's great hall.

She stood at the center of the cavernous space beside the wooden platform that carried workers and materials to and from the ever-growing tower and its scaffolding. "As long as you're on time and within budget, Cadoc, you can get bird crap, bat shit, and dust everywhere. I only care about that hole in the roof being closed before fall dumps rain and snow on our heads."

"We're making good progress, Your Ladyship," the head mason replied. "We'll have the fifth floor walled and roofed by summer's end." A wiry Beseran man with blue-black hair and dark freckles, Cadoc stood as high as Halina's nose and had a habit of rising on his toes. While nervous around the margrave, he'd proven a wonder at redesigning and overseeing the complexities of deconstructing five levels of the castle, reinforcing them with new columns from the undercroft up, and extending the height of the massive stone structure. No surprise that; he'd presented impressive credentials, including a letter of recommendation from the steward of Ystwyth Castle, the home of Gethen's Beseran brother King Zelal.

Halina started across the hall. "Excellent, that's all I need to hear. Eugen, what news do you have for me?"

Lining up behind Gethen, servants shifted from foot to

foot. They couldn't squeeze past him on the narrow stairs and none had the guts to ask him to move. He glanced over his shoulder then continued upward. With a flick of his wrist, he launched a ball of mage fire overhead and allowed it to stretch the length of the stairwell, filling the space with its warm glow. Murmurs of thanks and awe followed in his wake as the parade of servants resumed, led by Quoregna's Sun Mage.

Reaching the top floor, he passed through the iron-banded double doors that separated the keep from Halina's personal apartment, strode the narrow hallway that accessed all its rooms, and entered the bedchamber. A fire roared on the stone hearth, two servants were setting out food on a table before it, and a copper-hued surcoat lay across the canopied black oak bed. More servants moved past him into the bathing room and the study. One fussed over the bed curtains, another stacked wood in the firewood basket, a third mopped water that his compatriots spilled as they traipsed through the room to fill the tub.

"Where's Her Ladyship's green kirtle, Vi?" Philippa, Halina's only lady-in-waiting, called from the depths of her margrave's gown room.

"You put it aside because the hem was torn, Lady Philippa." Halina's slight, dark-eyed chambermaid Vika Kaleeda emerged from the bathing room, looked up, and squeaked as she nearly walked into Gethen. "Master Gethen! I didn't know you'd returned." She dipped into a deep curtsy then straightened and scuttled toward the bed. A native of Or-Halee, she'd come to Kharaton Castle with Halina after the Battle of Gurvan-Sum. Though she was the fourth daughter of Mahish, chief of the Dargani, she was merely a chambermaid here.

Philippa appeared in the doorway. "Well, dark blue looks better with that gown anyway." Her fair brows arched as she spied him. "So you're back, Master Mage. I suppose that's testament to a heart's folly."

"Or resolve," he replied as he handed the bottles of mead to Vi and nodded toward the table before the fireplace. "It's always such a pleasure to see you, Philippa." He curled his lip at the woman.

She sniffed, offered him a sidelong look, and returned her attention to Her Ladyship's clothes. She was a handsome woman, a few inches shorter than her mistress, a few years older, too, with green eyes, a hawk's sharp gaze, and an even sharper mind. She withstood Halina's formidable personality with the stern grace of an oak in high winds, bending so she didn't break and occasionally snapping back. She was King Vernard's choice to wait on the margrave, thus split her loyalties between father and daughter, an unenviable position.

Halina entered the bedchamber and surveyed the hurry-scurry of her staff. She offered a warm smile to Vi and Philippa, squeezing the lady-in-waiting's arm and murmuring her thanks. Her gaze went from the mead to Gethen. "Eugen hates it when you pilfer from the wine cellar."

He smiled. "Eugen is over-keen on his job."

"Maybe so, but I'm subject to his spleen when you step on his toes. And his tongue's just a little sharper than the dagger he keeps in his boot." She tossed an unopened letter on the table then surveyed the clothes and food that had been prepared for her. "Thank you, all," she said to her servants. "You may leave." They curtsied, and bowed, and filed past her as she gazed at him. Her hands hung at her sides. And her braids had come loose, again.

He moved to stand before her as Philippa, last to leave, closed the door. He brushed her auburn curls back from her face. "Your hair's lighter and muddier." With even the lightest touch, heat surged from his fingers to his brain and quickened his heart.

Her blue eyes held him prisoner. She reached up and traced the dark circles that rimmed his eyes. "You look tired." Her touch left a trail of heat and stoked his desire.

"I don't sleep well when you're away from me." He captured her fingers and brought them to his lips, fueling the passion they shared to burn hotter, higher. His voice thickened. "You smell like horses and sweaty soldiers."

Her eyes darkened with desire. "I only cuddled Abelard while I was away."

"Really? I tupped every dock trollop I could find."

Halina laughed. "Liar." But her smile disappeared and she touched his lips. "I missed your magic, Mage."

Gethen cupped her jaw. He tilted her head back. "And I missed yours, Militess." She opened her mouth as if to say more but he stole her words with a slow, soft kiss that she deepened as she shoved her hands into his hair and pulled him against her. Gethen grunted. She still wore her plate armor and it was cold and hard against his ribs.

Halina released him and began tugging at the buckles that held her vambraces around her forearms. "Feels like a cage."

"Let me do it." He caught her hand and arm and she surrendered to his nimble fingers. He quickly removed the vambraces, the metal pauldrons that protected her shoulders, and the tassets that protected her hips. He fingered the raised sol avuus — the winged sun symbol — that adorned the front and back of her body armor before that, too, came off. "Is Magod progressing?" he asked.

Halina sighed as he unbuckled and lifted her chain mail shirt off next. "I forget how heavy all of that is until it's off." She groaned as he removed the gray leather tabard that she wore between the armor and over her clothes. "Magod will only ever be adequate with a sword. However, he's quite terrifying with a battle ax."

"As you predicted," he replied.

"As I predicted."

The shift and trouzes she wore were stained with sweat and dirt from days of riding. She bore a collar and cuffs made of grime, and when he removed her boots, he revealed brown stockings that had once been white.

"All was uneventful?" he asked.

Halina stared at him for a long moment, a frown creasing the dirt on her forehead, then she shook her head and replied, "All was muddy."

"What's wrong?" he asked slowly.

She avoided his question. "I'm so filthy I could grow weeds." She padded into the bathing room, stripping down to bare skin and trailing clothes behind her. She climbed into the sheet-lined, wooden tub and submerged in the liminth-scented water.

Desire hummed through him and obliterated his will to pursue the question. Her graceful body was strong and muscular. She didn't hide or make excuses for the scars and halved fingers that revealed her soldier's life. She'd fought her way across every major battlefield during the War of the Winds and her scars proved it.

She surfaced and shook water from her hair. "Don't stand there gawking." She pointed at the soap and towels upon a stand by the bathing room door. "Let's have some of that tokay while you scrub my back."

He bowed then grabbed the bottle and two glasses. "You won't be disappointed." The letter's black wax seal caught his attention. It bore her father's bear symbol. "Ah, the monthly threat from His Majesty." He poured the mead and served her.

"I'm in no hurry to read it." Halina took the glass, savored her first sip, and closed her eyes. "Gods, that is so good." He raised his glass in a toast to her when she looked at him again. "All I drank on the road was bracket, and it was swill." She savored another sip. "This is liquid joy."

Gethen laughed and toed off his boots. "Am I forgiven?" He stripped off his stockings and removed his belt and brigandine.

"For bringing only two barrels? Absolutely not. Two are not enough." She rested her arms on the edge of the tub, her chin upon them, and closed her eyes.

Gethen stripped, grabbed the bar of honey soap, and climbed into the tub. He scooped water over her back and soaped her skin. Every stroke sent a bolt of lust through him and even now, more than half-a-year since they'd first touched, she gasped and her skin heated beneath his fingers.

His love for Halina was born of equal parts desire and respect. Her mother was a Beseran concubine, her father was the king of Ursinum. Freckles covered her face, shoulders, back, and breasts — proof of her bastard heritage — and she was considered homely by the standards of the ladies of the Ursinum court at Tatlis where she'd grown up. But Halina was the most beautiful, most powerful woman Gethen had ever held. Though most of her scars were silver with age, a few remained pink, and one in particular he avoided completely. It was a short, straight exit wound he'd given to her, along with its longer mate above her navel, and it still horrified him.

Lust held in check, Gethen finished her back, shoulders, and arse. "Lean back and I'll wash your hair." Halina finished her mead and obeyed, murmuring appreciatively as he worked the soap through her curls.

"Why did I leave?" she asked with a sigh.

"Because you're a diligent lord to your tenants."

"Oh, yes. Perhaps I should rethink that."

"Hand?"

She raised her palm and he placed the soap cake on it, then he slid his fingers into her soapy hair. "You have the most beautiful hair, Halina." Gethen massaged her scalp from crown to nape and down her neck to her shoulders. The warmth of their touch sparked the sun magic within him, and his skin burned as she absently stroked his thigh and continued the quiet, appreciative noises in the back of her throat. He grabbed a small bucket from the bench beside the tub, dipped it into a barrel of rinse water the servants had left within reach, and gently tilted her head forward. Four buckets of water had her hair clean.

"Soap, please," he said.

Eyes still closed and limbs languid, she held up the cake. Gethen took it, dipped it into the water, and reached his arms around her from behind. "Beautiful hair." He tipped her chin back until her head rested against his shoulder, then he slid the soap down her neck, between her breasts, down her belly, between her legs. "Beautiful skin." His lips found her jaw. He nibbled his way to her ear as his hands soaped her scarred breasts, belly, hips. "Beautiful woman."

Halina moaned and moved beneath his hands. "Gods, I missed you." Her right hand stroked his jaw as her left hand stole the soap and threw it out of the tub. She turned her head and captured his lips then her body followed and she twisted in the tub until she faced him and straddled his lap. "I want you inside me," she said into his mouth. He was hard for her. Halina shifted down upon him and Gethen slid into her, guided by her hand.

They moaned and moved. He held her hips and buried his face in the place where her neck met her shoulder, smelling soap, tasting desire, savoring her sweet skin. Halina ground against him, demanding that he fill her, demanding that he match her intensity, that he give her everything. She arched back and his mouth found her breasts. Her nipples were salty and sweet, tightening beneath his tongue as she held his head and urged him on with her moans.

Gethen followed the arch of her throat with his lips, nipping and licking, until he reached her mouth. She opened to him, kissed him with passion and ferocity, their tongues twining, teeth biting. Halina laced her fingers together behind his neck and rode him hard, sloshing water from the tub, flooding the floor. Each down thrust shot a lightning bolt through him from cock to skull and she panted a rhythm that sounded like prayer.

Suddenly she jerked upright, cried out, and then stiffened against him. Her body spasmed and her muscles contracted around him so powerfully it pained him. A surge of red-hot blood magic exploded through her and into him, so unexpected and violent that the fire that always smoldered behind Gethen's chest blazed into a conflagration and obliterated his control. He groaned and came deep inside her. A release of power flared between them and flashed through the room, setting everything aglow with amber mage fire.

They clung to each other as the heat and sorcery spun out, climbed the walls, and made the wooden shutters across the windows creak and chatter before it dissipated. Panting, muscles trembling, Gethen gently rocked Halina as her body spasmed and she whimpered, overwhelmed by her own release. Finally, she quieted and folded her arms against his chest. He held her tight, her head tucked beneath his chin, eyes closed. Steam rose in curling wisps from the damp floor.

After a few minutes, Halina stirred. "The water's foul."

"Mmm-hmm."

She drew back, cradled his face between her palms, and kissed his eyelids, his forehead, his nose, and his lips. "Thank you. That was lovely and, gods, I needed it. I'm sorry it was so brief."

Gethen smiled though he kept his eyes closed. "Short but sweet."

She stood and climbed from the tub. "Come on, Mage, I'll rinse you. And then we'll finish that bottle of tokay while I eat."

He opened his eyes to the glorious sight of a naked militess pouring water over her pale, scarred body. He followed her example and bit back a curse as the tepid rinse water cooled what Halina had heated. They dried off and he pulled on his trouzes as she returned to the sleeping chamber. Ignoring the kirtle and surcoat that Philippa had laid out, she dragged a wine-dark blanket off the bed to wrap around her body then tucked into one of the chairs before the hearth and started eating.

Gethen poured more tokay then combed her damp hair while she worked her way through bread, cheese, cold chicken, and sunberries. The letter remained on the table, untouched and taunting. "Let's have the news from Tatlis," he said as he worked on a large snarl with her wooden comb.

Halina studied one of the yellow, round berries before popping it in her mouth. "Ranith's berries are better."

"It's the decaying bodies. They add character to the berries I harvest from the citadel's graveyard."

She laughed. "That must be it." She retrieved the king's

letter, broke its black seal, and unfolded the parchment. "My dear father says— Ouch!"

"Sorry. This is a nasty one. Did you comb this mess at all while you were on the road?"

"No." She took a sip of mead and scanned the letter. She grew still. Then she put her glass on the table. "Khotyr, take me." Gethen stopped combing. The letter crackled as it crumpled in Halina's fist. "The Bear King is coming to Kharaton Castle."

CHAPTER 3

To my daughter and servant Halina Persinna, Militess of the Order of the Red Blade and Margrave of Khara, from the most eminent Vernard, rightful King of Ursinum, Archduke of Tatlis, and Duke of Eskis.

Greetings Daughter,

I am outraged to find my commands disobeyed by one I heretofore considered unerringly faithful. A marriage agreement was signed by Sun Mage Gethen of Ranith, the Duke of Rhyshis in absentia, yet its terms have not been fulfilled as you have failed to enforce them. Furthermore, you audaciously demand funds from my coffers to aid your people when their woes were caused by the Sun Mage's conflict; battles which in no way involved Tatlis. Your insubordination and temerity at the expense of Ursinum are intolerable.

You have cast a pall upon my sovereignty, which I see can only be lifted by my coming to Kharaton Castle. Your compliance will be absolute in all matters of kingdom and crown, Daughter. Do not make me doubt your loyalty.

Your King, Commander, and Father, Vernard, Ruler of Ursinum

"The old bruin's hackles are up." Halina stood and dropped the blanket while Gethen read the letter. "He can roar all he likes, as long as he brings the money Tatlis promised for Kharaton's renovations. The rest is pointless grousing because I'm forcing his capitulation." She dressed, went down the hall to her study, and pulled open the doors to the balcony. She stepped into the soft light of sunset.

The sky and the Silver Sea were indigo and orange, and a thin golden line crested the horizon to set the world afire before daylight failed. Mockingbirds and nightjars chirped and crooned goodnight to the sun, while the eerie squawks of night herons echoed across Kharaton Harbor.

Gethen appeared in the doorway wearing trouzes and the blanket. He was lean and muscular, fit from months of deconstructing the basilica at Ranith — hard labor to punish himself for his own perceived failures. He'd removed an outer wall, replaced shattered windows, cleaned the massive open space of all bones and ash — traces of a witch's brutality — and turned the space into an open stable for the animals that were slowly repopulating Kharayan Tor.

Halina shivered with the evening chill and her king's anger. Gethen moved behind her, wrapped his arms and the blanket around her, and rested his cheek against her ear. He was quiet, waiting for her to speak. She leaned back and sighed, stroked his dark-stubbled cheek and reveled in his nearness. She'd put off the inevitable bad to savor a few more moments of good. "I'm glad you're with me."

"Why? So you have fresh meat to bait the Bear King with?"

"Ha! I'm bait enough."

"What then? You need me?"

She didn't miss his teasing tone. "I don't need anyone. I *choose* you." But it was a lie. She'd needed him from the moment she'd passed through Kharaton Castle's gates a month ago. With every passing mile, she'd felt diminished by the distance separating them. The blood magic she'd earned in battle, and that Gethen said protected her, had lost the strength it had gained when he'd entered her heart. And the way it had mixed with his sun sorcery and roared back as they'd made love, nearly burning her from the inside out, proved how dear he'd become to her.

He tightened his arms around her. "That's why I'll always have your back." He cupped her breasts as he added, "and your front."

She covered his hands with her own. "It's not a bad front."

His breath tickled her ear as he said, "Mmm, not bad at all."

She laughed, low and quiet.

"Your blood magic's stronger." He nuzzled her neck.

"I noticed."

"My sun magic and your blood magic work well together."

Halina turned in his arms. "Why is that?" She liked the look of him and traced the brown lines of pigmentation — the Beseran stripes — that wrapped around his arms, followed his spine, curved around his ribs, and swirled over his chest.

He shrugged. "I don't understand magic, Halina, I just practice it."

"Ah. Do you realize that makes no sense?"

"No? How does the sun rise and set? What makes lightning? How can birds soar?" He kissed her forehead. "Magic. And why are we connected?" He shrugged again.

"Magic?"

"So it seems." He gazed toward Besera and the setting sun's glow reflected off the sea to make his gray eyes golden. "Or, perhaps, it's only lust." He turned those eyes on her and whispered, "Either way, let's keep that knowledge between us."

She nodded and kissed him. "Or my father will make it a weapon." Her lips brushed his as she spoke. He hugged her tighter, slid his face into her damp hair, and inhaled slowly, deeply. He was strong, so strong. Halina reveled in his touch, his smell, his taste. She closed her eyes. For the first time in her life, she had something other than battle and duty.

Somewhere in the village, a dog barked and neighboring hounds joined in. The sound made Halina think of shrikers and dead children. She cursed beneath her breath.

Gethen rubbed his cheek against hers and murmured, "He can't force me into his court."

"I know that."

"Then why are you cursing?"

"Because there are rumors of shrikers killing in Sokos that I don't want him to hear."

"What?" He stiffened, all nonchalance gone. "When? Why didn't you tell me immediately?"

She leaned back. "Why would I? They're only stories."

"What proof was offered?" He imprisoned her with his arms. "Have children died?"

"Yes, but—"

"Skiron's bones," he said through clenched teeth. "Where there're shrikers there's necromancy, Halina, and real or not, suspicion falls on me. Right?"

The wood of the balcony bit into her back. "Yes, Gethen, but—"

"You should've sent Enor to me."

"About a rumor?"

"Yes."

"No," Halina snapped. She flattened her palms against his chest and pressed him back. "I left Thaksin to gather accounts from all the families who suffered losses. I'm sure it's illness among feral dogs. He and Earl Sokos's soldiers will destroy them and that will be the end of it. I'm not—"

A fist pounded on her apartment door, hard enough to rattle the iron hinges. Gethen cursed. Halina muttered, "Gods, what now?" She tried to continue. "I'm not going to—"

The pounding repeated.

"Bollocks," she snarled then shouted, "What?"

"A message for Your Ladyship." The answer came from Eugen.

"Can't it wait?"

"No, Margrave."

She bared her teeth then captured Gethen's face with her hands. "We'll finish this conversation." She hated how their pleasure had devolved so quickly.

"When I return from Ranith."

"But you just got here."

"I came to see you, not to stay. Some of the beehives need splitting before their queens swarm."

"Your Ladyship?" came the muffled call from the apartment's outer doors.

"Gods, Eugen, keep your trouzes on. I'm coming."

Gethen added, "And now I need to pull information about shrikers from my library. They're not something I'm familiar with, despite everyone's assumptions."

"It's a wild rumor I intend to crush swiftly." Halina caressed his cheek and ran her fingers through his thick black hair, tracing the silver strands that highlighted his temples. Those hairs hinted at the early aging all necromancers suffered, a price they paid for wielding dark magic. "I'll send Thaksin to Ranith when he returns. Give him the information you gather. I've ordered him to dispel the whispers and innuendos. We need to resolve this before my father arrives."

The steward banged on the door and Halina shouted, "Knock again and I'll cut off your bollocks!"

"You expect your love-sick captain to do something that benefits me?" Gethen's jaw shifted with an audible *crack*.

"Absolutely. Thak hates you because he's jealous, but he's no less devoted to me. That makes him a better tool than you."

Gethen sneered. "And you want me to cooperate with that *tool*."

"Yes, I do."

He scratched his stubbled jaw then huffed a sigh. "Fine." His sneer became a wolfish grin. "But what's my reward for playing nice with your captain?"

Halina slid her fingers around his bare waist and dragged her nails up his spine. "What do you want?"

"Marry me."

She laughed. "High price for a little research."

"There's always a price to pay for knowledge."

Her hands drifted down to cup his arse. "Well, you'll soon have an opportunity to take that up with the king."

Gethen nodded. "Oh, yes. I plan to renegotiate with your father. I dislike his terms."

"You both can talk until you're blue in the face, but I'll decide whom I'll marry." She kissed him, ending with a slow sucking bite to his lower lip that made him growl, then she slipped past him and into the study. "I have a long list of negotiated suitors to choose from thanks to His Majesty."

Gethen followed. "I don't give up easily, Militess."

Eugen pounded on the door; the man was fearless.

"That's what makes you the right man for the job, Mage," she said over her shoulder as she headed into the hallway. She yanked the misericord from its sheath on her wrist and jerked open the door. Her steward stood with a thin, sweaty boy who wore the black and red uniform of a Tatlis messenger, and whose eyes widened as he spied the dagger. Gethen appeared in the hallway behind her and the boy's eyes looked like they'd tumble from his skull.

Blood and bones. The food and tokay in Halina's gut soured as she beheld the messenger's clothes. "Word from His Majesty?"

Eugen nodded and elbowed the boy to speak. The youngster bowed then relayed his message: "I bring greetings, Your Ladyship, from His Majesty, King Vernard of Ursinum, who travels east from Tatlis and will arrive at Kharaton in five days. His Majesty brings a retinue totaling one hundred eighty-six, including the Countess of Vala. Accommodations for their persons and their aides are expected to last for a fortnight. Additionally, His Majesty demands that Sun Mage Gethen Rhysh, Duke of Rhyshis in absentia, be in attendance upon His Majesty's arrival." He spouted it out without taking a breath as if the words were daggered and they'd been cutting him.

Khotyr, take me. Careful to keep her composure, Halina nodded. "I thank you for your diligence in delivering this news with haste." She turned to Eugen. "Please see to this youngster's needs, send riders to gauge the king's distance from Kharaton, then return to my study." The steward nodded and she added, "Put the king's soldiers and servants with our army in the causeway; we can only accommodate minimal staff in the south wing. If His Majesty doesn't approve, he can suck eggs."

The messenger gawked at her, but he was smart enough to remain silent.

Eugen frowned. "Captain Thaksin will object, Your Lady-ship. It's a risk to have so few soldiers in the castle with such important personages visiting."

"Not my preference either, but His Majesty knew we were under construction when he left Tatlis." She jerked her chin at the messenger. "Feed the boy before he drops dead."

Eugen turned, pulled the messenger around by his collar, and propelled him toward the kitchen stairs as Halina closed the door and began cursing. "Five days?" She strode past Gethen back to the study and flipped her heavy, black oak desk. Papers, inkpot, maps, and books scattered across the floor. Glass smashed, wood splintered. "That rat-faced, rump-splitter gives me only five days to prepare for his arrival?" She kicked a stool across the room. It crashed against the cold grate. She retrieved it and obliterated its remains upon the stone mantelpiece.

Bottle and glasses in hand, Gethen watched Halina destroy her study. She threw books, kicked cold braziers across the room and back again. The coal scuttle tipped and blackened the floor. She upturned the reading chairs and gutted one before her fury was finally controlled. She stood in the midst of the destruction, eyes closed, fists clenched, breath heavy.

With a spirit's quiet tread, Eugen reappeared beside Gethen and surveyed the room. "Are you finished, Your Lady-ship?" he asked.

Halina looked up at her steward's calm voice. She shoved damp hair back from her face, leaving coal-black streaks in her copper hair. "Yes. Thank you for returning so quickly. Can you have this castle ready for the king and Lady Vala in less than a week, Eugen?"

"Yes, Margrave." The man had served Halina for almost a decade and had grown up in the castle. "I'll find space for their retinue. We've enough supplies in the buttery and undercroft, thanks to Besera's generosity." He offered Gethen a slight bow with those words. "There's nothing to be done about the construction, but we can clean up the castle well enough. His Majesty and Her Ladyship will find Kharaton Castle drafty but welcoming."

Halina squeezed the man's forearm and left black prints on his pale sleeve. "Thank you. Take whatever you need. If anyone questions you, send them to me."

"I'll rouse the servants. There's much to do and little time to do it." He glanced past her. "And I'll send two chamber-maids to set right Your Ladyship's study."

"I can always rely upon your efficiency, Eugen."

"Yes, you can." The steward bowed then strode back into the hallway, closing the apartment doors behind him.

Halina kicked the coal scuttle across the room again. It pinged off the stone wall and spun away, sending up a small cloud of ashes and soot.

Gethen offered a full glass of mead.

She accepted it, drained it, and held it out for a refill. "I'm going to get drunk." She drained it once more and he refilled it. "With my family, there always has to be a complication."

"My love, your family *is* a complication." He wiped coal from her forehead with a spit-damp thumb and followed her into the bedchamber.

She snorted. "You should go home, Sun Mage. Go home and stay there. Find me the information I need to disprove the existence of shrikers in Sokos."

"I don't run from fights."

"You're not running. You're giving me room to battle and

you're solving a mystery for me. If Vernard wishes to command or condemn you, he can march his arse up the tor and knock on your front door himself. I recall how well that worked last time."

"And I recall that he sent you knocking."

She drained her glass. "A choice he regrets to this day." She went to a small cabinet beside the bed and fetched a dark brown bottle. "Ever had Schorvalan soma?" She uncorked it and offered the bottle to Gethen. "A gift from Militess Odruna Schlaar; her family's specialty." He sniffed and made a face like he'd smelled death. Halina nodded. "Tastes even worse. It's only good for obliterating your mind before death or surgery. The Schorvalans drink it with every meal."

"I'll remember to remain on the good side of any Schorvalans I meet."

She snorted. "Always a good idea." Her hands wavered just a little as she poured a shot. "You'll meet Odruna soon. She's bringing me another gift this summer." She frowned and peered into the half-empty bottle. "Hopefully, my father will be gone by then. They're not friends."

Gethen's brow was furrowed, his lips a hard line, his eyes harder. He captured her left hand, raised it to his lips, and kissed her blunted ring finger and pinky. "Vernard's used your loyalty before—"

She turned her hand to cover his mouth. "It's not all scars and death. His demands brought us together."

He pulled her hand away. "Halina—"

"Promise me you'll go to Ranith and not return until Vernard leaves." She tightened her fingers on his. "If you love me, Gethen, if you want us to be together, you'll stay away."

"You can't expect me to agree to that."

"I can and I do." She pulled back. Scars on her skin she

didn't mind. But the ones on her heart bled longest and hurt most. She didn't want more of those. Halina downed the shot, shuddered, refilled her glass. "I know it's unreasonable." She met his gaze. "But so is the Bear King when he gets his claws and teeth into something. He'll forgive my stubbornness. He'll give me the money Khara needs. He'll even accept our marriage on our terms. But if he believes necromancy is to blame for dead children in Sokos, none of that will happen because he'll label you Ursinum's enemy and order me to kill you."

"You're asking me not to defend myself."

"I'm asking you help me defend you." She leaned forward, pressed her lips to his, then murmured, "Just as I always have."

CHAPTER 4

Gethen spooned green powder from a small jar into a dram of mead and stirred the mixture. He padded on bare feet to where Halina slouched upon the sofa. She was squinting at the morning sunlight cutting a sharp line through the wooden window shutters, a pained scowl on her face. Crapulous after a night of drinking, she'd dressed in trouzes and tunic, moving like a wounded woman and cursing worse than Kharaton Harbor's dock trollops.

"Drink this."

She accepted the cup and downed the tincture without looking up or protesting, a sure sign that her head was torturing her.

He handed her a full tankard. "This, too."

Halina took a gulp then eyed the liquid, her scowl deepening. "Water?"

"Yes."

"Why am I drinking water? No one drinks this stuff."

"Everyone should." He tapped the container. "It's clarified and it'll help ease your suffering. Trust your healer and drink."

She muttered a curse but followed his advice and gulped it down. When she'd finished she said, "I'll spend half the day in the jakes with so much water sloshing around in my gut."

"Better your arse on the seat than your face."

"All right. No time for self-pity. The king arrives too soon." Halina stood. "We'll need more mead. How many barrels can I buy from Ranith?"

Gethen sat on the bed. "The great mead's not ready, but I have a dozen barrels of bracket."

"I'll take them. Can you send Magod today?" She stepped in front of him and he wrapped his arms around her hips.

"I haven't named my price."

"I'm sure it's unreasonable."

"Of course." He tried to pull her down onto the bed, but she resisted. "What? No partial payment?"

"Bad idea; I may puke on you."

"I see your point." He released her and fell back amid the blankets. Orange foxes stalked gray coneys upon the frescoed ceiling. He looked back at her. She retrieved her sword belt from the armor stand and buckled it at her waist but left off her sword and scabbard. Instead, lost in thought, she fingered an edge where the worn leather was tearing. He asked, "Why did you become a soldier?"

She smiled ironically. "To learn how to kill my father." Gethen snorted, but Halina nodded. "Truthfully."

He sobered. "What did King Vernard do to gain your hatred at such an early age?"

"It's not the king I hate. His Majesty is an outstanding ruler — wise, generous with his people, willing to do anything to protect them and benefit Ursinum. It's my father I'd like to kill.

"My mother set me in his path every chance she could from the moment I was born. But he ignored me; he had no intention of giving me legitimacy. He'd wanted another son, not a freckled, freakish daughter who pulled the limbs off her dolls."

"Did you really?"

"Every one, despite the beatings I received for it. I hated their staring eyes and fake smiles, so much like the women of the court.

"My mother knew I was a warrior, cut from the same cloth as the king and his sons. But Vernard saw weakness when he looked at me; I was just a girl. After my second cousin Waldram pushed me into the oubliette at Tatlis, my father taunted me about being afraid of the dark and the water. I was only six, but I hated him for that, for siding with that prick. So, I buried a quill in the back of his hand." Gethen's brows arched, but Halina continued. "He slapped me across the room then sent me to live in the barracks as a page. And made me one of his heirs."

"He saw that your mother was right."

She inclined her head and twined her fingers with his, considered their hands for a moment, then asked, "Why'd you remain neutral during the war?"

"I didn't."

Halina's gaze sharpened.

Gethen continued. "I was consulted many times by the kings. Each asking how he could kill the others. The only advice I offered was a method for killing Nalvika's necromancers. That kingdom's royal sorcerers were the enemy."

"Many people still think necromancy is the root of all evil."

"Yes. They prefer to think that mages and witches aren't also men and women just like them." He ran his hands over hers, calluses over calluses, from brewing and brawling. "Tell me everything you heard in Sokos."

Her expression twisted into the one she wore when she had something nasty to discuss. "There are fourteen dead children from the town and its tribute villages. It's one of the few areas in Khara not devastated by floods." She sighed. "Where does the misery end?"

"The killers will prove to be a dog pack. They'll be hunted down. And it will be over."

"I keep telling myself that, but the witnesses are so certain it's shrikers."

He shook his head. "Death from feral dogs I'll believe, but Skiron's revenge? No. There's no reason; I would know if there was."

"Could other necromancers be behind this?"

"No. I'm the only one with that much power."

"The villagers asked what I'd do if you summoned the shrikers."

"And you said you'll gut me?"

"Yes," she replied in a small voice.

He met her gaze evenly. "I should hope so. You're their protector."

She rubbed her eyes. "I need answers before the king arrives, Gethen."

"I'll make every effort to get them to you." He hooked his finger into her belt and tugged her into the circle of his arms. "Before I leave, I want to put a shadow on you."

"A shadow? No, thank you. The scars still ache from the last fight I had with one of your wraiths."

"This is an ambit, not a wraith. All it'll do is follow you."

"An idea which I'm to pretend isn't at all disturbing." Halina crossed her arms, squinted at him. "What else?"

Gethen returned her suspicious gaze but braced for her

reaction. It wouldn't be good. "Permit you to summon me if there's trouble when we're not together."

Her expression and her voice turned stony and she escaped his embrace. "I have an army at my back."

He grimaced and rubbed the back of his neck. "It's not a sign of weakness to accept my protection, Halina."

"If I need it, I'll ask for it."

"Exactly—"

"You think I can't keep myself and my holding safe?" The look she gave him would've made a lesser man piss his trouzes. "I *earned* Khara. I *earned* my title. And I *earned* fear and respect. It wasn't just my enemies' blood I shed in battle. I gave up plenty of my own, too."

"I know that," he said, his patience slipping. "We fought together. I made you bleed. I watched you die. Do you think I've forgotten?"

"I think you've decided that proves I'm weaker than you." Her hand dropped to her belt where her sword usually hung as she leaned toward him. "Every man thinks that at some point, then I'm forced to demonstrate how wrong he is. I thought you were different."

Gethen ran his hands through his hair. "You know I don't think that, Halina." She was too damned stubborn for her own good. Which, of course, was what had kept her alive through so many battles and made him love her. The woman did not back down from a fight. "Do you think I can't protect you or that others are more deserving of protection than you are?"

Her eyes narrowed. "What did you just say to me?" Anger shimmered off her, like heat rising from a sun-baked cart path. His lover had been replaced by the soldier who'd rallied her fleeing troops against overwhelming numbers while clutching her torn belly to keep her guts inside. And he'd overstepped the line by a mile. If he didn't back up, he'd lose his bollocks to her knife. It'd be worth it, though. Halina's piss and vinegar and relentlessness charmed him, fool that he was.

Gethen exhaled a long, slow breath and met her angry gaze evenly. "I'm here for you, Halina. Be vulnerable. Be weak. You have nothing to prove to me. I know your power."

Pain twisted her expression, there and gone in a blink. "I — can't. I don't have the luxury of weakness. My needs are my kingdom's needs. My wants are my citizens' wants."

"Then let me do this because I'm one of your citizens and I want and need to do it. Let me do it because I love you."

Halina stared at the floor, pain on her face again. Then she sighed, all emotion gone with it. "All right." She met his gaze and added, "But only if you agree not to return unless I summon you."

"You have my word."

"And," she held up a finger, "after the shadow's in place, you'll go back to Ranith, send the information about the shrikers with Magod, and not worry about me."

He cocked an eyebrow. "Asking me not to be concerned when people are dying and the king's on his way with his trouzes in a twist is asking a lot."

"It's all or nothing."

"I will try not to worry," Gethen said as he padded on bare feet into the adjoining chamber, his stillroom at Kharaton.

"I don't like this idea of being shadowed by your wraiths."

"I told you, an ambit is different from a wraith," he called over the sound of bottles rattling and metal clattering. "It has no intellect and prefers skulking to confrontation." He returned, put an armful of items down on the table before the fire, and shifted her empty bottles and glasses to the mantel-piece. "Light a torch and this shadow will flee; block all light and it will be swallowed by the dark." He slid his hand up her arm to her shoulder then stroked her cheek. "The worst it can do is make you cold."

Halina's expression screwed up like a cat that had smelled something rotten. "I had a lifetime of cold last winter." She kissed his palm then slipped beneath his arm. "It's shadow magic, Gethen. I've seen the harm that comes from that."

"Shadow magic saved your arse more than once." He understood her reticence. One of his own shadow wraiths had beaten her to the brink of death. "The only way this ambit can become a weapon is if I alter it. In this form it's harmless."

"It isn't necessary," she muttered as if she hadn't heard him. "I can handle my own affairs."

He arched a brow at her. "Halina, humor me."

"I wish you wouldn't worry." She collapsed into one of the chairs beside the table, looked up from beneath her brows. "But I'm glad you care."

Gethen started sorting the bottles and equipment. "More than is wise, I'm sure."

She gave him a half-smile. "That's the fate of a man who loves a militess."

"And for a woman who loves a mage." He returned her smile. "This won't take long."

She cocked her head to peer into the containers Gethen had spread out on the table. She reached toward one that held a combination of white crystals and black dust.

"Don't touch."

She glanced up. "Is it dangerous?"

"No. I just don't have much black salt and there isn't time to make more before I leave."

Halina curled her lip at him but clasped her hands in her lap and watched as he scooped some of the mixture from the container into an open copper pot. "Rainwater," he said uncorking a dark brown bottle and adding its contents to the salt. He suspended the pot over the grate and coaxed the banked coals to a steady flame.

"Is black salt hard to make?"

"Not really. It's ash mixed with salt, but I'm particular about the source of the ash."

"Oh."

He added a few more ingredients — a dark, viscous liquid, dried leaves, some yellow powder that stank of rot.

He crooked his finger, indicating she should follow him to the window. Halina hissed and squinted as he opened the shutters. Sunlight spilled through. "Turn so that your shadow is cast on the floor." He crouched in the sunlight and reached into her shadow. "Stand still." Gethen slid his fingers just above the floor and murmured an incantation as he scooped his hand through her shadow, closed his fingers into a fist, and yanked his hand back into the light.

Halina shivered, but he smiled as he straightened. "Come." He returned to the small pot, hooked the poker around the iron pot crane holding it, and swung it away from the fire. He held his fist above it and droned another incantation. Amber light glowed between his closed fingers but disappeared when he opened his hand. Instead, black pooled in his palm, something that was at once both vapor and liquid. When he tipped his hand, it turned back on itself, defying nature and refusing to fall until he gently blew it off and into the pot.

Halina gave a little grunt and shivered.

"That was a piece of your shadow imbued with my soul." He stirred the mixture with a copper stick then put it down and reached for her hand. "There's one more thing I need from you," he said as he chose a small misericord from the items on the table.

"Please tell me it's a lock of hair." She placed her hand in his, knowing it wasn't.

He gave her a tight-lipped smile, held her hand over the pot, and sliced her pinky just enough to make it bleed openly. After three drops, he released her hand, scraped ash over the fire, and added more rainwater to the mixture. He stirred it ceaselessly and continued his incantation while Halina pressed a rag to her pinky and watched. Finally, satisfied with what he saw, Gethen poured the liquid through a straining cloth into a copper flask, dipped a glass pipette into it, and dropped a small amount of liquid into his palm. He rubbed it against his skin then nodded and wiped it away with a cloth. "This ambit connects us. With it, as long as there's enough light to cast a shadow, you can summon me."

"From where?"

"Anywhere in Quoregna."

"Huh. Can anyone else use it?"

"No. It obeys only you." He met her gaze. "Which means I can't summon it to bring you to my bed in the middle of the night."

She arched a brow. "Too bad."

They returned to the window and, once again, he had her stand so that her shadow stretched away from her. With another incantation he poured most of the liquid into her shadow. Rather than splatter the floor, it spread and dissipated, becoming a part of the darkness. Gethen commanded a fragment of it to slip free of the rest.

It followed the movement of his fingers and Halina shuddered. "You're certain it's harmless?"

"Absolutely." He swept his hand over the wisp and it

rejoined Halina's shadow. "Until you use it, it'll remain part of your shadow." He capped the copper flask and slipped it into a pouch on his belt. "For my part, a drop in each eye will let me see where you are."

"You drop that stuff in your eyes?" She looked aghast.

"Ambit's tears. They're horrifically painful, which is why I rarely employ this form of magic." He patted the flask within the pouch and began closing the jars that held his ingredients. "If you need me, summon the shadow and direct it to find me."

"Summon it how?"

He smirked. "Say, 'Ambit, bring Gethen to me,' and it will."

"It's that easy?"

He looked up from beneath his brows. "Yes, but don't use it lightly, my love. Ambits are single-minded and forceful. Once it grabs hold of me, there'll be no stopping it from fulfilling its task. I'd prefer not to be yanked from a bath or out of the jakes without just cause." He straightened. "And don't use it if another sorcerer's ward stands between us."

"It'll pull you across?"

He nodded. "And kill me quite painfully in the process." He gave her a sly smile and added, "You know this is just a means of watching you undress, right?"

She laughed. "You have the morals of a pig's intestine."

He gathered her into his arms once more and scrutinized her face. "You're sure I shouldn't stay?"

"I'm sure." She caressed his cheek. "And I have too much to do on a day when I want to hide my head in a bucket." She kissed him deeply, a little desperately, then pushed him back a step. "You have your shadow, Mage. Now get me some answers, so I can keep you safe from my king."

She turned, but he grabbed her left hand to stop her. He raised it to his lips and kissed first her stunted fingers then her palm. His lips brushed her skin as he said, "Don't let pride prevent you from calling for my help."

"Why can't you trust me when I say I won't need it?"

"It's not you I distrust, Halina." He closed his eyes and pressed her palm to his cheek, murmuring, "It's the rest of the world."

Massive black oaks and silver pines creaked as wind whooshed through their branches, the sounds centering Gethen with the termination of his travel spell. He and Magod stood at the edge of the heavy, dark woods of Kharayan Tor. Amber mage fire whirled around them, dissipated to reveal the edge of the black cobblestone ring that marked the boundary of his land and its protective magical ward.

He crouched to touch the stones. As he did so, his hand entered the ward he'd placed around Kharayan Woods. Heat surged through him before mellowing to a comfortable warmth. Had he been an uninvited guest, the ward would've incinerated flesh and bone, a merciless and agonizing death for any fool who violated the privacy of Quoregna's Sun Mage.

Beside him, Magod waited. After twenty-three years in his master's service, he knew better than to cross a mage's ward line without an invitation.

Gethen stood and crossed the stones. The air wavered and the ward pulled against him, an unseen hand snatching him back. But, like the heat on his hand, the ward knew its maker and released its hold upon him as quickly as it had captured him. Satisfied with the strength of the incantation, he reached through, caught Magod's sleeve, and yanked the younger man safely across.

The groundsman yelped, shook himself, and remarked, "Nice day for a stroll," as they set forth into the shadowy woods.

"That's why I decided to arrive at the circle instead of inside the bailey or the hall." He knew Magod enjoyed the woods and had missed them during the months he'd been at the castle. "I understand your training's going well."

Magod grinned and made a stunted-fingered fist, showing forearm muscles like steel ropes. Losing parts of his fingers and toes to frostbite hadn't slowed him. "Am more skilled with the ax than many of Her Ladyship's seasoned soldiers, so she says." He was shorter than Gethen with large brown eyes he'd inherited his from his mother Noni and the peculiar speech pattern that called out their Ayestran heritage. But he stood a bit taller after six months of combat training. He threw his barrel-chest out and easily matched his master's long stride.

"I'm glad Halina took you on." Gethen's servant had let his chestnut hair grow long enough on top to braid it from forehead to back. He still kept the sides shaved close — in the Beseran style of his master — but the braid was an adaptation of an Ursinum warrior's style. Gethen tugged the plait. "It suits you."

Magod's grin widened. "Hair or ax?"

"Both."

The path was wide and sun-dappled. Black squirrels scrabbled around tree trunks and through the bushes, a woodpecker knocked high up in the canopy, and song birds serenaded each other and their woods' master.

"Tell me what you've heard of the deaths in Sokos."

Magod sobered. "Fourteen children gone, plus four adults."

"Any similarities among the deaths?"

"All heard dogs howling but not moving outside before the attacks. Children's bodies were undisturbed; adults were torn apart."

"Hmm. And all the villagers insisted the beasts were shrikers? Were the bodies dragged off and consumed?"

"No."

"None?" Magod shook his head. Gethen frowned. Wild dogs consumed what they killed. So did wolves. "Fear could explain the children's deaths; their hearts stopped."

"All of them?"

Gethen's frown became a grimace. "Unlikely," he admitted reluctantly.

A distant wolf howled, silencing the forest. Another answered. It was a lonely sound, even with two animals. There'd been a large pack, twenty-six strong, roaming the woods a year ago, before a powerful witch slaughtered them with most of the tor's other animals.

After a walk that took them from creaking, shadowy forest to winding, wind-swept stone path, Gethen and Magod reached Ranith Citadel's outer defenses. A wave of his hand and an incantation raised the iron portcullis then clanked it down behind them as they crossed through the barbican and beneath the empty guardhouse. Stubborn patches of scrubby, green grass and chunks of fallen stone and mortar made the path through Ranith's abandoned village treacherous. Wind whistled past the rotting buildings, as eerie and forlorn as the wolf calls. Gethen raised the hood on his travel tunic and was grateful for the thickness of his leather brigandine. Even at the height of summer, the ceaseless wind was chill atop Kharayan Tor, blowing westward from the Silver Sea.

The citadel's black iron gate creaked in protest as the men pushed into the small bailey enclosing three quarters of the tall stone tower. It wasn't a large building and housed only a stillroom, a library, and some cramped quarters. There was a kitchen and a few outbuildings — stables, storage, and an extraction room for processing the honey that Gethen and Magod harvested, the remains of the basilica and its berry bush-infested cemetery. The top of Ranith Citadel offered a clear view northward to Kharaton Castle and the craggy seawalls encircling the harbor. To the east were Besera's purple mountains. From his cliff-side home, Gethen saw his past and his future.

He crossed the bailey. Red-and-white speckled hens clucked and flapped their wings as they bustled back and forth across his path. He kept the brainless creatures for their eggs and feathers. "Hello, lazy beasts," he said to the animals housed within the citadel's protective walls. There were three newly acquired goats and two pigs. An ass grazed in the corner with the goats, working its way through the tough green scrub grass that grew along the verge.

Like his master, Magod had gone quiet as they'd entered the village. He headed for the extraction room. "Will pull aside the bracket. Think it's best to load those barrels before doing the splits, Master."

Gethen nodded. "A good plan."

Duesh and Gwyn, the only surviving wolves from Kharayan's pack, raised their heads to acknowledge the return of the men to Ranith. But they didn't move from a pool of sunshine in the middle of the bailey. "Laziest beasts of all," Gethen murmured as he ran his hands through their fur, leaving trails of amber sparks behind and shivering at the wild power of their souls. "I enjoyed your greeting." They yawned, flopped back, closed their eyes. He stood and continued toward the extraction room to roll out the barrels of bracket with Magod.

~

Gethen and Magod sat in the bailey surrounded by disassembled bee boxes and frames.

"Five-years go over there." Magod jerked his chin toward a pell-mell stack of wooden hive frames he'd removed from the empty bee boxes. They were the frames that had been used over a five-year period and now they'd become firewood, pulled from circulation to reduce the risk of contagion spreading among the bees.

"Are there enough new frames?" Gethen squinted at the stack.

"Built more than enough. Wasn't much else to do over the winter with you at Kharaton."

Gethen grunted and scraped reddish-brown propolis from the lip and inside walls of the box before him. The bees made it from tree buds and used it to seal their honeycombs and hives. It built up on the boxes and frames and had to be removed each spring.

Magod handled the majority of the labor around Ranith and Kharayan, and Gethen envied his freedom to come and go about the citadel and forest. It was an ease Gethen didn't feel in Kharaton. Curiosity and caution followed his movements in the town. Mothers turned their children away from the necromancer and men watched him with suspicion. It was only Halina's obvious and very public trust of him that prevented them from chasing him from Kharaton with pitchforks and torches.

"How do the splits look?" Gethen knocked resinous propolis from his curved metal scraper.

"Better than expected. Thought we'd lose more hives 'cause of the nasty winter, but spring's been good. Will split a third of the hives. Most will get new queens, not just eggs."

"Good. Is there enough honey for an early harvest?"

"Small one. Could take more out but think it's better to leave extra in the hives. Let them rebuild after the long cold season."

"Agreed."

They fell into companionable silence, comforted by the rhythmic scraping of the blades on wood, the whoosh of wind, creaking of trees, the calls of the sea crows wheeling high overhead.

"Staying tonight, Master?"

Gethen nodded. "If we work tonight and tomorrow, we should complete the splits, then you can leave for Kharaton the following morning."

Magod peered up at the gray stone citadel. "All right if I leave the bracket with Her Ladyship then come back here?"

"Not interested in rubbing elbows with a countess and a king?"

"No."

Gethen laughed and bent over the box.

"Think it's good we're away from the castle," Magod muttered.

Gethen studied the groundsman from beneath his brows. "Why?"

Magod stopped scraping, pulled a green rag from his pocket, and wiped sweat from his face as he peered up at the midday sun. "Thaksin's jealousy is a threat, Master. Even the margrave said to avoid him."

"You should or I should?"

Magod tapped his own chest with the scraper but said, "What's the difference?"

Gethen grimaced. "Heed her advice."

"Envy never brings any good."

"Thaksin's jealousy is outweighed by his loyalty."

"Sure about that?"

"No." Gethen went back to scraping. "Which is why I agree that you should be here instead of Kharaton. Tensions will be high with King Vernard in the castle. Best if you're not an available target when the captain returns from Sokos."

"True."

After they'd finished cleaning and sorting the frames, Gethen dropped a bucket into the well and brought up water for washing. The propolis took a great deal of scrubbing to remove from the scrapers and their hands. As they cleaned, he considered his groundsman's stormy expression and hunched shoulders. "What's got you so bent?"

"Nothing." But Magod's brow furrowed deeper.

"Bollocks it's nothing. I've known you your whole life. Something's under your skin."

Magod leaned back to take in the full height of the gray citadel looming over them. "Want to be free."

"You have more freedom than I do."

Magod nodded. "But am not a free man."

Gethen looked around the bailey. The chickens clucked and scratched, the ass and goats dozed in the sun, their tales swishing lazily, and the wolves had moved to the shade. He shrugged. "If it troubles you so much, I release you. But I hope you'll stay to oversee Ranith. At least until I can find a replacement if you intend to leave my service."

Magod stared at him. "A jest?"

Gethen shook his head and dug propolis from beneath his fingernails. "No jest."

Magod looked from his master to the citadel and woods. "Hadn't expected that."

Gethen laughed. "Truthfully, I'd planned to release you after last winter's struggles but delayed it when you started training."

Magod looked thoughtful for a moment then grinned. "Thank you, Master, ah, Master Gethen."

Gethen clapped him on the back. "You're meant for greater things than beekeeping, Magod. I've always known that."

Magod considered the tools he'd cleaned. "Eh. Bees keep me satisfied."

Gethen snorted. "They're simpler than women and politics."

Magod grinned. "Yeh."

CHAPTER 5

Kharaton Castle had been abuzz around the clock with the ordered chaos of cleaning, cooking, and construction since the news of the king's imminent arrival. Four days later Halina surveyed the cavernous great hall. Chairs and tables clattered and scraped across the blue-gray tile floors. Servants cleaned the lowered iron chandeliers, the braziers, and sconces. They spread linens across the tables, polished and set plates, goblets, and cutlery. They beat a year's collection of dust from the tapestries and rugs. Servants washed and wiped the windows, inside and out; others swept and toted the ashes from the massive, white marble fireplace. The kitchen and bake house were operating non-stop and the castle smelled of yeasty bread, roasting meats, bubbling stews and soups.

Masons loaded wood beams as thick as Halina's thigh onto the lowered construction platform. Cadoc spied her and started barking orders at his workers: "Don't overload that platform," and, "Move that weight around, numbskulls, there's more room!"

She frowned. Castle construction was a mystery to her and she didn't question the foreman's building methods, but browbeating and second-guessing the people under him was lazy leadership.

"Watch out!"

"Ai! I just washed there!"

"You're getting mud everywhere, you lout!"

Halina turned at the protests. A soldier wove past servants and scullions scrubbing the floor on their hands and knees. He left a trail of dirty boot prints and kicked a bucket in his haste. Several servants were wet and cursing.

"Your Ladyship!" the young man called as he hurried toward her. He stopped, proffered a stunted bow, and said, "I was ordered to find you without delay."

She looked past him. "Does 'without delay' also mean without respect, Umniris?"

Confusion twisted his fair brow then he followed her gaze and looked contrite. "I'm sorry," he called to the servants. Their gestures said his apology was too little too late.

Halina pursed her lips. "What have you come to tell me that's put you on the bad side of the scullery maids?"

"The Bear King's banners were spied on the Valmerian Plain this morning."

She nodded. "Right where I expected them to be by now."

He braced visibly as he added, "Nalvika's white stag flies beside the black bear, Margrave. And Crown Prince Waldram's black stripe tops Nalvika's orange banners."

"*Nalvika?*" Halina suddenly couldn't feel her hands or face. She took a deep, steadying breath and swallowed acid spit. "Why in the names of the gods is that swine Waldram with my father?" She grabbed the front of the young soldier's blue-and-gold tabard. "You're certain about that stripe?"

The knob in his throat bobbed. "Yes, Your Ladyship."

She shoved him away and unleashed a string of epithets. A tic fluttered high on her right cheek, tugging the corner of her eye. "Find Eugen and tell him to join me in the Weather Tower. Now."

"Right away, Your Ladyship." Umniris paused by the servants to offer his apology again but received a flung wet rag in return.

"Semele's blood." Halina cut through the small eastern courtyard where masons were preparing mortar beneath a canopy. She slipped through the narrow alley that led to the Weather Tower's stairs. She needed air. She needed to smooth the twitch and shake the numbness that came with the prospect of facing Crown Prince Waldram.

She needed to see the dark tower of Ranith Citadel.

Why had she sent Gethen away? She wanted him with her, not at Ranith with Magod. "Damn. Damn. Damn." She took the spiraling stone stairs two at a time and ignored the wide-eyed watchman who turned as she passed through the tower to the battlements. She emerged into sunshine and a strong breeze, crossed the wood-covered walkway, and came to rest against pale stone crenellations, their regular pattern like teeth atop the castle.

Halina's shadow fell across the stone and she looked from its darkness to the distant citadel. Gethen was only a thought away, easily brought to her side. "Don't be an idiot," she muttered. "Since when have you needed a man to save you?"

She scowled and answered her own question. "Since last winter." The damnable Rime Witch would've killed her if Gethen hadn't pulled her back from the Void. She'd felt fearful since that day. Doubtless he knew it. Certainly that's why his shadow ambit rankled her so much; allowing it was an admission of weakness. She lifted her chin, squared her shoulders. "I don't need a necromancer to protect me from a nimwit."

She worked a pebble of cream-colored stone away from the crenellation, wiggling it back and forth as she looked from gray Ranith to the colorful buildings of Kharaton. Blue-and-gold pennants fluttered atop many thatched and shingled roofs. Khara's largest town was a patchwork of color overlaid by a spider web of interconnected streets and alleys radiating outward from the castle perched atop its own rocky island. Awash in vivid hues — blue, green, yellow, purple, orange — the heart of Khara was called Ursinum's Painted City, though in truth it was smaller than Ahlas to the south and impressive only for its patchwork riot of colors and its cursed luck.

"Your Ladyship?"

Halina turned at Philippa's voice. "What?"

The woman stood in the tower doorway. "Have you thought about your gown for His Majesty's welcoming feast?"

"The king's feast? I think I'll wear his blood."

Philippa's eyes widened like a spooked horse and Halina bared her teeth, annoyed by her discomfort. She didn't share Halina's ease with violence, especially when it was directed toward King Vernard.

Eugen appeared behind the lady-in-waiting. "Margrave, let's go someplace where we can speak privately."

"Pick out any damned dress, Phila. As long as it's something I can fight in."

Philippa curtsied and retreated down the tower stairs. Eugen indicated for Halina to precede him and they made their way to her apartment and the small parlor that adjoined her study. She gripped the pommel of her steel sword, centered by its cool solidity. She was a militess, a margrave, the Red Blade of Or-Halee. The king and crown prince were no more dangerous than the swords and axes she'd faced in battle, a few of which had been wielded by Waldram.

"I understand Nalvika's crown prince is on our doorstep," the steward said. "Presumably to reassert his right to marry you in the face of Lord Rhyshis's claim. Where's the Sun Mage?"

"I sent him away."

"Ah. Will you summon him to return before the king's arrival?" Eugen hid his worry well, but Halina knew what the little up-pitch in his tone meant. "His Majesty was clear about wanting the duke here, Your Ladyship. And it seems prudent with Prince Waldram's unexpected company."

"Lord Rhyshis will return when he pleases, not when His Majesty commands."

"If he's not here to rebuff the king and the crown prince, how will you turn aside Nalvika's marriage contract?"

Halina drew her misericord, slammed it into the table before the couch, and left it there. The blow traveled up her hand, stinging, aching. She let none of the discomfort show on her face. "What makes you think that's the reason for this visit? Perhaps my father and my second cousin miss my charming personality." In the adjoining room, Philippa snorted. "Let's worry less about the crown prince asserting his marriage claim, and more about keeping the rumors of shrikers from entering the king's ears."

"Agreed." Eugen nodded. "Lord Rhyshis does have the greater claim. He holds a signed and sealed contract from His Majesty."

"So do many others and Nalvika's is the oldest," Philippa called. "Does that necromancer have enough influence with the Council of Kings if the crown prince pursues his claim, Your Ladyship?"

Quoregna's ruling body, the Council of Kings consisted of four seats occupied by the rulers of its four kingdoms — Vernard of Ursinum, Besera's King Zelal, Arik-bohk of Or-Halee, and Nalvika's King Hjalmer.

Halina glared toward the gown room from which her lady-in-waiting spoke so boldly. "*That necromancer* certainly has the power of fear on his side. And if he invokes his right as the Duke of Rhyshis, in absentia or not, he'll have the standing, even if his brother recuses himself from judging."

Eugen asked. "What of Crown Prince Ilker? Does your brother accept His Lordship's claim?"

Halina rolled her eyes. "Ilker wants to see me married and the idea that I could be bound by Beseran fidelity laws likely gives him great joy."

Philippa barked a laugh as the steward cleared his throat and murmured, "A fair conclusion, Margrave."

Halina pushed up from the sofa and Eugen stood, too. "Nalvika's marriage claim may be why the crown prince is here, but that's not what motivates my father."

"He's here to push for the Sun Mage's allegiance?" the steward asked.

"And to punish me for not sending Gethen to Tatlis. Eugen, keep your ears open for word among Nalvika's retinue. What's the news from the North? Phila, do your best to keep me from killing my father and my second cousin."

Eugen stopped in the doorway. "You're going to marry Lord Rhyshis, with or without the king's consent." It was a statement, not a question.

"Yes."

"Why?"

"Because I love him, Eugen."

He considered that for a long moment. "I agree with

Captain Thaksin in objecting. You're in danger of losing your command to a foreigner, Your Ladyship, a necromancer. The last one to occupy a ruler's court nearly destroyed Quoregna. And you."

"This one saved my life three times."

"He endangered your life three times."

Halina spoke deliberately when she asked, "Are you capable of fulfilling the duties of Kharaton's steward or not?"

He stiffened, comprehension dawning on his face. He'd overstepped a line that he hadn't realized he was toeing. "I remain your most loyal subject, Your Ladyship."

Her mouth tightened and she cocked a brow at him. "Are you?"

"Yes. I am. I'm devoted to serving you and Khara."

"Then don't question my choice of husband."

Eugen grunted as if she'd punched him but didn't back down. "I will continue to question you, Lady Khara, as is my duty, until and unless you choose to relieve me of my position and my responsibilities."

Halina gripped her dagger, worked it back and forth to free it from the table. She considered the fine blade, considered her steward, slid the misericord into its sheath and snarled, "Dammit, Eugen. Go do what I asked."

He ducked his head and obeyed. She dropped into a chair before the hearth, tipped her head back, and sighed. How could she expect her father to see the validity of Gethen's devotion when her own trusted steward and captain rejected it?

Philippa appeared in the doorway. "Crown Prince Waldram's considered a very attractive man, Poppet." No other person had ever given Halina a pet name and kept their teeth — the king's habit of calling her Girl didn't count. Of course,

Philippa was smart enough to use it only when they were alone.

Halina's gaze slid to her lady-in-waiting. She strangled the urge to slap the dear woman. "Crown Prince Waldram is a loathsome, back-stabbing jigglestick and he drools in his sleep."

Philippa laughed. "How do you know that?"

Halina sneered. "Childhood horrors." She rubbed her eyes. "What am I going to do if that prick pushes for a union, Phila? The king's thrown me into every treaty and agreement he made since I was a nursling."

"And your father has always supported your rejections of those suitors, made excuses for you, ignored their protests. What makes you think he'll do any differently now?"

"Something's changed. Gethen accepted the offer. I accepted Gethen. But His Majesty is demanding he go to Tatlis and swear his fealty to Ursinum knowing damn well the Sun Mage can't do that. Even if he weren't Skiron's servant, the ripple of such power being pledged to one kingdom would tear apart Quoregna's fragile peace. It's as Eugen said, the last time a necromancer occupied a high seat in a king's court, the War of the Winds resulted."

Philippa sat opposite her. "Your father respects your strength. I believe he's testing you. Your half-brother soon will become king. Vernard wants you to push back, harder, to prove your mettle again, prove you can lead all of Ursinum's troops under Ilker."

"Maybe. I'm just afraid that this time I'll stab him with something much deadlier than a quill."

Philippa leaned forward and touched Halina's hand. "Then I have just the right weapon for you." She stood and returned to the gown room.

"Weapon?"

"Court armor, really," she called.

"I don't think you'll find anything in my gown collection that's strong enough to knock back our king."

"He was saving it, but I don't think he'd object to its use in this battle," the woman murmured as she returned to the parlor with a gown in her arms. She laid it across the sofa. "I suggest this for the welcoming feast. It should make a strong impression upon King Vernard and Crown Prince Jigglestick."

Halina stared. The color of the surcoat was the soft blue-gray of the autumn sky. Its elaborate gold embroidery winked in the sunlight shafting through the parlor windows. She stood and moved closer to inspect it. "Where did this come from?" She touched the shimmering flowers, bees, and vines that followed the collar and flowed down the split front. Her fingers paused upon the embroidered sol avuus that came together as a closure at the chest. "Is this Beseran blue silk?"

Her lady-in-waiting's expression remained maddeningly bland as she glanced at the surcoat and replied, "Yes, Poppet." She cocked her head and added, "It does send a powerful message, doesn't it? Wearing such a gown to a feast with the king and an unwanted suitor."

Beseran brides always wore this specific type of blue silk, a fabric so expensive that only royalty could afford an entire gown cut from it. Most women were happy to display a ribbon at their wrist or neck, a treasured heirloom handed down from mothers to sons, and gifted from grooms to their brides for many generations.

"I'm told you have a smaller waist than Queen Cerys and Queen Tegwen, but your shoulders are broader. That had Ystwyth's seamstresses in quite a pique until more silk was obtained." She carefully turned the surcoat over and pointed out the stitching. "All the embroidery on the back was added to hide the new seams. And the motifs on the front were changed to reflect the combined heraldry of the House of Persinna and the House of Rhysh."

The gown Philippa had brought was a Beseran royal treasure.

Hands on her hips, Halina said, "That fen-sucker."

Philippa stared at her, confused, worried. "Is there a problem?"

"How long have you had this hidden in the vault?"

"A fortnight."

Halina shook her head. "I'm missing the obvious even when it's right under my nose."

"You've been distracted."

"No wonder he wanted to confront the king." She shook her head. "I'm too stubborn for my own good."

"You and Lord Rhyshis are equally iron-willed," Philippa replied as she began loosening the gown's ties and separating its layers. "Well-matched in mulishness."

"I thought you disliked Gethen."

"Unlike Thaksin and Eugen, I see the good Master Gethen does you, though my observations are more concerned with your emotional well-being and less with Khara's strategic gain." She curled her lip. "Your steward and your captain are men. As much as they respect you, they'll never truly believe you fully control Khara, because you lack a cock."

Halina blew out a sigh. "I don't want to believe that assessment, but Thak's possessiveness makes me wonder if he thinks I can't manage without him. And Eugen siding with him against my choice of husband surprised and...disappointed me."

Philippa nodded. "In truth they need you to need them."

Halina fingered the embroidery again. "Come to the feast. I want you to see that rat-sack Waldram's face when I appear wearing Beseran blue. His expression will be almost as priceless as this gown."

"It will be my pleasure, Poppet." She gestured for Halina to remove her sword and belt. "Let's test the fit."

"Only an idiot would love a mage, Phila."

The lady-in-waiting nodded. "It would take someone equally idiotic to love a militess." She considered the gown. "Ystwyth's seamstresses did a fine job."

Halina chuckled. "He's a devious man. And you—" She gave Philippa a withering glare. "I'll keep a closer eye on you, too."

CHAPTER 6

Gethen slumped in a gray chair in his stillroom staring at the faint blue glow emanating from the vat of podagra unguent he'd brewed that night. An owl hooted beyond the room's closed wooden shutters. A buzzbeetle circled the room, the sound of its wings rising and falling with every pass. Ranith reminded him of Halina. The infirmary door was closed, but the room beckoned. Beyond it was the bed where she'd lain wounded and wanting aid; the desk where she'd composed a message condemning him to her king; the place where he'd first touched her, kissed her, and unleashed the heat of their shared magic.

His body ached from the breakneck pace he and Magod had set to finish the work in the bee yards. His eyes were bleary from the hours he'd spent scanning book after book from his library's shelves to produce, ultimately, a scant handful of notes on shrikers. He was exhausted, but he didn't sleep well in Ranith anymore. It wasn't the cold of the citadel, but the lack of Halina's warmth in his bed. Most nights he avoided the bedchamber altogether, choosing to fall asleep on the worn leather sofa in the solar. Tonight even that room hadn't helped him rest. He'd come to the stillroom to brew tinctures and mix unguents.

He stood, opened the shutters, and rested his arms on the windowsill. The sky was more blue than black as night surrendered to morning. He groaned and rubbed his hands over his face. "Bollocks." He stretched, yawned, and retrieved the glass of mead he'd left on the desk. He'd worked his way through a bottle of melomel overnight, a sample from a barrel he'd brewed for Halina at the end of winter using the last of the dried ebonberries. It had more vinegar than he liked, but he'd not waste a bottle and she'd like its bite.

He drained the glass then summoned the meager fire from the hearth to light his way as he trudged down to the first floor. The sooner he completed his research and reading, the sooner he'd have answers for Halina. At the bottom of the tower's wide, stone staircase, Gethen encountered Magod.

"Heading out, Master." He shoved half a hard-boiled egg into his mouth.

"Gethen."

Confusion screwed up the groundsman's face then morphed into a sheepish, eggy grin. He swallowed. "Will take time to get used to that."

Gethen nodded. "Safe travels. The ward will yield to you. Tell Halina I'll send more information about shrikers as I uncover it." He continued to the library, ushered by the distant thud of the kitchen door closing as Magod left for Kharaton Castle.

As with the other rooms in the citadel, the library floor was covered with thick, colorful rugs. Shelves occupied most of the wall space. Two large wing chairs took up the area before the hearth, and a dark blue, worn sofa rested beside one wall, sagging sadly where Gethen's necromantic predecessors had lain upon its length and contemplated death.

At his gesture, mage fire fueled the hearth, braziers, and wall sconces. Gethen went to the section of books about beasts and demons, scanned the spines, and selected three. Although dusty, the tomes lacked the taint of evil that came from some of his books, particularly the ones about necromancy. Those he avoided as much as possible. Though he was a necromancer, Gethen preferred a less corruptive form of the practice. Not that Quoregna's general populace knew that; their fear guaranteed his privacy. And drove their paranoia.

A quick scan confirmed the books contained no new information about shrikers. The notes he'd sent were limited but complete. Skiron had created the beasts after Or-Halee's great warrior king Kurmun-bohk proclaimed that he and his kin were as mighty as the gods and slaughtered anyone who defied their will. Death's dogs stole the souls of the king's son and daughter. Kurmun-bohk, his queen Baihanai, and his brothers tried to retrieve the children. The adults were mutilated by the shrikers, ending Kurmun's dynasty.

Gethen sat back. He considered the shelves. He knew every book in his library. Not one contained the spells necessary to summon shrikers. Yet, if rumor was truth, someone had unleashed the beasts. "I need more information." His gaze went to a cabinet in the corner. He scowled and stood. The best source of knowledge about necromancy outside of Ranith's books was from Gethen's shadowy predecessors.

Which meant consulting the dead.

He knelt, unlocked the cabinet, and opened the black

metal Reliquary of the Mages stored within. Swallowing his gorge as the stench of death and the thick taste of dried blood and evil intentions wafted from the metal box, he quickly accessed the shelf that held a braid of Sun Mage Sulwen's silky black hair. He fingered the lock, familiarizing himself with his predecessor's warm, powerful spirit, then returned it to its shelf and hastily closed the reliquary and cabinet, glad to lock away centuries of curses, death, and the darkest forms of magic. Except for himself and Sulwen — the only other sun mage — the Voidline's previous guardians, all shadow mages, had been a brutal and bloodthirsty lot.

Rubbing his hands on his tunic to remove traces of evil, he headed back to the great hall and turned down the low, narrow hallway that led beneath the bailey and into Ranith's ancient basilica. The site of suffering and murder during his childhood and of Halina's near-death not even a year ago, it had been transformed from an enclosed space into a three-sided shelter for Kharayan's animals. Songbirds perched in its rafters and two does considered him with large, dark eyes before returning to their midday nap.

Gethen strode to the edge of the apse, to the rectangle of honey-colored marble that covered Sulwen's tomb. He knelt, flattened his palms upon the floor, and began the incantation that would summon her spirit. Experience told him this would be an arduous process, so he didn't lessen his droning spell, even as the muscles cramped across his back and shoulders. His fingers and feet grew numb. His voice grew hoarse. And just when he thought it wouldn't work, that her spirit had truly fled too far from the mortal world to be brought back, a cage of amber light shot up through the cracks between the golden slab and its surrounding white marble. Light enveloped him, warmth suffused him, and Sulwen's mellifluous voice filled his mind.

"I did not expect your summons, Sun Mage Gethen."

"I regret this disturbance, but I seek knowledge that isn't available in Ranith's library."

"How can I help?"

"Tell me how Skiron made his shrikers."

There was a pause. *"It is detailed in Yarvi's fourth and fifth* Chronicles of the Unmaking.*"*

"Yarvi's chronicles? I've never seen anything like that, only a few references to the Unmaking in various books."

"You have read everything in the library?"

"Every book, scrap, and diagram. All I know from that event is the tale of Kurmun-bohk."

"The Chronicles *should not be missing."*

Gethen sighed. "No, they shouldn't, but that will wait. Right now I need to know how Skiron created his shrikers."

"Why do you ask about the soul stealers?"

"Because evidence suggests they're hunting in Ursinum again."

"Impossible."

"So I thought, but the witnesses give credible details. I need more information. Could necromancers summon the beasts?"

"Yes, but it requires more power than even you wield. If this has happened, it will draw Skiron's attention to the mortal realm and the god will not appreciate what he sees. All will suffer the consequences, you most of all, Sun Mage. Find and destroy the shrikers and their summoner."

"That much I figured. So tell me how the beasts are made."

"They are rattling bones and rotting flesh, found in a boneyard

and animated with spells written with their master's blood upon their bones."

"Which draws them back to their creator?"

"Yes. An anchor to him or to a place of his choosing. This is very powerful necromancy."

"More powerful than my own?"

"Possibly. Though I do not see how such a mage could exist without your knowledge."

"Neither do I. Just another part of this mystery." He stood. "I thank you for answering my summons, Sulwen."

"My knowledge is yours."

He bowed and dispelled the incantation that had summoned his predecessor from so far beyond the grave. The sun had reached it zenith and the basilica was growing uncomfortably warm. The deer were gone to seek the cool shadows of the forest, replaced by the quiet hulks of Gwyn and Duesh. Time always passed strangely when he summoned Sulwen. He stretched, his spine and joints cracking, muscles aching. His tunic stuck to his skin, damp with sweat, and his hands and feet prickled.

He frowned and thought about Skiron's anger. Gethen had come face-to-face with his god twice; the first time when he was five years old and, again, the night he murdered Shemel. Both left him with indelible terrifying memories. He had no wish to repeat the experience, even less desire to garner the god's wrath.

It was time to visit Sokos.

As if sensing his need, the wolves came to his side and sat, their amber eyes full of patience and wisdom.

"You're good friends and I only require a little," Gethen murmured as he ran his fingers through their thick guard hairs. Beneath his strong, pale hands, the wolves' silver spirits shimmered and mingled with his amber mage fire. A gentle tug freed the power that resided within the animals. It flowed into the man and restored his strength. He released the wolves. They settled into the rushes that covered much of the basilica's floor, curled together, and slept as he headed for the bailey to saddle Remig.

CHAPTER 7

Flanked by her captain and her steward, Halina stood on Kharaton Castle's wide stone stoop and watched her father and second cousin ride between the barbicans. "Khotyr, take me," she muttered as she spied Vernard's scowl and Waldram's smile.

"Steady, Your Ladyship," Philippa murmured.

"One of us will be dead within a fortnight."

The party included King Vernard and Nalvika's crown prince, several guards and body servants, and the carriage transporting Halina's sister and her three ladies-in-waiting. There were too few soldiers to protect a king, but he'd been forced to leave the majority of his defenders with Halina's and Waldram's in the causeway outside Kharaton Castle's defensive walls.

As the king's black courser halted, Halina and her household knelt and bowed their heads. She watched from beneath her brows as her father — his hair now more gray than red — dismounted with the ease of a man half his age and strode toward her. As barrel-chested and surly as one would expect of a man called the Bear King, he'd given his auburn locks, blue eyes, and stubborn disposition to all of his children. His black boots kicked up dust and the sun flashed deep in the large red ruby set into the pommel of his long-sword, a bloody eye almost as baleful as its owner's. The king stopped and contemplated her for a long moment before saying, "Rise, girl."

Halina's lips tightened. She bit back the urge to reply, "Don't call me girl." She stood as the king held out his hands. She took them and bowed, pressing her forehead to his knuckles. He leaned forward and kissed her lowered head. They straightened from the show of fealty offered and accepted and Halina said, "We welcome you back to Khara and Kharaton Castle, Your Majesty."

Vernard's keen eyes roamed the gathering as her household staff regained their feet. "Where's your mage?"

"He's not *my* mage."

"You sent him off the moment you received my message, eh?"

"He comes and goes freely, Your Majesty."

He smirked. "Lovers' quarrel?"

Halina leaned close. "Are you trying to get killed today?"

"Many have tried and failed. What makes you think you can succeed?"

"Because you think I can."

Vernard's gaze sharpened. Behind him, Waldram dismounted from his horse. The king snapped, "Greet your second cousin then walk me to my chambers. I will speak with you privately."

His Majesty moved to greet Eugen, leaving Halina to face her pale, ermine enemy. "Your Grace," she said and bowed her head to Nalvika's crown prince. He didn't offer his hands. She wouldn't have touched them if he had.

Waldram considered her with keen, silver eyes. "You're looking dangerous, Halina." His smooth, bard's voice turned heads at court; his sharp, handsome face and sharper mind kept that attention.

"You would know."

His smile widened. "Indeed. You gave me an impressive set of scars at Gurvan-Sum."

"Back for more?"

His grin remained. "No. I have something else in mind, dear cousin."

"Daughter, attend me," the king called as he strode toward the keep's open main entrance. "There's much to discuss about your future."

Halina cursed beneath her breath. "My steward Eugen will escort you to your room, Your Grace." She slid past Waldram and caught up with her father in a few long strides.

Vernard scowled at the construction in the great hall. The masons paused in their efforts and knelt before their king. "Damned mess you've made. Glad I'm only staying briefly." They emerged into the east courtyard and threaded through the rose garden to the Weather Tower. Their booted steps echoed off stone as they ascended. "You've got me in the same musty, old chamber?"

"Yes. I'm not giving up my quarters for you."

The king snorted and took the stairs two at once.

They reached the double doors of his temporary apartment. Once inside Vernard stripped off his gloves and said, "I used to like that you'd battle me, Halina. You were the only one of my children who'd fight back with claws and teeth. But I could always count on your loyalty. I never doubted that you placed Ursinum first."

She met his gaze evenly. "I still do."

He poured a glass of mead from the bottle her servants had left in the parlor and sat on the room's wine-dark couch. After downing it, he said, "Very fine tokay," and refilled his glass. "Your mage's brew?"

"Gethen's work, yes." She watched him drink. "Where's Khara's money?"

"Where's that mage?"

"Really, old man? That's the game you want to play?"

"I'm not playing games!" He slammed his fist on the arm of the couch. "Hjalmer, Zelal, and Arik-bohk are watching Ursinum with eagle-eyed interest, wondering if I miscalculated when I sent you to Ranith." His finger stabbed at her like a dagger. "Wondering what Margrave Khara and the Sun Mage are plotting."

"Plotting?" She dismissed the idea with a wave of her hand. "Ridiculous."

"Is it? The strain of our relationship is well-known, Halina. It's not a long stretch for many to believe your intimacy with the most powerful mage in Quoregna gives you an advantage over your king. And that his intimacy with you increases his advantage over all of us."

"What are you saying? I have neither cause nor will to move against you, Your Majesty. And Gethen of Ranith serves all of Quoregna. He has no reason to use me against Ursinum or the other three kingdoms. Who sold you that set of lies?"

"You did. Your letters told me how he plotted with Besera against Ursinum, how he manipulated your mind into perceiving an imminent freezing death that didn't exist, how his own wraith nearly killed you, so that he had to come to your rescue. You told me how he stabbed you, sent you into the Void, and saved your life again." He leaned forward, his gaze sharp, wary. "You told me how he was the only man you'd marry — after rejecting the very idea of marriage for over a decade. And you refused to enforce the terms of our agreement which required his allegiance to Ursinum. Since when has the Red Blade of Or-Halee rejected the lusts of many for the affections of one? Since when has she chosen one man over her kingdom?"

"Since I discovered love. And when did my love become proof that I'm plotting against Quoregna, Ursinum, and my king? Do you think I'm such a fool, Father, that I would fall in love based upon lies?"

"Truth or lie or love, none matter. It's perception that bears weight." He combed his fingers through his neat gray beard. "You say you place Ursinum above all things, but I say you mislead yourself and me because the Sun Mage controls you."

She planted her hands on her hips and faced him squarely. "I am, and will ever be, loyal to Your Majesty, whether you're a pillock or not. Everyone knows that."

Vernard grunted. "Knowledge doesn't always sway the masses. A fact well understood by those who would twist ignorance and gullibility into an advantage; well understood by a necromancer who trained to be a king. Perceptions shape reality, girl."

"And kings shape perceptions."

"So do mages."

"I know truth from fiction."

"Oh?" He arched his shaggy brows. "Tell me, that second cousin you loath so much, do you still think the cruelty you suffered as a child went only in one direction?"

"What do you mean? Waldram's brutality toward me was unquestionable."

"True, but you've forgotten what a pack of badgers you and your brothers were toward him."

"He earned it."

"Are you certain?"

She crossed her arms. "Some scars never fade."

"Waldram was the youngest of five boys and treated cruelly by all. I brought him to Tatlis to buy his loyalty with kindness. Instead, my own children made an enemy of him."

"Tirius, Ilker, and Halion were protecting me when I couldn't fight back."

"Maybe Waldram didn't know any better, Halina. He certainly wasn't encouraged to be anything but brutal by his second cousins."

Instead of responding, she poured her own glass of mead and went to the window. King Vernard watched her, waited, and sipped his own wine.

The king had admired Nalvika's crown prince when he was a boy. He'd liked Waldram's ambition and said so whenever it was proven that Waldram had, indeed, done something vile to Halina — pushed her down the Black Stairs at Tatlis, knocked her from her horse at full gallop, shoved her into the oubliette. Vernard had shrugged it off, said, "He was just being a boy. He forgets his own strength. Boys are like that. The girl'd better get used to it, if she wants to be a soldier."

But Ilker had always come to her defense, and so had Halion and Tirius. After the oubliette incident when she nearly drowned, her brothers had beaten Waldram until he coughed blood. King Hjalmer had been angry about the thumping his son had received, and even angrier that the crown prince had failed to hold his own against three older, larger boys. Halina would've felt sorry for him, if he hadn't sought every opportunity to pinch, push, cut, wound her, if he hadn't always been a monster.

The Boorsooks encouraged their children to fight and be

cruel from an early age. But power and cruelty didn't have to go hand-in-hand; Gethen was proof of that. He'd been subjected to far worse torture under Shemel's tutelage than Waldram had faced at home — burns, beatings, bloodletting — yet he was kind, generous, a healer, and a good man at heart. He had the power to summon the dead, to cross from life to death and back again, to control spirits. Yet he refused to take lives, human or animal, to empower himself. So Waldram would get no pity from her.

Finally, she asked, "What's the point of your sad story, Father?"

"*Perception.* You perceive Waldram to be a man born a monster. I perceive a man shaped by the monstrous treatment of his own kin. Your perception has shaped your reality, but is it an accurate reflection of the man Crown Prince Waldram is?" He shrugged and added, "More germane to my visit, you perceive the Sun Mage to be your lover and ally. I perceive him to be a growing threat."

Halina considered Ranith Citadel through the window, gray and foreboding even under the summer sun. She shook her head. "Your demands put Gethen in an impossible position, Your Majesty. The sun mages and shadow mages predate Ursinum. They've always dwelled in Ranith upon Kharayan Tor. They've only served one master. Skiron." She faced her father. "If Gethen goes to Tatlis, the perception that you'll have more power than the other kings will reshape their reality and threaten to launch another war."

"The only threat of war comes from a powerful union, which I and my fellow kings don't control, between the Red Blade of Or-Halee and the Sun Mage. You were sent to gain the mage's trust and fealty. Instead, he's manipulated you to gain command of your sword and disguised his actions as love."

Astonished, she stared at him. "The love Gethen and I share is true, Father. Power doesn't motivate it. Control of each other or of Quoregna doesn't motivate it. What more can I do to convince you there's no threat in our union?"

The king savored another sip of mead and his tone was measured when he spoke again. "Nothing. My distrust solidified with every demand you turned aside, Halina. With every decision you made that was contrary to the faithful daughter I knew. The Sun Mage demonstrates far too much sway over you. With him at your side, your motives are no longer clear to me. So I have voided the offered marriage contract between you and Lord Rhyshis. And I have agreed to terms with Crown Prince Waldram. You will go to Drevya Linna to become Waldram's third wife and Nalvika's future queen."

A noise escaped her, part gasp, part grunt, like the sound she made when she took a blow on the battlefield. Hands curling into shaking fists, she choked back a retort that surely would've gotten her tongue removed. Instead, she snarled, "I won't marry that weasel-faced horse's arse."

"Yes, you will," Vernard replied with calm certainty. "I made you, Militess, and I alone will wield you."

"Wield me? I'm not a tool! I have wants and needs that I've long set aside in service to my kingdom. Am I nothing more to you than a means to an end?"

"It's done, Halina. You will go to Nalvika."

"Waldram's a snake."

"That may be true, but I'll take the asp I can control over the dragon I can't."

She ground her teeth. "Your paranoia is based on conjecture and old news. If you doubt Gethen's neutrality so much, request that he pledge his duty equally to the four kingdoms of

Quoregna before the Council of Kings, independent of your influence and mine."

Vernard stood and came to the wide window beside her. He leaned against the ledge and folded his arms, the leather of his black brigandine creaking. "Should you seek to weasel out of this command, I've placed a wedge against you. Waldram will have a new queen from among my daughters. If it won't be you, Arevik is most agreeable though not as skilled. She'll give me the influence I require once she's conceived a child by the crown prince."

Halina's fingers curled around the hilt of her sword and she moved away from her father lest she stab him. "You made that agreement knowing I'd never allow Waldram to have her." He nodded and lifted his glass, a grim salute. Vernard knew Halina would do anything to stop the crown prince from touching Arevik, breaking her, making her his third dead wife.

She stared at the floor and swallowed bitter regret. How many opportunities to kill her father had she let slip? Always swayed by duty, gratitude, even her own reputation as loyal to the end. Now he had her cornered, just as Gethen had warned. "You're a heartless, fen-sucking swine," she said through clenched teeth.

"No, girl, I'm a bear.

CHAPTER 8

S okos thronged with refugees. Men and women, crying babies, children chasing dogs and herding goats, elders riding upon the backs of their sons, horses and oxen pulling carts piled with the meager possessions of dispossessed people. Everywhere Gethen looked filthy faces bore masks of despair, and exhaustion bowed shoulders more heavily than packs did. He hadn't seen so much misery since the war. He gave Remig free rein to pick his way through the crowds and along the village's rutted cart paths.

He passed up the first inn. It sat just inside the town's gates and the crowd around it was six-deep and seething. The second, third, and fourth were no better. He continued until he found a quieter tavern at the western edge of the town. Gethen tied his horse to a post outside the Red Blade Inn and ran his hand over the gelding's soft chestnut nose. "I won't be long."

Locals and a good handful of travelers filled the dim, rickety building. Conversation rumbled and drinking cups clanked. He crossed the small room to a scratched wooden bar, just another stranger in their midst, and only the barmaid eyed him as he passed, doubtless assessing the size of his coin purse, among other things.

The innkeeper, a lean man with a small, bent nose and pale green eyes, served up two tankards and said, "If you're looking for a room, keep going to Kharaton. There are none to be found in Sokos."

"Why's that?" Gethen dropped a coin upon the bar and added, "Pint of bracket."

"No one wants to sleep in the open." The innkeeper took the coin and poured a cloudy, acidic pint.

If Gethen hadn't been so thirsty, he would've demanded his coin back. But swill was better than dust on his tongue and he downed it quickly as much to quench his thirst as to clear his palate of the taste. "Because of thieves?"

"Shrikers. Haven't you heard? The woods are crawling with them north and west of Delkati and all the way to the Selga."

A man who'd entered the tavern behind Gethen leaned on the bar and nodded toward the innkeeper. "The usual, Jax." He studied Gethen from head to toe. "What's a Beseran doing on this side of the Silver Sea?" He sounded more curious than hostile.

The best way to dodge an answer was to provide an alternate truth. "I heard Khara could use an itinerant healer's services after the floods and that bitch of a winter."

The man glanced toward the door then cocked an eyebrow. "You ride a fine horse for a vagrant warlock."

Gethen nodded. "Itinerant doesn't mean incompetent. I take payment in many forms, including a very fine steed from a Beseran landgrave whose wife took ill after childbirth." All irrelevant facts.

"I see she survived."

Gethen tossed another coin upon the bar. He nodded

toward the fellow's drink to indicate that he was paying for it. "Alive and the mother of another son as we speak."

The barkeeper collected the coin and the man raised his drink. "Here's to that fine woman's health and to the generosity of our neighbors from across the sea."

Gethen smiled. "Perhaps you can suggest a place for this healer to set up safe camp and offer his services to the neediest travelers."

"Your best bet is Kharaton, sir," the innkeeper repeated and the other man nodded. "Unless you travel with soldiers and archers who can take turns at the watch."

Gethen sniffed. "I've traveled most of Quoregna and never encountered a rumor I couldn't dispel."

A wiry woman at a nearby table said, "It's not a rumor, Beseran. It's the truth. I've heard and seen them. Only last night they killed my neighbor's husband and her son and left her near dead."

Gethen considered her. She believed what she'd said, true or not. "The woman survived?"

The people around her table nodded and another woman, bent with age and a hard life, replied, "Not for long."

"Perhaps I can help her."

The man at the table shook his head. "There's no money or trade to be had in saving a woman whose family is dead, Healer. You'd be better off applying your trade among the refugees on the road to Kharaton. At least they can offer some meager food or drink, a filthy blanket, or a rotten turnip in payment."

Gethen pushed away from the bar. "That may be true, but I can afford to offer my services to a widow, if it will save her life." He shrugged and added, "Besides, it's not every day that a healer gets a chance to defeat Skiron's dogs."

The people around the table shook their heads.

"Let the god of death have his prize," the wiry woman muttered.

But the man at the bar turned to Gethen. "I know the woman who was attacked. I'll take you to her cottage."

Gethen thanked him and they left the tavern. He untied Remig and led the horse through less crowded streets, passed between Sokos's western gates, and veered north to a small farmstead. A cow, an ass, and several sheep and pigs milled about the pens, untouched by whatever had torn the cottage door from its leather hinges and strewn its pieces across the road.

His guide paused on the doorstep. "It's an ugly sight."

Gethen murmured a lie about serving during the war, but the slaughter that greeted him would've made even Halina blanch.

The woman, though alive, was insensate. She lay upon a pile of bloody blankets in the corner of the room, her breaths alternating between rapid and still. The right side of her face was torn away to reveal bone and teeth. An elderly woman crouched at her feet, quietly crooning a tuneless dirge.

Death was dawdling.

Blood, bone, flesh marred every surface of the small hut, from floor to ceiling. What few furnishings they'd had were splintered. Feathers and down from pillows swirled about and stuck to blood with Gethen's passing steps.

He crouched beside the dying woman and met the gaze of the elder. She was Sokos's hedge witch, Dima. Her eyes widened with recognition, but she continued her song as he shook his head. He sandwiched the cold, limp hand of the dying wife between his own palms, her soul's hold upon her flesh tenuous, a feather snagged upon a leaf and wanting only the slightest breeze to pull free, float away.

"She cannot be saved," he murmured. Silently, he tugged her spirit from her body. Slowly, it circled the room.

Dima stood, leaned forward, and closed the woman's remaining eye. "Her suffering is over." The man removed his yellow hat. Gethen bowed his head. With ashes from the broken hearth, the hedge witch blackened the dead woman's eyelid and placed two black dots upon her forehead, one above each eye socket, to symbolize the blindness of death and the opening of the spirit's eyes as it entered the Void. "Let go of the heart that no longer beats," she murmured. "Do not try to see through eyes that are blind. Step free of the flesh that no longer breathes. You, spirit, whose ties to this mortal body have been severed, rise and depart from the realm of the living. Your place is no longer with your family. Cross the Voidline and step onto the path that awaits you. Your journey through the Void begins." She covered the body with one of the blankets and the spirit passed into the Void.

Gethen stood. "Where's her son?"

The healer jerked her thumb upward to indicate a sleeping loft, the ladder to which had been destroyed.

"You confirmed he's dead?"

The healer shrugged. "I was told he is. I can't climb up there."

"Has it occurred to anyone that the boy could be hiding and terrified?" She shrugged again. He jerked his head at the man. "Give me a leg up." The fellow did so and Gethen hoisted himself into the loft.

The child remained tucked in his bed, undisturbed by the horror that had occurred only feet from his resting place. His soul was gone, but there was no sign of any assault upon his small body. However, when Gethen lifted the child's eyelids the evidence of a shriker attack became irrefutable. The child's pupils were so large that only a sliver of his brown irises ringed their black edges. While his body had slept peacefully, the shriker had scared the life out of him.

"Well?" Dima called. "Is he dead or not?"

"Dead and soulless." Gethen close the boy's eyes then wrapped the small body in blankets, passed it down to his guide, and slipped over the edge of the loft. He scowled as he considered the bloody disaster. "Burn the house."

The man asked, "Will that keep the shrikers away?"

Gethen shook his head. "No, but there's not enough left of the father to bury and their scattered ashes should become part of the land they worked together."

"That's for the family to decide," Dima said. She closed her eyes and began her dirge anew. It was pointless now.

Gethen followed the man from the cottage. "Any idea where the beasts came from?"

"Some people are blaming the margrave's necromancer."

"Do you agree?"

"No. The creatures came from the north. I served under Lady Khara in Schorvala during the war. I'd follow that woman across the Voidline if she asked it of me. If she says the Sun Mage didn't make 'em then I believe her. The Red Blade's word is better than the king's, in my opinion."

"Your margrave inspires an astonishing level of loyalty from her citizens and soldiers."

"She does indeed, Lord Rhyshis," another man answered.

Gethen turned at the familiar voice. "I wondered when our paths would cross, Captain."

Thaksin sat astride his horse, Khara's gold sol avuus emblazoned on the chest of his blue tabard. He looked like he'd been sucking sour berries as he leaned forward in his saddle. "Why are you here, necromancer?"

"Her Ladyship asked me to provide information about shrikers. My research brought me to Sokos."

"She told you I was here?"

"Yes, and—"

"Your services aren't needed. Slither back to your tower. My soldiers and I can deal with these things." He paused. "Your Lordship."

Gethen cocked a brow at him. "Slither?"

From the corner of his eye, he saw his Sokosian guide blanch. The man looked from him to Thaksin and retreated toward the town's gate. There was great wisdom to be found in farmers, Gethen decided.

"We don't need a sorcerer to get rid of diseased dogs. We've already killed one."

"Show me."

Thaksin scowled. "What? The dead dog?"

"Yes."

"Why?"

"Because you're wrong."

The captain came off his horse, his mail ringing and his boots squelching in the mud. "Bollocks I am. The problem is that Lady Khara sees sorcery motivating everything now. But I find less mystery in the intentions of *some* people."

Gethen folded his arms. He wasn't interested in arguing with the jealous lout, but the man's insults were getting nettlesome. "There's no mystery or magic in your intentions, Captain. You're as transparent as glass and just as fragile."

Thaksin's dagger slid from his belt.

But Gethen's hand was around the captain's wrist.

"Get your hand off me, Mage."

"You've seen what happened in that house, haven't you?" Gethen replied, his grip unrelenting. "You know a dog didn't do that. You know Halina wouldn't believe such a lame answer. Do you really think you can stop that kind of savagery without my help?"

Thaksin glanced past Gethen's shoulder then jerked his wrist free. He pushed the knife back into its sheath. His voice lowered to a snarl. "Of course monsters are to blame, but I don't know who created them, and I'm trying to prevent all-out panic. You're my prime suspect, but Halina won't condemn you without solid proof. The question is, do you plan to stop me?"

Thaksin and Gethen matched in height, but the captain had him beat in brawn and in experience crushing men.

Gethen grinned. "I plan to help you, Captain."

"Wonderful," Thaksin muttered.

Taking the higher ground wasn't always easy when your opponent was slinging mud and hacking at your pride, but his fight wasn't with Thaksin. The man was battling for Halina's affection. Gethen had already won that war. "What information have your efforts yielded?"

Thaksin remounted his horse, leaned over, spat at Gethen's feet. "Why would I share that with you?"

"Because you'll look like a self-serving, incompetent arse when I inform Halina that you withheld knowledge from me."

The captain looked away, tight-lipped, scowling. "It's the same story again and again. Attacks preceded by dogs howling. Creatures emerge from the shadows. Adults slaughtered. Children dead, their bodies undisturbed. It makes my skin crawl."

"It should." Gethen considered the shattered door from the hut. "Did any of the survivors describe the beasts in detail?"

"Some." He looked back at Gethen. "Why? What're you looking for?"

"Spells written on their bones. The incantations that animate them and anchor them to their master."

That brought more than a glint of interest to Thaksin's eyes. "Really? Can the sorcerer be identified from the marks?"

"No, but I could follow the beasts back to their summoner by tracking their trail of tainted magic."

"And catch him?"

Gethen leveled the captain with a cold stare. "And kill him."

"You can hear the beasts on the Nalvik side of the Selga, even in the day."

Gethen was treating the feet of an elderly refugee who'd hobbled through mud and destruction for weeks. The man and his family had come south from a village near the river that separated Ursinum from Nalvika.

"But your village isn't located on the Selga."

"No, no, of course not. Ah! That's much improved already, healer." The man flexed his gout-swollen toes as Gethen applied podagra unguent. "We were two days south of the river but stories travel faster than feet. Especially these old feet."

The man's adult daughter said, "They may be old, but they got the job done."

"True, true." He squinted at the mass of refugees milling around the ever-growing camp. "Can't believe the Boorsooks are messing with necromancy again."

Gethen kept ministering. "What makes you think they are?"

The man screwed up his face, looking like a wrinkled blackapple doll. "Who else, eh?" He jabbed Gethen's shoulder.

"You know I lost two sons in the war? Killed in the siege on Drevya when those Nalvik necromancers released their wraiths. Monsters killed anything that moved — soldiers, citizens, animals." He spat on the ground and wiped the back of his grimy hand over his mouth, leaving a dirty smear behind. "Damned sorcerers."

Gethen grunted. This was the tenth claim he'd heard of the shrikers coming south from Nalvika. Separating truth from rumor was impossible.

The woman grimaced and patted her father's shoulder. "Now, Appa, not all magic is bad."

"Eh?" He looked up at her then at Gethen. "You know what I mean, healer. I don't mean your kind." He shook his head again and muttered, "Thought all Nalvika's magic folk fled that kingdom."

"All the decent ones did," his daughter said. She avoided Gethen's gaze.

The man nodded. "You know Hjalmer blamed them for the misery the war brought? *He* wouldn't take the blame, even though he ordered the conscriptions and hired necromancers from all over Quoregna." He spat again. "Skiron's lickspigot, that man is."

Gethen straightened and wiped his hands on a green rag. He knew all about the Boorsook's blame game. He also knew Nalvik hedge witches and healers who'd been slaughtered by soldiers and citizens alike. The few who'd survived eked out quiet livings on the edges of the kingdom, always ready to flee. "Keep your feet wrapped and warm." He handed a small jar of liniment to the man. "Wash them twice daily and rub this on afterward until it's all used. Also, drink more water."

"Water?" the man looked horrified.

"It'll flush the acids from your body. They're what's causing your pain and swelling."

The man's daughter helped her father stand. "I'll be sure he drinks it, healer." She offered a small blue egg. "I'm sorry we haven't more payment."

Gethen took it. "A man can be sustained for a day on such a payment. It's more than enough." She smiled then steadied her father as the next refugee appeared before Gethen, a blonde girl with blistered feet and tear-stained cheeks. He grimaced and stretched his shoulders, arched his back, then turned and washed his hands in the basin of water on a stool beside him. Someone had changed the water while he was busy with the elderly man. He glanced around, looking for the person to thank, but whoever it was had been swallowed by the sea of refugees, off to handle another of the camp's endless odious tasks.

Ragged, muddy tents dotted the landscape like mushrooms, creating a camp that soon would rival the village in size. Thaksin had helped organize the area to reduce the spread of illness. Cooking took place in the center, cleaning elsewhere, refuse and waste dumped at a distance.

Dogs barked, goats complained, and children squalled. Soldiers and citizens shouted at the children, the dogs, the goats, and each other. The noise was incessant, but the smell of so many unwashed bodies in the sun was worse. Dung from horses and livestock added to the stench of people and cooking fires to create a miserable miasma, equal parts putrid, acrid, and rancid.

The girl held a baby on her lap and stared at him, her blue eyes enormous in her gaunt face. Dirt matted her hair; caked the cracks and crevices of her neck, elbows, wrists, knuckles; made her tear tracks stand out where the salt of her misery had flowed down her cheeks. She wore rags and filth on her body, nothing on her torn feet. The baby stank of swaddling cloths long overdue for changing. Standing behind them was a boy of no more than twelve years, equally dirty and destitute, cradling a brown-and-gray fox sparrow in his palm, gingerly stroking its head and wings but watching Gethen like a sparrow hawk. He had the same blue eyes and hollowed face as the girl.

"What's your name?" Gethen examined one torn and bleeding sole. She said nothing, did nothing, until he murmured an incantation to ease her pain. Then she gasped. Tears welled in her eyes and muddied the tracks on her cheeks. "Better?" he asked. She nodded. He cleaned her wounds, treated them with unguent and bandages, carried her and the baby to a nearby tent for orphans. The boy followed, still petting the bird, still silent.

Gethen had spent the day among the miserable, gathering stories and rumors, treating the wounded and weary, planning his hunt for the beasts killing Khara's children. His services were needed in Sokos but better spent cutting off this misery at its root. More and more he was convinced that shrikers had been unleashed. That meant a necromancer with far more power than the average hedge witch, maybe more power than him.

There was one possibility. A sorceress named Lauma lived near the border between Nalvika and Schorvala. She'd fled the royal court after the War of the Winds. She was the only necromancer with enough power even to attempt summoning a shriker; the only one besides him, of course. He squinted at the hot late-afternoon sun. "But where could she have gotten those incantations?" he muttered and struck off toward the horse pickets.

He regretted his promise to not use the ambit's tears to observe Halina. Seeing her would be fortifying after all the misery, not to mention Thaksin's ceaseless suspicion. Hot sun turned to dappled light as he reached the pickets at the edge of the woods and entered shadows. He found Remig, fourth down the line. "A promise is a promise, right?" He ran his hand over the horse's flank. The gelding nickered gently then tossed his head. "Right." Gethen untied the reins.

"Who'd you promise what to, Mage?" Thaksin had been waiting among the horses, waiting for him. He emerged from the picket, his own courser saddled and prancing.

"I promised Halina I'd track down whatever's killing Khara's children." Gethen mounted and settled into the saddle. "And I'd not kill you in the process."

"Then I wish you speed and success." Thak mounted. His horse pawed the trampled pine needles around the picket. "And I'm sure you won't mind some company in the task, since we're helping each other."

"That'll make the not killing you part of my promise more difficult to keep."

"You'll manage."

"Maybe I don't want to manage," Gethen said beneath his breath. He turned in the saddle. "I'm going to visit an old friend in Nalvika. I don't need an escort, Captain. I won't be gone long."

"I'm not escorting you. I'm waiting for you to make a mistake."

"Blood and bones, man, I—"

A chilling scream cut him off, a sound to make a man piss his trouzes and lose heart and hope. Something massive and stinking bolted from the shadows. Remig reared and struck out. The horses on the picket panicked, screamed, yanked at their leads. Thaksin's warhorse snapped its teeth at the creature as it passed.

"Gods! What was that?" the captain shouted.

The monstrosity charged down the hill. Jagged claws tore up chunks of earth. Gnashing teeth snapped at everything and everyone. Its pale, glowing bones rattled, maggoty flesh flew. It crashed into the camp. It charged toward the orphans' tent. Panic rippled outward, destruction and chaos in its wake.

"Yah!" Gethen spurred Remig after. Thaksin was on his tail. Around torn tents and upturned carts. Past huddled refugees and fearful faces. Through scattered belongings and abandoned campfires. Ashes and sparks flew. Swords glinted. Villagers scattered. "Faster!" Remig bore down, streaming mane, flying hooves.

The shriker smashed through tents, crushed people, tore flesh and cloth, broke bones. Two soldiers went down, bleeding, groaning. Children ran, stumbled, fell, screamed.

Gethen was off Remig and in the tent before the horse had stopped his headlong rush.

The girl, the boy, and the baby.

Gone. So fast.

"Damn!" He kicked an upturned stool, sent it spinning away.

The fox-sparrow circled inside the tent, lost, confused, frightened. He raised his hand. The bird came to him, small heart hammering, hammering. He cradled it in his palms, murmured peace, held it close.

"Where is it?" Thaksin demanded. His sword pointed at Gethen's chest. "Where'd you send it, Mage?"

Gethen stepped to the tent flap, opened his palms, and the tiny bird flew free. Sobs came from outside. Screams, groans.

He turned, knelt beside the children, and closed their staring eyes. "They're traveling through the shadows."

"The children?" Thaksin hadn't lowered his weapon.

"The shrikers, idiot."

"They can do that?"

Gethen nodded.

Thaksin asked, "Can you?"

"Yes." Gethen grabbed the captain's tabard and yanked him into utter darkness and bitterly cold, airless nothing.

CHAPTER 9

Halina's footsteps resounded in the halls as she headed for the king's welcoming feast. Most of Kharaton Castle's rugs and tapestries had been removed and placed in storage until the construction was complete. Dust danced in the light that shafted through the windows and swirled around her gown's swinging hem. She missed the usual shouts and laughter, the ring of steel on steel as her soldiers trained in the bailey. The castle seemed empty and vulnerable without their boisterous presence.

With the king's, crown prince's, and countess's retinues spilling over from the guest wing into the servants' quarters, she'd divested Kharaton Castle of all but the most necessary staff to prepare meals and baths and to maintain the fires. It didn't help her mood that only eight of her own militairs patrolled the ramparts, each shadowed by a soldier from Tatlis or Drevya, and that she carried no weapons but her misericord. The dagger was inconveniently strapped to her ankle as the kirtle's dark sleeves were too fitted to accommodate it.

"His Majesty can fetch his own damn meals, light his own

damn fires, draw his own damn bath," she said to the dusty hall. It echoed agreement.

Magod stood outside the great hall's eastern entrance wearing a new brown tunic and staring at her, a basket of bread in his arms. His eyes widened as he beheld Halina dressed in the Beseran blue gown. He bowed. "Will make Master Gethen the happiest man in Quoregna, Your Ladyship."

Her face heated. "Thank you, Magod." She'd worn the gown out of spite, knowing this could be her only opportunity to flaunt it in her father's and second cousin's faces. It was petty, but she was seething and more than willing to fling mud.

"Your Ladyship is powerful and strong but equally beautiful. Khotyr and Semele must be jealous and proud of their mortal daughter."

A smile curved her mouth. "Take care you don't snag a woman with that honey-coated tongue or you'll be hers forever. Much as Lord Rhyshis is my captive."

Now Magod blushed. "Can only hope to have Master Gethen's fortune."

Halina squeezed his shoulder. "Thank you for fetching the bracket from Ranith." She nodded at the basket he held and added, "As well as staying to help. I know you wanted to return home. The cook is grateful for your aid, as am I."

Magod and Ranith made her think of Gethen and the sparse notes he'd sent about shrikers. She wondered if he'd gathered any more information. She wondered if he missed her as much as she missed him, knew he did, and shoved all thoughts of her lover away. That path only led her to bitterness and the filleting of her father and second cousin.

He grinned. "Know how it is to juggle many tasks with little help, Lady Khara."

"I'm sure you do." Her voice echoed as they entered the barren great hall.

As the door closed behind them, a girlish squeal drew Halina's attention. Arevik, her sixteen-year-old sister, rushed toward her, pale green skirts rustling an excited chorus. Remembering her manners as she reached Halina, the countess stopped and curtsied. "I'm so pleased to see you again, Lady Khara."

Halina arched a brow. "Spare me your pretty manners." She turned to Magod as Arevik rose, her gown swirling around her like a blossom. He was gawking, wide-eyed like he'd never seen a girl before. Halina smirked. "May I present Magod, Lady Vala? He is a particular friend of mine and an associate of Lord Rhyshis."

"A pleasure to meet you," Arevik said and held out her hand.

A little strangled sound escaped Magod. He looked at Arevik's outstretched elegant hand like she might stab him, shifted the basket like a shield between them, and looked at Halina. "Uh. Excuse me." He turned and escaped to the high table.

Halina snorted. "You're far more dangerous than I am, Arevik. You just destroyed a good man without even touching him."

Arevik giggled as she considered Magod from head to toe. "He's a fine example of mankind." Her gaze snapped back to Halina. She circled her sister, staring at the gown, Magod forgotten already. "Is that Beseran blue?"

"It is."

"From Lord Rhyshis?" She brushed her fingers over the gold embroidery.

"Yes."

"Mother will be disappointed to have missed this. She wanted to come, too, but she's gravid and the king wouldn't allow her to travel."

"Quite so. She couldn't possibly have stomached that loathsome warthog, Waldram."

Arevik stifled a laugh with a bejeweled hand. She had perfect, slender fingers. No callouses. No split nails. No scars. No missing joints. Lady Vala was fair and flawless. She sobered and grabbed Halina's wrist. "Does our father know you have this?"

"Not yet."

"But he and the crown prince negotiated throughout this trip. You're to become Nalvika's next queen. His Majesty won't permit you to defy his command in this matter."

"I'll always defy stupidity, Arevik, especially when it endangers Ursinum and Quoregna. I have no ambition to be a queen, nor will I see you sent to the frozen north in my stead."

"Granted the mage was born a crown prince, but now he's hardly more than a pauper." She bit her lip. "I know you're grateful to him for aiding you against the Rime Witch and turning Besera to our favor, but would you give up the chance to become a queen for such a man?"

"What's wrong with a mage?"

She swayed her viridescent silk skirts around her legs. "Nothing's wrong with having him in your bed for pleasure, but that's not the kind of man who makes a good lord and husband."

Halina looked at the deconstructed ceiling to keep from rolling her eyes. "I'm not interested in having a lord over me, and you won't hear me complain about having a mage under me." She folded her arms. "When did you become so worldly?"

Arevik's eyes narrowed. King Vernard's younger daughter was beautiful, charming, a princess coveted by kings because she was exactly what a princess should be — to the casual observer. She had sharper wits than most men credited her with. "A holding the size of Khara needs a man who can defend its borders and extend its reach."

Halina swallowed irritation. "You've been chatting with Queen Ambrosine." Ursinum's queen was a powerful woman, if somewhat tradition-bound. She didn't approve of Halina's "antics." "I can handle what I've got just fine. I don't need a man's protection."

"She's very wise about wielding power, especially as a woman. Ursinum's reach is exactly why Waldram's here. How can you say no to becoming his queen?"

Halina leaned close. "Watch me."

"Her Highness and our mother would say you're being foolish. And the king won't permit it." Halina began to answer, but Arevik continued, "Father offered me first, but the crown prince asked for you."

Halina curled her lip at her sister. "Proving he's too stupid to marry." She strode toward the high table, the heavy silk of her gown and underskirt making a satisfying rustle. The dress had weight. It implied wealth and authority. And it delivered a message that couldn't be ignored.

Arevik followed. "Your refusal will be disregarded. Her Highness says women will be treated like imbeciles while there's a cock on the throne." Arevik's expression turned shrewd. She'd spent all her sixteen years in Tatlis and knew the schemes of royalty even better than Halina did. She leaned closer. "Of course, the king knows you won't tolerate Waldram for long. I think he's counting on your knife to make you a widow and a ruler."

Vernard was a fool if he thought his daughters were ignorant of his stratagems. Halina sighed. "I'm tired of repeating myself, Arevik. I won't be Nalvika's next queen or our father's pawn." She'd put an end to this idiocy, even if that meant sticking a blade in Nalvika's crown prince during the meal's first course. He was far less likely to pursue a union if he was dead.

Arevik cocked her head. "Do you love this mage?"

"Certainly more than I do Waldram."

"I'll take that as a yes, and it's very romantic how you met."

"Is it? Being possessed by a witch and stabbed in the gut isn't my idea of romance."

Her sister ignored her sarcasm. "You know you'll be married to the crown prince. There's no escaping it. Love and duty are opposites in our world. However, that doesn't mean you can't have your mage." She met Halina's gaze and murmured, "Waldram told Father he'd permit you to keep your lover. He doesn't want to force your separation. He understands how strongly you feel for him."

"How. Thoughtful. I'm sure using me as leverage over Gethen never occurred to Crown Prince Jigglestick." Arevik's eyes widened and she giggled, still naïve enough to be scandalized by her older sister. Halina hugged her. "I love that you want to find good in everyone's motives here, but believe me, our father won't allow Nalvika to have access to that kind of power again."

As they'd spoken, the masons had lowered their platform and filed out of the great hall. Halina noticed. She scowled. "Cadoc." The foreman stood by the main doors. He turned and bowed. She signaled him to approach and he did so with his hat in hand. "There are at least three more hours of daylight. Why are your men leaving?"

"Your Ladyship, I thought it best to send the workers home." Cadoc's green hat folded between his fingers.

"Are they ahead of schedule?"

He looked up and down, as if hoping a favorable answer would suddenly appear from the Void, then shook his head. "No, Margrave. But we're not behind either. It's just that," he twisted the hat, "I thought you'd prefer to dine without the noise." When she failed to respond he quickly added, "And all the dust. Surely His Majesty and His Grace would prefer less dust and debris in their meals?"

"The king and the prince are here at my inconvenience. I require an enclosed roof and inhabitable barracks before summer's end. If that means they eat dirt, bugs, and shit, so be it." Halina pointed at the ceiling. "Your men will work their usual hours."

He bowed. "Yes, Your Ladyship. I'll recall them from their break."

The king's valet appeared at the great hall's main entrance, interrupting their conversation. Halina noticed Cadoc taking the opportunity to dodge her critical gaze. The valet clapped his hands. Halina and Arevik turned and gave him their attention. His voice loud and clear to carry from one end of the room to the other, the man announced, "Presenting His Majesty King Vernard of Ursinum, Archduke of Tatlis and Duke of Eskis. Also presenting His Grace, Crown Prince Waldram of the House of Boorsook, Duke of Linna and heir to the throne of Nalvika."

Gods, why was he announcing them? There was no one to care but her and her sister. And Halina was trying *not* to care.

Both men strode into the room, cocks assured of their station among the hens. Eyes only for Halina, they crossed the great hall to stand before her. She curtsied, matching her father's cold, blue-eyed gaze; a gaze she'd inherited from the man and perfected. "I trust you found your apartment comfortable, Your Majesty." She turned to Waldram and added, "And you, as well, Your Grace. Kharaton Castle is a bit dustier than usual, but I'm sure you appreciate the need to improve our defenses."

Tall, wiry, but broad-shouldered, Crown Prince Waldram's reputation as a fierce combatant preceded him on the battle-field and off. As did Halina's memories of the cruelty she'd suffered at his hands as a girl. He'd grown up to be a man who was comfortable in any setting and more than willing to cut out the hearts of anyone who stood in his way; something his older brothers would attest to, if they still drew breath. The crown prince offered a deep bow to Halina and a smile that many considered charming. He had the white hair of Nalvika's oldest families and the peculiar luminous gray eyes typical of the Boorsooks. He was the son of Vernard's cousin, so Halina's second cousin, but they shared no family resemblance.

Smooth as Beseran silk and just as expensive, Waldram caught Halina's hand and kissed first her knuckles then her palm. She suppressed the urge to put her misericord through his skull as he gazed up at her, that broad smile curling his pale lips. "You and your castle are as formidable as ever, cousin. Your reputation as a fierce opponent on the battlefield and elsewhere continues to grow. I relish the opportunity to become reacquainted."

"I don't." Halina yanked her hand from his and turned to her father. She did nothing to veil the disgust and irritation she felt for both men. "You'll have to live with the dust and debris. I didn't anticipate a visit from either of your courts this summer." She stabbed her finger upwards toward the wide hole in the keep. "I can't afford to delay construction on a new, taller watchtower for the castle. I must provide the greatest strategic structure in order to keep my holding, my people, and Ursinum's border secure." Her gaze slid to Waldram's face as she added, "You never know when an enemy will try to creep beneath your nose." The crown prince's bland expression didn't change.

"A load of crap." Vernard glared at the sawdust and dirt, the broken wood and dry mortar, the loose feathers and bird shit that had plummeted through the opening in the ceiling when the platform had descended. But his gaze landed upon her, took in the gown, and he stabbed his finger at her surcoat. "This is insulting." He stepped closer until their faces were separated only by inches and added, "Defiant as always. I see our discussion meant nothing to you."

Halina began to turn away, but her father seized her arm and yanked her back. "You will obey me, girl. It's time to put aside your childish selfishness." He glanced at Waldram and added, "We have an agreement."

"Like the one you have with Sun Mage Gethen?" Her arm ached beneath his solid grip, but it only made her want to stab the man again. He held her with the hand she'd wounded as a child. The scar remained where she'd dug the quill into his skin, a stain from the ink still marking the place where her hatred had first been displayed.

King Vernard began to release her, but Halina seized his wrist, held him close, and whispered, "I stopped being a child in my seventeenth year when you sent me to Or-Halee and I nearly died thanks to your ambition. I learned early what betrayal feels like, Your Majesty. I've done my duty by letting you live. I'll continue to do it by stopping you from shattering Quoregna's peace." She released his hand even as he shoved her away.

The cook's arrival with two servants trundling a plated suckling pig between them broke the tension as Vernard's manner lightened. "Ah! You remembered my favorite. And are those spiced blackapples?"

"Yes, Your Majesty. Caramelized with onions. And we have magluba," Halina said through her teeth.

"Amma Xana's recipe?" the king asked as he stopped the servants, lifted covers off of dishes, and sniffed appreciatively.

"The very same, made with her chingis spices."

Vernard pointed Waldram toward the high table before the hall's wide marble hearth. "Sit, Your Grace."

Still all smiles, the crown prince offered his arm to Arevik. "Allow me to escort you to your seat, Countess." With a practiced smile plastered to her face, the young Countess of Vala accepted the offer and Waldram's arm.

Vernard leaned close to Halina. "Wearing Queen Tegwen's gown will not alter the course I've set for you."

"I set my own course."

"Do you think to provoke me?"

"I don't have to think about it, Your Majesty. It's second nature after a lifetime spent under your thumb." Halina looked past the king's shoulder to meet her second cousin's sharp gaze as he seated Arevik. He recognized Beseran blue and comprehension was clear in his narrowed eyes. But he was a master at court games and he pulled back Halina's chair as she reached the table. "That's a lovely shade of blue, Margrave. It complements your auburn hair and fair skin quite strikingly."

"Beware honeyed words," Arevik murmured and Halina snorted.

The king yanked back the chair on Halina's right as Waldram sat to her left.

Vernard said, "This kind of food is what Nalvika lacks, Waldram. I don't know how you remain so lanky eating sausage, root vegetables, and pickled fish. Your northern food lacks flavor."

Arevik reached for her goblet and frowned into its emptiness. Magod was the closest person available to serve her. Eyes downcast, he took up the wine pitcher and began pouring bracket.

"Who is this man, Margrave?" the crown prince asked, eyeing him from head to toe. "Why isn't he dressed in your colors?"

"Magod is Ranith Citadel's groundskeeper and a friend to Lord Rhyshis," she replied.

Waldram's gaze slipped over Magod and landed upon her. "Friend?"

Halina murmured her thanks to the cook's assistant as the young man carved and plated food. "Yes. The Sun Mage associates with kings and commoners." *And you can't hold a candle to him.*

"Was His Lordship's slave until yesterday, Your Ladyship," Magod said. "Am a free man today."

She smiled up at him and began to offer her congratulations when Waldram interrupted. "You dare speak to the margrave?" His bland expression folded with irritation and his fist came up.

But Halina was faster. She intercepted his wrist and slammed his arm to the table, pinning it there. Her voice was calm as she said, "Magod is also *my friend* and an invited guest, Your Grace. He's serving us tonight because my castle is understaffed." She met the prince's glare and added, "He's doing me a favor."

Magod had continued down the table as if nothing had

occurred and Halina released Waldram's wrist. Doubtless she'd left a bruise. The thought was deeply satisfying.

The crown prince picked up his full goblet, studied her over it, then drank.

King Vernard lifted his fork as a plate was set before him. "Where's the Sun Mage, girl?"

"Not here."

He brandished the fork like a weapon. "You'll defy me no more. Your refusal to relinquish the sorcerer was a wasted effort. Refuse my orders again and I'll have your head."

"Enjoy seeing my blood on your sword, Your Majesty. I won't marry a fen-sucking leech and you damn-well know it. You're a son-of-a-bitch for negotiating that first marriage contract with Hjalmer and I should have agreed when Halion asked me to help murder you."

Arevik stared at her from beyond the king's shoulder, her blue eyes looking ready to fall from her skull. The cook and servants beat a hasty retreat from the battle brewing in the great hall. Halina envied them.

Waldram turned to her. "Pity Lord Rhyshis isn't here. I'd hoped to speak with him again."

"His duty to the four kingdoms supersedes social events."

The crown prince's eyebrows arched. "He considers himself above his king and lady?"

"Considers?" She stabbed a pink summer potato onto her fork then scowled at it. She'd ordered the cook to prepare a variety of meatless dishes at all meals to accommodate Gethen's unique diet. Her fork clattered on the plate as she dropped it. She had no appetite. She met Waldram's bland, silvery gaze and said, "The Sun Mage is above all of us. He serves Quoregna, not kings."

"But he's your lover, cousin. Do you believe he would turn

away should you be threatened?"

"I believe he'd do what was best for the four kingdoms. I'm sure that's beyond the comprehension of a self-serving rat like you, cousin." She leaned forward. "And I'm more than capable of defending myself. Remember?"

Waldram smiled. "You're always so charming, Halina. Do you speak this way to all your suitors?"

"You're not a suitor, Waldram, you're an opportunist," she replied.

He leaned in, too. "Since we're being blunt. Our union is meant to block Ursinum from using the Sun Mage against Nalvika. I anticipate that Lord Rhyshis will refuse to move against his beloved Militess Halina."

"Mm-hmm. And the chance to utilize his power through me never crossed your mind?"

His smile widened. "Of course it has."

"Forget that. It'll never happen, just like this marriage. The Council will block it."

Cadoc and some of his men quietly filed into the great hall through its main entrance. With a show of care, they moved toward the platform and listened as their foreman murmured instructions and pointed toward the ceiling, scaffolding, and doors.

Waldram blew steam from the potato he'd gutted. He glanced up at them then at the hole in the ceiling. "Kharaton Castle's drafty but pleasant enough for a minor holding, if you don't mind something so small."

Halina sneered. "I prefer it. There's less room for monsters to fester in dark corners."

"Do you enjoy being so isolated, cousin?"

"I enjoy not being surrounded with weasels, asps, and sycophantic toads."

"Drevya Linna has no asps. In fact, there are none in Nalvika at all."

"How ironic."

Vernard leaned in and said, "It's too cold. Only creatures with ice in their veins survive in the high north."

Waldram chewed, swallowed, and said, "The Schorvalans are further north than even Drevya Linna, Your Majesty."

"I've seen them fight," the king replied. "Cold-hearted brutes. Exactly the kind of soldiers I like on my side when I'm at war." He tore a hunk from the bread roll on his plate and added, "I believe one of your Red Blade militesses is Schorvalan, right, Margrave?"

"Militess Odruna Schlaar, the daughter of the Count and Countess Nervei. She fought with me at Or-Halee and Gurvan-Sum. Surely you remember her, Your Grace. She stabbed you in the arse."

"Left thigh." Waldram took a sip of bracket before continuing. "She's quite memorable. As are most Schorvalans, I find."

The king barked a laugh. "I bet you do. They've repelled Nalvika's attempts at occupation more times than I can recall. When is Hjalmer going to give up?"

Halina snorted. "Nalvika doesn't give up, Your Majesty." She drawled, "They lose," and gave the crown prince her best impression of Gethen's wolfish smile.

Waldram's pale face flushed pink, but any reply he may have offered was cut off by a multitude of echoing thuds as the keep's doors slammed shut. The sound rang through the cavernous room with finality.

Halina's gaze jerked away from her second cousin. Cadoc stood in the middle of the room. The construction platform had been raised. His masons stood at the doors and they were armed.

CHAPTER 10

Warmth, light, and sound returned. Following instinct and the faint traces of a strange necromancer's tainted magic, Gethen had left Sokos behind to arrive at an uncertain destination.

Captain Thaksin, his involuntary companion, stumbled and cursed, shaking from the cold. He hadn't pissed himself and Gethen had to give him grudging approval for that; he'd lost his bladder and his lunch the first time Shemel had yanked him through the shadows.

They'd emerged from nothingness into a tiny, dark village. Huge trees arched overhead, swaying and creaking. A single dirt path led to the small, open square where they crouched, watchful, careful. Rickety wooden huts with thatched roofs surrounded them, green with moss and gray with rot. Stars blinked in a bruised sky. Nightfall. Snow clung to the edges of gardens and hid beneath bushes. They were north of where they'd been. Far north.

Thaksin murmured, "Where are we?"

Shrieks answered — some human, some blood-curdling and unearthly.

"Run!" a woman shouted.

Gethen raised a rolling wall of fire as the shriker lunged from between two buildings.

"Bollocks!" Thaksin's sword now faced their real enemy.

The beast screamed again as it encountered the fiery spell. Its cries were answered by others. Gethen spun out a silencing spell to steal its mind-numbing shriek, and finally got a good look at one of Skiron's monstrosities.

The enormous dead dog was all raw, jagged bones knotted together with gray ligaments, stretched yellowed skin, and patches of mangy fur. Its head was mostly exposed skull with brown teeth, maggoty jaws, and jaundiced, pus-filled eyes. A pallid glow lit it from within, visible through its parchment flesh — the incantations a necromancer had carved into its bones to animate his mindless, undead puppet.

"How many of these damned things did you make?" Thaksin asked.

Gethen's answer was a deep growl. The captain was dancing with death.

Blood and spittle flew from the shriker's jaws as it lunged again and again at the scribed wall of flames.

Gethen called, "Lauma?" He'd recognized her voice and the village, Grimbu. It was a tiny Nalvik hamlet near the border of Schorvala, and home to Nalvika's last sorceress.

"Here!" Her voice was high and tight. As if reading his mind, she added, "They're not my doing, Gethen. I swear it!"

Thaksin peered around quickly. "Who's that?"

Gethen ignored him. "How many?" He saw her now, under a cart, a dark pool spreading beneath her slight body.

"Two, maybe more."

"Get her inside, Captain."

"You don't order me, Mage."

"No, I protect you." Gethen summoned shadows from doorways and the tree line. He shaped their darkness into iridescent armor that encased his body and moved with his muscles, rippling and shifting like a living thing. "Get inside, Thaksin. You're not equipped for this fight." He drew his long-sword, dropped the mage fire, and braced as the shriker sprang at him.

"Gods!" Thaksin fell back.

Gethen raised his hand. He scribed an amber spell in midair forming a round, sorcerous shield. It flashed as it deflected the shriker. He slashed low with his sword. The beast leaped away and kept its legs. It prowled and shrieked, its piercing cry still silenced. Gethen kept his shield up and strengthened it with another heat incantation. The creature couldn't feel pain, but setting it on fire might slow it.

"I'm not useless, you know," Thaksin said.

"You're distracting, is what you are," Gethen muttered.

The shriker lunged and dodged, snapped daggered teeth, launched itself again and again against the amber shield of magic. The spell flashed and squealed with each impact.

Gethen hacked off the beast's tail and some toes, but he couldn't land a strike that would sever its spine or remove its head.

"Cut off the head, Mage! Isn't that obvious?"

"Shut your mouth." Gethen snapped his hand toward Thaksin, stealing his voice with a spell, too.

Instinct and a scrape on stone made him pivot from the jaws of a second shriker. "Bollocks!" He drove it back with an incantation but was set upon by the first beast. Gethen dodged its claws. The creature plowed into him. His shield spell disintegrated. He hit the ground, lost his sword. He rolled away from the monster's snapping teeth. Not fast enough. It seized his leg and shook. He slammed into Thaksin, knocking the captain across the square. He struck something solid, knocking the wind out of him. The beast stopped and Gethen started kicking its head. He lost armor, but the shriker lost teeth as Thaksin staggered into the fray and joined in kicking until it let go.

The second monster came at them and Gethen snarled, "Enough!" He called down the sun's power and unleashed a surging incantation that exploded outward from his hands, an arc of blue-white lightning that threw both shrikers back and flattened the captain.

The first beast hit the village's defensive stone wall and landed in a heap of bones. Gethen grabbed his sword as he pinned it with a weighty incantation. The second beast rose and leaped at him, but Thaksin was up. He cleaved its head from its neck; one monster down. Gethen lopped the legs off the other. As its cohort's body meandered aimlessly between the wall and Lauma's cart, the beast struggled to stand. It snapped at the captain impotently. A blow from Thaksin's sword severed the spine of the legless monstrosity and Gethen removed its head. The pallid glow of its maker's incantations faded to black beneath its leathery skin.

Gethen caught his breath. That was two shrikers dispatched. He assessed his leg where the monster had seized him. The shadow armor was twisted and torn but had done its job. He straightened and tried to work a hitch out of his lower back as he took in the devastation the beasts had wrought.

Flesh and blood littered the market square. Grimbu was small and only a few families lived there, but many came to the weekly market to buy tinctures from Lauma and seek her advice. Few mages remained in Nalvika. After losing her status as a royal sorceress and healer for the Boorsook women, Lauma had returned to the forgotten village of her birth.

Thaksin mouthed something. He scowled as Gethen turned and pushed him toward the cart. Lauma hadn't moved, but her blood had painted the dirt red. Her guts were open, her right arm a bloody stump at the shoulder.

She bore the sharp, pale features of the Nalviks but the black hair of Schorvala's populace, heavily braided with brightly colored ribbon. Blood congealed in the strands of knots she wore around her neck. It coated the keys, beads, and bones hanging at her wrists. Her green dress was muddy and bloody. Gethen lifted her hair from her face.

Lauma's eyes opened. "Too late," she rasped.

"I'm sorry."

"I know." She began to shake.

He held her hand and stroked her blood-soaked hair. "Who made them, Lauma?"

Her eyes glazed and lost focus. The words she struggled to speak bubbled between her lips, bloody froth. She stiffened and died. Her spirit lifted away from her flesh, circled Thaksin, passed through Gethen, its touch a lover's caress.

"You may enter the Void," he said. Her soul obeyed.

Thaksin stood. Gethen glanced at him and returned the man's voice with a flick of his fingers.

The captain bared his teeth. "Bootlicker."

A third mutilated shriker — the one they'd followed from Sokos — still struggled in the dirt square, wandering aimlessly and lashing out whenever it made contact with something, living or not. Gethen retrieved his sword from the ground and hacked off its legs. He followed with an incantation and a swirling gesture, invoking a fiery whirlwind spell that pulled the three broken monstrosities into its center where bones, flesh, and evil incantations became ash.

The firestorm dispersed and the ashes drifted on the wind, gray snow, cursed snow. Gethen felt a gaze on his back. He wiped his sword, returned it to its scabbard, and said, "You can come out. The beasts are destroyed."

Thaksin pivoted, his sword ready to strike.

"Is Lauma dead?" asked a young boy. The captain lowered his weapon.

"Yes." Gethen spied him in the shadows of the doorway beyond the cart. A scrawny child with an almost-adolescent girl beside him; both fair Nalviks, both with haunted, pale eyes.

"There are more in the woods," said the girl.

Thaksin asked, "How many?"

"I think I saw six."

"We destroyed two, plus the one we followed here. That leaves three unaccounted for. Unless someone destroyed them before we arrived?"

The children shook their heads.

"No," Thaksin said, "we're not that lucky today."

Gethen frowned and surveyed Grimbu. Less than a dozen stone huts with thatched, mossy roofs surrounded the dirt square. One road led to and from the village. The Ballard River to the north marked the border between Nalvika and Schorvala. Dense forest hemmed in the village in the other directions. And shadows overhung all of it. Color was so muted that he felt strangely at home; as if he was walking in another part of the Void and not northern Nalvika. Grimbu was well named and he understood why Lauma had left it for Drevya Linna as a girl. The place had more chickens than it had ever had residents, and most of them — folk and fowl — were dead or fled.

"All right." He turned back to the children. "Hide until we come back."

Thaksin nodded, grim resolve all over his face.

The children withdrew into the hut's darkness, ghostly faces and wide, pale eyes that receded into nothingness.

Gethen retrieved Lauma's body, brought it to the center of the square, and set it aflame. While it burned, he and Thaksin searched the houses. The captain found two destroyed shrikers. "Four and Five are down."

Gethen discovered a dying man whose gaping wounds assured his death.

"Kill me before another comes," the man whispered.

Gethen ended his suffering quickly before the captain saw and objected. "Spirit, I give you permission to cross the Voidline; find solace and relief from your pain." He found another victim, a woman, also too horrifically hurt to save, and released her soul. All the other adults and children he found were dead — the adult bodies mutilated, the children not.

When he reemerged into the square, the remaining shriker was circling Lauma's burning body and the captain was nowhere to be seen.

"You must be Number Six."

The beast turned its rheumy gaze on him, shrieked, and charged. Gethen raised his sword and brought his empty left hand back to hurl an incantation. Pain shot up his arm, into his shoulder. He was yanked backward. He hit the ground.

A seventh shriker had hold of his arm. The fall saved him from the charging beast, but the one holding him shook its head. Gethen cursed his luck. He crashed from side to side, once again a child's toy in a monster's jaws. His sword swung out. He got lucky. It caught the first shriker as it came back around and cleaved its jaw from its skull — *clonk* — and sent it skittering under a bush.

The beast stopped. It turned a circle as if looking for its missing face.

Gethen's shoulder burned. He gritted his teeth, tried to pull free. Something popped out of place. His hand went numb as pain flared across his back and chest. He smashed his right fist into the beast's skull. Its left eye exploded, a mass of yellow pus and maggoty gore. But it didn't let go.

The other shriker remembered Gethen. It forgot its jaw.

He was trapped between two deaths, neither of which was pleasant in the least. "Semele's blood." He summoned the sun's fire into his left hand, its mass into his right. He filled the throat and mangy body of the beast holding him with heat and flames, boiling the creature's purulent innards. He hurled the weighted spell at the other shriker, pinning it to the ground. It shrieked and struggled. His incantation snapped its glowing bones, crushed its skull, snuffed the spells motivating it. Pus oozed from its belly, a bilious stain that stank of rotting meat.

Finally, the monster released his arm. It went to its knees. Its flesh bubbled and erupted as it cooked from the inside out. Gethen gagged. The stink, the pain, both were too much. He sucked a breath. It didn't help. He puked. So much for his breakfast.

"Gods." Thaksin stood at the edge of the square, sword in hand, eyes wide as a spooked horse, sleeve over mouth and nose.

Gethen spat, and spat again. "Seven. Not Six. Seven shrikers." He straightened and considered his trembling left forearm. The monster's massive jaws had crushed his shadow armor, driving its unearthly substance into his flesh. Blood ran down his arm, dripped from his twitching fingers, pit-pat, pit-pat into the dirt. Moving his shoulder brought a new level of searing agony, a pinprick of lights, another mouthful of acid spit.

He retrieved his sword, staggered past Thaksin to the hut where the children hid. The captain followed and pounded on the door. "Open up. The shrikers are gone."

Muffled footsteps. The girl's voice. "Gone? Dead?"

Gethen spat again. "They were always dead. Now they're in pieces. Open the damn door."

The locks slid home and she let them in. "You're hurt."

"Get water and clean rags," Thaksin ordered. Gethen crossed the room and swept everything off the work table that dominated the space. Herbs, roots, mushrooms. Bottles and jars. A copper still. This was Lauma's house, he realized. *Finally, some good fortune.* He crooked a finger at the pale wisp of a boy. "Come. I need your help." He closed his eyes and the children gasped as he dispelled his dark armor.

"You'll shield the cottage?" Thaksin asked.

"Ward it. Sorcerous shields and armor are for battle; wards protect unmoving people, places, and things," he said as he safeguarded the house.

The boy came to his side. "You're a sorcerer."

"You and your friend have a great grasp of the obvious but run a little short on the details," he said through clenched teeth. The child stared at him, face blank, jaw open. Gethen clarified, "Yes, I'm a mage and, yes," he looked at the girl, "I'm injured."

Thaksin said, "And there were seven shrikers, not six."

"Precision matters." Gethen sat on the table and, with some effort and a great many swallowed epithets, managed to turn onto his stomach. He let his shoulder and arm hang over the edge. He directed the girl to wrap a rag around his arm to stanch the bleeding wound then had her tie another one to his wrist.

Thaksin said, "I should reset it."

"You're too heavy. The boy's a better choice."

"What do you want me to do?" The child watched, his eyes and voice holding no small measure of suspicious.

"Sit on the floor, grab the rag hanging from his wrist, and slowly let your body weight pull his arm downward," Thaksin explained.

"My shoulder's out of its socket," Gethen said. "You're going to help it move back into place. But don't jerk it. Understand?"

The boy nodded and did as he was instructed. The pulling shot pain through Gethen's whole torso. He breathed and focused on not puking again. After a few minutes and many slow, deep breaths, the shoulder popped back into place and his pain eased. "Gods," he groaned. "Let go."

The boy sat up. "That fixed it?"

Gethen nodded. He rolled onto his back. "There'll be some swelling, but I've got all the tinctures I need here." He jerked his chin toward Lauma's medicinals then reached across his chest to grip his sore shoulder, closed his eyes, and focused a low, susurrus healing incantation upon his own injured muscles and ligaments.

The children gathered herbs and containers as he directed, set a lantern so that Gethen could see his wound, and brought more rags and clean water. The girl Feddie had the gangly look of early adolescence and the boy Elof was no more than ten. They wore stained, ragged clothes; hers a nightgown. His hair was shaved short like a kitchen slave's. She had a long, messy plait that she dragged over her shoulder and re-braided again and again. That reminded him of Halina, which made him aware of need. He hadn't spent enough time with her to assuage his cravings after their month-long separation. His hands and feet still prickled and now his skin itched. He grimaced and scratched his stubbled jaw. That itch would become an internal one that he couldn't ease.

"Are you related to Lauma?" Gethen sponged blood off his arm. Pieces of his armor remained embedded in his flesh.

Feddie shook her head and tucked her hair behind her ears.

The boy glanced at her. "Lauma was my aunt." He paused then added, "Feddie's my friend."

Gethen pulled a thick sliver of something glassy and iridescent from his forearm with tweezers. It wavered and dissipated as it came free of his flesh. The tweezers clattered in the bowl. He poured a cleansing tincture into the wound. "Lauma said she didn't create the shrikers. Is that true?"

Elof replied, "I don't know," but Feddie said, "No."

Thaksin leaned against the wall, arms folded, watching. He said, "No, she didn't, or no it's not true?"

The girl chewed her lower lip. The boy stared at the floor.

Gethen put down the bottle. The fire on the hearth flared as his sun sorcery threatened to spin out of control. He clutched the table's edge. Pain, battle, the captain being a sliver in his arse, the dead children, his growing need for souls; all made controlling his magic a struggle. He raised his right hand, opened his palm, and pulled the flames from the hearth, candles, and lantern. It formed a ball that hovered in the middle of the room and radiated intense heat.

The children cowered. Sweat beaded their brows. Thaksin stepped forward, his hand on his sword grip.

"When the Sun Mage asks you a question, you answer it *honestly*," Gethen snarled. His fingers twitched and sent the flames home. "Did Lauma summon the shrikers or not?"

"I don't think so." Feddie's voice was a whisper.

Gethen stood. The table rocked behind him. Bottles tipped. Fouled water sloshed from the bowl. The girl gasped. Elof scuttled behind her. "Now you don't know?" He was losing all the cool control of the Shadow Mage to the fire of his sun sorcery. "I don't have time for your lies."

The white bones of the boy's knuckles pressed against his skin as he clutched Feddie's arm.

Thaksin raised a hand. "Calm down, Mage."

Gethen bared his teeth at the man. He was damn tired of Halina's captain.

"Stop scaring Elof." The command came from the girl. A surprising show of strength. She stood taller, facing him with the kind of authority he expected of Halina.

"No." Gethen loomed over them. "You're keeping information from me and innocent people are dying while you dither."

"They followed us from the castle," the boy blurted. "I thought Lauma could protect us."

Thaksin growled, "Which castle?"

Feddie said, "We won't go back."

Gethen snarled, "Which castle?"

She balled her hands into fists. "You can't make us!"

He grabbed her upper arms. "This isn't about you, girl. Lauma is dead. Other children and their parents are dead. I need to know the source of the shrikers or they're going to slaughter a lot more people. Tell me what you know."

Thaksin's sword was in his hand. "Let her go." The edge to his voice was as deadly as the one on his sword.

"Feddie," Elof begged. "Tell them."

She snarled and bared her teeth, a cornered possum more willing to fight than play dead. "We're not going back. We're not going to die like our families did. We're not!" Her spit flecked Gethen's face. Her ferocity was driven by fear. It showed in her wide, wild eyes, in her trembling body. And it cooled his anger. He released her. Straightened.

"No," he said. "I won't force you to return to danger." He looked pointedly at Thaksin's long-sword. "Captain Thaksin will escort you to the Ballard River Garrison. You'll be safe there." He ignored the captain's obstinate expression. "But, first, tell me which castle the shrikers came from."

The girl considered him through narrowed eyes. "Do you swear by Semele that you'll send us to the garrison if I tell you?"

Gethen met her gray gaze. "I swear by Skiron, the god I serve. Captain Thaksin is Lady Khara's most trusted soldier. He'll do all he can to assure your safety." He met the captain's glare. "Right, Captain?"

Tight-lipped, Thaksin could only reply, "Of course, I will."

Feddie folded her arms and looked at Elof. The boy nodded. She chewed her bottom lip. She sighed. "Drevya Linna. That's where they came from. But that's all I know. I don't know who summoned them."

Gethen scowled. "The Boorsooks have no sorcerers," he said mostly to himself. "But they do have enemies."

Thaksin asked, "True, but which ones?"

"I told you I don't know who created them," the girl repeated.

Gethen held up his hand. "I understand that. Did the shrikers come from within the keep?"

She glanced right and shrugged as Elof nodded.

Another lie. Some of the Boorsooks may be dead. Gethen sucked his teeth. Now he had no choice but to travel to Nalvika's capital city. "We'll sleep here tonight. The garrison is less than a day away. You'll leave at sunrise." Ignoring the sour expression on the captain's scarred face, he retrieved the tweezers and returned to picking shadow armor from his flesh. If he could find the guilty necromancer quickly, he could return to Kharaton and deliver the prisoner to Halina. The Council of Kings could oversee the trial and the destruction of the remaining shrikers. A quick end to the chaos, his name cleared of suspicion, Halina spared her father's doubts, and no unwanted wrath from Skiron.

Thaksin crossed his arms. "You shouldn't go alone."

"I didn't think you cared."

"I don't, but Halina will want to know how you died."

"Will you tell her it was by your knife in my back?"

"If it's true."

Gethen nodded at his bloody arm. "You still doubt me?"

"I will until you prove it was another sorcerer."

"Gods, you're an arse. I don't know what she saw in you."

"I say the same thing about you every damn day."

Chin on her chest, Feddie eyed Gethen from beneath her brows. "She spoke of you often, Sun Mage."

"Lauma?" He met her gaze. She nodded. Elof escaped her shadow and stared avidly at him. Magic wasn't strange to them. "Did she call me friend or foe?" He sponged blood away from the gaping wound then snagged another shard from deep within the striated muscle. Pain — sharp, burning — shot up his arm, but he welcomed its distraction.

"Both," the boy answered and Feddie said, "She wished she had your power."

Gethen grunted and didn't look at Thaksin. The children weren't helping his cause. "Lauma was my friend." They'd lain together many times since he'd become the master of Ranith Citadel. Had Elof claimed her as his mother, he would've wondered if he'd fathered the boy. It was as likely as not. He extracted the last shard of shadow armor, tossed the tweezers into the bowl of bloodied water, and rinsed the wound again. Then he smeared a healing unguent in it and found the sewing kit one of the children had fetched. "Which of you can sew?"

Feddie held out her hand. "I can."

Thaksin said, "I've more experience."

Gethen ignored him. "She can do it."

"Not well." Elof said, "You'll have an ugly scar."

Gethen laughed. "You've reminded me of a militess I know. She isn't troubled by scars, nor am I. We both wear them proudly. Sew it up, child."

She set to work while Thaksin dropped into a creaking chair and scowled at the fire. She was slow and the boy hadn't lied about it being an ugly job. But it was better than an open, festering wound. While she worked, Elof set out striped beans, dried fish, eggs, bread, and cheese. Gethen murmured his thanks and their unlikely party settled down to eat as the room darkened with the setting sun.

Afterward, he strengthened the ward. "Don't cross the threshold. The ward is deadly." He and Thaksin refused to take Lauma's bed from the children.

The captain said, "No telling where you'll sleep at the garrison. Take a bed while you can."

Elof brought them blankets and small, woolen pillows. "I couldn't find anything that wasn't scratchy."

Thaksin started snoring as soon as he'd stretched out. Gethen settled on the other side of the room. "This is fine, Elof. I've slept in worse places without even a rag for warmth." He rolled in the blanket, raised his hood, and closed his eyes. But the boy still crouched at his side. Gethen peered at him through a half-lidded eye. "What?"

"Feddie said we should watch you for fever during the night."

"Did she?"

"She says you're tetchy because you're ill from the shriker wound."

"Huh. Feddie is kind, and were I not a necromancer and a healer she'd likely be right. But I am and she's not. I'm *tetchy* because I'm chasing shrikers all over Quoregna with Captain Cockswallow instead of feasting at Kharaton Castle."

"Oh."

Gethen closed his eyes. "Go to sleep, Elof." After all the travel, fighting, wounds, and healing, his body hurt everywhere. He was spent. Too spent even to set a ward around himself against Halina's captain.

"Thank you, *Herra-tomruma*," the boy said and shuffled to the bed. Feddie already softly snored under the quilt.

Thaksin shifted, rolled over. "What's that mean?" he muttered from the dark.

Bones. Of course he'd been listening. "What?"

"Herra-tom-whatever. What the boy called you."

"Herra-tomruma. It's Nalvik. It means Voidmaster. Shadow Mage Shemel favored it, which is why I don't."

Thaksin grunted. "There's something I've been wondering. If you're the most powerful mage in Quoregna, why can't you just, I dunno, snap your fingers to destroy the shrikers?"

Gethen rubbed his eyes. "That most-powerful-mage reputation is carefully propagated gossip. I keep the Voidline. My power is formidable to the spirits, but it's only a little greater than any other necromancer's among the living. You don't have to be significantly more powerful to make the claim, you know. You just have to convince people you are and let their imaginations do the rest."

Thaksin sat up, a shifting mass in the darkness. "You're a conman!"

"Don't underestimate me, Captain. I'm an extremely capable sorcerer with far more knowledge of potions and incantations than my peers. But people will believe anything if you put enough flash behind it."

"I saw the wards around Kharayan Tor. Those things are nasty."

"Wards are meant to be deadly. Any decent mage can spin up a brutal ward with the proper training and a good power source to draw from."

"Power source?" The captain lay back, boots scraping, leather creaking.

"The tor yokes the souls of all the previous shadow mages. There's a lot of spiritual power humming beneath that hunk of rock." Gethen folded his hands behind his head and stared into the dark. "But sorcery demands a price equal to its strength, Captain. And the greater the magic wielded, the greater the danger to the mage. More so if that magic is necromancy."

When he was fifteen years old, Shemel had taken Gethen to Besalee Portcity. They'd stalked the dank, twisted streets of the pleasure district, visiting all the nocoli dens where the seeds and roots of that smoke weed were crushed, powdered, snorted, rubbed into gums, poured into veins, shoved up arseholes. Shemel bought the souls of addicts for pennies, for the cost of a last exquisite high. Sticky, sweet, sickening smell, sweat, vomit, and piss. Black-eyed, slack-faced, drooling, wheezing, twitching skeletal humans, their skin hanging on their bones, pale lips stretched over rictus smiles, crying, laughing, screaming all at once. Dying slow, harrowing deaths, they'd do anything for a nocoli haze, anything. Even sell their own souls to a necromancer.

Shemel took them. Gladly. Cheaply. With a laugh and a copper coin. He drained the life from them, one-two-three at a time, leaving human husks, bags of bones to rot in the streets. He forced Gethen to subsume one. "There's the source of real power, boy!" Shemel had crowed and laughed, sent blood-red magic snaking through the streets, enslaved men to murder for his amusement, women to whore for his pleasure.

Gethen had run from the madness. He'd run from the exquisite high of a human soul coursing through him, run from the monster than Shemel wanted him to be.

He still ran from it.

He'd only taken one other human soul since that day — Shemel's, after stabbing the master necromancer more times than he could count. That was how he became the Shadow Mage, the keeper of the Voidline, Skiron's servant. He'd slaughtered his master and stolen his power, his knowledge, and battled the mania that came with it ever since. He'd hoped his transition to sun sorcery would ease the urges, but it had done the opposite and he ached for the power of human souls more acutely than ever.

Only Halina dulled the razor edge of his cravings.

He was dreaming of Halina. Dressed in red armor, she sat in the great hall and said, "I don't want you here," over and over as he circled her chair. Beyond them, all was dark and voices murmured, but he couldn't understand the words, couldn't make out figures or faces. "I don't want you here. I don't want you here. I don't want you here." Something poked his leg. He looked down. A shriker had hold of him, maggots squirming from its mouth, its eyes. "I don't want you here." Its jaws clamped down, broke his armor, his skin.

Gethen came awake with his dagger in hand.

Elof jerked back and landed on his arse, eyes-wide, hands raised to stop a blow. "Sorry, Master! I'm sorry! There are soldiers here, in the square. The captain says you need to lower your ward."

"My ward?" Gethen scrubbed his hands over his face and groaned; even his eyelids ached. "Yes. All right." Feddie stood beside Thaksin, peering out the window. "Are they Nalvik or Schorvalan?" Gethen asked.

"Schorvalan, I think," the captain replied. "Hard to be sure in the dark."

Voices murmured outside, horses snorted, armor jangled and creaked.

Gethen stood and waved the children closer. He removed his dagger and its sheath from his belt and gave it to Elof. "To defend yourself and Feddie. It's small but ensorcelled and more dangerous than it looks. Use it only if you must, and not for cutting anything but enemies."

The boy slid the sheath onto his belt. "Thank you."

Thaksin folded his arms. "What are you doing?"

"Taking precautions." He hung his sword belt around Feddie's narrow hips, looping it twice to take up the extra leather before giving her his long-sword in its scabbard. "Have you ever handled a sword?"

She nodded. "My brothers taught me."

"Good. This is spellbound, too. Keep Elof safe. Don't hesitate to use it if you're threatened. Adults will assume you're helpless. Surprise them; that's your advantage."

"Yes, Herra-tomruma." She slid the weapon into its sword

frog and kept her hand on the grip to tilt it forward and off the ground.

Through a narrow window he saw the black, shapeless wall of night-wrapped forest. "Elof, fetch the lantern." The boy did and Gethen placed it upon the floor at their feet. "I can use a spark from your souls to create mage fire that will obey you." He met their gazes. "Will you allow this?"

Now Thaksin drew closer, curiosity clear in his keen eyes.

"Will it hurt?" Elof asked.

"No. The spark is a little power I draw out of you." They exchanged a glance then nodded together. Gethen held up his left palm. "Place your hands on mine." They did and both started a little as he pulled the smallest spark from their souls, a soft green flash. He raised a bright ball of amber mage fire over his left palm, murmured an incantation of eternal light, and brought the two sparks into the flame. It took on a greenish cast until he opened the lantern and set the mage fire inside. There its glow returned to a normal yellowish flame. Gethen handed the lantern to Elof. "Tell the flame to go out."

The boy looked from him to the lamp and said, "Flame, go out." The lantern went dark. "Flame, return," Elof said without prompting and the mage fire returned. The children's smiles vied with the light for brightness. "Will it work for Feddie?"

Gethen nodded. "But no one else."

Thaksin murmured, "Useful trick."

Horses snorted, armor clanked, and voices broke the eerie quiet.

"Drop the ward," Thaksin said. "I'll speak with the soldiers."

Gethen motioned for the children to remain behind as he lowered the hut's ward. He stepped into chill air behind the captain and reached for the now-familiar mania of the shrikers. All was calm.

An armor-clad woman rode forward. "Thak? You're far from home."

Thaksin held his arms wide. "I go where I'm needed, Odruna."

"And what made you think you were needed in Grimbu?"

"I did." Gethen stepped forward. "And a lot of shrikers."

The militess was built like her warhorse, tall and muscular with a tense discipline that bespoke tightly harnessed power. She and her soldiers had the brown skin, black hair, and blue eyes of the Schorvalans, an anomaly among Nalvika's northern tribes, the rest of whom were almost uniformly pale. She wore her hair in row after row of thin, tight braids, each banded at intervals with narrow metal rings. Like Halina, the militess was scarred, though she followed the Schorvalan practice of tattooing her scars with black ink. Her most pronounced one slashed her jaw, crossed her throat, and descended diagonally below her collar. Her white tabard displayed Schorvala's black wolf, and the red sword embroidered beneath the animal proclaimed her a member of the Order of the Red Blade.

"Who are you?" she asked.

"The bloody Sun Mage," Thaksin muttered.

Gethen said, "Gethen of Ranith, Duke of Rhyshis in absentia."

"Also far from home, Your Grace." The woman leaned forward in her saddle. "Is Margrave Khara with you?"

"No," Thaksin said. "She's at Kharaton, called upon by His Majesty King Vernard."

Odruna considered the charred and scattered remains of the shrikers. "Your doing, Master Mage?"

"Their destruction, yes. Not their creation. I'm here by the margrave's request to hunt and kill the dung heap who unleashed them."

"Was it the Nalvik sorceress Lauma?" one of the men asked.

"No. She's dead."

"Convenient that," the man muttered.

Gethen's gaze slid to him. "Not for her."

"Enough, Paick." Odruna nodded toward the doorway where Feddie and Elof stood. "Whose children?"

"Orphans from Drevya," Thaksin replied. "Driven out by the emergence of the shrikers there."

The militess voiced a long and colorful string of epithets. "The shrikers came from Nalvika's capital?"

"I'm only certain that's where these children first encountered them," Gethen said. "I'll follow that lead in hopes it'll bring me to an unfamiliar necromancer whom I can kill."

She grimaced toward the black woods. "We can't go with you. We're already too far into Nalvik territory."

Thaksin quickly replied, "We're not asking for aid or an escort but do request that you take Feddie and Elof to your garrison and keep them safe."

Gethen scowled at him. The damned weasel wasn't willing to be sent down a hole.

She nodded. "Paick. Reider. Take the children. We'll return directly to the garrison."

Gethen and Thaksin set the children on the horses behind the soldiers. "May the gods keep you safe," Gethen murmured.

The patrol headed toward the Ballard River, none looking back.

Gethen returned to the hut, followed by the captain. In silence they packed what was left of the food, gathered blankets and a bottle of bracket. Gethen sat on the edge of the table and closed his eyes.

"What're you doing?"

"Remembering."

"Remembering what?"

"Drevya. It's been many years since I was last there."

"Why is now the time for nostalgia?"

Gethen exhaled irritation. "Because an incantation can't take me to a place I've never visited, don't recall, or have no magic trail to follow."

"Oh. Bollocks. Not that spell travel again."

He smiled, wolfish, eyes still closed. "Worse."

CHAPTER 11

Halina scowled. Where were the servants? She'd been so busy baiting the crown prince and snarling at the king that she hadn't realized the flow of food had stopped. Two courses were finished, but no one had plated the remaining dishes. Only Magod remained of the serving staff.

Cadoc stood in the center of the room, flanked by two baby-faced Nalvik adolescents and a dozen burly, armed carpenters.

Her chair screeched across the stone floor as she stood. The men at the doors drew their swords. Vernard and Waldram rose, too. "No one gave your men permission to carry weapons, Cadoc." Her hand went to her waist where her sword should've been. "Remove them from my great hall."

The head mason stepped forward with his men. "Apologies, Your Ladyship, but that's not going to happen."

Halina's head cocked to the side. "Why not?" She glanced at her tablemates. Vernard's expression was as black as her mood, Waldram's was as cold. Arevik looked like a startled doe. Magod stepped between the countess and the builders, his hand on the grip of the knife he always wore at the small of his back. Halina liked his instincts.

Cadoc met her gaze, a confident smile curving his mouth. Gone was the nervous foreman who'd worried his cap and tiptoed around her. "Because I've ordered them to keep you and your companions in this room."

"You've ordered them?" Vernard said, his voice dead calm.

"Yes, Your Majesty. My soldiers and I must impose upon Your Lords- and Ladyships for the remainder of the evening."

"Because?" Halina reassessed him.

"We're being handsomely paid to do so." He gestured around the room at the armed men. They'd been masons and carpenters until only moments ago, men who'd moved freely about the castle, learned the comings and goings of its soldiers, and overheard Halina's affairs. She'd trusted them. And they were betraying her.

The atmosphere in the room warped and crackled. The hair on Halina's arms stood. She stared at Cadoc's two pale, Nalvik companions. They had the gangling appearance of pubescence and stood back-to-back, eyes closed and stringy arms raised. Their hooded black cloaks swayed with some unfelt breeze. She knew a magical ward when she felt it. And she could see it if she didn't look directly at it, a faint shimmering in the air like heat rising from cobblestones under the summer sun.

"They've warded the hall," the king snarled.

Halina pivoted and punched Waldram in the skull, knocking him off his chair. "Nalvik battle mages! You pallid turd!" She lacked a sword, but even a fork became a deadly weapon in Militess Halina's hands. She brandished hers, ready to remove his eyes and his liver. Waldram scrambled to his feet. She yanked her misericord from the sheath on her ankle and kicked aside his toppled chair. "I'm going to carve you like that suckling pig."

Cadoc's laughter rang through the hall. "As much as I enjoy watching you beat the future king of Nalvika, Lady Khara, you're mistaken." He jerked his thumb at the baby mages. "Britta and Vins are hired mercenaries, just like the men blocking the doors and killing all of your servants. They work for me, not Crown Prince Waldram." He strolled toward the table and the sorcerers came with him. "That they're Nalvik is an amusing coincidence. Unfortunately for my two young companions, being a mage in their homeland makes them unpopular. Fortunately for me, that makes their services quite affordable."

"What do you want?" King Vernard's voice rumbled dangerously and the table creaked as he leaned on it.

Cadoc clasped his hands behind his back, cocksure and comfortable. "We want money. Our employer wants war." His associates threw back their hoods to reveal dark hair, light eyes, and mottled skin. Beserans, every one, and thick brutes all. Cadoc's workers had come from all over Quoregna, but only his countrymen stood with him now. They'd mingled with the regular builders and spent months studying Kharaton Castle. Then the king and Waldram had arrived and handed them opportunity on a platter.

"Only a madman would want war." Halina stepped forward. Two Beserans blocked her with raised swords. The other mercenaries fanned out to intercept Magod, the king, and Waldram.

"Who's this lunatic with deep pockets?" Vernard demanded.

Halina noted the men to her right and left. One of them watched her, but the other's attention strayed to the king.

Cadoc smiled. "Gethen of Ranith, of course."

"A damned lie!" Magod lunged at Cadoc. He was blocked by a mercenary blade at his chest but not through it.

Halina crossed her arms. "It takes big bollocks to throw out such a bald falsehood."

"Well, I've got a nice pair, Militess." Cadoc laughed and cupped his crotch. "And I don't care if you believe me or not."

Halina stuck her fork in her distracted guard's thigh. He howled. She followed up with her dagger. The blade slid through the gaps in his weak mail, puncturing femoral artery, kidney, heart. She ducked his companion's sword and yanked the dying man's body between her and the other armed builders.

Her companions waded into the fray. Shouts and grunts followed. Fists struck flesh. Bodies hit the floor.

"Stop, Margrave." Cadoc's voice rang above it all. "Or I'll slit your little sister's pretty throat."

Halina shoved the dying man away, caught his sword as he fell, and stuck it in her other attacker's gut. She strode toward Cadoc, marking him for murder.

His blade bit Arevik's pale skin. Blood oozed from the wound. She panicked. "Halina, please!" She was too afraid. She didn't trust that her sister could put a blade through a man's eye at twelve paces. She was struggling and frightened and would end up dead. Cadoc's smile widened. He knew he had something Halina wouldn't risk.

The king, the crown prince, and Magod still battled their captors. Halina withdrew the sword and thrust it into the back of a man attacking the king. She released the weapon's grip and raised her hands. "Stop, my lords. We can't win against these numbers." Facing Cadoc she added, "Release Arevik, my family, and my servants. If it's a fight you want, then you don't need these captives. I've more than enough piss and vinegar to take you all down alone."

Cadoc kissed Arevik's cheek. "That's obvious, Margrave. You just executed three of my men without putting a hair out of place. So I'll keep this nice shield of innocent and influential victims around me while I'm awaiting the Sun Mage's next command."

"Proving you're a coward and a liar."

He showed her his teeth. "Proving I'm a survivor." He nodded toward one of his men, who came forward and took Halina's misericord. "I have patience, a cunning mind, two battle mages," he indicated the boy and the girl standing nearby, "and the advantage. That's why His Lordship chose me for this job."

She glanced at the king and found his shrewd, angry gaze fixed upon her. *Khotyr, take me.* Cadoc's lies were bolstering her father's paranoia about Gethen.

"Now." The head mason accepted the misericord from his man and surrendered Arevik to him then nodded at another mercenary. "Ren, get rid of Magod. That'll complete my control of the great hall and Kharaton Castle."

Ren turned, reached for Magod, and got knocked flat. "Not leaving the margrave and the countess," the groundsman said.

Cadoc jerked his head at two more mercenaries. They took on Magod as their leader strolled to the head table. He turned Halina's dagger this way and that as he considered the food and his men fought. He sampled some magluba and licked his fingers. "That's delicious." He roamed the length of the table, lifting covers off various dishes, sniffing appreciatively, sampling white cheese from a cutting board and a potato from Halina's abandoned dinner plate. He cut a piece of steaming meat from the haunch of the suckling pig.

"That's even better." He cut more and licked grease from the dagger.

"Not leaving this room!" Magod fought. Two more men joined the fray.

Waldram said, "Halina, order the man to leave. He's going to end up dead." It was the first smart thing the crown prince had said all day.

"He'll end up dead anyway," Vernard replied. "We all will." That was even smarter.

Halina started to speak when, quick as an asp, Cadoc pivoted and stabbed her honed knife into her father's neck. "No!" she shouted. Two mercenaries caught her, threw her to the floor. A third joined in. The prince and Magod fought, cursed. A fourth man piled on. Halina snarled, kicked, scratched, bit. "Father!"

The keen blade sawed through cords, ligaments, flesh. King Vernard stared at her. Stared, pawed his gaping throat, and found the hole. He made a wet, sucking sound. He opened and closed his mouth, a fish needing water. Arevik screamed and screamed. Halina's heart pounded in her ears. Her father's knees buckled. Arevik ran to him. The high table toppled. Metal clattered, crockery broke. The countess sobbed. She pressed her hands to the king's throat, desperate, pointless. His feet scraped the stones, jerking like a frog on a hot pan. Blood gushed between Arevik's fingers, bright red on green silk, bright red in gray beard, a spreading crimson stain on the floor.

It was hopeless. Halina fought anyway. Her skull slammed into someone's face. Bones cracked. Blood splattered her face. Her fist met a man's groin. He squealed, went to his knees. Her elbow laid him flat. But for every mercenary she shook off, two more piled on. She raged. She struggled. They crushed her to the stone floor and her father's life bled out between her sister's elegant fingers. King Vernard's legs kicked, twitched, went still.

"Enough," Cadoc said. His men backed off as quickly as they'd come on. "Now our hosts understand our intentions. There'll be no misperceptions here."

Magod shoved free from his captors and scrambled to Arevik. He put his arm around her shoulders. "King's dead, Your Ladyship." His tone was soothing, like he was calming a startled horse. "Come away." He gently pulled her up. Sobbing, she turned into his arms. Magod eased her back from the body and the mercenaries.

Cadoc watched them, eyes narrow, calculating, shrewd. "Magod stays. Having his life in my hands may prove useful." He crouched before Halina; his men hadn't released her yet. Someone's meaty hand pinned her head to the floor. Others manacled her arms, her legs. Someone's knee pressed into her back. "Now that I have your undivided attention, we'll discuss next steps."

Her spittle hit his trouzes, blood and phlegm and hatred splattering the dusty material. "Dead men never have anything worth discussing."

"Still snarling? I thought you'd have learned from the Bear's end." Cadoc straightened. "Get her up." Then he called, "Vaughn! Owyn! Send them down!"

Yanked to her feet, Halina followed his gaze upward to see movement around the deconstructed roof and, moments later, the construction platform descended. The pulleys and tackle squealed. The wood groaned. Halina saw its load. "Son of a bitch." Bloodied bodies clad in blue and gold, red and black, orange and white were piled upon the lowering platform.

Their throats had been cut, their skulls crushed. She ground her teeth. "I'll kill you, Cadoc."

"You'll pay for this," Waldram snarled.

Cadoc glanced at the bodies and shrugged. "So you see, no one's coming to your aid anytime soon." He filled a glass with bracket from the bottle upon the table and savored a sip. "Is this one of the Sun Mage's brews?" He peered at the liquid and said, "I've been hearing for months how good it is, and the claims aren't exaggerated." He drained the cup. "I'll ask Lord Rhyshis to add a few barrels to our bargain." He grinned and drank deeply.

"Obviously, you don't know Gethen."

"Obviously, *you* don't." He turned to his mercenaries and his voice gained a sharp edge as he said, "Clear this table and anything that can be used as a weapon from the hall. Search the castle from top to bottom, inside and out. Kill everyone you encounter and bring me any keys you find." Then he headed for the south door. "Britta, Vins, and Trefor, come with me. The rest of you get to it."

They'd removed the tables, chairs, benches, braziers, even the logs from the hearth. Halina stared at the pile of dead soldiers. She knew every Kharan man and woman, knew their families, had sung songs and drank with them on the ramparts and on battlefields. She'd lain with some of them on cold nights. They were her family as much as Vernard was, maybe more.

"If I hadn't panicked, he'd still be alive," Arevik said, cowering against Magod, the last word ending with a sob.

Something that had gone askew in Halina snapped back into place. It slammed a lid down on grief and shoved it into a crowded, seething corner of her mind. Determination swamped the void. This was how Militess Halina, the Red Blade of Or-Halee, stayed alive and won battles. "Enough, Arevik," she snapped, her voice harsh. "The Bear King is dead because Cadoc slit his throat. Don't lessen the crime by taking the guilt. And stop crying for our father. He was a great soldier. He died on his feet, fighting to protect his family and his people. Don't dishonor him with self-pity and snot."

"But I was a coward," she mumbled, misery in every symbol.

Halina looked away, stomped on a surge of rage at her sister's weakness, drew a steadying breath. *Arevik is inexperienced.* She caught Waldram watching her and hated that it wasn't his throat that had been cut. She turned back to her sister. "You were scared. You've never been in a fight, for which I'm grateful."

Magod used his sleeve to wipe blood from Arevik's hands. "Couldn't've won against two battle mages."

Waldram offered her a handkerchief, orange silk edged in black with a white stag embroidered in the middle. "For your neck."

She took it. "You're very kind."

Halina's gaze narrowed. Blood stained his pale gray tunic, his neck, his knuckles. He *was* too kind for Waldram. She didn't like Kind Waldram, Brave Waldram. She didn't trust him. "Keep pressure on the wound and the bleeding will stop." Magod removed his brown coat, folded it, and settled Arevik against the wall, close to the hearth. Halina touched his arm. "Thank you."

He ducked his head and crouched beside the countess, his back against the wall, his eyes on the mercenaries guarding the doors.

Waldram asked, "Where's the Sun Mage, Your Ladyship?" He was bleeding from a wound on the back of his skull. He didn't seem to notice. Kind Waldram was still oblivious to pain, just like Monster Waldram had been when they were children, and when they were adults on opposite sides of the battlefield. Though, back then it'd been her pain he'd ignored.

"Ranith," Magod replied.

She looked away from her bloody second cousin. "And not due to return here for weeks." She couldn't use the ambit. Gethen had been clear about not summoning him across a sorcerer's ward. He'd be killed. She couldn't lose him, too.

Quietly, hesitantly, Arevik asked, "Are you sure of his innocence, Halina?"

"Yes," she snarled. Her sister winced as if bitten. Contrite, she stooped to inspect Arevik's wounded neck and her voice was gentler when she said, "It's just a scratch, thank the gods."

"I'll thank you."

Halina kissed her head. "Pull your guts together, Arevik. I need a countess, not a coward."

Her sister covered her mouth with Waldram's handkerchief, hiccupped little sobs, and nodded as she struggled to find bravery. "I'll be all right, Halina. I will."

"Of course you will." She caught Arevik's hands in hers. Squeezed and squeezed harder until the girl gasped and tried to pull away, her eyes round, brows twisting from pain. Halina's voice was steely. "You're a Persinna." Her voice was cold. "The Bear King's daughter." Her voice was as sharp as the dagger that had killed the king. "Don't forget it." She let go and stood. "The dead need tending." Arevik clenched the handkerchief and swallowed, her expression controlled at last.

Waldram murmured, "Magod and I will move the king."

She nodded, folded her arms. "He should not have died."

"It was a coward's act," Waldram replied as Magod closed the king's staring eyes and wiped blood from his pallid face.

She nodded then turned to dealing with her soldiers. Two of them clung to life, though it was impossible that they would survive. "Arevik, comfort the dying." The girl put on a stoic face and came to sit between the soldiers, holding their limp fingers. Neither was conscious, and that was a gift from the gods.

Halina, Magod, and Waldram moved the dead soldiers to the windowed wall. She arranged them to lay side-by-side and closed their mouths and eyes.

"What're you doing?"

She ignored the mercenary named Ren but found it harder to ignore his heavy mace, its flanged head still bloody, bits of pale hair and flesh stuck in its grooves. He'd mixed mortar for her castle's walls, up to his knees in lime, halite, and lard, always quick to offer a nod and a smile.

"Cadoc didn't say anything about moving them. Go sit down." He shoved her.

Halina's hands curled into fists. She straightened and slowly turned to face him. "Maybe you don't care about the dead, but I do. Interrupt me again and I'll feed you your teeth."

He crossed his arms and sneered. "You don't frighten me."

"Because you're an idiot."

There must have been some glint of madness in her eyes because Ren blinked and stepped back. "Finish with them. Quietly. I'm sick of all the wailing."

"Your ancestors must despise you." Halina spat on his mortar-crusted boots.

He snarled, lunged. She dodged, pivoted, snapped her fist out and struck his nose. His head snapped back. His shout became a gurgle. Her elbow struck his face once, twice, a third time before another mercenary pulled her away. This time it wasn't fresh Ursinum blood that stained blue and gold.

"C'mon, Ren," the man said and shoved the wounded, cursing mercenary away. "You'll get your chance at her. We all will."

Halina spat at them, wiped her mouth, and turned to the dead. Without a hedge witch to perform the Voidline crossing, the ceremony fell to her. As an in-field commander, she'd directed many fallen soldiers' souls to seek the Voidline.

As she whispered the words and marked their faces with ash, cold regret and heated anger mingled within her. "Revenge," she imagined the fleeing souls whispering. "Murderer," they said. She almost felt their reluctance to leave. "Monster." Almost felt their rage, their despair, their betrayal.

"Your deaths won't go unavenged." She raised her head imagining she could see the spirits hovering around her, a shimmering mirage straddling the mortal and immortal realms. She blinked and the illusion was gone. Halina bowed her head. She remembered her father's powerful presence. "I'll find the person behind this, Your Majesty. I'll have revenge." She shivered as if his soul passed through her to cross into the Void. She was left with a powerful resolve. Cadoc was a dead man, and whoever paid him, too.

With the ritual complete, she turned to help the wounded. One of the soldiers had died. She performed another crossing and they moved the woman's body to join her compatriots. Blood pooled beneath the other soldier. He wouldn't survive much longer. Halina knelt and took his hand. He slowly opened his remaining eye.

"You'll ruin your gown, Your Ladyship," he rasped.

"Too late to worry about that, Umniris."

"Your army approves of the union. Did you know that?"

"The union?"

"You and Master Gethen," he whispered.

"Oh." Halina's shoulders hunched and heat flushed her cheeks.

"He's good for you." His response came through clenched teeth. His body stiffened. "And...Khara."

She leaned forward and kissed his forehead. "Let go."

"Failed...you."

"No. You die with honor."

His eyes lost focus. His last breath escaped. Umniris's soul went with it and crossed the Voidline. Halina closed his eyes. He wasn't even twenty. Regret clogged her throat.

Arevik knelt beside her. "We shouldn't have left so many soldiers outside the castle walls." She smudged ashes on Umniris's eyelids and forehead. Halina choked on that bitter pill, held her breath, forced down guilt. Arevik glanced toward the bodies. "If we're lucky, the soldiers in the guardhouse heard the fighting."

Magod crouched on Halina's other side and shook his head. "Bell would be clanging."

Halina said, "We're on our own." She stood as Magod and Waldram moved Umniris's body to the windows. She and her sister followed.

Waldram said, "We'll all be lined up here, if we don't escape soon."

Arevik twisted the handkerchief around her knuckles. "But they said they want money; they need us alive for ransom, right?"

"Wrong." Halina stared at the dead. "They said what they want us to believe. Something to sow doubt among us."

Waldram nodded. "If war is their goal, killing a king is a decisive step toward it." The crown prince wiped his hands on his gray uniform, adding more red streaks. "We need to work together to escape."

Magod nodded. "Agreed."

Arevik chewed her lower lip. It was a habit the king abhorred and the only reason he'd ever raised a hand to his younger daughter. "If they want war, why attack Kharaton? Why not go to Tatlis?"

"Because war is expensive and many kingdoms are still recovering from the War of the Winds." Halina touched Arevik's lip both to make her stop biting and to avoid looking at their second cousin. "Create disorder in your enemy's camp and the odds will favor you when you attack." She studied their captors. "Cut off the head and the body stumbles and falls." Beseran mercenaries who moved like they worked together often. "But I'm not convinced war is their goal."

As if reading her thoughts, Waldram said, "Someone wants this job done right, is willing to pay well for it, but wants no ties to it."

Arevik bit her lower lip again. "If it's not to start a war, then why do this?"

Halina frowned at the torn and bloody threads of her priceless gown. Cadoc had pinned the blame on her lover. "Whoever planned this attack wants to turn sentiments and swords against Gethen of Ranith. Someone wants the Sun Mage dead."

"How does killing our father accomplish that?"

"Or discredited," Waldram said. He was watching Halina, a strange look in his eye. "They've set you up to fall, too, Halina."

"I see that," she murmured.

"Well, I don't," Arevik said, her voice high with frustration.

"Conflict between the margrave and King Vernard is well-known," Magod said.

Waldram nodded. "It's not a big leap to think she saw an opportunity to ally with Quoregna's most powerful mage, murder her father, and take control of Ursinum."

Arevik stared at Halina. "No one who knows you would believe it. Your loyalty is unquestionable."

Reflecting upon her father's accusations, Halina wished that were true. "Nothing is beyond question." She looked at her sister from beneath her brows. "It only takes a few doubts to erode certainty and reveal opportunity."

CHAPTER 12

There was only one way in and out of Nalvika's capital: two iron gates wide enough to permit one of Teleyansk's massive thirty-two-oared trade ships to pass right through, oars extended, sails full, with room to spare. Gates so heavy each had a team of oxen to lift and lower it, so heavy it was said they'd flatten a man to the thickness of parchment if he were beneath when they dropped. One gate to enter, one to leave, separated by a thick stone wall, sharing one broad gatehouse, and a long passage beyond.

Those two iron gates were shut.

And the sky was pissing.

Thaksin stood scratching his skull beside Gethen. "Semele's blood. I heard they were impressive, but never imagined something like this. How'd Feddie and Elof get out alive?"

Blinking away fat raindrops, Gethen craned his neck to see the top of the ancient stone walls surrounding Drevya. They towered far above, thick as five horses standing flank-to-flank, moss-slicked, topped with a saw-tooth line of steel spikes that mirrored the jagged heights of King Hjalmer's saw-tooth castle, Drevya Linna, and the purple, saw-tooth Skerp Mountains rising above that.

Mutilated bodies and a handful of wandering spirits guarded the gates, and none up to the task. Gethen scowled. "This city is dead."

Thaksin stopped scratching. "What do you mean?"

"Skiron's abandoned it. The few spirits who've escaped being consumed by shrikers wander here, lost, unable to cross the Voidline because the god has barred the way to them."

"The god will not appreciate what he sees. All will suffer the consequences, you most of all, Sun Mage." Sulwen's warning.

"Why would he do that?"

Gethen studied the massive gates, trying to understand the mechanism that lifted them. There was a lock he couldn't see but needed to disengage. Mechanical sorcery was easier when he could see what he was doing. And when he wasn't distracted by the temptation of so many needy souls. He clenched his teeth.

"Mage, why would Skiron abandon the dead here?"

"I don't know and I don't plan to ask him," Gethen snarled.

Thaksin folded his arms. "Why not? He's your god."

"Not even I want Death's attention on me for too long. But, if you're volunteering, I'll gladly cut your throat and send you into the Void to ask him yourself." The captain gestured rudely but kept his mouth shut. Gethen moved into the shadow of the massive stone tunnel. He peered up into the darkness, placed his palms against the cold, iron gates, and mentally felt for what he couldn't see. There were thick chains and huge wheels and two enormous cranks with locking pins. "Ah, I see how this works," he muttered.

"What?"

"The gate mechanism. Get ready to move. I'll raise it just enough for us to slip beneath."

Thaksin blew out a long breath and looked from the mutilated corpses, to the gate, to Gethen. "You sure you want to go in there?"

"I'm sure I have to."

"Can't we just wait here and pick off the shrikers as they show up? What's in there that's so important?"

"Maybe their boneyard. Maybe their necromancer." He sniffed. "Maybe nothing." He wiped his wet face with a wet sleeve then split the focus of his magic between moving the pin that held the gate shut and raising its massive iron weight. "Maybe my death," he added through gritted teeth. "Maybe yours."

Shuddering, squealing, clanking, the gate slowly rose. Sweat joined the rainwater on Gethen's brow. With just enough clearance to stoop and shuffle beneath, Thaksin slipped into Drevya. Gethen followed, his focus on keeping the crushing iron mass aloft. Once past, he let the gate fall. The ground jumped beneath their feet, mud splattered their boots and trouzes. The sound left his ears ringing.

The way split. Stone walls hemmed them in. They were forced to turn right and follow a chute topped by parapets from which soldiers could kill any invaders before they ever reached the town. Nalvika's wealth was in the iron mined from its jagged mountains. Hard labor performed by hard people exploited by harder rulers. Attacks on Drevya Linna by its own citizens weren't unique. The Boorsook family ruled by being more hard-handed than their citizens. They'd come to power by being more hard-hearted than their predecessors. Many peers had been slaughtered in their sleep, oldest to youngest, immediate family to the most distant relations, in one bloody night in Drevya.

"What's a boneyard?" Thaksin asked as they escaped the chute without encountering anything living.

"A birthing ground for nightmares."

"Wish I hadn't asked."

"Wishing you hadn't joined me?"

"Don't recall you giving me a choice."

"Don't recall you pissing off when I told you to."

Thaksin grabbed the front of Gethen's gray brigandine and shoved him into a wall. "I'm going nowhere, Mage. Halina may trust you, but I don't and I won't. Nothing good ever comes from sorcery. She fought enough of your kind during the war to damn-well know that. She has the scars to remind her, the newest ones compliments of *you*." He jabbed a hard finger into Gethen's chest. "So I'm here and I'm watching you. When you slip and show your true intentions, I'll stick a sword in you and end this ugly affair." His finger turned into a fist. "I won't let you hurt her again. You getting to her was my failure. I'll fix it. That's a promise I made to the gods and the king."

Gethen's eyes narrowed. So, King Vernard had played a part in the captain's hostility. "Does she know you're Vernard's puppet and don't trust her judgment?" Thaksin blinked. His scowl deepened. Gethen had guessed right. "Halina won't appreciate that."

"I've faced her rage many times. If it gets rid of you, it's worth the pain."

Gethen seized his wrist. "Keep giving me reasons to send you across the Voidline, Captain."

"Keep giving me reasons to open your gut, Mage." Thaksin pulled his knife and pressed it to Gethen's stomach.

It was a mistake.

Gethen murmured ancient words and pain twisted Thaksin's face. "Halina trusts you on the battlefield and off." The man's eyes widened, his mouth gaped, his hand shook. "She calls you a friend, a trusted advisor." The knife hit the ground between them. Gethen stepped on it. The captain's knees buckled, his body arched. A thin line of blood ran from his right nostril into his beard. "I'm glad you care about her." Gethen still held Thaksin's wrist, his grip light yet deadly, burning the man's skin. "I can tear your soul out, Captain." Gods, it was tempting. "I can clot the blood in your veins, stop your heart, cramp your muscles until you piss yourself from pain." Gethen released him. "I can boil your guts inside your skin." Thaksin went to his hands and knees, panting, drooling, cursing. "Halina is the only reason you're still alive." Gethen stepped over him and started the long walk toward the castle. "Don't test me again."

The ancient Nalvik town was a maze of narrow stone streets sandwiched between crooked stone buildings. It stank of rotting corpses, piss, smoke, and fear. Every path led to a blind curve. From every direction came the distant screams of men and horses, the shrieks of undead dogs. Black smoke rose from the Iron Quarter on the city's western flank and, standing tall and sharp above it all, Drevya Linna's heights were silent, still, its windows shuttered. The castle's orange-and-white banners stirred little on a scant breeze.

Sword in hand, rancor seemingly in check, Thaksin crept ahead of Gethen, flattened to the wall and as tense as a hunted hare. Sound carried strangely through the helter-skelter streets and alleys. They rounded a corner. The captain halted.

A group of soldiers battled a shriker. The militair leading them turned and shouted in Nalvik: "Get out of here! We don't need more dead idiots underfoot!"

Thaksin held his ground. "You don't need more dead soldiers either. We can help."

The militair brandished his sword. "I told you to clear out."

Gethen raised a glowing mass spell. "And I suggest you get down." He hurled it at the shriker. It flattened the soldiers and slammed the beast into the building behind them with enough force to collapse a stone wall upon its bony carcass.

The Nalviks regained their feet. "We don't want more trouble from mages," one of them snarled.

"I didn't bring trouble." Gethen gathered shadows from the street's cracks and crevices, from doorways, windowsills, and the arches of Drevya's winding way. Dark, nacreous armor formed around his body, settled, tightened. "I brought battle magic." The soldiers stared, mouths and eyes wide. He jerked his thumb at the captain. "And him."

Thaksin grinned, bright-eyed battle madness blooming across his scarred face. "A truce, Mage, until these beasts are finished. Then I'll kill you."

Gethen sneered. "Watch your back, Captain. I wouldn't want you to get in my way *accidentally*."

The Nalvik militair looked from the broken shriker to Gethen to Halina's captain. "Ya, we could use a battle mage and a maniac." He stretched out his hand. "I'm Nikolaus."

There was a shout. "Watch out!"

Another shriker dropped from an arched overpass above the street a dozen feet from their position. It charged the soldiers and three more beasts followed. Thaksin's roar nearly shamed the monsters as he brandished his sword and charged, screaming his bloody head off, and swinging like a lunatic.

Gethen held back and studied the man's technique. Thaksin waded into the fray, a hungry dog invited to a cockfight, sword hacking, slashing, inelegant but effective. He had to admire the man's commitment to slaughter. No wonder Halina kept him on. He was a formidable enemy.

Gethen shrugged. He missed the reassuring weight of his sword and borrowed one from a dead man. Then he raised his shield of amber magic, dodged, pivoted, slammed spells into dead flesh and set fire to mangy fur.

Their group fought their way into the stricken city. They passed streets barricaded with carts, crates, barrels, boards. Passed shattered doorways, blood-encrusted windows, obliterated homes that had failed to keep shrikers out. They passed mutilated adults and untouched, dead children. Black smoke and the stench of Skiron's undead dogs curled around corners. Screams, shouts, crying bounced off crooked walls, jumbled along crooked alleys like tumbleweeds made of terror. Riderless horses charged out of the smoke, snorting fear, eyes rolling, whites showing. Dogs fought over carcasses, teeth bared, tongues flicking, hackles raised. Men fought over safety, teeth bared, lips curled, fists flying. Gethen gained new callouses, new aches, new injuries. Their group lost some militairs to the mania of the soul stealers. And they gained more fighters from the refugees, some experienced soldiers, some merchants, butchers, bakers. Anyone armed and willing was swept up in their tide as they drove the shrikers into the burning Iron Quarter.

Gethen set a ward to keep the fire and the monsters contained. Five crooked city blocks were becoming smoke and cinders and blackened, jagged skeletons of building. Flames licked, spat, snapped. Sparks twisted into the nightmare sky, blotted out the early evening stars, and turned the crescent moon bloody. He spun the ward tight and anchored it with the souls of the soldiers, men, and women he'd fought beside. He fueled it with the fire that burned through the buildings and the beasts. "Stay here until the flames die out and the ashes go cold. Then the ward will disintegrate." A dozen people had volunteered. A dozen more had agreed to bring food, water, blankets, and to set a watch for keeping the chosen wardens safe until the shrikers were nothing but ash.

Gethen leaned against a stone wall, his face heated by the flames beyond the ward. His hands shook, bloody and black, shoulders slumped. Muscles cramped across his back. His left arm burned where he'd been chewed by the shriker in Grimbu. His dislocated shoulder joined the chorus of complaints. Fatigue made sorcery an agony and sorcery created a bone-aching fatigue, especially battle magic. It was why battle mages fought in pairs and teams, to spell and support each other. Sweat chilled his skin beneath his brigandine and a headache was gaining strength as it hammered the insides of his eye sockets.

"Tired already? It's early yet." Thaksin slapped him on the injured shoulder. Gethen winced and considered killing the man for his soul. The brightness hadn't left the captain's green eyes, made more vibrant by the soot and blood coating his face. He looked like something Skiron had brought forth to punish the world. The power coursing through him could make Gethen near invincible, if only briefly.

Perhaps Sulwen's prediction was coming true and his suffering was beginning with Halina's man. *That would be damned ironic.* "On this side of the Voidline, sorcery's only as strong as the man who wields it. Care to find out what I can do on the other side, Captain?"

Thaksin slid his finger across his own throat, a clear

message for Gethen. He turned and strode to where a group of farmers milled around, brandishing pitchforks and scythes.

Nikolaus leaned against the wall, nursing a leg that'd met a shriker's claws. "You're not friends, I see."

"No." Gethen tongued his teeth. A few of the lower molars in his left jaw were jangly. Shrikers hit hard.

"A few times I thought he was aiming for you." The man's pale face and hair were soot-smeared.

"He was."

"If you're going to stick around and fight with us, I should know how bad the trouble is between you." He fiddled with a silver ring on his left hand, twisting it around and around the way Halina sometimes did with her black band.

Halina. Gods, how he missed her. Gethen couldn't see the harm in telling Nikolaus the basic truth of Thaksin's resentment. "He wants the woman I have."

"Oof." The Nalvik militair's brows arched. "That's some nasty business. You take her from him?"

"It was her choice to make. She made it. He doesn't agree with the choice." Gethen pushed away from the wall and groaned. He opened and closed his fists, trying to work out pain and stiffness.

"Probably explains his battle joy," Nikolaus said. "I'll send him off to reconnoiter the field walls. The castle's our next target. That's where the shrikers first appeared on Nimnight."

Gethen didn't like the sound of that. "From inside the castle grounds?"

The militair nodded. "At least their numbers have slowed. At first they were pouring out like wasps from a nest. We've had no communication from the royal family, no signs they're alive. Fortunately, Crown Prince Waldram left three days before this madness began."

"Where'd he go? Was a message sent to him?"

"To Tatlis and, yes, of course. But if the prince sent a reply, the man who carried it is dead. Nothing ever came of it and I can't spare the men to deliver another message."

"Tatlis, eh?" Waldram had likely missed King Vernard and was still sitting in the court, twiddling his thumbs, resentful of the wait and unaware of the chaos that had seized his city.

Nikolaus nodded. "He would've returned by now if he'd received the news."

"Skiron's bones." Gethen's curse ended with a yawn. "I've got to sleep. I'm next to useless, can't spell-cast effectively when I'm this tired."

"I'll join you. The castle's eastern gate barracks are a few blocks down and still secure." Nikolaus led him and several soldiers along the streets and through the gates of a compound. Archers with crossbows, infantrymen with maces, halberds, pikes stood guard against shrikers and their own desperate citizens.

Once inside, Gethen slumped in a corner and pulled his hood over his eyes. "How long until we go back out?"

"We have four hours." Nikolaus dropped a blanket on his lap and indicated a nearby bunk. "Take a bed, Mage, you've earned it. Eat and rest. Tomorrow we'll try for the castle. With a battle mage in our midst we finally have a chance of reaching the keep."

Gethen considered sleeping where he was, but the thought of a bed inspired him to drag his bones off the floor. He dropped heavily to the cot, groaned, and nodded his thanks to the soldier who'd given it up.

"It's a strange thing," Nikolaus muttered as he studied Gethen, who returned his regard through bleary eyes.

"What's strange?" he slurred, his head muzzy with the need to sleep.

"With all the day's madness, I never got your name. What should we call you besides Mage?"

"Sorcerer. Mage. Friend. They're just as good as any other name I've been called and better than most." Gethen yawned and rolled toward the wall as the soldiers laughed, a weary, half-hearted sound. He whispered a ward around himself, a brief dull shimmer of symbols that faded as fast as a breath. His thoughts drifted to Halina. He wanted to see her, to know she was safe and surly and untroubled by shrikers and her father. Why'd he agreed not to use the ambit's tears?

I could do it anyway; she'd never know. He closed his eyes and sighed. *But I would.*

The floorboards creaked beneath her feet as Noni scuttled into the infirmary. "Gods, Master. She dead?"

"Nearly. Put the water on the table then give me the towels and the medical kit." He cut the straps holding Halina's bloody, battered armor to her body. She was cold, clammy, pale, her breathing shallow and rapid. He had to get the blade out of her thigh, but she was bleeding like a stuck pig and removing the dagger would hasten her death if he didn't close the wound quickly.

Noni handed him a damp towel and started working on the pauldrons protecting the militess's shoulders and upper chest. "Told you that wraith would be trouble."

The metal and leather were blood-slicked. Gethen finally got the steel tasset protecting her left thigh unbuckled. "I'll regret that later. Thread a needle." He glanced up as Magod entered the room. "Grab a towel," he said to the groundsman. "As soon as I lift this tasset and the dagger away, bear down on the wound or she'll bleed out." With the armor loose, Gethen slid his own belt around Halina's thigh above the wound. Quickly, quickly, they had to work quickly.

Noni offered the threaded needle. Magod stood poised with the folded towel. Gethen pulled the tasset and misericord away from Halina's flesh. Her blood geysered. Magod covered the wound and Gethen tightened the belt. "Semele's blood." Her own blade had nicked her artery. "Skiron, spare her," he murmured as he worked to close the wound before blood loss took her leg or her life.

The room darkened and Gethen looked up from his stitching. Where were Noni and Magod? He looked back down. Halina was gone, the infirmary, too. He was crouching beneath a table, hidden by a heavy tablecloth. Two voices echoed in a vast room, the sound dissipating into the rafters and behind columns. One of the men was his father. Except that was impossible because Gethen's father was dead. The other man's voice was strange, wispy, both familiar and unfamiliar. He, too, was dead — by Gethen's hand. How could he know that if he didn't know the man? Gethen shook his head.

His father said, "She was formidable without the Sun Mage's power at her beck and call. Now, she's undefeatable. That makes her our most dangerous enemy."

"Or our greatest ally."

"She'll refuse."

"How can you be certain?"

"That hatred had deep roots."

"Fine. Then use her strength to destroy him." Their voices receded as they moved away.

"Agreed." A door creaked open. "The deaths begin tonight." It thudded closed.

He hugged his knees, cold in his nightshirt. He'd be beaten if they caught him out of bed. He crawled out from beneath the table,

cautious, all senses alert. He stood and blinked. He was in Khara-
ton's great hall.

"I don't want you here." Halina was circling him. "I don't want
you here. I don't want you." She grabbed his arm.

Gethen awakened, dagger in hand. A pale, young page
squawked and jumped back, surprised by the blade and the
bite of the ward he'd broken.

"My hand's dead!" the boy cried, cradling the limb against
his chest like a baby.

"Consider yourself fortunate," Gethen growled. He sat
upright and dropped the ward with a wave of his hand. He
yawned, stretched, still felt fatigue in his bones, the itch of
craving beneath his skin. His rest had been much too brief.
Bollocks. Being around so many souls had him on his mettle.

"But—"

"Stop whining." He snarled and jabbed the dagger at the
boy. "It'll last only long enough for me to slit your throat." The
blade shook. His hand and body trembled from need and craving, both worsened by fatigue. That was the trouble with
necromancy. Drawing power from an animal's soul was easy
and easily controlled. Taking it from a human? That was too
easy, too powerful, too addictive. Once started, it was agony to
stop and few necromancers had the will and strength to give it
up after that first taste. Many friends, families, villages had
fallen to a necromancer's craving for human souls. That ache
was why Gethen was a hermit, why he warded Kharayan Tor,
why he needed Halina. She eased his cravings, siphoned off
the madness, soothed the itch.

"You have some interesting habits, Mage." Nikolaus slid his
own sword into its scabbard. "Last night I was surprised you
trusted us enough to sleep in our midst." He donned leather-
and-steel gauntlets and added, "I see you didn't."

Gethen sheathed the borrowed misericord on his belt and rubbed his hands over his stubbled chin. "I trust fewer people than Lady Khara has fingers, and myself least of all." That raised a few eyebrows from the men around the room.

"Instincts shouldn't be ignored when you're dealing with a mage," Thaksin said. He sat at the long table, peeling a black-apple with his dagger. He had a new gouge running from his temple to his ear. Blood crusted his nostrils and his nails. Soot dirtied his fair hair and dulled his uniform.

Nikolaus tossed Gethen a hard roll, a boiled egg, and a mealy blackapple. "It's not much."

"It's better than hunger." Gethen ate quickly, gathering the shells and core into a neat pile while Thaksin watched him with bright eyes and rabid suspicion. He felt prickly, achy, a man made of glass shards waiting to splinter and cut. "I need a horse."

"Going somewhere?" Thaksin asked.

Gethen ignored him. "One that doesn't need to carry a load today."

Nikolaus frowned, puzzled. "Why?"

"Not enough rest to restore me. I need to draw strength from an animal's spirit." That was met with uncomfortable silence. Gethen looked around. His gaze settled on Thaksin. "Unless you want to volunteer."

Halina's captain curled his lip but didn't offer his soul, the coward.

"You're a necromancer," one of the soldiers said.

Thaksin snorted. "He's *the* necromancer." His boots clonked on the floor. His chair feet clattered as he pushed back from the table. He stood and bowed with a flourish. "Skiron's lackey. Death's doorkeeper. Quoregna's very own Sun Mage.

What did those children call you? Tomru-something-or-other?"

Someone muttered, "Herra-tomruma." He didn't sound happy. The soldiers stared, slowly stood. Swords and knives came out. Fists flexed. Nalviks weren't fans of necromancers. Thaksin sat, heels on the table, chair tipping back again. He peeled his apple, quartered it, shoved a piece in his mouth.

"You're a rank old codpiece," Gethen said.

The captain's bright blue eyes watched the room change as he chewed, swallowed, shrugged. He indicated their surroundings. "I told you nothing good ever comes from sorcery."

"Is this a game to you, necromancer?" Nikolaus snarled, his long-sword a promised threat.

Gethen backed toward the door, aware of the soldiers moving toward him, aware of Thaksin's growing smile. "Do I look like I'm having fun?"

"You come to watch your handiwork play out?" another soldier growled, two daggers in his hands.

Gethen reached the doorway. He found it blocked by a hulking Nalvik with a hulking mace. "Skiron's bones." He raised a protective shield, its heat enough to set the barrack's wood walls smoking and drive his sudden enemies back. "Suit yourselves." He offered Thaksin Halina's favorite rude gesture, invoked a travel spell, and put himself just inside the castle's closed eastern gate. As the amber glow of the incantation dissipated around him, Gethen rattled off a long list of expletives. "I'm going to kill Captain Thaksin, whether Halina wishes it or not."

CHAPTER 13

"Halina?" Arevik motioned for her. "This isn't working." The princess knelt behind Waldram, pressing a strip torn from her own gown to the back of his skull, chin up, focused on her task, and pointedly not looking at the corpses by the windows. Her hands shook and silent tears still welled, trembled, spilled, and left shining tracks on her cheeks, but she was making an admirable effort at self-control. Poor girl was out of her element, under water, and sinking fast. She needed assurance. She needed Halina's strength. Just like when she was a little girl and afraid of thunder.

She'd crawled into Halina's bed during storms and asked, "Is Khotyr angry?"

Halina had always hugged her close. "No, Arevik, that's Skiron's laughter. Khotyr's tickling him. See the rain? Those are his tears; he's laughing so hard he's crying."

Now Halina knelt beside her young sister, stroked her hair, kissed her temple. She swallowed all her own uncertainty, stuffed it down, made a hard pit of it in her gut and showed only confidence to give Arevik a solid base upon which to build some of her own. "What's the problem?" Good. Her voice was steady, solid, strong.

"I can't stop the bleeding." Arevik lifted the cloth. The back of Waldram's pale skull and pale uniform were crimson and slick, his white hair matted.

"Because that needs stitches." Halina moved behind her second cousin. "Do you have a needle and thread?"

"Of course." The girl always carried such things in her girdle pouch and she gave them over. "But how will you see with so much blood?" Halina quickly threaded the needle and knotted the string.

"You don't have to see to stitch a wound." She felt the gash through the prince's bloody white hair, a flap of scalp, loose as a sail in a slack breeze. "This was made by a mace. It has a distinctive pattern. If there wasn't so much blood, you'd see that the blow glanced off his skull and tore his scalp in a crescent shape." Halina deftly stitched. Waldram barely flinched. She finished and bit off the black thread, leaving a few inches dangling in his hair, and passed the needle back to her sister. She gave the thread a gentle tug. "Look, now we have him leashed."

Waldram snorted. "A dream come true?" he asked. Arevik blanched, swallowed, looked away, not ready to stomach her sister-soldier's black humor.

"If only it was so simple to collar a Boorsook, Your Grace." The wound wept only a little. Halina pressed the cloth into the crown prince's hand. "Keep steady pressure on it until the bleeding stops."

Arevik stared at the bloody needle, her expression a mixture of disgust and horror. She pawed half-heartedly at the girdle pouch's flap, looked at the needle, looked around, and stuck it into the black trim of a large tapestry sagging off the wall, its torn fabric piled on the floor. Halina didn't care. It was called *To War for the Gods*. She'd always despised the thing, which was why it remained up during construction. It depicted two dozen armed soldiers hacking each other apart, blood splattering and spraying, with a picturesque castle on a flower-dotted hillside in the background and a shepherd giving a jaunty wave as he took his fluffy white sheep out to forage. Stupid tapestry, stupid choice for the hall where she dined, stupid soldiers and stupid shepherd. She looked down at her hands. She hated having blood beneath her fingernails.

Arevik mumbled, "I thought I'd make it worse since I couldn't see what I was doing." She tore more fabric from the hem of her green gown and held it out. Halina wiped her hands and passed it back.

"Clean his face, neck, and hands as best you can."

Waldram caught Halina's wrist as she straightened. "Thank you, Your Ladyship." He trailed his stained fingers down to stroke her palm.

She yanked her hand away. "I suggest you stay still. That blow addled your brain."

"Possibly." Waldram shrugged. He fingered the sleeve of Halina's surcoat. "Beseran blue. Have you been betrayed by your groom?"

Arevik gasped and the prince smirked.

Halina leaned close, their faces within inches. "Have you been betrayed by your own stupidity?" She straightened and looked her cousin up and down. His left eye was blackened and his lip was swollen. Blood stained his pale gray tunic and trouzes. He didn't look so pretty now. She nodded toward his face. "I like what Cadoc did. It's an improvement."

Arevik gawked.

Waldram grinned. "I wear war almost as prettily as you do, Red Blade."

Halina curled her lip. "You haven't changed, Waldram. Still a snide, little prick."

He scowled. "I've changed. You just can't see it," he said. "You love playing the savior and the martyr, the militess who fought her way out of the cesspool of her bastard blood to stand atop the dung heap of her royal family. Queen of her own castle." He waved dismissively at the great room. "Well, you're not the only one who's fought and struggled. You don't know the difficulties that Nalviks have faced every day since the war."

"Difficulties from a war the Boorsooks started." She stabbed a finger at him.

"And one no one lets us forget."

"Why should we? Halion and Tirius died during the Boorsook's war. I still have pain and scars from the Boorsook's war. I'll never bear a child because of the Boorsook's war." She folded her arms. "Why should I believe any of the Boorsooks have changed? You're all so good at smiles and charm while knifing everyone else in the back."

Waldram's scowl deepened. "You're not the only person with scars. Ursinum isn't the only kingdom that suffered from my family's mistakes, but the rest of Quoregna's permitted to move on. We're constantly reminded of our misdeeds. Our children starve. Our countryside remains war-torn. We face the sanctions the rest of Quoregna holds against us all these years later, though we've done everything that was asked of us after we surrendered."

"Oh, you plead a sad story that I might've swallowed if you hadn't been trying to kill me since we were children. Nalvika's citizens suffer because of your family's cruelty, greed, and ambition. Not because the rest of Quoregna wants to see them miserable. The sanctions have eased. I've been party to those negotiations. Don't think I'm ignorant of the politics of the four kingdoms because I'm a woman; only Nalvika treats its women like imbeciles and property. Your people shouldn't be starving and they shouldn't be miserable. They have all they need, unless, of course, the wealthy Nalviks are keeping it for themselves."

Arevik was staring at her. Magod was staring at his feet. The mercenaries were sneering. Halina should've stopped, should've shut up, walked away, but Waldram brought out the worst in her. Always.

His fists clenched. He glared at her, hate, jealousy, hunger in his eyes. Maybe he'd strike her. She squared her shoulders. That would prove amusing. Instead, he shook his head, relaxed his hands. Calm overtook his expression and his voice was even when he replied. "Yes, there are problems with corruption. Just as I'm sure there are in Ursinum, Or-Halee, and Besera." At the last, he nodded toward the mercenaries. "The other houses aren't perfect, Halina. Not at all."

"I'm far from flawless. I'm also far from believing your act of innocence. I faced you in battle more than once. I've a few scars from you and I know you have plenty from me." She stuck her fist in his face. "Better get off your high horse and swallow your lies or I'll give you a few new scars."

As she turned Waldram said, "I've changed for the better, Halina. You'll see." He was accomplished at hiding his intentions. There'd been so many times when she'd been forced to endure his cruelty as a child, then watched him play the innocent boy. He'd even been praised for freeing her from the very traps he'd set. It had always been the young crown prince's word against the little bastard bitch's. It still was.

"Changed for the better?" She snorted. "Right. From maggot to blowfly. Both eat shit and love death."

Waldram's cool cracked. He cursed her in Nalvik and stalked away.

"If you think I'll honor my father's marriage agreement after we get out of this, you're an idiot," she said to his retreating figure.

The room's atmosphere warped, like a sudden wind sucking past her. She turned to the great hall's closest entrance. Cadoc was there with a handful of his mercenaries and Britta and Vins. The baby mages had lowered the ward. That explained the draft; all the decency was fleeing the room. Halina glanced at Arevik and Magod, wishing they could be pulled out with it, the only good and decent people present.

Cadoc had been gone for hours but now made straight for her.

"You didn't have to kill those soldiers," she said, crossing her arms and shoving aside the uncomfortable knowledge that she'd have done the same thing had she been him.

He stopped in the middle of the room. "Of course I did and you know it. Playing the fool doesn't suit you, Margrave." He bit into a blackapple, its crisp snap punctuating his sentence. He regarded her with a cool, steady stare and chewed.

"Have you come to kill me next?"

He swallowed and wiped juice from his lips. "In due time." He picked fruit from his teeth, considered what he'd pried loose, ate it, and gestured at her with the blackapple. "You'll get to die in a most interesting fashion. Lord Rhyshis promised it." Another bite. Juice dribbled down his chin. He wiped it on his sleeve and threw the apple core at the hearth. It splatted against the stones, spreading seeds, juice, flesh. "And don't expect a rescue to come from outside. My mages warded the perimeter of the castle, too. No one gets in or out without our knowledge."

Two men appeared at the northern servant's doorway, but they didn't enter the room. Cadoc jerked his chin at them. "Well?"

"The servants are gone and castle's secure."

"Any keys?"

One of them held up several large rings of keys. "All we found."

"Start trying them." Cadoc snapped his fingers at his men. "Someone bring two chairs. Our host and I need to have a little chat." He winked at Halina.

"So it begins," she muttered as Cadoc continued toward her gathering the battle mages and four of his men, a glint in his eye, a smirk on his lips. She itched to smack it off with a sword.

Magod stepped up to her right. "Why keep us alive?"

"I think we're about to find out."

He moved between her and the approaching mercenaries, folded his arms, and glared at them. "Come no closer."

Cadoc paused, brows arched. "Touching but stupid, man. Don't make me kill you."

Halina caught Magod's shoulder. "I'm grateful for your loyalty." She eased around him and tightened her grip when she saw his angry gaze. "I can't allow anyone else to die, especially in my defense."

"But—"

She dug her fingers into flesh until he winced. "Don't argue with me." She dropped her voice to a whisper. "I need you alive." Her gaze darted to Arevik behind them, to Waldram scowling beside a pillar, back to Magod. "I trust you to protect my sister from Cadoc *and* from Waldram."

His glare slid from her to the two men and hardened into acceptance. "With my life, Your Ladyship."

She nodded, turned, stepped forward. "Why did my father die, Cadoc?"

"Aside from the massive blood loss? I thought that was made clear. Nothing starts a war faster than a dead king. We're being paid to start that war." The man folded his hands and tapped his fingers to his lips almost as if in prayer then gave her a smile she didn't trust. "Now. Let's have a conversation."

"You need two mages and four murderers by your side just to chat?" Halina sneered at Ren's bruised face as he set two chairs between her and Cadoc.

The mercenary leader gave a funny little laugh and a bit of a shrug, almost self-effacing. "You've proven your reputation as a killer, Lady Khara. And since I like my skin and bones attached to my body, I've decided protection is wise when I'm in the same room as you. Like your late father, you remind me of a wild bear — fascinating from a distance, deadly close-up. Another reason I killed him quickly."

"If that's supposed to be flattery, you can shove it up your arse."

The four thugs moved around her, shoving Magod back. Arevik tried to grab her hand, but Halina wouldn't take it. She met the girl's frightened gaze and shook her head, a silent command to step back and not endanger herself. Arevik glared her defiance, but Magod wrapped an arm around her shoulders and eased her away from danger. Halina trusted him with her life and something more precious: her little sister.

Cadoc sat and indicated the other chair. "Please, Your Ladyship. Will you sit?"

"And if I would prefer to stand?" Halina folded her arms.

He crossed his right leg over the left, frowning at rust-brown blood streaks on his trouzes. "We may be conversing for a long time. I'm certain you'll be more comfortable if you sit. And I'm positive I'll be safer. So humor me."

Halina's neck crackled as she tilted her head to the side. The man was interesting, dangerous, and certainly going to cause her a great deal of pain very soon. She glanced at the chair, at the two mages who flanked it and the huge, hard-faced mercenaries who flanked them. "Fine. Let's pretend this'll remain civilized for a little while." She sat.

With a whispered incantation, both mages combined their power. It skittered across her skin, cold and prickly, like rat claws. It was nothing like the seductive caress of Gethen's warm, powerful incantations, but effective enough to make Halina's body obey. She yelped as her muscles cramped. Her fingers gripped the chair arms. Her feet flattened hard against the floor. Her spine straightened and her head cracked against the chair back hard enough to spin stars across her vision. Breathing was painful, moving impossible. "A very little while," she said through clenched teeth.

Cadoc raised his fingers and the spell's grip eased. "Now you know what they're capable of." He leaned forward, rested his elbows upon his knees, and steepled his fingers under his chin. He held her gaze, a faint smile playing across his lips. Chapped lips, she noticed, chapped and pale. "I want the keys to the castle's treasury," he said. "Tell me where they're hidden."

"I thought you were being well compensated by your patron."

"Yes. Your fortune is part of it." He waggled his fingers at her. "Keys."

"No."

He blinked, arched his brows. "No?"

"Piss off, pissant." The keys weren't kept in the castle. Even if Cadoc got them and opened the treasury, he'd be disappointed. It was almost barren. Halina had distributed much of her wealth among Khara's villages after the long, harsh winter, and had invested the rest in the castle's renovations. It galled her to realize she'd already filled the mercenaries' purses.

He sighed and, for a moment, seemed like the awkward mason again. "I respect you, Margrave. I do. But our familiarity after these many months working on your castle won't prevent me from hurting you to get what I came for."

Halina set her expression. If she told him the keys' whereabouts, she and her companions would all too quickly end up company to the corpses by the windows. Best to stall for time, for ideas, for her soldiers outside the walls to come up with a plan of attack. "I won't make this easy for you." Let Cadoc and his pillocks waste hours trying keys, hammers, and torture to gain access to Kharaton Castle's formidable treasury. Its six-foot-thick walls and three doors, each with multiple locks, had never been breached.

"Too bad." He sat back. "Vins, Britta, get her up. Trefor, take that gown off Lady Khara. It's worth far too much to see any more damage."

The mages motioned upward in unison. Halina squeaked as her muscles obeyed and brought her to her feet while her mind wondered what was happening and how. *Get used to it, brain,* she thought.

Trefor chuckled, an oily sound. He wiped his lips and leered. "That'll be my pleasure." Halina scowled; clearly, the beady-eyed prick was thinking of taking more than the dress. He pulled a wicked little knife from his belt.

"Just the surcoat, idiot," Cadoc said. "We're not animals."

Behind her, Arevik started crying. Trefor slit the laces at

the back of the gown, each releasing with a *snick*. The man's breath was as sour as rotten cabbage, his body odor worse.

"Turn around, Arevik." Halina treasured her sister's tender heart. She was the child who put spiders high up in the castle's windows so they could catch flies and not be killed by the servants. The girl who saved mice from Tatlis's cats then stole kitchen scraps to apologize to the cats for letting their dinner escape. She'd never seen torture or war. She believed in romance and chivalry. And Halina never wanted her to grow bitter.

Her sister said, "No. If you can endure this, Halina, so can I."

Trefor pulled the sleeves off, tossed them to Cadoc.

Halina rolled her eyes toward the ceiling. "Make her turn around, Magod."

The groundsman's voice was soothing but firm. "Lady Khara's right, Countess. Don't watch her suffer. Will only make things worse for her."

Trefor grasped the front of the surcoat, his fingers too friendly, his pocked face too close. His leer widened. Halina matched it with her own dead smile then cracked his nose with her forehead. He shouted, cursed, bled. Arevik screamed. Halina saw stars and would've staggered a step if the mages' spell had allowed it. Ren and the other mercenaries started laughing. Trefor brandished his little knife. "Rotten bitch."

"Am I the only one who understands how dangerous the margrave is?" Cadoc muttered and yanked him back. "I'll get the gown." Halina lifted her chin, pursed her lips, and glared down at the leader as he removed the surcoat. He quickly stepped back, thrust it into Trefor's hands, and shoved him toward the doors. "Don't bleed on the Beseran silk, idiot. It's worth far more than your life." Trefor retreated, cursing, snuffling, the gown over his shoulder. Cadoc crooked a finger at Ren. "See if you can inspire Lady Khara to share her wealth."

"Halina?" Arevik's voice wavered, squeaked.

Halina growled. "I told you to turn around. *Now*, Arevik." It must've been her tone. Her sister's next hiccupping sob was suddenly muffled and Magod's voice turned soothing, their scuffing footsteps moved away.

Ren stepped forward, rolling his sleeves. He was a mouse haired brute with a scrubby beard and forearms the size of mutton legs. Halina met his sneer and steeled herself. The first blow was always the worst. And he owed her.

CHAPTER 14

Gethen stood inside Drevya Linna's secure grounds, his back to the lowered portcullis. He raised mage fire to illuminate the barbican. Structured like the city's entrance, the castle's entry and exit led visitors through two high-walled chutes. To his left was a mountain of stinking, slaughtered corpses. Disembodied arms reached through the iron lattice of the lowered gate, fingers grasping, clutching, desperate to escape but trapped by their own castle's defenses. He looked up. The chain and pulley for the gate mechanism dangled, broken, useless. Someone had dismantled it, probably to keep the shrikers trapped within the castle grounds. "Semele's blood," he whispered. It was a terrifying show of self-sacrifice.

To his right was a shifting, pacing wall of shrikers, their bones dully glowing with the curse that animated them. He stared at them. They returned his black regard. "Skiron's bones." There was no retreating into the city; Thaksin had Drevya's soldiers looking for him. There was no going up; the walls were blood-slicked and canted inward. "Forward with fire, then."

As if sensing his resolve, the shrikers screeched and came at him, bones rattling, rot flying. Gethen gritted his teeth, raised a shield, and hurled a massive ball of mage fire at them. He covered his face and huddled behind the shimmering amber spell as shrikers caught fire. Some stopped, confused. Some turned back. Some attacked each other. And some kept coming, snapping flames and shedding fire, flesh, fur. He strengthened his shield and added to his ever-growing list of regrets his decision to give his sword to Feddie.

Three shrikers held together long enough to reach him. They screamed and threw themselves against his shield, were repelled, regrouped, attacked again. The jolt of each hit ran through him, almost physical in its impact. His muscles ached. There was a massive crack, screeching, and a wave of heat. He was knocked arse over elbows. An ungodly stench smothered him. Gethen raised another shield and used a mass spell to slam the last two standing shrikers across the chute — left wall, right wall, left, right. He released them. They collapsed in a smoldering jumble of flesh, bones, ashes.

"Bollocks," he muttered and staggered around the piles of putrid, smoking corpses. He exited the entrance chute into a wide, cobbled stable yard and a scene of more carnage. It looked like every horse, cow, goat, and chicken had been shredded like day-old meat and spread out to dry in the sun. The smoke from the rotten corpses behind him combined with the stink of the rotting corpses in front of him. Acid bile surged up his throat. Gethen swallowed his scant breakfast a second time. So much for the Boorsooks' stables and livestock. He covered his mouth and nose and took in the tall spires of the castle.

Tall and sharp, Drevya Linna bit at the sky. It was a beautiful castle, built on the ruins of an ancient fortress, with gabled roofs, elaborate carved stags posing majestically over lintels and at downspouts, and tall, jeweled windows. Terraced gardens spread out from the northern bailey to follow the sheer cliff upon which the castle perched above the Jera River Gorge. Mist and rainbows shimmered up from the cascading waterfalls and snaking river. Green-and-white river gulls soared out over the water and the turrets, their croaking calls heard from dawn to dusk. They nested among the ancient cliffs and caves that were the castle's foundation.

Gethen scratched his stubbled jaw. Tall enough to accommodate double a normal man's height, the white doors of Drevya Linna were propped open by the headless torso of a dead pikeman. It wasn't a welcoming vision. It grew less inviting as he neared and his mage fire revealed the doors were speckled pink with misted blood. Perhaps it was good that he'd had a meager breakfast. He secured a rag around his mouth and nose, brightened the mage fire's amber glow, then entered the castle, bracing to see worse. He wasn't disappointed. A healer sees many parts of men that few others see, but he'd never seen them like this and prayed to the gods that he never would again. The butchery was endless. Not a person left alive, not a soul unconsumed by the shrikers.

He'd last been in the castle as a very young boy and had a vague memory of the royal quarters occupying the northwest corner of the keep. He was right. First came four dead royal guards, their armor dented, torn, twisted and unrecognizable, like their bodies.

Next he found the adult princesses Sigveig and Yrsa. They'd died in the hall outside the nursery.

Gethen entered the apartment where sixteen children,

ranging from infant to almost adult, normally slept in four adjoining rooms. Four governesses had suffered the same fate as Sigveig and Yrsa, but the Boorsooks' youngest children remained untouched. Only their souls had been ripped away. The littlest ones had huddled in a corner while two older boys and a girl tried to defend them. A noble but fruitless attempt. Heartbreaking.

Gethen dropped onto a made bed, rubbing his temples. His head ached, a pounding behind his eyes. The entire Boorsook family slaughtered in one night. Only Crown Prince Waldram — now King Waldram — still lived, the only luck that had visited Drevya Linna, and not much of a showing in Gethen's opinion; the new king was a vicious lout.

He scowled. Elof and Feddie had said the shrikers came from Drevya. The soldiers said they'd emerged from the castle. He looked around. "Where's that boneyard?" It couldn't be far. The midden? Seemed like a logical place to start but not large enough to produce so many shrikers. He was looking for a place where many dogs and animals were dumped.

Sound reached his ears. He held his breath, hoping it was gulls outside the window. He waited. Listened.

Voices. Not gulls. Soldiers inside the castle. Smoke from the burning shriker bodies must have given away his location. His destruction of the beasts had provided Drevya's men with safe passage. Cries of horror and rage echoed up the stairs.

"Time to go," Gethen muttered.

A man shouted, "Where's the king?"

Didn't the idiots realize Drevya Linna was a tomb? A little quiet respect for the dead was in order. Not to mention quiet caution. If more shrikers lurked in the castle, the soldiers' squawking surely would bring them.

"Check the nursery!"

"Princess Yrsa!"

Boots stomped up the back stairs.

"Find the children!"

Armor clattered in the hall.

"Gods! Is *that* Princess Sigveig?"

Gethen stood. There was no escape the way he'd come. He snuffed the mage fire and stepped into a shadow.

Doors creaked, slammed.

"The children!"

"No! Gods, no."

He emerged into a massive chamber and exhaled. He raised his light. King Hjalmer was dead in the middle of the room, his chest and torso opened, emptied. Queen Ektrina never made it out of bed. Their souls, trapped in the mortal realm by Skiron's will, raged around the room, unable to speak, unable to cross the Voidline. They knocked books from shelves, rattled the shutters, threw candles, and pulled the blankets off the bed. Noticing him, the spirits directed their wrath and objects his way.

"I didn't do this," Gethen hissed, trying to calm them without bringing the soldiers back to the king's chamber. Too late. Shouts and the sound of running feet carried in from the hall. He leaped for the bedchamber's open door, slammed it in a soldier's face, and threw the lock.

Behind him the spirits raised a vortex of swirling debris and rage. "Calm down. I didn't kill anyone."

"Sure you didn't, *necromancer!*" the soldier snarled.

"I'm not talking to you, idiot!" he shouted back. Then to the king and queen, he said, "I'm here to find out who did. I'll get word to the crown prince." The vortex grew, throwing off candles and cups, a hairbrush, a hand mirror. Behind him, weapons and weight struck wood. The door creaked, groaned, cracked as the soldiers assaulted it. A book smacked the side of his head. He ducked a crystal decanter but felt the sting of its shards as it shattered against the wall above him.

Gethen growled and raised a shield. Or tried to. His sorcery was strong but not infinite and could be devitalized by demand and Gethen's own fatigue. The spells shimmered. They wavered, warped, and died. "Bollocks." Another try resulted in even worse fizzling results and his mage fire sputtered with it. "Bollocks!" Damned unfortunate timing for his sorcery to be exhausted. He'd have to rely on wits and strength until he could rest adequately.

Drevya's soldiers roared insults and assaulted the door.

"Death's spawn!"

Thud.

"Skiron's lickspigot!"

Thud.

"We're gonna skin you alive!"

Crack!

"And leave you for the gulls!"

Gethen made for one of the windows. He opened the creaking shutters and looked out into a rocky gorge. He peered up, down, left, right. Just his luck. Pale moonlight revealed a six-story fall to be smashed on the castle's rocky foundation, followed by a four-story plunge into the Jera River to drown. Above him, machicolations protruded from the side of the building, overhanging the walls to afford clear views down into the churning whitewater through their murder holes. Putlog holes, dark squares against the dark wall, ran at regular intervals around the tower below the machicolations. And, beneath them, some of the keep's other windows were open.

A mighty thud, a mighty crack, and the glinting edge of an ax appeared on this side of the door.

Gethen sat back on his haunches and gripped the stone sill. "I'm too old for this." He was strong, but he was no acrobat. As a boy, he'd often climbed through Ranith Tower's windows to escape Shemel's fists, but it had been a dozen years or more since he'd scaled walls. "It's reasonable not to want to die this way," he said to the angry spirits, even as he pulled off his boots and stockings. "Damned unreliable sorcery." He buckled the boots together and hung them off his belt then sat back against the stone wall and absently rubbed his healing arm. If he lost his grip, he didn't have enough power to invoke a travel incantation and save himself from being smashed on the rocks then drowning.

Another massive blow to the door and its latch pinged.

"Skiron's bones." Gethen swallowed, climbed over side of the cold, stone sill, and blindly felt for toeholds.

Thud-thud-thud.

His right foot found purchase. Its brother located a divot in the wall.

Crack.

He eased his body below the sill, rain-slick cracks and aching fingers and toes his only hold on life.

Hide here, wait for them to search the room, climb back in. A simple plan. Simple was always best.

Bang.

Another huge jolt and the door flew open. It swung and hit the opposite wall.

Slam.

He clung just below the ledge as the soldiers stormed the room. Their cursing and bristling turned to confusion. Gethen twisted his fingers deeper into crevices. He flattened his body to the stone. Wind whirled around the corners of the keep, gusting wildly up from the gorge, whipping, biting. It snapped at his tunic and trouzes, found gaps between the cloth and his leather brigandine, stung his exposed feet.

It was damnably cold and he didn't dare look down. Though not afraid of heights, he didn't seek them out either, and hanging precariously above a ten-story drop to a churning river threatened to shrivel his bollocks.

Like a dark spider clinging to a light tree trunk, he was too exposed. So, though the effort made him shake even more than the cold, the wind, and the height, he commanded what little shadow magery he could muster to cloak him in its darkness. The sorcery came but sullenly — pushing at his demands, twisting and turning to escape his hold — a petulant, overtired child pressed to obey. It threatened to disintegrate like dust on the wind or explode outward as an oil fire plumes when water touches it. Either would catch the soldier's attention and bring death at the end of something sharp and pointy.

There was movement and the clatter of metal on stone. "Where'd that bastard go?" A soldier stood at the window only inches above him. Flickering torchlight made the man's shadow dance precariously across the sill.

Gethen wasn't a religious man, but he knew when to call upon the gods. *Please, Skiron. I'd like to live through this day.*

"Search the castle! He's using sorcery to outwit us."

"I'm gonna ram my sword up his arse! See if he can magically outwit that!"

With a curse, the soldier slapped the ledge, sending bits of dirt into Gethen's face, then disappeared back into the room. The window closed on screeching hinges. The latch scraped home.

"*Bol*-locks." So much for a simple plan.

Sucking in a steadying breath, Gethen felt for a handhold

near his waist, found one, then shifted his left foot until it found purchase between the window he'd left and its nearest closed neighbor. His other hand and foot followed and he eased his way over until he was clinging to irregularities in the stone. His route was sideways from there, past two more closed windows, then up to one of the dark openings and safety. He reached, pushed, stretched, found another notch in the stone, scraped moss and slime away, shifted a little closer to his target. Pinching notches, pressing his body flat, finding cracks and crevices, finger- and toeholds, he inched across Drevya Linna's unbreachable face.

Now he reached a stretch of smooth marble, no holds readily found. His fingers and toes ached, his wounded arm burned, and his muscles shook. This was the crux, the worst of the challenge. He took a moment to breathe and risked a dim spark of light to search out the closest crack. He found it, parchment-thin with a little weed sprouting from it. He'd have to push and reach for it. Gethen surged up, stretched, slapped his fingers against the stone, caught, slipped, cursed, and somehow snagged it with his trembling left pinky. His other fingers followed and wormed into the space. He brought his left foot up, his knee almost to his chest to go over the stretch of slick marble. He discovered another notch for his toes, pushed, pulled, snarled, begged. And made it over the line. He found a more secure handhold and took another moment to catch his breath, a moment to assess his location. Two more moves and he'd reach safety.

Gethen pressed his face to the wet stone, dragging in hard, painful breaths, eyes closed. A chill passed through him. The muscles in his left arm spasmed, his fingers cramped. The chill hadn't been from the wind but from the return of King Hjalmer and Queen Ektrina. They'd found him and drifted close, their need, anger, despair palpable enough to make his guts churn. "I told you I didn't release the shrikers. I'm trying to find the sorcerer who did. I'm trying to—"

Metal scraped stone. "Wait," a man said from somewhere above Gethen. "Did you hear something?"

"Hear what?"

The conversation echoed downward. He looked up. He was directly beneath a murder hole and his gaze met that of a Nalvik soldier, the man's face lit by flickering, yellow torchlight.

Another face came into view. "Well, look at that. Drevya Linna has a spider."

"Get me a rock. I'm gonna smash it loose."

Bollocks, bollocks, bollocks. Gethen focused on the wall to his left as he stretched for another toehold.

"Forget a rock. Let's shoot the bastard."

"Just hand me a rock. I'm gonna bash his face in."

"Find your own rock. I'm getting a bow and bolt."

"Just hand me — Skiron's bones, Arped, you're such a prick."

Gethen found a hold as the men's voices receded. He took it with his left hand, reached for another with his right hand, and swung his body away from the murder hole just as a rock plunged through it from above. The stone caught his boots and knocked them free from his belt.

The king and queen circled fast, frantic.

"Huh," said the man on the rampart above, his voice echoing down the hole.

"What?"

"Got his boots."

"Boots?"

"Yeah." Bits of mortar dribbled past Gethen as the men

stood around the murder hole and gazed through it to where his boots clattered and bounced off stone, cliff, stone, and splashed into the river far below. "Guess it's your turn."

Blood and bones. Those were his favorite boots.

"Let's see how well our spider clings with an arrow in his skull." The bow creaked, string sang.

The spirits slammed into Gethen. Fiery orange power surged through him. He slipped. An arrow twanged off the stone where his face had been. Tiny stone shards cut his forehead, stung his cheek. He tumbled backward, arse-ward, forward, backward toward the churning Jera. He saw walls, stars, torchlight, water, walls, stars, torchlight, water. Power surged through him, burning from his chest, through his brain, down his spine. He invoked a shield spell, saw the water, slammed into the river hard enough to make his whole world hurt, hard enough to make everything go black.

CHAPTER 15

Midday and the basilica was as hot as a bread oven. Halina strode between its columns, her skirts swishing around her legs, stirring up dust. Gethen swung a heavy sledge into the crumbling southern wall. Mortar and stone fell thudding around his feet. He'd removed his tunic. The planes and valleys of his back shifted with his muscles. Dust discolored the mottled Beseran stripes encasing his ribs and dulled the sheen of sweat across his shoulders.

He straightened. "Sneaking up on me, Militess?"

She swallowed. She'd come to offer him wine. But seeing him dirty and half-naked stirred her desire. She licked her lips. "No." Her voice sounded husky. His gaze sharpened, darkened, grew predatory.

Halina left the wine bottle and glasses on a stool and went to him. She pressed against him, her body tingling, heating at his musky, masculine scent, the hardness of his muscles, the silk of his skin. Her hands slid into his trouzes, her tongue was in his mouth. "I want you inside me."

Gethen moaned. He locked his arms around her, turned and pushed her against the unbroken wall. He raised her skirts. Halina loosened his belt. He lifted her body. She burned beneath the heat of his touch. Her back was up against the wall, his shoulder was in her mouth, his hands gripped her arse, opened her to him. The basilica echoed with their moaning, their panting, growled words of love and lust as he entered her, hard, deep, slow. He pinned her to the wall and stopped, held still, all muscles straining as he pressed his face to her neck and inhaled, slowly, his lips against her skin. He raised his head, looked into her eyes, and began to move, to grind and slide.

"Oh, gods," she moaned.

He smelled of sweat and dust, of sex and desire. She ran her tongue up his shoulder to his neck, licked the sweat that beaded his skin, his whiskers rough, his flesh salty-sweet. Animal noises escaped her, lustful, needy, commanding.

Gethen thrust into her, a slow, steady rhythm that stoked the fires burning between them higher with every stroke. She trapped him with her legs, locked them around his hips, twisted her fingers in his hair, sank her teeth into the bulge of muscle capping his shoulder.

"Deeper. Harder," she growled against his skin.

He did. Her every command was met, surpassed, until she thought she'd catch fire, burn and break apart. His mouth was on hers, tongue pushing past her teeth, twining with hers. Panting into her, pushing into her. "Gods. You. Feel. So. Good."

Halina moaned and drove back against him, met each thrust with a squeeze of her legs, rocked her hips forward against him, felt his cock inside her, filling her, sliding, surging. His nails dug into her flesh, painful, exquisite.

"Open your eyes," he said. She obeyed, met his gaze. He touched her face, kissed her mouth, a hard, bruising kiss. She trembled, arched. She closed her eyes and moaned, tension building, heat and ache growing with each rhythmic thrust.

"I told you to open your eyes, bitch."

She blinked and struggled to move, but she was held tight, pinned to the wall, to the chair. He slapped her.

Then he was gone. She was left trapped, exposed, raw, confused. "Gethen?"

Cold water splashed her, sudden, shocking. A bucket of it in her face. Another slap. More cold water.

"I said, open your eyes."

She awakened wet, spluttering, hurting. The memory's warmth and pleasure disappeared. She was shaking and cold, aching, angry. "Prick."

Ren dropped a bucket at her feet. Its hollow thud hurt her head. She was still trapped in the chair. He grabbed her hair, yanked her head back. "You look like shit and smell worse."

"If you treated me better, I'd look and smell better, arsehole."

He slapped her again then looked at his hand. "Nasty." He wiped it on her dark, wet kirtle.

She blinked down at the soaked underdress, confused. Where was her blue betrothal gown? Gethen loved her. He was going to marry her. She'd worn it to show Vernard and Waldram that she wasn't for sale.

Then she remembered. They'd taken her beautiful, price-less surcoat. They'd cut the laces, slit the seams, and folded the silk. They would tear it into pieces, sell each at a cut rate and still make a fortune. A wave of regret surged through her, threatening to trigger tears. She sucked a breath. It tried to be a sob. She swallowed and hiccupped instead. *Don't cry. Don't you dare cry.*

A thread of sound wormed around her and into her brain. "Release her." The words a sweet song, like the rustle of wings in Ranith's rafters, a lullaby sung by her mother.

Ren stopped and stared, bloody fist cocked for the next

blow. "Eh?" he said. Halina could only see out of one eye, but the mercenary looked as stupid as ever, maybe even more.

"You will not raise a hand to Lady Khara."

Arevik. It was Arevik's voice. Halina smiled, or would've if it wasn't so painful. Their mother Ianthe was a whisper witch, a sireah, capable of influencing others with the sound of her voice. Halina hadn't inherited a lick of the ability, but Arevik had the rudimentary skill and was giving it a go.

"What she said, arse-licker," Halina mumbled.

Ren looked down at her, the same slack stupidity on his face. "Eh?" She swiped her tongue around the raw insides of her mouth, rolled it, spat blood, mucus, and a tooth in his face. He blinked, befuddled.

But Vins barked a harsh laugh and pointed at Arevik. "So you're a sireah." He sneered. "Not a very good one. Right, Britta?"

His sister mirrored his sneer and nodded. "You can't control *us* with your voice."

"What?" Ren shook his head. He and the other mercenaries stared at each other, slack-jawed, stupid.

"Release Lady Khara," Arevik whispered, but her voice was losing its command and gaining a warble. She had a long way to go in her training before she had even a tenth of the skill their mother possessed. Halina thought that was a damn shame. A full-strength whisper witch would've been more than welcome just then.

Vins snapped his fingers at the men. "Gag the little sorceress and tie her to that Ayestran lout and Crown Prince Idiot." He stretched, yawned, and elbowed Britta. "I'm bored with blood and bone. Time to try this our way."

The mercenaries shook their heads, snarled at their own

stupidity, then bound and gagged Arevik. They'd restrained Magod and Waldram when Halina's torture began.

The baby mages giggled like lunatics. Britta dragged her toe through a puddle of blood. She smirked at Halina. "Death comes for some of us sooner than others," she sang, her voice soft, sing-song, insane. Vins pointed at Ren and another man. "Flatten the margrave's right hand." They pinned Halina's palm on the chair arm. Vins swaggered forward and pried the black band off her ring finger, the gift from Gethen. She always wore it. Always.

She growled at the young mage. "Give. It. Back."

"Don't worry, Your Ladyship." He passed it to his sister. She held the ring between her finger and thumb, peering at Halina through the hole. Vins said, "Britta will." The ring glowed orange in his sister's grasp, though she made no indication that it burned her fingers. She smiled and slipped the sorcery-heated band back onto Halina's hand.

She knew better than to fight the agony of torture; being brave only pushed the brutality to greater heights. She screamed. She sobbed. She struggled to escape the searing pain and the stench of her own burning flesh. Yet when she looked at her finger and the ring, expecting to see blistering flesh and white bone, there was no wound. The pain existed only in her mind, an illusion, sorcery. But she'd experienced this kind of dark magic before and, illusion or reality, the suffering was the same.

Vins watched her, his expression impassive, even bored. "Tell us where to find the treasury keys and the burning will stop." Britta touched the ring and its color intensified from orange to yellow and the heat and agony worsened.

Tears blinded Halina, tremors shook her. She gagged as

pain radiated up her arm. But she only shook her head and gritted her teeth so she wouldn't bite her tongue.

"Hmm." The girl mage touched the band again and it became white-hot.

"Keys for relief," Vins said.

The agony radiated across Halina's chest and back. She'd have pissed herself if she hadn't already done that hours ago. She clutched the chair arm. "Screw you," she growled through clenched teeth. She turned away from the pain in search of palliation and found the memory of Gethen holding her cold, dying body in Ranith's basilica.

Don't give up, Halina. You never give up.

Gods, if only she could use the ambit. Gethen would return and slaughter her tormentors. She shook her head. She couldn't. He'd die. Two wards stood between her and rescue, two deadly wards that would kill her lover if she sent the ambit for him. She had no choice but to endure and find her own escape.

Arevik sobbed. Halina struggled to block that sound. Her sister's terror was the worst torture.

Waldram cursed, kicked the knees out from under the mercenary guarding him, then lunged from his chair and slammed into Vins like a bull stomping a cur in its corral. The boy went down hard and sent his sister sprawling. Her face cracked against the floor, blood spurted from her nose.

Halina's pain suddenly ceased. Relief surged through her and she cried out. The brute, Trefor, tackled Waldram and Cadoc's men piled on. A few minutes of vigorous pummeling left the crown prince bleeding from the mouth and nose.

"That was stupid," Vins snarled as Britta smeared blood across her face with a wipe of her sleeve. The boy turned on Halina. He gripped her neck. It was only a light touch, but her throat constricted. She gasped, squirmed to escape his touch, desperate for air and staring Vins in the face as the boy mage leaned close, a delighted smile twisting his swelling lips. "We heard you're afraid of drowning, Margrave."

The weight of fluid filled her lungs. It pressed against her chest. She arched and thrashed. *Illusion! It's illusion!* she screamed in her mind, but that didn't lessen the terror and panic. Pinpoint lights sparked before her vision.

Vins blew air across her face. "The keys for a breath." Britta started her insane giggling.

Halina couldn't. She wouldn't. They'd kill her and Arevik and Magod, if she did. The world was tilting. Her ears were ringing. She shook her head and closed her eyes. *Not drowning. Not! Real!*

"It must feel terrible to not be able to breathe." Vins straightened and drew a long, slow breath, blew it out. "We can make it stop so easily, Margrave."

Halina opened her eyes. The arrogant nimwit stood too close. She kicked out. Her foot crushed the boy's little bollocks and he squealed like a stuck pig. The spell broke. He doubled over, clutching his crotch. She dragged in a breath, and another. "Little prick," she gasped, drooling, snot running, eyes watering. She kicked again, this time catching him in the ribs and knocking him onto his back.

"You bitch!" Britta screeched.

Ren punched Halina in the face. Pain erupted through her skull and blood splattered her kirtle. It had been stupid to kick the little fen-sucker. She swallowed more blood, more tears, more snot, and mumbled, "Worth it."

Arevik was cradling her and sobbing when Halina regained her senses. She peered at her sister through the slit of her right eye and mumbled, "Don't cry. I'm not dead yet."

That only made the countess cry harder.

"You're *not* trying to kill her?" a man shouted. "You could've fooled me." Halina craned her head and was surprised to see it was Waldram.

"Of course not, Your Grace," Cadoc crooned. "We've been going easy, trying to tickle the whereabouts of those keys from her. I'd hoped she'd be reasonable, but I still don't have my treasure, the day's grown long, and my patience has thinned."

"You're monsters."

"You think so?"

"I know so."

Cadoc laughed. "Just wait."

"I don't wait on murder." Waldram bared his teeth. "It's best served in the heat of the moment."

Halina mumbled, "Or maybe I *am* dead." Waldram defending her? This was a strange reality she'd awakened to.

"If Margrave Khara dies, you'd better kill me too."

"Vengeance? For the cousin you notoriously hate? How surprising. I guess blood binds tighter than I thought."

Waldram bared his teeth. "I guess it does."

"We'll soon see how tight those bonds remain, Your Grace."

Britta and Vins appeared in the doorway. The girl peered at Halina. "That bitch got what she deserves."

Cadoc slowly turned. "Meaning?"

"The locks were tricky, and there were a lot of them, but we finally got 'em open."

Vins grumbled, "I told you we're not much good at mechanical sorcery."

"The treasury's open?" Cadoc headed toward the mages, his mercenaries at his heels like dogs. The ward warped and dropped as he reached the doorway.

When the rush of magic ceased behind the re-established ward, the captives were alone in the great hall.

"He's in for a disappointment," Halina mumbled.

Waldram eyed her. "Why?"

"Khara's treasury is barren. I spent most of it on feeding my starving people, rebuilding their flood-ravaged villages, and renovating this castle."

He stared, shook his head. "That won't go over well."

She shrugged then winced. "He didn't ask."

"We need to get you out of here."

Halina squinted at Waldram through her good eye. Perhaps he *had* changed. She almost laughed at the ridiculousness of that. The last thing she expected was a softening of her second cousin's stony heart. The man had no compassion for anyone or anything. If he was defending her, it was because he gained more from her life than her death.

Arevik stroked her hair, tried to re-braid it, but it was too snarled and knotted. She plucked absentmindedly at her own ruined dress. "I can't believe they stole your betrothal gown."

The sadness that cracked her sister's voice nearly broke Halina. She slowly sat up and waited for the world to stop lurching. Her ribs screamed, her face felt fat and broken, her teeth jangly. Everything hurt. Everything made her want to cry. She breathed through her mouth to settle her stomach as nausea rolled through like tempest waves. Puking on the battlefield was normal. Puking on her sister was more than the girl deserved. "Have you checked the crown prince's wounds?"

"No. Will you be all right?"

"I need a moment alone."

"Oh." Arevik stood, reluctant, chewing her lip, watching Halina.

"Go on." When she did, Halina buried her face against her knees. Tears dampened her cheeks. Gods, the last hours had been a long, awful blur of pain and horror. She needed nerve and will to outlast and outwit Cadoc. Both felt in short supply.

Magod kneeled beside her. "What do you need, Your Ladyship?"

Halina shook her head and winced. "Just, ah, just give me a moment."

He leaned close and whispered, "Master Gethen will kill them." He stood and retreated.

Again and again as they'd tortured her Gethen's words had kept her strong. *"Don't give up, Halina. You never give up."* He loved her. As Cadoc's mages had twisted her mind and his men had beaten her body, she'd held fast to that love. They'd lied about his involvement. She knew it, knew him. He could never betray her this way.

But they'd planted a seed of doubt, and even in barren soil it tried to root beside the one her father had sown.

She turned her head and spied her shadow dancing in the firelight. *Skiron's bones.* A tiny piece of her berated Gethen for giving her the ambit, a powerful tool she couldn't use without killing him. Knowing freedom and revenge were within her grasp yet utterly unattainable was its own kind of torture.

Arevik returned with a cloth in her hand. "Let me clean your face."

Halina straightened and stood, hissing at endless, throbbing pain. She shoved the cloth and her own frustrations away. "Got to get us out of this mess. Got to get those wards down." Somehow.

"Please. Let me help you." Arevik tried to wipe her face

again. Halina stared at her sister's hands, stared at Magod, at Waldram.

"They untied us?"

Magod nodded. "Was wondering about that."

Waldram caught her elbow, his grip firm but, surprisingly, not unkind. "I don't like it."

"Neither do I, but let's not squander the opportunity." Halina took the cloth from Arevik. "Look outside. I want to know what's happening in the bailey, on the battlements, and beyond the field walls. Where are our soldiers? Are the portcullises down?"

Arevik nodded and went to the window. Magod followed her. Waldram said, "You can't take much more of this."

"They'll really get going when they return from the treasury. But don't worry, cousin, I learned how to endure torture at an early age." Halina wiped her broken nose, cursed the sharp pain that followed, and scowled at the bloody smear it left on the rag. "Your cruelty has served me well."

He grunted and turned away, arms folded and expression — hurt? Halina considered her second cousin's tall, trim figure. Had she finally dug deeply enough to touch a nerve? "Why do you care if they kill me? Cadoc's right; everyone in Quoregna knows we hate each other."

"Politics, Halina. You're more useful to me alive than dead." He smiled ruefully. "For now at least."

Arevik strained to see the movements beyond the windows.

"Magod?" Halina waved the groundsman over.

"Yes, Your Ladyship?"

"When you see a chance to escape take it. Get my sister out of the castle."

His large brown eyes were steady and solemn. "Swear on

Mummin's grave to keep the countess safe and get her free, Lady Khara."

"And do not come back for me."

For a moment she thought he'd argue as his shoulders hunched, but his mouth flattened into a straight line. He gave her a short, sharp nod. "Yes, Your Ladyship."

She squeezed his arm, finger burning, bones clicking with the movement. "Thank you."

Several mercenaries returned to the hall and hovered outside the door beyond the ward. They glared at Halina. Arevik meandered around the room as if in prayer, pausing to offer obeisance to the gods at each compass point, with the final offering to the light and the dark. The mercenaries spared her a cursory glance then turned away, more interested in Halina than her younger sister's piety. She returned to Halina's side. "It's quiet in the bailey. The portcullises are down. There's a lot of activity beyond the curtain walls. I think the soldiers know we're in trouble."

"They should by now. We've got to break those wards so they can get past the walls."

Magod nodded and met her gaze evenly. "Kill the mages."

"Exactly," Halina replied.

Arevik said, "But they're younger than me. They're—"

"A threat to Ursinum," Waldram said as he rejoined them.

"To Quoregna," Halina corrected.

He nodded. "Cadoc will start killing the moment he realizes the wards have failed."

Arevik worried her lower lip with her teeth. "Why would he kill us before getting what he came for?"

"Because that's what I'd do, if my primary defense was compromised," Halina replied. "I wouldn't leave any witnesses alive to attest to my guilt. I'd kill every single one of the hostages." She touched her chest and added, "Starting with me."

Waldram nodded. "A handful of dead peers and a looted treasury will guarantee their war."

Cadoc reappeared at the doorway with both baby mages in tow. They lowered the ward and entered the hall. His gaze ranged over the group before settling on Halina. He muttered something to the mages and they nodded, their boot heels tapping a sure rhythm on the tile floor as they approached.

Waldram turned to the mercenaries and Halina studied him. His arms were folded. His scowl was fierce. He stepped between her and their enemies, and for the first time that she could recall, she felt conflicted about her second cousin. Could her father have been right about him being a better man than she realized?

Cadoc circled, just out of reach, six armed mercenaries keeping sharp eyes on her and her companions, their hands on their daggers, swords, axes. "You're a devious woman, Margrave." He stopped and considered her from head to toe. He tutted. "Ren, Vins, and Britta have done quite a job on you. But Britta's right, you earned it. I must admit you've endured far more suffering than I ever imagined any soldier could take. Shocking, considering you knew we'd be disappointed once we got into the vault. An admirable, if extreme, attempt at buying your soldiers time to find a way around our wards." He shrugged. "Too bad it failed."

Halina slowly straightened. Sharp, burning pain shot up her spine and through her shoulders and hips, but she did it anyway, and knew it showed on her face. She smoothed down the front of her dark, damp kirtle, aware of the betrothal gown's missing weight, aware of the violation that taking it had become. They'd stolen Gethen's commitment to her and hers to him. They sought to make his love a lie, a fool's fantasy.

The bloody, arse-sniffing pillocks didn't know whom they were dealing with.

Her swollen mouth and missing tooth garbled her words, so she took her time, enunciating carefully. She didn't want Cadoc to misunderstand. "You are the biggest, dumbest nutsack I've ever met." Something like consternation crossed his face. "You won't get any satisfaction from me. I've had worse." She raised her right hand and slowly folded all but the middle finger.

The man looked down, pressed his lips into a straight line, then said, "You're right. This is wasting our time. Your suffering's grown tedious and pointless."

"Boo-bloody-hoo."

He stepped back. "You haven't met all our friends, Margrave. I think it's time we made an introduction." He snapped his fingers at Britta and Vins. "Release them." The baby mages grinned and began an incantation. "Put the margrave out in the hall." Cadoc's men shoved and menaced Waldram, Magod, and Arevik back, steel and teeth bared. Halina cursed as Ren and Trefor seized her arms, their hands like vices. They propelled her toward the doorway where the mages had parted the ward. Cadoc said, "Wait. Let's give her some company." He looked over his hostages and pointed at Waldram. "The crown prince." Waldram was forced through the doorway after her.

The ward snapped back with a hair-raising crackle. "We'll keep the princess and the pauper, in case we need to trade," Cadoc said. He smirked "Have fun playing with our other friends."

Halina stared at the shimmering wall of deadly magic as Cadoc shut the door. "What's his game?"

"I don't—" An unearthly, blood-curdling shriek cut Waldram off. The hair stood on Halina's arms and neck. He grabbed her hand. "Can you run?"

"Like a damned horse, if I have to."

"You do."

A shriker rounded the corner from the eastern wing of the servant's hall. Rheumy, yellow eyes tracked them. Another beast appeared behind it.

Cadoc's *friends*.

CHAPTER 16

Gethen lay on the riverbank beneath a canopy of
trees. Moonlight winked through the swaying
branches, bathing the black woods in an eerie silver
hue. The unsaturated surroundings felt like the colorless Void
and, when he'd first regained his senses, he'd had a moment of
panic, thinking he'd died and crossed the Voidline. The fall
had scared the piss out of him. The impact had felt like being
kicked by four heavy warhorses then trampled afterward for
good measure.

He was alive and intact thanks to King Hjalmer and Queen
Ektrina. They'd given him enough power to shield his body
from the impact with the river, from the pummeling of the
whitewater and rocks, from drowning.

"You saved my life. Why?" he croaked as they circled. They
were a little fainter, a little weaker, but no less persistent in
demanding his attention. He drew a breath, tried to sit up,
changed his mind. "Oh, no-no-no, not yet." The forest, stars,
and moon spun, tilted, and his guts twisted in the opposite
direction.

Gethen closed his eyes. Halina's face came to mind. That was a pleasant distraction and he let his mind's eye wander over her freckles, her blue eyes, the faint old scar that followed her jaw. He remembered the baths at Gurvan-sum and how she'd bared her body to him. That look in her eye, her certainty, her desire. He sighed. Ursinum society may have labeled her ugly, but he saw only beauty in her power and confidence. And, scarred or not, her strong, muscular body was the most beautiful thing he'd ever seen, held, explored. Smiling hurt his bruised face, but he didn't care. He couldn't help but smile when he thought of his lover.

Voices, distant but insistent, wiped the smile off his face. Shouting. Splashing. Soldiers. Maybe looking for him, maybe not. It didn't matter because he didn't want to be found.

"Is this a jest, Skiron? Just a taste of my punishment if I fail to find the necromancer?" With a groan, he pushed upright, got to his knees, and stood, swayed, stumbled into the dark woods. The spirits followed. Of course. Gethen hadn't solved the riddle of their company yet and the Voidline was closed to them.

He hadn't gone far before he was blocked by cliffs. He was in the Jera River Gorge and much of the water flowed swiftly past sheer stone walls. He'd been lucky King Hjalmer and Queen Ektrina had directed him to a rare bit of riverbank. Without them, he'd still be treading water and heading toward the Bay of Ayestra. Or he'd be dead.

Bats fluttered past; nocturnal friends whose wings brushed his face. The cliffs were pocked with small, black openings. River gulls nested there, watching him with red eyes, suspicious, protective. Unlike Ursinum's gulls, which nested among the marsh grasses, these chose the high caves to avoid predators, like Nalvika's wild dogs.

The soldiers were louder. Closer. He glimpsed torchlight flickering through the trees. The Nalviks were on the river upon a barge, peering into the forest, jabbing pikes into the water, looking for him — or his body — it seemed. Moonlight glowed on their plate armor and steel weapons. He wondered if Thaksin was among them. If so, he hoped the prick fell overboard and drowned.

Gethen studied the cliffs. Among the many small caves a few larger openings gaped, like dark mouths in a face of many empty eye sockets. "Up this time." He climbed, using the smaller caves as hand- and footholds. It was easier going than traversing Drevya Linna's face, though his burning, trembling muscles didn't appreciate the exertion. The gulls were put out by his passage, too. A few ruffled their feathers, a few poked at his hands and feet. He murmured reassurances, took care not to disturb their nests and hatchlings, and they settled around him.

He reached his chosen cave, a tight squeeze but doable and still below the tops of the trees so he was hidden from Nalvika's soldiers. He dug his fingers into a little lip just above the opening, pulled his body up, and slid in feet first. He wormed back, surprised by how deep it went and that no other occupants fled his intrusion. He sensed that it widened as he went back but had no reason to keep going. He was hiding, not exploring. He pulled his dark hood over his head, folded his arms into his sleeves, and rested his face against them, eyes closed.

Voices came near, men thrashing through the trees. The gulls swooped and called, protesting the intrusion. The soldiers complained back at them, stomped around, retreated. Their shouts faded.

Gethen rolled onto his back, pressed his shaking hands to

his chest, and stared into utter darkness. As he'd fallen from the castle's face, he'd had time only to draw a small amount of strength from King Hjalmer's and Queen Ektrina's souls. But even that minute, human spark, already spent, left him prickly and aching for more.

That was the danger of his sorcery. "I don't want this," Gethen groaned, not for the first time, not for the last. "I didn't ask for it." His voice cracked. He crushed the heels of his palms against his eyelids. He was a necromancer, but he didn't practice necromancy, not in its purest form, anyway. To do that was to abandon being a man for becoming a monster.

He lowered his shaking fists. Battling the urge to consume the pure energy of the king's and queen's spirits, he reached for his memories of Halina, again, craving her like a nocoli addict craves a water pipe. He brought her face to mind, her throaty, full laugh. She had a lustful, shameless laugh, a laugh that made men roar with her. Halina and her laugh made him think of life, made life worth living. In spite of his position in a hole, in spite of the dirt in his mouth, down his tunic, up his nose, in spite of his aches and pains and struggles, he laughed, thinking of how her face and her chest gained a rosy flush and her breasts bounced, just a little, when she laughed.

Gethen laughed harder, shifted, spat dirt and winced as something poked him in the arse. He reached down, thinking it was a root, found something with angles, and pulled it out of the dirt. A bone. Long, thin, curved. A rib. "Boneyard." In his quest to remain in one piece, he'd forgotten about that search. He felt around and found more bones. He wormed further back into the cave until his feet crossed open space and the roof widened up and out. Gethen sat up slowly and raised a ball of mage fire, looked around, and gawked.

The cave became a wide, shallow cavern. Bones riddled the

floor. Animal bones mostly, but he spied more than a few human skulls grinning among them. He slipped down the small embankment, hit the cave floor, and his knees buckled. He cursed as he fell forward, landing on his hands and knees, up to his wrists in old, broken bones, grimacing as they snapped beneath his weight. A carpet of bones and teeth spread out before him. He shoved away, stood, and sagged against the cave wall.

Around the perimeter, small alcoves and wide shelves had been gouged into the walls. Skulls and bones perched upon them, arranged carefully with unlit candles, dried flowers, dusty figurines, books, platters, goblets — shrines to Skiron. A glint caught his eye. He gave more light to the mage fire. The glint multiplied. Gethen stared at a wall of pearly black nacre and yellow-white teeth. The black oyster shells had been carried hundreds of miles from Ewell Bay, the teeth torn free of hundreds of jaws. So much effort to create a massive mosaic depicting Skiron summoning his shrikers.

"Buh."

Hjalmer and Ektrina captured his attention as they circled the cavern, faster and faster, flashing past him, excited. Gethen raised a trembling hand to brush dirt from his face. "This is the necromancer's boneyard." The spirits still circled, circled, circled. "What? What more do you know?" He couldn't think clearly. He was too tired, in too much pain. His sorcery was too spent, his cravings too intense. "Blood and bones, just show me!"

The souls veered off course and slammed into him. The impact knocked him off his feet. Power surged through him, exquisite, potent. Orange and blue like fire, it burned the fatigue out of every organ. Magic exploded outward from where it had retreated within his chest. It surged through every nerve, set off a festival of colors, sounds, smells in his brain. He lay on his back, jerking, sweating, moaning, insensate with the high of subsuming two human souls.

∽

"Agreed." A door creaked open. "The deaths begin tonight." It thudded closed.

She hugged her knees, cold in her nightgown. She'd be beaten if they caught her out of bed. She crawled from beneath the table, cautious, all senses alert. She stood and blinked. She slunk across the throne room, a nervous little night creature hoping not to be seen by the predators. She slunk over the long dark tongue of carpet, not looking at the king's chair. It scared her almost as much as the man who sat in it did. There was a sound, high and thin. She stopped, listened. She stared into the dark, eyes wide, body tense, like a rabbit ready to run-run-run.

An urgent whisper. "Feddie!"

She squeaked, turned, heart in her throat.

Elof beckoned from the servant's door, a wicked grin on his face. "Scared you!"

She bared her teeth at him, vicious like a dog, like she'd seen her father do in the practice square. "Don't make me stab you, servant boy," she hissed, so low it sounded like the wind.

His grin widened. He bowed, sweeping his hand low like an emissary from Teleyansk. "My apologies, Your Ladyship."

She giggled. "Better." She grabbed his hand and her nightgown's hem. "We have to run. The crown prince is walking the halls. He'll skin us if we're caught."

"I never get caught." Elof pulled her toward the door the men had gone through.

That high, thin sound came again. Feddie froze, her feet rooted, the hair standing on her arms and scalp. "What was that?"

Elof tugged. "Just some wild dogs. C'mon! We'll miss the dancing lights, if we don't hurry. Tonight's the best night to see them. Lauma said they were purple and green last year and filled the whole sky."

"Okay, but—" That sound returned. Louder, closer. Crashes followed. Screams. Doors slamming, armor clattering. Shouts. Elof's eyes widened. "What's happening?" Feddie whispered, not feeling adventurous or brave anymore.

"I don't know." Elof pulled her into the hallway and into chaos. Soldiers charged past. Horrible, high-pitched screams followed them. He yanked her into the parlor and found the hidden door in the wall behind the Snow Queen's Court tapestry. Elof knew all the passages within the walls, knew the caves and the woods. Lauma had shown him. She knew all Drevya Linna's secrets, and had lots of her own. Down, down into the darkness, into the caves, their breathing the only sound. That and the cracking of bones beneath their feet. Cracking, crunching, shifting bones beneath Drevya Linna. Feddie hated all the bones. It was like living atop a cemetery.

Gethen awoke and the dream fragmented, like the bones under his body. He felt lingering fear, saw a glimpse of armor, heard a terrible sound, but none of it held together to tell him its story. He raised mage fire again. The boneyard. The necromancer. Shrikers. *Right.* He was covered in mud and dust, cold in clothes that were still damp. Like it or not, the spirits' sacrifice of their power had him feeling strong, clear-minded, formidable. He'd worry later about the pains and cravings that would come roaring back to fill the gap when their gift was spent. The sorcerer responsible for the shrikers had to be nearby. Maybe back in the castle, maybe hidden in one of these caves. "I'm coming for you, pillock. You can't hide forever."

He climbed back up to the entrance ledge and sat. Something was nagging him. The necromancer had created the shrikers in Drevya and sent them to Khara but, apparently, nowhere else in Ursinum. King Vernard would've said something in his letter to Halina, if they'd been spotted in other parts of the kingdom. The beasts were mindless. Without a necromancer's guidance, they devolved into chaos. Gethen squinted into the darkness. "That means Khara was targeted." He wanted to find the shrikers' creator quickly but was going to break a promise first. He had to know that Halina was safe. "Sorry, Margrave, but you knew I was a liar when you fell in love with me." He fished the little flask of shadow tears from his belt pouch and uncorked it. He set a deadly ward, tilted his head back, and put a drop of inky liquid in each eye.

It felt like his eyeballs were freezing. Nauseating pain followed burning cold. He breathed through his mouth to calm his roiling gut. The world blurred, his vision tunneled from gray to black. He blinked, blinked, blinked. Cold tears streamed down his cheeks and his vision began to lighten. Shapes appeared, colors, and finally he discerned the wide main stairwell of Kharaton Castle's east wing, jolting movement, and a world that was stretched and distorted by the ambit's position. Gethen willed the shadow to focus on Halina from its place on the floor and wall. It obeyed.

"Gods!" He jerked hard enough to hit his head on the cave wall. Dirt showered him, but he hardly noticed for the shock of seeing her. Bloody, beaten, bruised, she'd stopped at the entrance to the servant's hall, one arm wrapped protectively around her ribs, her face a rictus of pain and fear. A man was with her, pale, sinewy. A Nalvik. It wasn't the king or any of Halina's militairs. Something looked vaguely familiar about him and Gethen realized with a start that he was Crown Prince Waldram.

So he'd reached Tatlis and traveled with King Vernard. That explained his failure to reply to the message his soldiers had sent. Halina said something. Waldram shook his head, argued. The ambit stretched out to give Gethen a better view. Both of them started and looked toward the eastern stairs. They sprinted down the hall toward the kitchen, Halina struggling, Waldram holding her hand and carrying a bent pike. They reached the heavy kitchen door. He pushed her ahead, shouted something, slammed it shut between them.

Halina struggled to drag one of the heavy tables against the door, shaking her head, angry, upset. Probably cursing herself. Or cursing Waldram. She jumped back as something slammed against the door. She pushed the table into place. The door shuddered. The table hopped but held.

She stumbled to the window, looked into the bailey, left, right, left. Stopped. She looked over her shoulder toward the door, back into the bailey. She grabbed a butcher's knife from a table and limped into the bake house.

Gethen lost the ambit. The light was too low to maintain its form. "Damn!" He found his water flask and upended it onto his face, flushing the shadow tears from his eyes. He blinked them away, ignoring the potion's sting. He had to get to Halina. He didn't know what was chasing her, but it wasn't something as simple as a few armed opponents. He'd put money on it being a shriker. That made his blood boil and his heart fear. No matter how tough she was, Halina couldn't destroy a shriker with a knife and no aid. Gethen had barely won his battles and had needed that prick Thaksin's help more than once.

He set Kharaton's bake house in his mind, the two arched

brick ovens, the long worktable, flour drifting on the air and dulling the light, the smell of fresh brown bread baking. He invoked a travel incantation to carry him to her side. Dirt and mud mixed with amber magic, a whirlwind of sorcery and soil. But something didn't feel right as the spell took him from the tunnel, as he slipped between space, as he approached the castle and its great hall. Something pushed back against him, burned and bit.

A pair of wards. *Blood and bones.* Wards he hadn't set. Gethen altered his destination, a dangerous but necessary change to the travel spell. He landed in a heap outside the lists, surrounded by startled Kharan militairs, his ribs stinging from meeting a wooden railing. Swords appeared, their sharp ends pointing at his chest. He wiped his muddy face with a muddy sleeve and looked at the castle. The portcullises were closed. The ramparts were empty.

"Lord Rhyshis?" Eugen yanked him up.

"Why are you out here?" Gethen snarled. He surveyed the field before the walls. Horses, tents, soldiers. The standards of Khara, Ursinum, and Nalvika waved gently in the afternoon breeze. "Why aren't these soldiers inside the castle?"

"We're trying," the steward snapped back with unusual heat. He waved toward the drawbridge. Several bodies lay between the two barbicans. "But *we* can't get past a sorcerer's ward."

Gethen grabbed the front of the steward's tunic and yanked him close. "Halina's in there and she's injured." He jabbed his finger at Kharaton Castle. "Someone brought battle mages into the castle while you were sitting on your arses out here."

"Someone like you, maybe?" snarled a militair clad in

Ursinum's red and black. He found himself on his face in the dirt, Gethen looming over him with a bloodied fist.

"Don't ever question my devotion to Lady Khara." There was something deadly in his calm voice and cold eyes. He heard it and saw realization reflected in the soldiers' faces.

Eugen pulled Gethen back. "If Lord Rhyshis wanted the margrave dead, he'd have killed her by now." His wary expression didn't quite support his assertion. "Do you know who's taken Kharaton Castle, Your Lordship?"

"No. But I'm sure there's more than one mage. Their magic has a strange, raw duality." Gethen surveyed the surrounding militairs and said, "Walk with me, Eugen. I must speak with you alone." He started toward the wooden lists at the edge of the footbridge. The steward followed, waving the soldiers back. When they were side-by-side again, Gethen asked, "Did the crown prince retain any servants inside the castle? I just returned from battling shrikers in Drevya."

"They're real?"

"Yes." He lowered his voice. "With the exception of Prince Waldram, the entire Boorsook royal family is dead."

"All of them?" Eugen stared at him, unable to hide his shock. "Gods. The crown prince is in the castle with few guards. He and King Vernard left most of their soldiers out here."

"The mages who did this could be responsible for the shrikers, too." Gethen grimaced. "From what I've seen of Halina's predicament, one may be roaming the halls."

"Bollocks. Then we have a bigger problem than any of us thought." They stopped on the bridge well back from the bodies. The stench of burned flesh and hair wafted on the wind. Eugen's demeanor turned surprisingly cold, surprisingly deadly. He jerked his chin toward the castle. "How do we breach that ward?"

"Not by direct assault. That'll earn you more dead soldiers." Gethen clasped his hands behind his back. "Who's inside?"

"Halina, the king, the crown prince, and Lady Vala. The cook and I estimate two dozen servants, including Philippa. Cadoc with some of his masons. And your man Magod. He delivered a dozen barrels of bracket then stayed behind to help in the kitchen. We don't know who's alive and who's dead."

Halina and *Magod?* "No soldiers?"

"There were sixteen patrolling the ramparts, but there's been no sign of them for hours. We're assuming they're dead."

Gethen scanned the abandoned castle defenses. "Likely you're right." He folded his arms and looked down at the ground, studying Eugen's polished boots. The man was meticulous, predictable. Gethen liked that about him. "In addition to the ward outside the curtain walls, there's another surrounding the great hall." The two battle mages' sorcery was raw and wild, their application of their wards and power sloppy. That gave him an advantage. And it made him wonder how they could've created so many shrikers. Likely dumb luck.

The militair he'd knocked flat was striding toward them, glaring, a handful of his peers in tow. Unwilling to let go of suspicion, he stopped a little too close, his hand on his sword grip. "Swear before your god Skiron that you're not behind this, mage."

Gethen held the man's gaze. "I have no hand in this. I swear it before all the gods."

Eugen nodded toward the lowered gates. "What will you do while we gather an assault team?"

"Try to remove those wards."

One of the soldiers sneered. "Should be easy enough for the most powerful mage in Quoregna."

Gethen sneered back. "Only idiots think sorcery is easy."

A Kharan militess, Theola, slapped the arm of the soldier beside her. "I told you something wasn't right when I saw the portcullises close."

Eugen stepped between Gethen and the soldiers. "Caution is paramount and we need to work together." He nodded toward the lowered iron gates. "First steps, Lord Rhyshis?"

Gethen gave him a grim smile. "I test the mages' skill and strength."

"How?"

He stood an arm's length from the ward's edge. It shimmered like a heat mirage, vibrated like a nest of angry wasps. He glanced over his shoulder at Halina's steward and said, "The horrifically painful way," as he raised his hand toward the sorcerous barrier.

CHAPTER 17

Waldram had found an old, bent poleaxe and was leading the shrikers away. "Whatever you're going to do to bring down that ward, do it quickly," were his last words before he'd slammed the kitchen door in her face.

"Damn him," she muttered, unable to decide what was more annoying — that he was being self-sacrificing or that she never expected him to be self-sacrificing. She stood in the shadowy bake house, comforted by the solidity of the butcher's knife in her hand, horrified by the carnage at her feet. The room smelled earthy, yeasty, heartening. A faint dusting of flour covered the floor and tables, lumps of dough dried and stiffened as they awaited baking that would never happen. The baker, the cook and her young assistant, and the entire kitchen staff were dead, hacked apart and left in a pile like sacks of grain. Their blood mingled with flour, their guts twisted among the rushes on the floor.

Halina pulled her gaze to the window and the keep opposite. She had a plan, but executing it without getting killed in the process was the biggest hurdle to success. "This is madness."

This was, in fact, a nightmare. Kharaton Castle had never been breached. Its defenses had kept more than one large army out with very few soldiers defending it. If her militairs were to succeed in getting in, she had to destroy those wards.

Fire was her best chance and she surveyed the bailey. She considered and rejected the straw by the stables. "That'll burn too long and threaten the castle." She wanted something that would burn fast and extinguish itself quickly. The kitchen midden was rejected as too hard to light; the stable midden was out for the same reason. Lots of wood and sawdust in the carpenter's shop, but that abutted the stables, so it was a no.

She jumped as another shriek and a thud hit the kitchen door. Cracking followed. The table against it jolted, rocked, nearly tipped. The shrikers were back. Waldram was probably dead. She was surprised to find that she hoped not.

"Think, Halina. *Think*." She was running out of time.

She passed the bodies, silent, respectful, regretful, to get a better view of the bailey and spied the curve of the stone granary. The narrow tower was close to the guardhouse and self-contained. Grain dust was explosive, which was why it was kept in a stone tower and separate from the heat of the bake house and kitchen. Best of all, she could reach it by passing through the Captain's Tower and Thaksin's quarters, remaining unseen by anyone atop the ramparts. "That'll do."

Its hinges squealed as she eased open the narrow door into the tower. Halina stopped. Inch by agonizing inch she opened it, pausing, listening. Finally, she had it far enough to peer through. No one in the anteroom; no one on the spiraling stone stairs. She crossed the space. The door into Thak's quarters was ajar. She peered in. A mercenary sat at the table before the hearth, his back to her. A fire crackled and he was digging into a full supper plate, shoveling dripping meat into his mouth, sopping up the juices with bread he'd taken from her dead baker and boy.

Halina flexed her fingers on the cook's butchery knife. She slipped into the room on bare, aching feet, a shadow unseen, unheard. She stopped behind the man. Sometimes life meets death on the end of a sharp steel point. The fellow sat back, belched, licked pig grease from his fingers. Halina caught his black hair. She yanked his head back, thrust the blade upward through his jaw into his skull. She yanked it out, stuck it through his throat 'til it hit bone, yanked it out, and buried it in his chest.

The dying man overturned the table as he slumped and fell. Meat, bread, broth splattered the floor.

"I hope you enjoyed your last meal." Halina pulled the knife from his quivering chest, wiped it on his trouzes, and snatched the tinderbox from atop the hearth. She eased open the door to the bailey, scanned the grounds and battlements. No one.

Keeping to the shadows she crept to the granary. When she reached the stone tower, she opened the small door that allowed the bakers to scoop out grain. A puff of wheat dust greeted her. She greeted it back with a smile. She removed the char cloth, flint, and steel from the tinderbox and turned over the lid. The smallest spark would trigger an explosion, one that would come fast and hot. She was in danger of being caught by the blast and in the mood to take chances.

She struck several sparks onto the cloth, watched them spread, tiny orange flames licking at the edge of the fabric, leaving dark destruction behind. "Khotyr, keep me." She tossed the cloth into the granary and slammed the door shut.

Gethen braced for pain. Sorcery burned through his fingers, his palm, up his arm; his own magic was flaring as he reached for the ward. This would hurt, no doubt. How much? Well—

A sudden hiss filled the air. A booming explosion followed. Flames shot through the iron vents on the grain tower behind the castle's walls. Its roof blew off. Roaring sound punched him. Sharp pain knifed his ears. "Gods!" He staggered and clapped his hands over them, too late. Castle windows shattered. Town windows shattered. Mortar, dust, glass shards, splinters of wood, chunks of stone flew upward, outward, everywhere.

Shouts. Grinding. Rumbling. He looked up. The three-story, stone granary trembled. It twisted and buckled like a dying ox. It smashed through Thaksin's quarters. It obliterated the guardhouse. Gethen turned, shouting, "Run!" He couldn't hear his own voice.

Wood and stone crashed all around. The castle barbican groaned and squealed. The iron portcullis bent. With a tremendous snap, the lattice gate failed. Its massive chains whipped through the crumbling stone like the arms of a clanking, flailing beast. They obliterated everything. One struck a militair from the bridge. The man made a little "oof" and left behind a mist of blood, a clattering greave. The second chain splintered the footbridge. It tore away the balustrade. It splintered a raft in the moat. It splintered the fisherman on the raft.

The bridge shuddered. It threw Gethen on his face. He clawed at the boards as he slid toward the water. The bridge torqued and dropped. It held trembling, then dropped again and jolted to a stop at an angle. Gethen caught hold, toes and fingers gaining splinters. Soldiers tumbled past him, bellowing

for help. Some caught the slats and stopped. Others disappeared over the edge into the water. They sank, screaming and
flailing, dragged down by the weight of their mail and plate.

Eugen was sliding toward him. Gethen caught his arm. His
grip failed. He cursed and snagged the steward's wrist. Eugen
jerked to a stop. Pain stabbed through Gethen's shoulder.
Theola rolled toward them. The steward grabbed one of her
pauldrons. Gethen groaned at their combined weight. His
shoulders and arms protested the abuse, but he didn't let go of
the bridge slats. He didn't fancy another unplanned swim.

Now the second barbican squealed and jolted. Pulled from
its moorings by the failing bridge, it slowly rotated, a drunken
reel. It lurched toward the castle, taking a drunken bow. But it
didn't collapse. Its iron portcullis warped, screeched. It pulled
away from the bridge deck throwing wooden shards as long as
daggers across the bridge and into the camp. Militairs running
to help were cut down. Horses panicking on the picket were
impaled.

Gethen raised his head. The destruction of the bridge and
portcullises had opened gaps in the defenses large enough for
the soldiers to climb through. Even better, the castle ward
shimmered, surged, and winked out of existence. His grin was
equal parts grimace. "Thank you, Skiron, Khotyr, and Semele,"
he said through clenched teeth.

Halina saw double. She'd flown without wings and landed
without control. Her head had hit the cobblestones. She rolled
over, gasped as pain knifed her already painful ribs, coughed
as she inhaled dust and smoke. The bailey was shrouded in a
thick, unnatural brume. The castle wall was a ragged lump

where the gatehouse and granary once stood. Somewhere beneath the debris was Thaksin's flattened apartment. "Thak won't like that," she muttered, her voice hoarse, thin. She got to her knees, and staggered to the safety of the servant passage, trying to shake the ringing from her ears, trying to focus her vision.

Two mercenaries stood in the kitchen doorway with Britta, open-mouthed, squinting into the dust. They stared around, ghostly figures confused by the appearance of a sudden afternoon fog. Halina looked at them. They looked back. Realization registered on their faces. One of the men pointed, shouted. His voice was muffled in her ears.

"Semele's blood." Halina sprinted across the bailey, no time for pain, no time for wounds, no time to wonder if she was running toward the damned shrikers or even decide if she was moving in a straight line.

"The wards are down!" Gethen couldn't hear his own voice.

"What?" That's what he thought Eugen shouted back.

He gestured toward the broken gateway, hunched over to counter the bridge's tilt, and staggered across the line where the ward had been. He waved toward those soldiers who'd regained their feet. Eugen nodded. The militess stood, pulled him up, and more soldiers joined them.

A Tatlis militair wearing red-and-black said, "We have to get in while we can."

"Do you know who's taken the castle, Your Lordship?" Theola shouted.

He shook his head. "I only know Lady Khara and the

crown prince are endangered. And there may be shrikers loose in there."

That brought a heavy silence. Eugen broke it. "They can be destroyed by removing their heads, right, Your Lordship?"

Gethen nodded. He peered over the bridge into the water and rubbed his stinging palms on the front of his trouzes. Fishermen were pulling soldiers from the moat, some alive, most not. He looked back at the dust pluming above Kharaton Castle and had an idea. "Get as many soldiers as possible past the walls before that ward comes back. I need our enemy's attention kept here and their hands kept busy."

Eugen and the militairs nodded. "Where are you going?" Theola asked, a little suspicion creeping into her voice.

He bared his teeth. "Hunting."

Halina sprinted through the bailey, scrambled over debris, and charged up the North Tower stairs with the mercenaries right behind her. She'd lost her knife after the blast and was left with fleet feet, a hearty will to survive, and an uncanny ability to block out pain when her life was in jeopardy.

One of the soldiers fell back; the other brute came on at a full run.

She took the tower stairs two at once, hoping she didn't encounter any mercenaries or the shrikers descending. The pounding footsteps of the man behind her grew louder, closer. She ran up the spiraling stairs, around and around and around, hoping to put some distance between herself and the large man.

An opening to the third floor loomed and Halina took it, turned back, and slammed the arched door in the mercenary's face. The man ran face-first into the wooden door. He shouted, she smiled. She yanked it open and grabbed the top of its arch. She kicked out, catching his chest with both feet. Off guard and off balance, the man grunted before tumbling arse-over-elbows down the spiral stairs, his head cracking against steps and walls as he rolled, grunts and yelps escaping him.

There was no time to enjoy her small victory. Halina continued her breakneck pace, trying to buy just a few minutes and a little distance between herself and the other mercenary, needing a place to hide, breathe, strategize. She wouldn't stop until Arevik and Magod were free. And Waldram, if he still lived.

The northeast wing of the castle jutted out into Kharaton Harbor, its sharply angled taluses dropping off into the deep water, slick with dark green algae and moss. She swerved left as an open window loomed. She grabbed for the windowsill meaning to hop onto it and scale across the outside of the castle wall. If she lost her hold, at least she'd fall into deep, cold water, not onto sharp rocks.

The other mercenary appeared. He captured her around the waist and threw her across the hallway. She struck the inner wall. Her head snapped against the wood. Her teeth jarred together. The man's fist followed and Halina barely dodged a meaty blow. He had greater height, weight, and reach. She had speed, experience, and just plain meanness. She was battle-hardened and trained daily, relentless in her pursuit of more strength, better technique, greater speed. She blocked his blows. She turned aside his pummeling fists. She landed more than a few good strikes. But she was tired and injured, and if she didn't get away quickly, she'd be pummeled into a bloody mess.

Khotyr, however, hadn't abandoned her favored daughter

yet. Halina dodged a jab, a hook, and smashed her fist into the mercenary's collarbone. He gasped, stumbled back. She barged him with her shoulder. He hit the window ledge. She hoisted his legs and dumped him backwards out the window into the harbor.

She sent her thanks to the gods as she ran up the stairs to the fourth floor. She pulled the double doors to her quarters closed behind her, exhaled, took two steps, and shrieked. Sharp, burning pain shot from her feet to her brain. She slumped to the floor, swallowing a sob, and peered at her bloody feet. Glass shards jutted from both heels and the ball of her left foot. She'd run across shattered glass in the bailey, so focused on survival that she hadn't felt the pain. Until now.

A trail of bloody footprints led to the door.

Halina cursed, groaned, swallowed snot and sobs as she crawled to Gethen's stillroom in search of something to dull the pain and stop the bleeding. At the doorway she cursed even more. The room had been ransacked. The water pitcher and washstand were smashed, his cabinets opened and emptied. Their contents were scattered, smeared, and splattered across the floor. Tinctures and unguents pooled with herbs, powders, and ash to create a miasmic pool of wasted work. Even his mead had been pilfered or poured.

"Damn them." She closed her eyes and felt sorry for herself; there was only so much abuse a body could endure. But she forced the moment past. "Quit the self-pity," she said through gritted teeth. "Arevik needs you." Magod couldn't protect her sister from a roomful of mercenaries and those two arsehole mages. "Gods, I can't wait to kill those little turds."

Halina found a dry towel, shook debris from it, and pulled three long shards from her right foot, another two from the left. What she wouldn't do for some Schorvalan soma to ease the pain. But that was gone, too. Hasty stitches stopped the bleeding. Torn sheets and blood moss cushioned her feet inside a pair of worn boots. She limped, but she wouldn't stop fighting or start regretting. Not until Cadoc and his pillocks were dead.

Her gaze fell on the trail of bloody footprints. She'd been in the apartment long enough that the mercenaries should've found her easily. What was keeping them away?

As if on cue, the door handle turned, the catch clicked, the door eased open slowly, slowly.

Militairs scrabbled across the crooked footbridge and pushed into the bailey. Shouts, screams, the clash of armor and swords and axes rang across the bay. The sounds of battle competed with the knock and ring and rumble of trees being felled, split, rolled as soldiers and villagers cut them, hauled them into the moat, and pulled them to the bridge footings, reinforcements to prevent its collapse. The damaged structure shook and groaned with the weight of the soldiers.

Gethen stood to the side of the lists, arms crossed, studying the castle, considering each room and hallway, the undercroft, the ramparts, even the jakes. Where was the best insertion point? Where was he least likely to be seen? With the wards down, the challenge wasn't getting into the castle; it was getting inside unnoticed. He could stride into the center of the bailey amid all the fighting and make a spectacle, but if Halina was under the mages' control, drawing attention to himself would be idiotic. No one in the castle knew he'd returned to Kharaton. He could use that ignorance to his advantage. But only if he acted deliberately.

One of the Bear King's militairs came at him. "What are you waiting for, Mage?" Several other soldiers paused before the lists to watch and listen.

"The right time and place." Gethen kept a tight hold on his ire, but he was getting damned tired of people questioning his methods and his motives.

The man jabbed his finger toward the castle and snarled, "Now's the time. There's the place."

"Not yet."

The militair made to grab him but was stopped by Gethen's hand meeting his face, a straight-armed open grip with just enough power coursing through his fingertips to make the fool dance and jerk like a puppet on a wire.

Eugen pushed past the watching soldiers, grabbed the militair, and yanked him from Gethen's grip. The man stumbled, held up by Halina's steward then cuffed by him once, twice. "Idiot! Never touch a mage uninvited."

Gethen lowered his hand. He turned his head to look at them. "The battle mages don't know I'm here. Yet. What do you think they'll do to the king, the margrave, and the crown prince if I storm into the castle?" He leaned toward the soldier, bared his teeth. "I won't be the cause of their deaths."

Eugen nodded. He shoved the militair past the lists and onto the footbridge, said, "Good luck, Lord Rhyshis," and followed the man toward the castle.

"Good luck to all of us," Gethen murmured.

Rows and rows of tents spread toward the town from the harbor's causeway, some being re-pitched, some shredded by debris. Bodies of soldiers and horses were being piled for burning. Cries of suffering and sadness drifted on the breeze. The pall of smoke and dust swirled around the camp, hung above the castle, hovered over Kharaton Bay.

Gethen returned his attention to the castle. The solar. That's where he'd go in. A temporary storage room, it held furniture and linens displaced by the keep's renovations. The room was locked and otherwise unused, located on the southeast side of the castle. He checked the two borrowed daggers on his belt — both sharp steel, both made for murder — then summoned shadows from the trees and the tents. He wrapped darkness around himself, careful to control the evidence and flow of the magic. To make as small an impact as possible, he'd enter without his armor formed and without a shield. He visualized the room with its stacks of furnishings, crates, and trunks as he performed a travel incantation and kept a tight hold of the sorcery. The effort made him shake and expended more of the power from Hjalmer and Ektrina than he would've liked, but the bleed couldn't be helped.

The solar appeared, his sorcery spun out, faded. Boots scuffed stone. A man cursed.

Gethen jerked around as someone charged him from the open doorway, dagger in hand, teeth bared like a rabid dog. He didn't even have time to rue his rotten luck as he countered the attack with his own blades, returned each strike, each curse. He withstood blow after blow from his larger opponent.

Power, dark and deadly, filled him. Halina's enemies were his enemies. His rage spun out and loosened his control. A rope of darkness whipped forward from the hall's shadows and wrapped around the man's wrist. It yanked the attacker backward through the doorway. It slammed him against the wall. Again. And again. And again. Bones splintered. Blood splattered. The white-washed walls cracked, chipped. The man's face was a rictus as the shadow pinned him to the wall. A silent plea for mercy moved his lips. Blood flecked his chin, ran from his nose.

But Gethen felt no pity as he recognized the man. "Trefor." He'd cut and carved stones for the keep's growing walls and played a wooden recorder when the masons took breaks. The masons Halina had invited into her castle, the builders she'd trusted, listened to, laughed with. "You shouldn't have come here." The cold and death of the Void filled Gethen's voice. His murmured mass incantation slowly crushed the life from his enemy. The man's eyes rolled into his head and he exhaled a last, wet breath. Gethen retracted the shadow magic. Trefor's body hit the floor. The mercenary's confused spirit circled but received neither regret nor guidance from the keeper of the Voidline.

Gethen's sorcery, fueled by Hjalmer's and Ektrina's souls, was set ablaze by a stark hatred that he'd rarely tapped since the night he'd murdered Shemel. He bared his teeth. "Gods damn it." A conflagration burned bright, hot, and fierce within him. Sorcery pushed outward, threatening to obliterate his control and tear him apart at the seams.

He looked down at the man, at his Beseran freckles, his Beseran stripes, and saw an even deeper betrayal. He bared his teeth, tore a loose leg from a broken chair, and beat the man's face to a pulp. Each blow lessened his rage until he regained control. He straightened, threw the wood back into the solar, and wiped his bloody, trembling hands on the dead man's tunic. His ears rang. His head pounded. He wrestled an overwhelming, seductive power back into the dark place inside himself from which it had emerged. He wouldn't follow his sorcery to its natural conclusion, a necromantic madness that would rot him from the inside out.

He refocused on his purpose. "Halina." She needed him and he ran to the servant's stairs in the middle of the hallway. He was on the top floor and paused to listen for anyone ascending. Voices rose from two men descending. He stole after them on bare, silent feet. Eugen had offered him boots; he'd deliberately rejected them. Stealth was his friend, made all the more necessary by his bellicose sorcery.

"*Ast gwallof hwunu*," one of the men said in Beseran.

"The margrave? Yeah, that bitch *is* crazy," his companion replied, also in Gethen's native language. "Can't believe the shrikers didn't get her yet."

The acrid scent of burning nocoli leaves reached his nose. He held his breath. Smoke sticks made him sneeze. He could see them now, slowly descending ahead of him, apparently in no hurry to aid their companions in the battle raging in the bailey.

"Crazy but tough."

"*Eeyei.* You think Cadoc underestimated her?"

Gethen bared his teeth. *Cadoc.* That cockrel's death would be gruesome and slow.

The smoker nodded. "Definitely. Watched men do it the first day she took Khara."

"How? You're not from here."

"My mother was." He exhaled a cloud of smoke. "I spied for the Boorsooks after the war."

"Ah. I didn't know that."

"I go where the gold sends me." The man dropped his smoke stick, ground it beneath his heel. "Always have."

His companion grunted. "Eh. Come on. Those little Nalvik witches are gonna loose the shrikers in the bailey."

Pulling his cloak of shadows tight, Gethen ran down the stairs, daggers in hand. The two men meandered ahead. He came up behind them, and neat as Eugen trimming his beard, stabbed both men through the neck, in below the ears, right-to-left, left-to-right, and meeting in the middle. Knives out, blood fountained up the walls, across the stairs.

Two mercenaries down. No notion how many more to go. Their spirits jerked free of their bodies, surprised to be out of their skin.

"Find your own way to the Void, pillocks," he snarled and took the stairs two at a time, his destination the bailey, his intentions Halina's freedom and Cadoc's death.

CHAPTER 18

Halina hefted a broken bottle by its neck, muscles tense, breath held, focused. She'd gutted more than one man with her bare hands. She wouldn't hesitate to kill another.

The bedchamber door creaked. She drew back the bottle. Through the doorway came a shadow, a hand, a whisper.

"Halina?"

She lowered the bottle. "Bones, Waldram, I nearly took your face off." Relief flooded her followed by confusion. She'd never been happy to see her second cousin before.

He slipped into the room. "Thanks for not." He jerked his head over his shoulder to indicate the bailey. "You caused all that chaos?"

She nodded. "Bit more effective than I expected." She felt off balance around him.

"Certainly got the job done." He frowned at the blood prints on the floor. "You're hurt?"

She looked down. "Ran through glass."

He grimaced. "Can you walk?"

"Walk, run, fight, kill." She limped into the hallway. "You escaped the shrikers or killed—" She stopped and stared at the open doorway to her study, seeing what she'd missed before. Blood congealing on the floor, in the tangled, honey-colored hair, around a pale hand. Philippa.

"Oh, no." Halina clutched the wall. "No-no-no," she moaned.

They'd slit Philippa's throat. Turned out her pockets and her belt pouch in search of the keys. They'd broken her nose, broken her teeth.

Then they'd slit her throat.

"Gods, Philippa." Halina couldn't breathe.

Waldram caught her beneath the elbow and jerked her around. "We can't stay." He shook her.

They'd slit Philippa's throat.

He raised his hand to slap her, but Halina caught his wrist. "Don't ever hit me." Her voice was deadly.

"Then let's go," he snarled, his face so close she could've counted the hairs on his upper lip. With a last regretful look at her dear dead friend, Halina followed Waldram from her quarters. Every step sent burning pain from her feet to her brain. Her hips, back, ribs, shoulders, everything hurt, her heart most of all. But she forced herself to move. *Gods, Philippa. I'm so sorry.*

Shouts, screams, the clash of steel on steel, the sounds of battle tumbled through the windows and up the stairs.

"Strike first," Halina muttered. "Strike hard. Strike fast."

"This way. We can escape." Waldram tried to steer her away from the great hall, but she tore her arm from his grasp.

"Don't let them think. Don't let them leave. Finish what they started."

"Halina, let your soldiers round up the mercenaries."

"Arevik and Magod," she replied over her shoulder.

"They're safe!"

She kept going. She had to see for herself.

"They escaped the great hall when the granary came down." He grabbed her elbow again. "Let's get out while we can. Shrikers still roam the halls."

She shook her head. "Cadoc. I'm gonna kill him. Him and Ren and those little prick mages." She pulled away and stumbled into the great hall. Dead soldiers. Dead mercenaries. The far doors were open and sunlight flashed on steel. Britta prowled the steps above the bailey, her arms raised, her voice shrill as she cast spells.

Waldram was beside Halina again. "Let your militairs handle this. You're injured."

There was a body with a dagger in its back. Halina shoved her cousin away, shoved pain and fatigue and heartbreak away. She stumbled toward the open doors, snatched the dagger free as she passed. She spun through the doorway and put the blade through Britta's face, cheek-to-cheek. The girl mage stiffened, jerked, pawed at the dagger. Halina was behind her now, arm across her chest, locking the girl against her, using her greater weight, height, and strength as weapons, too. She tore the blade free, sending a few teeth tinkling down the stone steps.

Britta screamed.

Halina pressed her lips to the girl's ear. "You're right. Death *does* come for some of us sooner than others." She slammed the knife into Britta's side, punching, punching, punching. The girl jerked with each blow. Blood leaked from her mouth, her nose. She made little gurgles with each brutal strike. Halina pushed her away, threw her body down the steps into the shattered bailey.

Her blood pounded in her ears. The scene before her spread out, everything clear and slow. She saw the battlefield. Battle joy spread through her, warm, strong, relentless. Gethen said that was the blood magic doing its work, keeping her upright, giving her clarity and speed, keeping her alert, alive.

Her soldiers saw her. They shouted for her. "Red Blade!"

Halina raised her arm, bloody to the elbow, the dagger glinting gore in the morning light. A red blade to rally them. Men in blue-and-gold, red-and-black, orange-and-white. "Bring me their heads!" she cried.

They answered, a throaty roar for their margrave, their Red Blade.

An unearthly shriek shattered the sound. The lines of soldiers failed. Triumphant shouts turned to horrified screams. Shrikers, two of them, charged into the midst of the melee.

Someone grabbed her, yanked her into the great hall. Waldram. "Go! *Go!*" he shouted and propelled her across the room.

They were running, stumbling through the hall, into the depths of Kharaton Castle. "The postern door," she panted, her surge of battle joy spent on vengeance and stunted by her fear of Skiron's dogs. "That's the closest escape." She tried to stop him, but he yanked her down the servant's hall toward the kitchen, his hand a manacle on her wrist, her legs too weak to resist.

"Cadoc, Vins, and Ren headed into the undercroft before I found you. We can surprise them, kill them, and hide from the shrikers down there."

"But—"

He stopped, shoved her against the wall. Her head smacked it. She saw stars. He snarled, "Don't you want to kill

Cadoc? Don't you want revenge for your king?" He slammed his hand against the wall. "For yourself?"

Halina stuck the dagger beneath Waldram's chin, the grip sticky with Britta's blood, shaking in her weakening fingers. "Back. Down." He raised his hands, stepped back. "I know what I want, what I can get, and when I'm close to breaking." Killing Britta, rallying her troops, that last surge of battle madness was gone. She was empty, hurting, stumbling and close to crying. It was all she could do to stay upright. "If they're in the undercroft, they've trapped themselves. My militairs will find them. They won't escape." She started toward the postern again, but a shadow fell across her.

"Oh, I can escape...with the help of a hostage." Cadoc. Sword in hand he stalked toward them, a sneer on his face.

Halina cursed. "Unbelievable."

"Give me your knife and keep going." Waldram stepped between her and the mercenary. "I'll join you after I kill this bastard."

"Stop being selfless," Halina mumbled as she gave him the dagger. "I don't know what to do with a caring Boorsook."

He laughed humorlessly and glanced over his shoulder at her. His gray eyes were dead. "Don't worry. I'll get back to being your enemy soon enough." He brandished the blade.

Halina wasn't stupid enough to stand around. Breathing hurt. Moving hurt. Staying upright hurt. She needed the head start he was providing and she stumbled toward the kitchen entrance.

"Haven't you had enough, Cadoc?" Waldram asked, his tone surprisingly casual. "I'd say you've done well, despite the toughness of the fight."

"You think I underestimated the margrave?"

"Absolutely. But don't feel bad. You're not the only one. Or the first. Even I'm guilty of that mistake."

Halina looked over her shoulder then slowed to a shaking halt. Waldram stood calm, relaxed, the knife loose in his hand as Cadoc approached. He acted like this was a game. Her gaze flicked from the prince to the mercenary. Her cousin couldn't be that fresh; he'd received a good share of beatings, too. And Cadoc had a sword.

"What do you suggest, Your Grace?" the Beseran asked conversationally.

"Throw her into the oubliette." Waldram started moving backwards toward her, still facing the mercenary. "That's what I'd do."

He can't be serious. Hands pressed against her burning ribs, Halina continued forward, focused on the kitchen doorway, focused on moving one aching foot after the other. She panted and winced, every step a worsening agony.

"That's an interesting idea," Cadoc said. "Is that before or after I kill you?"

"Neither, of course. I'm your hostage."

The men's voices were growing louder as they neared her.

"I think that should be my *choice*." Cadoc's last word ended in a strangle. Halina looked back. The man was arching sideways, as if in sudden agony. Waldram was watching her with a strange smile on his face.

"What did you do to him?"

"Appealed to his greed," he said. The crown prince winked then pivoted and buried the dagger in Cadoc's throat, yanked it out, stabbed the man low in the belly and dragged it up to his chest, spilling his guts. "It's astonishing how eagerly men will follow a promise of riches."

Halina stared as the mercenary collapsed on the floor, his

body a mess of blood and gore. His hand still gripped his sword. He hadn't even raised the weapon. She looked at Waldram. He was protecting her. Or so she thought. The eerie emotionlessness of her second cousin's eyes and the dead dog smile on his face made her doubt.

Waldram continued as if he hadn't just slaughtered a man. "They'll sell their own king and country." He seized the dying man's hand and pried off King Vernard's ring, the bear signet of Ursinum. He slipped it on, admired it. "They'll doom one royal family to disgrace and another to decimation. All for a few gold coins and the promise of many more."

Halina's perception of her situation started to twist along with her gut. She reached for Cadoc's sword, but Waldram stepped on it. "Thanks to your spectacular skill and stubbornness, Halina, I'm on the verge of destroying the House of Persinna and discrediting the House of Rhysh. And I just murdered the only person who could be traced to my culpability." His grin widened. "Except you, of course."

She tried to strike him, but he had far more reserve strength than she did. He blocked her blow, grabbed her elbow, and threw her through the doorway into the kitchen. The table she'd used to block the door had been moved, but still caught her hip. She yelped at the sharp pain, doubled over from it. She grabbed for a cleaver on the floor. He was faster, fresher. He kicked it away and stomped her hand. She shouted. He laughed and grabbed her hair, dragged her across the kitchen, and tossed her down the stairs into the undercroft.

"I'm not quite done with you, Red Blade."

Halina tumbled down the short, narrow flight and landed on her stomach. She got to her knees, drooling blood. "Ilker and Arevik still live. Heirs to the throne."

"Eh. Not for long." Waldram yanked her up, propelled her

into the shadows. Halina gagged. The stench of death and something putrefying filled the air. "Arevik still has a small but crucial part to play in this. She's escaping with that idiot Ayestran slave as we speak. Cadoc's instructions from *Lord Rhyshis* were clear on that; let the young countess go. She'll be called to testify before the Council of the Kings. Your sweet sister will attest to how hard I fought to protect you and your father. How I was beaten, too. How the mercenaries said your lover planned all of this."

"No one will believe that lie!" Even as she said it, Halina recalled her father's words: *"Truth or lie or love, none matter. It's perception that bears weight."*

"They'll believe the story I've created for them today, Halina, lie or not." He twisted her arm up behind her back. Her fingers numbed, her arm and shoulder burned. His other hand fisted her hair and he propelled her past the cold stores, the dry stores, past barrels and bags, toward the dungeon. Their feet splashed in the water that pooled, black and cold, at the castle's low points. "Ilker will ascend to Ursinum's throne, a perfect puppet until he's no longer useful. He'll help me line up Ursinum's troops to attack Besera for their treachery in killing King Vernard and his valiant daughter, the Red Blade of Or-Halee. We'll rally Or-Halee to the cause; your finest allies until the end. Then I'll turn on them, too."

"There are other heirs." She tried to pull away, but he threw her down another set of worn, wide steps. She came to rest at the bottom, seeing triple as her head cracked against the bedrock foundation. A new sharpness of pain was added to each breath and pressure suddenly squeezed the right side of her chest. She gasped and tried to rise. "Semele's blood."

"As for Arevik. I'll make her my third wife, produce a few

heirs, then poison her." Waldram's shadow twisted in the low light as he circled her.

Shadow. The ambit! She'd put it out of her mind when the wards were in place, but now they were destroyed. Halina inhaled to summon Gethen. Waldram kicked her in the gut once, twice, a third time. She screamed, coughed, and choked on acid spit.

He grabbed her hair and pulled her to her feet. "The House of Persinna will die and Ursinum with it." They'd entered the crypt. He spun her to face away and forced her forward until she stood at the edge of the oubliette. The cover was gone from it.

Blood and bones. She felt sick, dizzy. He locked her arms at her sides. She had nowhere to go. Her right hand found something cold and metal at his waist. The dagger.

"While I prefer my women pliable, I'd make an exception for you," Waldram pressed his lips to Halina's ear, his body against her back. She shuddered both from fear of the gaping black pit and the feel of his warm tongue as he shoved it in her ear. He eased back. "If you weren't so damn deadly."

Halina gripped the knife. She slammed her skull back into his face and pivoted. The blade flashed in the low light. It slowed as it found his flesh. Waldram roared, shoved her. She slipped off the edge into the gaping pit of the oubliette.

But she didn't fall.

"You half-breed whore!" Blood ran down his face, black in the dungeon's scant light. She'd missed his throat but had sliced him from cheek to chin, torn open his upper and lower lips, and just missed his eye.

He had his hands poised toward her, holding her up with an incantation — pallid, cold sorcery.

"How?" she gasped.

"Stupid cunny. Now you see who really should've been the Shadow Mage and the Sun Mage." Waldram began a susurrus spell.

Halina groaned as her body contorted against her will. Below her things moved in the darkness. Splashing, thrashing, the clatter of bones and the scrape of nails on stone rose through the darkness. Her voice cranked tight with agony, Halina said, "Ambit, bring..." Waldram leaned forward and tapped her forehead with his bloody forefinger. Her thoughts failed. She shook her head. "Ambit...I...I." She couldn't recall the simple spell. "No! Ambit... No-no-no!" She snarled like a cornered animal.

Waldram laughed. "Clever, Militess. But you don't get to use that particular trick. This is *my* game and I'm not ready for him to find you yet." He waved his left hand and a flicker of sickly green mage fire rolled off his fingers and drifted into the oubliette. Things moved down there, bones and flesh and teeth were illuminated then swallowed by darkness as the flame hit the water and winked out with a hiss. "I may not have benefited from the training Gethen of Ranith had, but I received gifts from my uncle Shemel. And I put them to good use."

Halina screamed as he made a twisting gesture with his fingers. Pain, sharp and fiery, surged up her spine. She arched and struggled to escape what was inescapable. There was nothing but agony.

"You don't get to escape or die yet, dear cousin. First, we'll have some fun. Then I'll bleed you. You have magic that I need."

Fear replaced pain as Halina plummeted into the oubliette amidst enlivened corpses. Black, fetid water filled her mouth and nose. She fought bony hands and bloated, fleshy fingers.

They grasped her kirtle and hair, pulled her into the depths away from the circle of dim light and dank air that were so far above her. She pushed off the bottom of the oubliette, escaped the slime-covered skeletons, and surfaced with a high-pitched wail. She tried to summon the ambit but failed again. She couldn't form the words, couldn't remember them.

"I don't know what's more satisfying, bastard." Waldram crouched at the ledge above, crowing and clapping. "Your inability to stop me from destroying everything you love or your terror as the dead I've summoned torture you." He spat on her and laughed. "The slaughter at Kharaton Castle will become your lover's downfall. All of Quoregna will believe you died here, too, torn apart by shrikers. Every battle you fought, every scar you earned, every life you sacrificed will benefit me. You'll suffer unimaginable agonies as I steal your blood magic one drop at a time to become the most powerful sorcerer Quoregna's ever seen."

"No one will believe you!" Dead things rattled and oozed around her. They grabbed her hair and clothes. She punched and kicked and fought as they bit and scratched her. Bony hands, slimy with algae, tried to drag her beneath the putrid liquid again.

"No? Are you sure about that? All the mercenaries Cadoc hired were Beseran. They accused your Beseran lover of plotting this whole attack. Arevik witnessed it. She'll testify to it. The most powerful mage and he never showed up to save the woman he loves? Tsk-tsk. How long do you think it'll take before the Sun Mage's royal brother is accused of plotting with him to overthrow Ursinum?"

"Whoremonger! I'll kill you!"

"Halina!" Gethen's distant shout cut a line through her

terror and rage. She looked past Waldram. Her lover was above in the great hall.

She inhaled to call him but choked instead, her voice stolen by Waldram.

"Not even a goodbye, Margrave." He stepped off the ledge to plummet into the oubliette with her.

CHAPTER 19

"Halina!" Gethen stood in the empty great hall and shouted for her, but the only reply was his voice echoing from the ceiling and the sounds of battle carrying through the open doors. She was near, of that he was certain. The soldiers in the bailey had been chanting her name. "Halina!" He listened. Again, no response. "Blood and bones, where is she?" he muttered.

He'd seen the dead king, the dead soldiers, all neatly lined up beneath the windows. The broken chair, blood pooling around it. He'd sensed spent magic, a crackle in the air, a smell almost like lightning released. It wafted from the dead Nalvik girl at the bottom of the keep's steps, reeking of necromancy. She provided half the duality of wild magic he'd sensed from behind the wards, but he doubted she could've summoned the shrikers. Too young. Too uncontrolled, untrained.

Once again, Gethen stretched his senses to locate Halina. He peered into the scaffolding. She was somewhere in the hall or — he looked down — the undercroft.

A sudden surge of wild, dark magic washed over him. He

raised a shield spell instinctively as an incantation exploded into the room. This kind of raw sorcery spread destruction like black powder — untargeted, undiscerning, bringing death and dismemberment to anyone too close.

"Bastard! I'll kill you!" It came from a second mage, an adolescent boy emanating grief and madness. He snarled and sobbed, flung spells and mage fire at Gethen, undisciplined and driven by despair, dangerous to everyone, including himself.

Gethen batted aside each incantation, his shield spell more than adequate against the grieving boy. "I'll give you one chance to ask for mercy," he said, his voice filled with the sepulcher tones of the Void.

"Mercy?" The boy spat and swaggered across the room, giggling like a madman. "Who said I want mercy?" His next spell went wide and exploded one of the hall's columns. Dust showered Gethen. "Mercy is for cowards!" Another spell blew a chunk of marble from a second column. More dust and debris scattered. "I didn't give that whore margrave any mercy. You should've heard her squeal!" He stopped and chortled, holding his sides. "So damn *funny!*"

The braggart's giggling drained the charity right out of Gethen. He captured the next incantation, imbued it with a mass spell, and lobbed it back. His toss hit the young mage like an anvil kicked by an elephant. It hurtled the boy across the room and into the hearth. A plume of ash blew outward, hung like fog, swirled in his wake as Gethen strode through it. The boy rolled out of the hearth groaning, bleeding, but still laughing.

Teeth bared like a mad dog, Gethen growled, "You think torture's amusing?"

"Of course it is." The boy stabbed at him with a shadow spell.

Gethen knocked it into nothingness. "My master tortured me. I slaughtered him." He caught the boy's collar and twisted the cloth to choke him. He dragged him free of the hearth and threw him toward the doors that opened to the bailey.

The boy landed in a tumbling, jumbling heap of gangling limbs and torn, bloodied cloak. "I should've killed that bitch!" he shouted, fists balled like a child's. He got to his knees and hurled blazing mage fire.

Gethen caught it. He subsumed it into his palm as he strode toward the young mage. "Those are my tricks, boy." The youngster tried to scuttle back, like a wolf's wounded prey. Gethen's fist met the lickspigot's face and knocked him on his arse. He wiped blood and phlegm from his knuckles. As the boy sat up, Gethen delivered a second blow. It knocked him back hard enough to bounce his skull off the tile floor with a resounding *crack*.

Drooling, the boy rolled over, got to his knees, and started giggling again. "Wish I'd choked that cunny whore and set her on fire."

Gethen twisted his fingers in the boy's collar. The young mage gagged. He pawed at the garroting fabric. Gethen dragged him through the doorway. The child snuffled, clawed, threw wild spells, but he was a rat in a trap. "You're a mean little prick," Gethen snarled as he stopped at the top of the steps and surveyed the chaos in the bailey. One shriker was down. The other lunged at soldiers and mercenaries, alike.

"I'm not scared of you!"

Gethen looked down. Blood and snot and ash mingled on the youngster's face. He bared bloody, broken teeth. Little animal. Little monster. Little Shemel in the making. Gethen curled his lip. "You say that as if I care." He hauled the boy up and threw him into the path of the shriker. "Brought you a parting gift."

The boy rolled, stopped on his back. He looked up. Stared, his eyes widening with terror as the shriker stood over him. Its shriek changed from an excited squeal to a murmur, a purr that raised every hair on Gethen's body. He wanted to turn away but forced himself to watch. The boy went lax, his chest fell, his eyes rolled back. His spirit lifted from his body as he collapsed. The shriker inhaled the soul, bone spells flaring brighter. It nuzzled the boy's slack face, stretched like a dog waking from a long nap, and shrieked.

Disgusted with the beast, disgusted with himself, Gethen lassoed the shriker with a shadow spell and whipped it across the bailey, back across to hit the keep's outer wall, across to the rubble of the collapsed granary. Mercenaries and militairs ducked and ran for cover. He released the carcass, came off the steps at a run, and slammed the thing with both mass and heat incantations. It exploded. Flaming flesh and fragmented bones splattered the bailey, the keep, the walls.

He snatched up a dropped, bloody sword. He pointed it toward the cowering men, bared his teeth. "Come on! Which of you cowards raised a hand to Halina?" Shadows writhed across the bailey, seeking, moving outward from the Sun Mage. "Who held her down so the others could beat her? You sons-o-bitches have less guts than she has whole fingers."

The crowd shifted and Magod stepped forward, ax in hand. He pointed the weapon across the bailey. "Ren deserves to die for what he did."

A big, hatchet-faced Beseran shoved past the small group of mercenaries. "I deserve to die for a lot of things, but I won't take on a mage. That's no fair fight."

Magod moved away from the soldiers. "Have the bollocks to face my ax?"

Ren glanced from Magod to Gethen. "If the sorcerer agrees to stay out of it."

"You're sure about this?" Gethen asked Magod.

"Watched him beat Her Ladyship. Never felt so helpless. Tried to comfort Lady Vala after they murdered King Vernard, but there's no way to escape meanness like that." He met Gethen's gaze, his own eyes calm, steady, steely. "Is my revenge to take, Master Gethen."

"Agreed then." He squeezed his man's shoulder. "Kill the prick." Magod returned the gesture and nodded at a young woman who stood surrounded by Tatlis militairs. Arevik. Halina's young sister. She nodded in return. Gethen stepped back.

Magod let the haft of his ax slide through his fingers as he moved around a loose circle. Ren mirrored his steps.

"Ren." A whisper of magic twisted through the air, seductive, distracting. A sweet, melodic voice murmured, "Ren, look at me." The Beseran's face went slack. He blinked, wobbled his head, turned. He stood searching, facing away from Magod. "Ren," the voice sang out.

Gethen scanned the crowd. *Arevik. A sireah, like her mother.*

Magod lunged forward. His ax thudded neatly between Ren's shoulder blades. The mercenary made a little *hurk* sound, crossed his eyes, hiccupped blood. Like a tower he crashed face-first into the dirt, dust, and blood of the shattered bailey. Arevik shouldered between her Tatlis militairs. She spat on the twitching body. "You forgot to say no witches, arsehole."

Magod yanked his ax free and grabbed her hand. "Promised your sister I'd get you free of the castle." He led her into the shadow of the destroyed barbican. "Aim to fulfill that promise, Your Ladyship."

The remaining mercenaries threw down their weapons and raised their hands. Eugen stepped up. "Bind these men. Search the castle. Margrave Khara's still missing, as is Crown Prince Waldram, and their leader Cadoc. There may be servants hiding, so take care. If you can bring in any mercenaries alive, do it. If they fight, kill them."

Halina. Gethen gave in to his rage and his sorcery. Magic exploded through Kharaton Castle. Its mass pushed against the walls and ceilings, drove the shadows from the cracks and crevices, and revealed everything to him. Everything except his lover. Nothing of her presence remained. It was impossible, but no matter how he sought, he couldn't find a trace of her in the castle or the village. With a snarl, he seized the tunic of one of the surviving mercenaries, yanked the manacled man out of line, and threw him on the cobblestones. His voice was dead calm when he asked, "Where's the necromancer?"

"Vins and Britta are dead," the man said, eyes wide and rolling, a frightened horse's eyes.

Gethen's fist cracked his nose. "The necromancer. Not the little pretenders. The one who summoned the shrikers."

The man blew a bloody bubble from one nostril. "I don't know who you mean!"

Gethen's next punch knocked out teeth. "Wrong answer."

One of the other mercenaries replied, "There were only the two kid mages and Cadoc."

"Wrong again." *Crack* went the man's collar bone and he shouted. Gethen remained cold, calm, a reflection of the Void itself. "Cadoc wasn't a necromancer. I spent enough time around him that I would've known it." He drew a shadow down from the eaves and twisted it into a dark stiletto that hovered before the man's eyes, deadly sharp. "This will worm up your nose, burrow through your eyeballs, and scramble your brain to help you remember who the necromancer is."

The acrid stink of urine wafted between them. The man was sobbing, eyes wide, nearly crossed as he watched the shadow's point. "You! Lord Rhyshis! Cadoc said you paid for everything!"

Other mercenaries echoed him.

"Me?" Gethen's body went numb. "Ungh." His brain buzzed. "I stand accused of causing all this destruction?" He stared at the blubbering man, shadow poised. He looked at the bound men around them. "Of plotting King Vernard's death?" The man nodded, eyes closed, face twisted with terror. "Of torturing the woman I love more than life?" Gethen sniffed. He blew out a slow breath. "You don't know who the real culprit is." The shadow dissipated. He wiped his bloody knuckles on the man's tunic, stood, and motioned for the staring militairs to take him.

Eugen watched. Gethen met the steward's even gaze and said, "I would never do this." He shook his head and snarled, "I have no reason to do this."

"I'm not the one you have to convince, Lord Rhyshis."

Gethen turned away. "Has anyone located the Crown Prince?"

"No, Your Lordship," Eugen replied. "He was last seen with the margrave, but they've both disappeared."

Gethen turned away and followed the faint traces of Halina's fading blood magic into the great hall, past the dead king, dead mercenaries, servants, and soldiers. It led him to Cadoc's mutilated body. Spent magic seeped from the man's skin, slippery and secretive. This wasn't the bold, crackling sorcery left behind by the two young mages. "The necromancer," he murmured. It coiled around her blood magic, twisting, constricting.

He followed the trail through the kitchen, down to the undercroft, to the very edge of the oubliette. The sour tang of her fear hit him and the sickly sweetness of the strange necromancer's excitement. Gethen inhaled through his mouth, tasted bitterness, terror, betrayal. He lit the narrow cell with amber mage fire but saw only his face reflected in the still black water.

"Halina is gone from the castle," he muttered. "Crown Prince Waldram, too." He cocked his head, curled his lip. "No, now King Waldram."

Gethen should've been relieved that Halina had escaped the torture and the shrikers, but he wasn't. Only a powerful sorcerer could've stolen her from the castle. One with enough power to summon shrikers, too. Puzzle pieces were snapping into place and he didn't like the picture they created. It showed him Drevya Linna's new king, whose uncle was a powerful shadow mage. A man who'd murdered his brothers to climb, step-by-step, to the throne. A man whose parents' spirits had saved Gethen, led him to a necromancer's boneyard, and now imbued him with a sinking certainty as he reached for the flask of shadow tears in his belt pouch and spun a very deadly ward around himself; a certainty that when he looked through the ambit, he'd find Halina in a dead castle with pale King Waldram crowing triumphantly.

CHAPTER 20

Halina slammed face down onto cold, dry stone. She vomited and coughed up the oubliette's foul water then looked around as she struggled for breath and shivered in the cool room.

Kharaton's dark undercroft was gone, replaced by white-washed walls and massive, white marble columns upholding a carved, arched ceiling. Pallid fire flickered on the stone hearth, in the braziers and sconces. A dark red runner led to... Halina stared. It was impossible. She blinked, but the scene didn't change. The red runner led from tall white doors to the Boorsooks' infamous skull throne.

She was in Nalvika, in the ruling family's castle, Drevya Linna.

"Gods, no," she groaned. Her breath bubbled in her chest, wet and tight. She'd been such an idiot.

Heels tapped marble then were muted by the rug as Waldram circled her once then strode up the runner that was so like an enormous lolling tongue. He mounted the steps and settled upon the red cushion within the gaping, toothy maw of the throne. Carved from a single piece of bone-white marble, the royal chair was an open-mouthed skull that looked either ready to masticate the Nalvik prince or vomit him out. "It is my honor to welcome you to my home, Lady Khara."

She pushed upright. The room was empty. The castle seemed empty. There was no sound of servants bustling, soldiers practicing, children calling. "Where's King Hjalmer?"

"Dead. Queen Ektrina, too. I slaughtered everyone, Halina. Family, servants, soldiers, peasants. Drevya's a dead city."

"Even your own children?" The thought made her stomach churn. "*Why?*"

Waldram shrugged. "I needed their souls more than they did."

"The shrikers are yours." Halina stood slowly, shaking, swallowing acid spit. "You're the necromancer."

He smirked. "Aren't you a bit slow today? Those blows must've addled your brain." He leaned forward. "Yes, dear cousin, I've been practicing necromancy since I was a boy. Guided by my uncle Shadow Mage Shemel." Waldram stood, turned, and spread his arms. Behind the throne, loomed massive, white statues. "There they are! The great carved kings of Nalvika." He pointed at one. "My father, the former King Hjalmer. He doesn't look so fearsome now." He grinned over his shoulder. "I can take you to the king's bedchamber, if you'd like to see what a dead king looks like." He turned to her, pressed his fingers to his lips. "Oops. That's right, you already know that kings piss themselves when they die, just like everyone else."

Halina's fingers twitched. She'd shoved the dagger up her sleeve. Had he forgotten it? Her fingers itched to hold the blade; she felt naked without a weapon in hand. "Why kill children? How could you be so heartless?"

His head jerked up and he pinned her with a stare so cold it spread chills across her scalp. She shivered in the wet, rot-blackened kirtle. "You don't know the power of a new soul, Halina," he said. "I wasn't born with the gift of sorcery, but I had the will to master it. Shemel taught me the basics. He gave me tools and brought me books from his library. Unlike your precious Sun Mage, I taught myself. I created my own ways to summon the dead and draw power from the living. I fought for it!" He waved dismissively toward the king's statue. "I sacrificed for it." He grinned. "My father always said children exist to serve their parents." He strode down the steps and passed her, went to the throne room doors and pulled one open. It groaned on iron hinges. Air whooshed in and carried the stench of carrion death on it. "But look at the wonders I've done with that power. And I've only just begun to unleash my abilities."

Her stomach felt like it would flee out her arse.

Four shrikers slunk into the room, bringing the stench of decay with them. Behind the nightmare horrors she saw a room riddled with corpses, a room painted in gore. Waldram trailed his fingers over their filthy, maggot-infested coats as they passed. Power shimmered beneath his hands, white and blazing. It wrapped around his arms, sank into his skin. He made a little noise and shivered like a man in ecstasy. But far more of the power lifted and scattered, dissipating and disappearing, embers flying from a fire.

It was like Gethen's practice with his wolves, only horrific and corrupt.

"Children's souls," he murmured. "But so much is wasted. You saw it escape? Of course you did." He clenched his fists as if to capture the fleeting power then met her gaze. "That's why I brought you here, Red Blade."

Halina staggered back. The stinking shrikers trotted forward, their glowing bones rattling. Maggots and bits of flesh dropped from them as they came, slapping wetly upon the floor. She swallowed her gorge and held still. They circled her, squealing excitedly like a pack of wild forest dogs with cornered prey.

Waldram rubbed his hands on his thighs, manic glee in his eyes. He was as excited at his monsters. "My pets bring me power, but your blood is the key to capturing it. It takes strength to gain strength. I want the power that flows through your veins, always eager to strike, defend, destroy. I want your blood magic, cousin."

Halina snapped, "It's not for sale."

"I'm not buying." He reached toward her and Halina's muscles stiffened. "I'm taking." He made a fist and her agony reached a new pitch.

Halina screamed as an unseen force jerked her into the air and slammed her against the ceiling. The force released her and she plummeted toward the stone floor only to be jerked to a halt just above Waldram's head. Her stomach lurched, her head throbbed, blood trickled from her nose, coated her tongue. "Gethen," she whispered.

Waldram's deep laughter echoed off the high ceiling of Drevya Linna's throne room. "Call your lover all you like. He's chasing his tail around Kharaton, looking for you. I wonder how long before he figures out you're gone and uses that ambit?" He shrugged. "It won't be soon enough to save you." He strode toward the door, the shrikers heeling like good dogs. "Don't go away. We have lots to do."

"Ambit..." She racked her addled brain for the phrase. "Ambit, find Gethen." Nothing. She wasn't sure if it was even still part of her shadow. She cleared her throat, sucked down snot and blood and terror, strengthened her voice. "Ambit, fetch Gethen for me." Waldram hadn't gone far; his footsteps were growing louder as he returned. "Gods! Please, work." The shrikers squealed. She didn't know if she had the phrase right, if the ambit understood her.

The beasts trotted back into the room and swarmed beneath her.

She focused, instead, on Gethen. With her mind's eye, she traced the Beseran stripes that encircled his arms and ribs, his back and his chest. She thought of his gray eyes and the way his wolfish grin could turn to pure joy and make her yearn. She tasted his tongue and his skin. He smelled masculine and clean, of honey, liminth flowers, wax, and maluk. And she felt his power, unheard, unseen, but always vibrating inside her like a hidden beehive. *Gethen, I love you. I should've said it more.*

Waldram entered the room with a wide, hammered-metal basin. He gestured at her as he approached and, against her will, her arms came up until they were just below parallel with her body and stretched in front of her, like she was reaching for something. He placed the basin on the floor beneath her, straightened, and kissed her hands. Then he stabbed both her palms with a misericord. She yelped, the shrikers yipped, he laughed and licked the dagger. He caught some of her dripping blood on his fingers and drew lines from his forehead, over his eyelids, and down his cheeks. It mingled with the blood that still oozed from the wound she'd opened across his face.

He was so close and so cocksure. If she could free her arms from their invisible shackles, she could slit his throat or stab him through the eye. Get free. Get away. Hide until Gethen found her. But she couldn't move. Her body wouldn't obey no matter how hard she willed it, cried, cursed.

Waldram toed the basin over to catch her blood. He arched a brow at her, slid her sleeve up, and took the dagger. "I admire your determination." He tugged her sleeve down. "I really do." He produced a jeweled box from an inner coat pocket, opened it, and snorted a pinch of brownish-green powder into each nostril. He shook his head, grimaced, and put the box and the dagger beside the basin. He stripped off his coat and tunic to reveal pale, scarred skin. He circled the room, shaking his hands and muttering. Every few feet, he stopped and sliced his skin with his own jeweled misericord, pushing himself to frenzy.

Halina's blood drip-drip-dripped as she struggled against her unseen bonds.

Waldram returned to the basin and let his blood drip into it to mingle with Halina's. He swirled it around, drank some, then poured the remainder over his bowed head. Halina's stomach lurched, twisting even more as he put down the basin and gazed up at her with an expression that was almost loving. He slowly raised his hand and his smile broadened. At his whispered incantation, Halina's arms raised above her head. A low chuckle escaped her cousin as he tightened his fist.

She gasped. Agony twisted through her, followed by nausea. Her world went red. The fluid in her veins began to move unnaturally and she felt the trickling of her own warm blood as it ran from her nose and wept from her eyes. She struggled to escape the confines of his sorcery, but she was too weak.

Her blood twisted into drops and lines that hovered in the air before her. They flowed toward Waldram. He reached into them, ran his hands through the blood, then sucked it off his fingers. His smile widened. "Isn't it beautiful? Your blood magic, Halina. So powerful, so rare, such a precious gift. It will be mine to wield against Quoregna. And you, dear cousin, will be dead." Waldram tightened his fists again and Halina arched. A high scream escaped her, a thin, animal cry, as blood ran down her legs and wept from the palms of her hands and the soles of her feet. She couldn't breathe, couldn't speak. The world grew red. It darkened around the edges. This was magic she couldn't escape, magic tearing her apart from the inside out.

Suddenly, a man shouted, "Arsehole! I'll *kill* you!"

The shrikers screamed.

Waldram snarled.

Halina blinked bleary eyes. A figure stood in the doorway, several figures. Thaksin and militairs. She didn't know how they'd found her, didn't have the energy to even wonder. She forced her brain to focus on the ambit. She needed to remember the spell. She needed Gethen, they all did.

More voices rang through the room. Men shouted. The shrikers attacked.

Words formed in her mind. She turned them on her tongue. Opened her mouth. They emerged thick and slow. "Ambit, bring Gethen to me." *Gods. Please.* Halina gasped as a chill rippled up her spine, a strange tearing as the ambit pulled free. There was a flicker of darkness, then it was gone.

Her head sagged. Tired. Too tired...to care...to fight.

CHAPTER 21

The ambit hit Gethen hard enough to knock him on his arse. Pain, suffering, terror, rage. Overwhelming emotion twisted through him, threatening to send his heart and his guts fleeing. It wrapped him in cold shadows, yanked him across Quoregna, and dumped him in the middle of chaos.

He landed hard, bit his tongue, tasted blood. Ambit travel was even more violent than he'd remembered. Halina's overwhelming agony and emotions increased this one's brute force. The ambit had amplified their connection once he'd tapped into it. Or maybe it was her blood magic doing that. Either way, he felt as raw as a skinned bull and just as angry. Angrier when he spied her.

Halina hung in midair, limp and lifeless. Her blood streamed from her body and flowed into a growing orb of liquid. Waldram was manipulating the blood, drawing glowing red power from it. He'd formed bright red living armor. Like Gethen's shadow armor, it shifted and moved with his muscles, rippling across his body in waves.

"Ah, the hero's arrived in time for your death, cousin." Nalvika's new king smiled, a skeletal rictus that disappeared behind a blood-red helmet. He threw back his head, crowed like a mad cock, then snarled an incantation to release three more shrikers into the throne room. They appeared from nowhere in a brume of ash and dark sorcery.

Shrieking, shouting, the clang of steel on stone, screams, agony and fear; all of it ricocheted around Gethen, blurs of violence and battle. Beyond the chaos were white walls, a red runner, blood, steel, death. He just managed a shield spell as a shriker attacked. Another beast joined the assault and the shield stretched, distorted. It squealed, adding to the room's cacophony. Gethen pushed more power into the incantation until it glowed orange like hot slag. He roared and swelled the shield suddenly, knocking the shrikers away like children's toys.

A dozen Nalvik soldiers battled four shrikers. Thaksin was there, Nikolaus too. They'd pushed into the cavernous throne room only to be trapped by two more beasts behind them. For every one they cut down, another appeared.

Instinct clawed at his spine and Gethen threw the shield across his back. Just in time as Waldram hurled an incantation at him. The spell knocked him to his knees, exploded outward off the shield in a hail of red sparks, hit two Nalvik soldiers and a shriker. All became flaming figures, then glowing cinders, then piles of black ash.

His guts roiled and his skin crawled. He was trapped and the shield prevented him from going head-to-head with Waldram. He needed to draw up his own armor, which meant a minute to weaken his shield. Thaksin stood opposite him. Their eyes met. "Keep him on you," Gethen mouthed and gestured. The captain nodded and drew an archer to his side.

Gethen knelt. The shield squealed as Waldram hammered it with another incantation.

A bow twanged. An arrow breezed past Gethen's left ear. A solid *thud*, a shocked curse. The stream of necromantic spells lessened. Not a fatal shot, but it bought him time. He redirected power from his shield to the shadows. He pulled them around his body and formed armor. It settled upon him, comforting, empowering, protective.

He dropped the shield and hurled a mass spell that knocked Waldram off his feet. The orb of blood collapsed, splattering columns, runner, marble floor. The incantation holding Halina aloft failed. Gethen hurled a spell and managed to break her fall, but she still hit the ground with a sickening thud. Her body sent a metal basin spinning and clattering in one direction, a jeweled box tumbling in the other.

Waldram snarled, rose, cast more spells. Gethen raised a ward between Halina and her second cousin, but shrikers stopped him from reaching her. He filled the monsters with heat, boiling them from the inside out. He set them ablaze, burning them from the outside in. The militairs cheered as each beast caught fire. Men set upon the monsters like hungry hounds on a rabbit, swords and axes flashing.

Thaksin and Nikolaus came at Waldram from opposite sides. He snarled incantations that flattened both men. Gethen charged him, but the strength of his enemy's next spell made him grunt as it exploded off his dark armor and pushed him back. The ward around Halina failed and she was jerked into the air. Once again her blood flowed and formed an orb. With her stolen blood magic, Waldram matched Gethen's power, maybe surpassed it.

Nalvika's king tried blinding him with shadow spells, tried

paralyzing him with fear incantations. Gethen countered each attempt. "You lack experience," he said.

Waldram cursed him in old Nalvik. He summoned more shrikers, directed his incantations at the soldiers, too, and blocked him from reaching Halina again. "*You* lack imagination," he snarled.

But Waldram was wrong. Gethen's challenge was sorcery stretched thin as he tried to battle Waldram, aid the soldiers, and protect Halina. He had to reach her, had to stop the prick from bleeding her, murdering her. Every time he got a step closer, Waldram matched him and forced him back. If he couldn't bring the magic to her, she'd have to bring it herself. "Halina." He couldn't tell if she conscious. "Halina, do you hear me?" Her head lolled to the side. She groaned. "I gave you a weapon in Kharaton," he said.

Waldram snarled, "I don't think so, Sun Mage." Another swirl of ash and black magic produced a shriker, a big one, and its rheumy gaze fixed on Gethen. It shrieked and sprang.

But Nikolaus lunged at it. His sword took its rear leg off. "Help her!" he shouted and dodged a swipe of the shriker's claws. One missing leg wasn't enough to stop it. Thaksin joined the fight. So did two more shrikers. These attacked the captain. He split the skull of one, but the other seized his leg. Bone snapped. The captain shouted. With admirable self-control, Halina's man severed the beast's head from its neck, but the monster held on even as its body was trampled by more shrikers. Gethen's next incantation tossed the monsters in every direction while Nikolaus levered the beast's jaws open with his sword and Thak kicked the head away with his uninjured foot.

The Nalvik militair raised his sword to strike another shriker. He jerked, trembled, eyes bulging, mouth gaping.

Thaksin and all the other soldiers were struck with the same paroxysm. The shrikers attacked, their frenzied shrieks echoing in the room. The militairs were helpless, held by a susurrus spell from Waldram.

Gethen formed a ball of sun magic. He hurled it at the shriker closest to Nalvika's mad king. It struck the beast, set it afire, and slammed it into the necromancer. Waldram stumbled and fell on the dais steps. The curse broke but too late for Nikolaus and four of his soldiers. Gethen's next mass spell crushed the remaining beasts, sparing Thaksin and two Nalviks.

He ignored a growing tremor in his hands, the first sign of strain. He was burning through the spirit magic he'd been gifted by Waldram's parents, skimming power from his own soul. But Waldram showed signs of fatigue, too. He'd stopped laughing, stopped snarling. His hands shook and his back curved under the weight of necromancy unleashed.

Gethen called, "Halina, listen to me." She raised her head, eyes blood-shot, bleary, unfocused. Bloody tears stained her cheeks. Blood oozed from her nose. "I gave you a weapon before I left for Ranith."

Cursing, Waldram unleashed an explosion of blinding ash and dark magic into the room.

The incantation knocked Gethen off his feet. He closed his eyes and protected his face from the scouring, blinding grit. He countered the spell, gathering the soot into a funnel cloud, dispelling the sorcery, letting the tornado collapse with a hiss across the floor. The dust cleared.

Waldram was gone. Halina was gone. The destroyed shrikers and dead soldiers were gone.

Thaksin groaned and slid down the wall. "Where'd that lickspigot go?"

One of the remaining Nalvik soldiers limped across the room, his arm hanging, blood dripping from his fingers.

Gethen knelt. He raised his palms over the basin of mingled blood. He whispered a spell and the ambit lifted from his flesh, a thing alive, a thing born of his soul and Halina's shadow. The weapon he'd given her. A weapon only she could wield.

Thaksin stood with the Nalvik's aid. "We can't just sit here, Mage."

"I'm not."

"Looks like you are," the militair grumbled.

"Shut. Up. I'm trying to work," Gethen snarled then lowered his voice again. The blood roiled and separated, some of it boiling over the sides of the basin. What remained — Halina's blood — rose to combine with the ambit, forming a shining, dark mist. Gethen continued the spell, rolling the mist, forming a tight orb the size and reddish-black hue of a blackapple.

His voice changed. It took on the sepulchral tones of the Void, the sounds less human, more inhumane, carrying death and disease and damnation. He closed his eyes. Had Thaksin seen them — his black pupils expanding to fill the whole orb — the captain would've run him through and asked questions later. This was necromancy in its purest, deadliest form.

Gethen drew a deep breath and exhaled a black, dense, rotting brume from deep inside his soul, a ropey, sinewy, and snakelike vapor, hissing and hateful. He sent this into the center of the orb. It turned from shiny to opaque, reddish hue gone, all light falling into it and failing to escape. It settled into his palm with a sound like an old man's dying wheeze. He closed his fist, squeezed, squeezed. When he opened his fingers, it was the size of a bean and vibrated with the pressure of its own lethal potential, fighting to be free, to attack, to destroy. The ambit was now a wraith leashed, imbued with necromancy and Gethen's desire to destroy Waldram, pulsing with Halina's blood magic and rage. A deadly weapon waiting for its mistress to unleash it.

"What's that?" Thaksin's voice was gruff with pain and suspicion.

"A weapon for Halina." Gethen kept his eyes closed and forced Skiron's necromancy to retreat back into himself.

The captain pushed away from the wall and hobbled over, grimacing and cursing. "How do we get it to her?"

"We?" Gethen stood, shook his head to a wave of dizziness, weakness. "Just me, Captain." He slipped the ambit into his belt pouch then indicated Thak's leg. "You're wounded. I'm exhausted." He didn't wait for a response but pictured his destination and raised a travel incantation. As the amber mage fire blurred Drevya Linna's throne room, something grabbed his arm, dragged on him. He pushed through it. The magic resolved, fell away to reveal the boneyard in the cavern, Waldram in his blood-red armor, Halina in a heap at his feet, a circle of shrikers and other undead things. Thaksin swayed beside him, his hand a clawed grip on Gethen's arm.

"Two where I thought I'd only get to kill one?" Waldram laughed. "What a pleasant surprise!"

Gethen raised a shield. "Don't know when to quit, do you?" he muttered to Halina's captain.

The shrikers and monstrosities attacked from every side. The shield squealed and warped. Magic, like lightning, flashed jagged over its surface with every strike.

"Never have. Never will." Thak pulled his sword, his eyes hard, glinting with that same battle joy and something else, something menacing. For a moment Gethen thought he'd stab him, wondered if the man's jealousy was really that destructive. Instead, the captain turned the weapon and offered it to him. "You need my help." His gaze went to Halina and worry joined the other emotions in his eyes. "She needs yours."

Gethen gritted his teeth. "I don't think you can help." His body trembled from the strain of holding the shield and his armor. Sweat beaded his forehead, trickled down his back, salted his upper lip.

"I've seen you take power from those wolves. I figure you can do the same with a man. Take what you need from me, Lord Rhyshis."

Gethen didn't have the energy to be surprised. "Halina will kill me if I kill you." His muscles burned.

"I always planned to die in her service." Gethen's focus wavered. The shield flickered. Thak snarled, "Damn it, man, don't be an arse. Take what you need to kill that pillock." He gripped Gethen's arm again. "Save Halina. Save all of us."

Gethen matched the captain's grip, grabbing his wrist. He met the man's sure gaze. He nodded, reached for Thaksin's soul, and found it eager, powerful, willing to sacrifice anything to protect Halina. It clawed into him, burrowed deep, burned hot with rage, jealousy, admiration. The high, the battle joy, the black desire to kill Waldram burned Gethen's body and brain. He tore his hand free of the captain, wrapped a ward around Thaksin's toppling body, and let the incredible power of the man's bright soul course through him.

He roared Thaksin's rage. He charged. The sword hacked at shrikers and corpses. His spells sent them exploding off walls in showers of splintered bones and torn parchment flesh. He threw the beasts at Waldram. He batted aside curses. He pushed closer and closer to Halina.

But Waldram held his own and his incantations grew deadlier, came faster, were more sophisticated.

Gethen sensed that duality again. The one he'd noticed at Kharaton Castle. The one he'd thought evinced the sibling mages. He suddenly realized he'd been mistaken. Waldram, alone, couldn't be powerful enough to summon shrikers and withstand Gethen's sun sorcery, especially fueled by Thaksin's soul. "Waldram, you arse-sniffing *imbecile!* You leashed the remnants of Shemel's soul?"

Nalvika's king snapped his teeth like an excited animal. "You're not the only one who can create ambits and wraiths, Sun Mage."

"Only a madman would tie his soul to that necromantic monster." Gethen scanned the deep shadows, searching for the telltale movement of a wraith. If Nalvika's idiot king had created an ambit, spinning it into a wraith was well within his abilities.

Waldram grinned as a thin, familiar voice slithered from the shadows. "For a man with so much raw talent, you're as slow as winter honey, Apprentice." Waldram reached toward Halina as Shemel added, "You were always weak when it came to people."

Her body jerked into the air again. She gasped. Not unconscious then.

"Still clinging to your *protector*?" the wraith sneered. "I don't see why. I told you she's not very good at the job." Halina screamed as her body contorted under Waldram's spell. "In fact, she's close to useless now."

Shrikers attacked Gethen, one from the left, one from the right. They snarled and snapped, lunged, shrieked. One latched onto his leg, but he'd learned that lesson already. He shattered its skull with a weighty spell and blasted the other beast across the cavern.

A flicker of movement, black against darkness, warned him to move. He lunged clear as Shemel's wraith form stabbed at him with a spear of darkness, missed, tried again. Gethen batted it aside. "You may have a wraith's form, Shemel, but you don't have Kharayan Tor's power to drawn on." He blocked another incantation from Waldram, even as his former master slid across the wall, slithering in the dark. "You can't even leave the shadows."

Waldram passed beneath Halina. There was something in her hand. He cleared her and moved just beyond her reach. Her focus followed him, sharp, deadly. Waldram had underestimated her endurance, her sheer grit.

"You did this before I killed Shemel," Gethen said to Waldram. He wanted to keep the man's attention off Halina.

"Of course, idiot." Nalvik's young king trembled as he summoned more shrikers. They circled Gethen, squealing, snarling. But their maker's power was fading fast, being siphoned away by Shemel's emergence.

"I knew you'd overpower me," Gethen's dead master hissed from the dark, revealing his location. "It was inescapable. But not permanent, as you see."

They were surrounding Gethen, moving to launch a simultaneous attack. "Nice try," he said as he reached up and stole all the light from the cave. The darkness was total. Shemel, as much shadow as entity, dispelled without the light to define him.

Waldram growled and raised a ball of mage fire. Gethen seized opportunity. He flared the fire, bright as the sun, hot enough to set the shrikers aflame. Waldram squinted, blinded by the sudden change. Gethen hurled the beasts into the cave walls. He charged. He snapped his fist into Waldram's face. The sorcerer king's head whipped to the side. He stumbled back and went to his knees in a skittering of bones. He snarled, stood, and raised his fists, his back to Halina, his focus on Gethen. "Now you're speaking my tongue, Sun Mage!"

But before Waldram could rejoin the fray, Halina tore free of her cousin's unfocused control. She raised a hidden dagger and screamed her rage as she slammed it downward into the crown of Waldram's skull.

He staggered, blink-blink-blinked. "Eh." He stared at nothing, mouth slack. A line of drool slipped from his lips. A rivulet of blood ran from his nose.

Gethen's next blow cracked Waldram's jaw and his own knuckles.

Nalvika's king staggered.

The spell holding Halina failed. She gasped. She fell. Gethen lunged forward and caught her.

Confused and frenzied, the remaining shrikers attacked each other, attacked the soldier corpses, who attacked back. None had independent will.

Waldram pawed at the dagger. He went to his knees, stared at Gethen and Halina with his right eye as the left eye slowly wandered, a lost ship on a fogged sea. He pitched forward into the clattering piles of broken bones.

Heat and light surged, smashed into cold hatred, and shook the cavern. The walls groaned, the floor jolted, bones juddered. The mural of Skiron fractured, fragmented, hurled slivers of iridescent pearl and teeth in every direction. Pallid mage fire and inky shadows raced up the walls and across the floor. Uncontained necromancy forced open cracks and crevices, exposed roots, sent rocks and dirt sliding.

"The cavern's collapsing!" Gethen lifted Halina, staggered

to where Thaksin lay. Rumbling, groaning, squealing assaulted their ears. Hand on the captain's back, he pushed the man's soul back into his body and used the last of his own strength to invoke another travel incantation as the shrikers turned on Waldram and the cavern showered them in dirt, rocks, and roots.

CHAPTER 22

Bright lines of early morning sunshine shot through the shutters in Gethen's Ranith bedchamber. Halina watched dust motes swirling through them, a lazy dance to unheard music.

Gethen lay on his back, his face toward her, relaxed in sleep. The room's warmth promised a hot summer day and he was naked beneath a thin sheet, one long leg akimbo and atop. Her gaze traced the mottled, brown stripes that wrapped around his arms and shoulders, delineated the arcs of his ribs, and whorled across his collarbones. A thin, pink scar distorted the stripe that wrapped his left forearm. He bore far fewer scars than she did and this one was new, a parting gift from a shriker. She traced the line with her finger.

"That tickles," he murmured, his eyes still closed, his lips curving into a slow smile.

"Better than hurting."

He yawned and stretched, rolled onto his side and considered her from head to toe and back again. "You're the expert on scars here." He reached out. Faint gold sparks skated across her pale skin, trailing his fingers as he connected the pink, puckered lines and dots that marked damage inflicted by Waldram and Cadoc, pain delivered by men and mages. "Khotyr's demanded a lot from you," he said.

Halina squirmed beneath his fingers, caught his hand. "No more than Skiron's asked of you."

He pressed her palm to his bare chest. "The gods seek to pull you into the Void."

"We all end up there eventually." Halina snuggled into the pillows. She needed more pillows on her bed at Kharaton, she decided. Pillows made any bed a luxury.

"Well, they can't have you. Not yet." He pushed up, leaned over, and buried his face between her bare breasts, his breath hot, his whiskers scratchy.

"Now you're defying gods?" She ran her fingers through his hair.

"Always." He pushed up and kissed her. When their lips met, heat surged through both of them. He pulled back and gazed at her.

She touched his mouth with her fingertips, ran them along his jaw, and gave his dark-whiskered chin a gentle tug. "Testing their patience?"

"Perhaps. Though it's their own fault. They made me this way."

She snorted. "And you won't let them forget it."

"No. I won't."

"We don't forgive and we don't forget, you and I."

"We're alike in many ways." He kissed her again, this time slower, lingering.

Her breath quickened. "I like you in many ways." She bit his lower lip.

He smiled against her mouth. "I'd like to have you in many ways." His voice was a little husky.

Halina growled. She shoved her hands into his hair, pulled him down, and turned play into passion with her lips and her tongue.

But Gethen wouldn't be rushed. He slowed her kisses, trailed his lips from her jaw to her ear, nuzzled her neck, nipped her throat. He laughed, low and throaty, when she squirmed beneath him, snapped her teeth at him. "You try to control too much," he murmured.

She locked her calves over his thighs, a little sweaty, a little slick with desire. "I thought you liked that about me." Her fingers found his chest. She purred, pleased to see him arch, hear him moan as she raked his nipples with her nails then teased them with her lips, her tongue, her teeth.

"I do." Gethen caught her wrists and pinned them over her head. "But you can't control everything, Halina," he said, his voice husky, carnal. "And sometimes, the harder you try, the faster it slips from your grasp." He opened his mouth, lips hovering over hers, pulling back every time she stretched for the kiss. She smelled and tasted desire on his breath. She pressed her breasts against his chest, her skin damp and slick against his, felt him hard between her legs. She panted, moaned.

The flame that always smoldered between them flared with his touches, his caresses. But it died as quickly as it rose. There was something cold in the center of her, something she feared to unfold and examine. Where there'd once been a constant fire, she found only cooling ashes. Halina knew it was where her blood magic had nestled, waiting to flare into a conflagration when she was endangered. But Waldram had left her cold, drained. No matter how she tried to spark the flame, it died back to a dull coal. She was terrified that the magic wouldn't be there when she next went to battle, when she next needed it to win, to survive, to protect herself and Gethen. The thought turned her colder. She stiffened, whimpered.

As if knowing what was twisting her mind, he tightened his hands on her wrists, painfully. He lowered his mouth, his lips caressing hers as he murmured, "There's still magic in you. He didn't take it all. He can't." She whimpered again, almost a sob. He released her hands, held himself over her with one hand, feathered his fingers over her cheeks, her lips. "You can still set that magic aflame, Halina. You can still burn."

"I — ohhh." His lips had found her breasts. His tongue, gods, he had a talented tongue. He nipped, sucked, held her waist, took his time. His mouth drifted lower, kissing down her body, tongue and lips finding her scars, circling her navel, even lingering on the pink wound he'd given her with her own sword, the one with the matching scar on her back. His hands found her hips, fingers tight, burning into her skin. He parted her thighs, kissed, licked, used his mouth to stoke those fires. Halina moaned, arched. Her hips trembled, her body desperate, on the brink of breaking. But he stopped before she exploded, surged up to kiss her, leaving the tang of herself on her tongue. Arms around her, he rolled to his back. She came up straddling him, aching to feel him inside her, desperate to feel his heat.

"Burn for me, Halina."

She closed her eyes. "Say it again."

"Burn, Halina. Burn for me."

She hovered over him, his cock just nudging inside her, teasing both of them, muscles quivering, animal noises in the back of her throat, in the back of his. Slowly, exquisitely, she lowered her body onto him. Her head hanging, hair swaying, eyes closed, lips parted. A low moan came from each of them.

"Gods, you feel so good," he murmured.

She breathed, "Yes," moved, ground her hips into him, felt every inch. "Like that." He arched his neck, the muscles standing out on his throat, sweat glistening, slick. She licked him, chest, throat, chin, salty-sweet and made him moan. She leaned back, loving the way he grabbed her hips and pushed up into her, filled her, stroked her, stretched her.

They'd come too close to losing each other. The thought that she'd never see him again had been too painful to allow during those long hours of torture. But since then, she'd cried in his arms. Cried from the pain of her wounded body. Cried from the pain of Arevik's terror, King Vernard's death, her soldiers' and servants' slaughter. Cried from the stupidity of trusting Waldram, and Cadoc and his mercenaries for months. Cried at the weakness and fear that losing so much control and magic had left in her. Cried hardest at how close she'd come to being killed, to never being held by Gethen again, never feeling his body against her, inside her.

Faint traces of blood magic stirred deep in her veins. She craved it, craved him. Even now, eight weeks since the siege, a month past when she should've returned to Kharaton Castle, she lingered in Ranith, reluctant to leave his side. Where was he going? Would he return soon? Could she go with him, sit with him, be his shadow, feel his strength, his magic? She hated this weakness. Hated it.

Gethen sat up, arms around her back and hips. He stayed inside her as he gently laid her over on her back, like she was something delicate, something precious. He pushed deeper into her, thrusting hard, deep, pulling back slowly. He watched her, gray eyes dark, lips parted. "So beautiful. So strong. Gods, I love you, Halina."

She touched his mouth. He sucked her fingers, licked, bit. His hips ground into her. His body heated hers, filled her. "I love you." She buried her face against his chest. "I need you, Gethen, I need you so much."

"I know."

What once had burned so hot and bright and deadly within her was only faint embers now. But as he coaxed her with his mouth and body, each touch and thrust awakened the fire. She craved her lover like a nocoli addict craves the leaf. It was his strength, his magic, that kept her darkness and doubt at bay. For a little while, his lips and body could stop her shaking, tears, and self-loathing.

"Burn for me," he whispered and stroked her, slow, steady, his breath and his body moving in, out, in, out. "Burn, Halina. Burn for me. Burn with me."

"I can't." Her voice cracked. She choked on the words, the fear.

"Yes." His mouth was on hers. "You can." His body was on hers. "Burn bright. Burn hot. Burn, my love." Every stroke of his cock built the fires, made her forget, made her crave, brave, burn. "Yes, you can." His fingers found her, slick, sliding. "Burn, Halina." Lightning danced along her nerves. Sparks. Heat. He moved inside her. His fingers stroked her. "Burn, Halina." It was a chant, a prayer, a spell.

She moaned. She pushed against him, rose to meet every stroke. Arched. Ached. Shook.

"Burn, Halina."

Magic exploded inside her. White-hot exquisite release. It seared her nerves. Set her soul afire. She screamed. She burned. Power surged through her and back into Gethen. He came inside her, groaning, releasing his own magic into her, into the room. It surged through the space, a wave of amber light and red sparks. The walls creaked. Heat undulated up them, hit the ceiling, spread shimmering mirages in all directions. The door and shutters popped as their hinges strained.

Halina collapsed, a ragdoll panting, sweating. Gethen kissed the sheen from her brow, her mouth. He gave a little laugh. "Our magic still works well together."

She nuzzled his neck, licked the sweat from his skin. "Have you figured out why that is yet?"

"Yes."

She gazed up at him, waiting. He tucked a stray auburn curl behind her right ear. "Because we're two halves of a whole. Powerful when separate, magic when united." He rolled off her, sweat making their skin slick, making her shiver. He pulled the sheet over her. She snuggled against him with a contented smile, blood magic buzzing behind her chest once again. He kissed her closed eyes, murmured, "I love you."

"I know." She sighed. "I owe you an apology."

"For?"

"Being a mule-headed idiot when you offered your protection before my father's arrival. You were right. It's not a sign of weakness to let someone else wear the armor and wield the sword. I don't know why I forgot that."

"You have nothing to prove to me."

She nodded. "I have to stop thinking I need to show my mettle to everyone else."

"Mm-hmm." His brow furrowed and he faced the closed window, he murmured a low incantation then brushed his fingers over her scarred shoulder. "Speaking of someone who has something to prove, Thaksin just entered the village."

"He's here?"

Gethen nodded. "With three companions."

"Damn. I wonder what brings him north."

Thaksin, Magod, and all the king's surviving soldiers had accompanied Arevik and King Vernard's body to Tatlis. Gethen had sent a written accounting of the events as he understood them to Halina's brother Ilker. Bedridden, she'd missed her father's cremation and her brother's coronation.

Halina sighed. She sat up and retrieved her white chemise from the foot of the bed, pulled it over her head, and absently braided her hair as she looked around Gethen's room. "Perhaps I should move Khara's capital back to the ancient citadel."

He tucked his hands behind his head. "Bit small."

"Bit drafty. And the current owner is trouble."

"So I've heard. Certainly more than he's worth."

"Oh, I don't know." She looked down, smoothed the fabric over her thighs. "He's proven handy in the odd scrape or two." She stood and stretched, winced, and muttered at aches that lingered. Gethen had told her what Thaksin did in the throne room and the cavern. These men kept saving her life. He dragged his trouzes across the bed and stood. She eyed the curves of his arse, the wide planes of his back, the whorls and stripes around his ribs. "And I never tire of the view."

He pulled up his trouzes and flashed that wolfish grin she liked. "The place is cursed with too many necromancers. Besides, Eugen's working hard to repair Kharaton Castle." He turned to the table beside the bed and uncorked the dark blue bottle sitting there. It was a metheglin he'd formulated to ease her pain, boost her blood, and speed her healing. "Militess Halina Persinna doesn't run from a fight." He measured some into a dram cup and held it out. "Drink."

He was right, though part of her wished he wasn't. Her gut

said this wasn't her last battle. "Militess Halina Persinna is weary of running into death." She downed the dram and grimaced. "Couldn't you make it taste better?"

"I could."

Her grimace became a scowl. "Why am I always surrounded by heartless mages?" She wrapped boned stays around her chest and added, "Lace me?"

Gethen clutched his chest. "Cruel words." There was a knock on the door. "Come," he called as he obliged her request and deftly, carefully tightened the foundation that encased her breasts and back.

"Not too tight."

"Captain Thaksin's arrived, Your Ladyship." Vi proffered two letters as she entered. "He brought these."

Eugen had sent Vi to help Halina, a role Philippa had filled for almost twenty years. Halina missed her lady-in-waiting's guidance, her acerbic wit, and honest tongue. The woman's death left her with regrets.

Halina took the messages, turned the first over, and bumped her finger over its white wax seal — a circle of four crowns. "From the Council of Kings." She broke the seal and read. "We've been summoned to Tatlis. They require our testimony."

Gethen said, "I'm surprised they waited this long."

"Me, too." She held it up for him to read over her shoulder. "Did the captain stay, Vi?"

"Yes, Your Ladyship," The young woman's lips quirked like she was fighting a smile. "He wishes to speak with you." She retrieved Halina's cream-colored underdress from the floor.

Gethen muttered, "I bet he does," as he finished the lacing. Louder he added, "If Captain Thaksin and his companions wish to remain tonight, I'll have to displace someone." He pulled a brown tunic over his head.

"Who's with him?" Halina asked as her servant helped her with the kirtle.

"Militess Odruna and two pages."

Halina's brow arched. "Odruna's traveling with Thak?"

Vi murmured, "Shriker hunting makes for strange bedfellows."

Gethen nodded. "A fact if ever I heard one." He tossed Halina's gray surcoat to Vi. "What's the other message?"

This one bore Ilker's bear-and-star seal. "It's from my brother." The wax snapped as she broke it. Halina read aloud:

"To Halina Persinna, Princess of Ursinum, Margrave of Khara, and Militess of the Order of the Red Blade, from her king and brother, Ilker, rightful ruler of Ursinum.

"Greetings and wishes for Your Ladyship's continued recovery and ongoing heartiness.

"It is with tremendous relief that I have read each update from your indefatigable steward on your continually improving health and the ongoing repairs to our easternmost defenses. I view your arrival in Tatlis with great anticipation, dear sister. There is much to discuss regarding His Majesty's death, the situation with Lord Rhyshis, and your future.

"Additionally, I have the pleasure of informing you that our sister Lady Vala will soon become Duchess Ostendra. Arevik accepted a proposal of marriage from Kieran Osten, the Margrave of Essendra and heir to the duchy. She has safely arrived into the care of his father, Duke Ostendra, with the dedicated protection of the Sun Mage's man, Magod.

"As for your marriage, there are many who seek to enforce our good father's agreements. I find the situation challenging. With the

attack upon Kharaton Castle fresh in my mind, and clear evidence
as to the guilt of men whom we so surely considered steady, the
fog of uncertainty clears. I shall prevail in choosing the path that
is good and right for you, for our dedicated allies, and for Ursinum.

    "Your deeply devoted brother, Ilker, rightful King of Ursinum,
Archduke of Tatlis, Duke of Ahlas and Eskis, Militair of the Order
of the Black Bear, and most faithful servant of the One God."

Halina lowered the letter. He'd sent Arevik away without
consulting her. She glanced at Gethen. He stared at nothing,
his eyes narrow, mouth pinched, arms crossed. "You look as
irritated as I feel."

His gaze came up. He gave a little shrug. "Hard to know
how to interpret a lot of that."

She tossed it on the bed. "Exactly. Which I don't like. Ilker's
always been transparent with me."

"He's king now," Vi offered.

"But still my brother." Halina twisted the black ring on her
finger and shivered. That finger still felt phantom pain, like
her missing fingers did. "Vi, tell Thak and Odruna I'll be down
soon." The young woman curtsied and left.

Gethen wrapped his arms around Halina. He gazed down
at her, his gray eyes serene again. "What are you thinking?"

"That I'm not looking forward to the court at Tatlis. As
usual."

CHAPTER 23

Gethen hummed as he descended Ranith's winding stone stairwell. At the bottom, he turned into the great hall, and stopped humming. Captain Thaksin stood before the wide stone hearth, hands behind his back, head down. He appeared to be studying the room's ornate wool rug or his own boots.

After the madness in Nalvika, the captain had spent two days unconscious in Ranith's infirmary, his wounds cleaned and stitched by Gethen. When the captain had awakened, he'd visited Halina's bedside then returned to Kharaton Castle with nary a thanks for the hospitality. A week later two nervous pages arrived at Ranith with Remig and Gethen's carthorses, but with neither words of gratitude nor apology.

Thinking to ignore the pignut, Gethen continued toward the keep's entrance.

"I never thanked you." Thaksin's bass voice was swallowed by the arched ceiling and the room's ancient tapestries; it made him seem small, weak. He looked up. "And I never apologized." He rubbed the back of his neck. "I was wrong about you, Lord Rhyshis. Very wrong."

Gethen didn't slow his stride. "Apology and thanks accepted, Captain. Her Ladyship will be with you momentarily."

"Bollocks, man, wait. I'm trying to have a conversation with you before she comes down."

Gethen didn't miss the chagrin in the man's voice. He stopped, turned, crossed his arms. "All right. Have your say."

"I made mistakes. I nearly got you killed. Nearly got Halina and everyone else killed, too." He narrowed his eyes, jutted his jaw forward, his lower teeth over the uppers. He looked like an ankle-biting rat dog, the kind farmers put down holes to kill badgers. "I won't come between you and her again." His capitulation came out in a rush.

Gethen stalked across the room, stopped toe-to-toe with the captain, bared his teeth. "Damn right you won't." He turned and headed toward the keep's front door and the bailey beyond.

Halina's voice echoed off the stairs and followed him. "You got off easy, Thak. I'd've killed you, if I were him."

Gethen opened the wicket door set into the citadel's towering, iron-banded front doors. Bright sunshine warmed his face, made him squint. He started humming again. In the sun by the front gates, white Gwyn and black Duesh raised their heads, regarded him with amber eyes, then returned to their rest. He smiled. The summer day was starting out quite well. First a very fine frigging, followed by an idiot's apology, and now? Maybe he'd ride Remig to the bee yards. He let his head fall back, felt the crackle and crunch of ligaments and spine, enjoyed the warm summer breeze.

"Morning, Master Gethen," a woman called. He opened

one eye and let his head tilt to the side. For a man who valued his privacy, Gethen was hip-deep in women who were hip deep in weapons and encamped in his bailey. While Halina recovered, they'd arrived, singly and in pairs, at the black stone circle around Kharayan Tor. The Order of the Red Blade, and Odruna made a dozen, if he counted Halina and Vi among them.

Vika Kaleeda — now, she'd been a surprise. He prided himself on reading people quickly, so he was taken off-guard when the timid chambermaid was revealed to be a dangerous assassin. "Not all members of the Order of the Red Blade wear swords and hold titles, Master Gethen," she'd said.

"Good morning, Marja," he replied to the woman who'd greeted him.

Before the open stable doors, Militess Odruna pulled the saddle and blanket off a magnificent black-and-white courser. A pair of small, dark-haired boys set to work with brushes on the stallion's back. "That's a fine horse, Militess," he called and snatched up an empty water bucket on his way to the well.

Odruna replied, "Indeed, he is." She paused by the steed's muscular shoulder. "Lady Khara out and about?" She swung the saddle into the arms of the taller page. The stallion tossed his head, the high sheen of his coat rippling in the sun. The children were pale and furtive like mice among cats. But Gethen recognized Feddie and Elof, even with their hair dyed dark and hers cut short like a boy's.

"Speaking with her captain. She'll be out soon to greet you." He set the bucket on the well's stone lip, sent the well bucket into the black depths of the cistern, then cranked it up and tipped water into the empty one.

Odruna jerked the tie loose on her pale arming cap, pulled it off, and shook out her banded braids. She surveyed the tents spread around the bailey. Elof finished brushing and led the horse into the stable.

Gethen swung the full bucket down and carried it to the stable door. "Why're Feddie and Elof still with you? Why's she disguised as a boy?"

Odruna took the bucket from him. "You'll have answers when I give them to Her Ladyship," she said over her shoulder as she carried the water into the stable for the horse.

Feddie reappeared, a long, narrow bundle in her hands. "The militess returns this with her thanks, Your Lordship." She left the bundle on a stool just inside the stable then retreated to the shadows.

Halina exited the kitchen and came toward him, a limp shortening her stride. Spying her, the other militesses put aside their tasks and joined her. Gethen offered his elbow. "Surprises await us in the stable, Your Ladyship."

She cocked a brow. "Should I run away, Your Lordship?"

"Would you if I recommended it?"

She snorted and took his arm. "Unlikely." They crossed the bailey but paused to let their eyes adjust as they moved from sunshine to shadows. Gethen picked up the bundle from the stool.

"Is that your sword and dagger?" Halina asked.

"Yes. I loaned them to the children I encountered in Grimbu." He buckled the sword belt at his waist, added the sword to its frog and sheathed the dagger. "I didn't expect to see them again."

"How did Odruna come to have them?"

"That's part of the surprise." It felt good to have the weapons' weight back on his hips.

"Khotyr, take me." Arms akimbo, Odruna stood before a

stall door and peered at Halina. "You look like Skiron chewed you up and spat you out."

"I've looked and felt worse."

Gethen folded his arms. "I'd hoped you'd take another week to arrive, Militess. Waiting for you meant rest and recovery for Lady Khara."

Halina rolled her eyes. "He's convinced he knows what's best for me."

He curled his lip. "One of us should."

She kissed his cheek then turned and offered her hands to her militess. The woman clasped them and bowed, pressing her forehead to Halina's knuckles. She, in turn, leaned forward and kissed her militess's bowed head. They both straightened from the show of fealty. Halina said, "I'm relieved to see you."

"Not half as much as I am to hold your hands and know you're alive, Halina." Odruna stepped back and bowed to Gethen. "It's my honor to be in your presence again, Lord Rhyshis. I speak for all the Red Blades when I offer my services and my thanks. We're in your debt, Your Lordship."

Gethen nodded. Movement in the corner of the stall caught his eye. It had drawn Halina's attention, too, and she asked, "You've taken a page?"

"Two," Odruna said. She considered the children and slowly nodded. She pointedly turned back to Halina. "The horse's name is Pedran. He's Schorvalan bred and Beseran trained."

"An excellent mount for battle then," Gethen assessed and Halina murmured agreement. He wondered why Odruna was withholding the information on the children.

Feddie passed the horse's bridle to the Schorvalan woman then closed the slatted stall door while Elof picked dirt from the horse's hooves. Pedran sloshed the water in his bucket before drinking. The militess said, "Indeed. He's been a pleasure to bring to Ursinum. I'll miss having such a fine creature between my legs."

Halina snorted. "I'm sure you'll find a willing substitute."

Odruna's smile was lascivious. "Been trying to break your captain. I'll ride that one hard and put him away wet, if he'll give me the chance." The militesses around them laughed. Gethen arched a brow.

Halina replied, "Be gentle. Thaksin's recovering from some fresh wounds."

"Then he'll benefit from Schorvalan soma and my kind of healing," Odruna said.

Gethen changed the subject. "Pedran's not yours, Militess?"

Halina smiled. "He's yours. From me." Surprise murmured between the gathered militesses.

Gethen looked from her, to Odruna and the women, to the horse and the children, then back at Halina. "You're giving me this horse?" His voice was low, his words deliberate.

It was an Ursinum tradition for women to give an animal — a horse, a goat, a chicken, whatever the family could afford — to a man whom she intended to marry.

"Yes. I'm giving you this horse, Gethen Rhysh, Sun Mage of Ranith, Duke of Rhyshis in absentia. Do you accept my gift?"

He stepped forward. He cupped her jaw and tilted her head back. "I accept your gift, Halina Persinna, Margrave of Khara, Militess of the Order of the Red Blade." He kissed her. The women clapped, laughed, nodded their satisfaction. He stepped back and considered the stallion with fresh eyes.

"Odruna selected him," Halina said.

He smiled at the Schorvalan militess. "You know your horses."

She nodded. Her gaze went to Halina and lingered before

returning to him. "I envy you, Master Mage." She bowed to them, said, "Come, boys. You can clean the tack after you've eaten." She left the stable with her pages and the other Red Blades in tow.

Halina looked away from his gaze. "I'm sorry they destroyed Tegwen's gown. It was beautiful."

"My mother hated that dress," he said. "She was terrified that she'd damage it."

Halina rolled her eyes. "If only she'd known what would happen when I wore it."

Pedran shuffled around in his straw then came to the stall door. Gethen looked back at the horse and asked, "When shall we be wed?" as the stallion snuffled his open palm.

"You and Pedran? There are laws against such things." Gethen laughed and she added, "Shame. Such a fine, strong, handsome beast should be someone's husband." Then she was behind him, her body pressing against his. She slid her hands around his waist and up his chest. Gethen pressed her hands close. "That's why I've decided to make you mine, Gethen Rhysh."

"Because I'm a beast?"

"Yes. And because I love you."

He lifted her hands and kissed her fingers. "Then I'll make you my wife, Halina Persinna. Because I love you."

They remained that way for a time and Pedran sampled hay from the manger.

Gethen pulled Halina around to tuck her against his side. "Gods, he's magnificent."

"The courser matches the man."

He ducked his head and captured her lips for a long, slow kiss. Then he slid his lips to her temple and whispered, "The man is fortunate, indeed."

Halina leaned into him. "So is the woman."

After a few moments of feeling the magic and warmth coursing through her body, inhaling the sweet scent of liminth flowers and honey in her hair and the faint, lingering musk of their coupling, Gethen tugged her away from the stall. "I need to speak with those children."

"Are they the ones you encountered in Nalvika?" They headed back into the bright sunshine. "I thought Odruna agreed to take them to the Ballard River Garrison?"

"So did I."

They found the militess in the kitchen with Elof and Feddie. She leaned against the wooden counter before the window and cut thin slices from a golden plum, sliding each from the blade with her tongue, and humming as she chewed. The children sat at the kitchen table, eating goat cheese and bread smeared with honey, and rolling another plum between them. The militess eyed Gethen as he entered. "Finish up," she said. "Lord Rhyshis has questions."

"Lord Rhyshis has suspicions," he said. Elof and Feddie obeyed Odruna and stuffed the rest of their meal down their throats like it might be their last. Gethen led the group to the library. Halina took a chair close to the fire and he sat opposite her.

Odruna refused to sit. "My arse aches from riding." The children stayed close to the militess and eyed him and the margrave, worry and defiance vying for control of their expressions.

Gethen began with Odruna. "What happened at the garrison?"

"We never reached it. There were too many shrikers in the woods between Grimbu and the Ballard. We headed east instead, crossed the Delta Islands and the Fist to the Great

Green. I got us passage on a trawler heading for Ayestra, then we crossed Besera's Throat to the North Selga. Took a barge to Sokos a week ago."

Halina asked, "But why not stay in Schorvala?"

Gethen was studying Feddie. She returned his regard with the same mixture of defiance and fear she'd offered up in Grimbu. He leaned forward, planted his hands on his knees. "Because the north isn't safe for Princess Federika Janne Boorsook." The girl's gaze flickered down, right, then back. She was a tough one. Her defiance and strength, and curiosity, had saved her life. "You never went to your bed on Nimnight. You snuck down to the throne room to wait for Elof. He'd promised to show you the dancing lights. But your father was there with a stranger. They discussed murder. You were afraid you'd be caught and beaten for being out of bed and Elof scared you when he snuck into the room. Then there were frightening sounds, struggling, fighting, screams. You were both afraid, but Elof knew all the secret passages under the castle. And I bet he knows a few simple incantations, like a travel spell his Aunt Lauma taught him."

The hearth's orange fire reflected in Odruna's blade as she drew her sword. "The only way you could know all that is if you were the stranger in Drevya Linna's throne room."

"Hold," Halina commanded. "That's not possible, 'Druna. Gethen was with me on Nimnight."

Feddie said, "The other man in the room was a wraith. I'd seen my father talking to him before. He lives in my father's shadow."

"Shemel?" Gethen asked.

She nodded. "That's his name."

Elof said, "He's why Lauma wanted me to stay at the castle,

Your Lordship. She wanted to know what he was doing with the crown prince and how he got there."

Odruna sheathed the sword. "Who's this wraith?"

"Shadow Mage Shemel is my former master," Gethen replied. "And King Waldram's uncle." He looked at Feddie. "Your great uncle."

Halina cursed colorfully enough to make a dock trollop's pimp blush. "You destroyed him in the Void, Gethen."

"Indeed. And before that I murdered him in the basilica and chained his spirit to Kharayan Tor. He has an annoying habit of escaping the grave."

"How could you know what happened?" Feddie demanded.

Gethen sat back in his chair. "Because you shared the memory with me in Grimbu when you stitched my arm. An experience that strong dominates your soul."

Odruna pulled both children against her, a gruff hug. "They can't go back to Nalvika."

"Of course not," Halina said. "We'll take you to the Council of Kings," she told them. "Gethen and I have been summoned to Tatlis to testify. We leave as soon as possible." She stood, straight, tall. She looked more like Margrave Khara than she had in weeks, Gethen thought. Having something to do, someone to protect, suited her. "Odruna, you'll continue to protect them. Assign an additional militess to each child and we'll bunk them in the infirmary. Vi, you'll stay with me."

"Of course, Halina." The maid militess appeared from the shadows. Gethen arched a brow. He'd failed to sense her presence, and not for the first time. He was beginning to suspect the woman had some magic in her; it wasn't unusual for assassins.

"Duesh and Gwyn can sleep in the stillroom," he said. Halina nodded.

"Who are they?" Odruna asked.

"Wolves."

Elof grinned. "Really? I love wolves. Can I pet them?"

"They're not pets," Gethen said. "But I'll ask them if you can scratch their ears."

"Aren't they yours?" Feddie asked.

"Of course not. They belong to themselves."

Odruna stood. "All right, little ones, time to get some sleep." The children grumbled, but only a bit, and followed Odruna and Vi from the library.

Halina started to follow as well, but Gethen snagged her hand. "About that marriage."

"Yes?"

Gethen hugged her to him, his arms around her hips, hands against the curve of her back. She felt good, right. "You trust Ilker to honor your father's agreement with me when the Bear King himself threatened to annul it?"

"I've always had Ilker's support. He wants to see me married. Better still if I'm constrained by Beseran fidelity laws."

"We don't live in Besera."

"That may be so, but a certain captain informs me you're a possessive lout with a foul temper."

Gethen's grip tightened. "A certain captain had to learn that I don't like to share."

As if on cue, boots scuffed stone and Thaksin appeared in the doorway. He saw them embracing, looked away, cleared his throat. Halina stepped back from Gethen and her captain said, "You left before our conversation was finished, Your Lordship. I brought something from Kharaton. It's for you, Halina, but really belongs to both of you. Seemed appropriate considering the horse Odruna delivered." He swallowed again and held out a large package of linen, wrapped with twine.

She took it, sat, and loosened the wrapping. She gasped when she unfolded the linen.

"I'm not sure what can be done to fix it." Thaksin shifted from foot to foot. "It was found down the garden well."

"Ai, gods," Gethen muttered as Halina held up Tegwen's surcoat. Largely intact, her blood had mingled with the well water to turn the front of the gown a sickly rusted-blue shade and one side of the skirt was stained blackish-green from the well stones. The water had damaged the fabric itself, stealing its sheen and loosening the silk to leave the gown limp, the color dull.

"Eugen had it rinsed with clean water, but no one knew what else to do. I think they were all afraid they'd make it worse." Thak grimaced. "Maybe Besera's seamstresses have some method for restoring it?"

Halina's hands were shaking as she bundled the surcoat back into its linen. Gethen squeezed her shoulder. She looked up and her face was calm. "Thank you, Thak," she said. "And thank Eugen for us."

"I will, Your Ladyship." The captain straightened, nodded at Gethen, and left the library.

Gethen watched the man's shadow disappear from the doorway. "Did he know you intended to give me a horse?"

"Yes."

"For how long?"

"Since the start of spring. Why d'you think he was being such a prick?"

Gethen grunted. "I assumed he was always that way."

CHAPTER 24

They camped for the night in the hills above the Persin Bridge, well off the road and away from curious travelers. Gethen, Halina, Elof and Feddie, Odruna, Marja, Jessavon, and Vika. The pass was clear of flood debris and they'd made good time, reaching the edge of Tatlis on their thirteenth day. Thaksin had wanted to accompany Halina, but she'd sent him back to Kharaton. "The people of Khara need their captain, Thak. Your strengths are wasted standing around the court at Tatlis." Besides, shrikers had been reported in northwestern Khara. So he accompanied her to the foot of the Valmerians then took a squad to hunt the beasts.

Gethen sat behind Halina, his back to a tree, comb in hand. They'd camped on the side of a rise where a thicket of dead gorse hid their fire. She watched the flames dance and let him work the snarls from her hair. She was reluctant to re-enter court politics, reluctant to leave the small paradise that Ranith had become. It's why they'd traveled by horse, rather than incantation. She wasn't hurrying. Sitting opposite them,

Odruna watched her and Gethen, her expression thoughtful. Feddie and Elof slept on either side of her. Marja and Jessavon played bones and bickered. Vi had slipped into the night, gone to find her brother — an artificer in the Iron Quarter — and hear the news of the city.

"'Druna, any soma left in your flask?" Halina asked.

The Schorvalan militess dug a metal canister from her haversack and tossed it over the fire. "*Til din helsch.*"

Halina caught it. She unscrewed the cap and saluted her soldiers in Schorvalan. "*Tele den helsche.*" The large swig burned all the way down and then some. She tossed the flask to Jessavon and wiped her mouth. "Tastes worse than usual."

"Homebrew," Odruna said and laughed as Jessavon swigged, gagged, coughed, and got walloped between the shoulder blades by Marja.

"You'll go blind drinking witch's bathwater," Gethen muttered.

Halina laughed. "Says the necromancer."

"My brews only cause harm when I want them to." He sectioned her hair for braiding. "How do you want this done? For beauty or for battle?"

"Better choose battle." The shadows disgorged Vika at the edge of the firelight. Halina saw Gethen frown. It bothered him a great deal that he kept missing the stealthy assassin's departures and arrivals.

Odruna tossed the flask to Vi. "What news, Assassin?"

"Flags fly over Tatlis, but only for Ursinum and Nalvika." She dropped cross-legged beside the fire. "No others."

Halina straightened. "No sign of Besera and Or-Halee? What's the word on the street?"

Vi swigged, squinted her left eye as she swallowed the soma, blew out. "Your favored allies were never invited. There's no Council meeting. According to my brother the rumor is there may soon be no Council of the Kings."

Halina rolled her tongue and spat in the fire. "Whose stupidity is that?"

"King Waldram's."

Silence smothered their little gathering, thick and heavy as winter wools in the summer.

Halina shifted to a crouch, her dagger in hand. She bared her teeth. "I stabbed that prick in the skull." She slammed her blade into the ground for emphasis. "He's dead."

"It's impossible," Gethen growled. "His shrikers turned on him. He's buried beneath a mountain."

Halina stood. "Did *you* see him, Vi?"

"No, but the gate guards claimed they did. And..." her gaze flicked to Gethen, "there's a deathmark worth fifty-thousand gold coins for your head, Master Gethen."

Odruna dismissed that. "Ninety-eight percent of Quoregna wouldn't recognize Master Gethen if he slapped them."

"It's the two percent we need to worry about," Marja said.

Halina bared her teeth, ready to roar, but Feddie's eyes were open, watching her, wide with fear. Gethen was standing behind her. She turned. "Get the children out of here."

"I'll get all of us out of here."

She shook her head and looked at her assassin. "Vi, you're with me. The rest of you will go with Gethen and the children." To him she added, "Take Duesh and Gwyn. Go to Gurvan-Sum, find Mahish, go someplace I've never heard of. Hide Elof and Feddie. Nalvika's next queen must be kept safe."

Gethen nodded. "Feddie, wake Elof. Gather your things. Be quick."

Jessavon said, "I'll ready the horses."

The camp was sober and bustling. Halina yanked her

dagger from the dirt and returned it to its sheath. Gethen grabbed her elbow and pulled her into the shadows at the edge of their camp. "You're determined to speak with Ilker, aren't you?"

"I have to try. I need to see what game is being played and who the players are. We need the information if we're going to keep you and Feddie alive and stay ahead of," she waved her hand, "whoever's pulling the strings."

"It's Shemel. You know how dangerous my old master is. There are other ways, other people who can spy for you. You don't have to be the one, Halina."

"Yes, I do. I'm the only person Ilker will listen to. And," she looked down, "I'm terrified of Waldram. I have to face that fear, Gethen." He ran his hands through his hair and cursed as she continued. "I'm going to Tatlis. I can get into the castle unseen. I'll—"

He grabbed her arms. "You'll make me walk away when you're in danger. Again." His voice was husky, tight with anger and fear for her.

She pressed against him. "Only a fool falls in love with a militess."

"Only a fool doesn't listen to her mage." She opened her mouth to protest, but he held up a finger. "I have one condition."

She arched a brow. "Which is?"

He removed the wraith pellet from his belt pouch. "You take this. Unleash it at the first sign of trouble."

"What is it?"

"A threat to anyone who would harm you."

She opened her palm. "Does it respond to my commands like the ambit?" He gave it to her and closed her fingers around it.

He shook his head. "If you need it, put it in your mouth, bite to break the shell, exhale. You'll release a wraith whose sole purpose is to kill anyone trying to harm you. He'll do that until all his energy is spent and he no longer exists. Remember the wraith that almost killed you in Kharayan Woods?" She nodded, looking from the pellet to his face. "This one's angrier."

She swallowed and put the pellet in her own belt pouch. "Let's hope I don't have to unleash him."

"If you're in danger, don't hesitate to use him then call upon your ambit to bring you to me."

"It can do that?"

"It can now."

"You changed it." A small part of her was annoyed that he'd broken his promise not to make a wraith and not to make the ambit more powerful. But a larger part was relieved to have a weapon and a means of escape. "All right. Go. Before I lose my nerve." Behind them, the militesses and children were astride their horses. She kissed him, hands in his hair, body pressed hard to his, a bruising kind of parting kiss, deep, a little desperate. She pulled away and pushed him back. "Go."

"I'll see you soon." He climbed into Pedran's saddle. He held Feddie's and Elof's hands; they clung to Odruna, Marja and Jessavon. With a low incantation, a swirl of amber magic, a flurry of leaves, he took them away. Halina stared up through the night-black tree canopy to the twinkling stars. Somewhere in Quoregna, a mage, three militesses, and two children had appeared astride horses. Had anyone witnessed their arrival? Would they be welcomed in Gurvan-Sum or by the Dargani?

"Swig?" Vi stood beside her, Odruna's flask uncorked between them, firelight flashing across its metal side.

"Definitely."

They crossed the bridge just as morning turned the sky from black to indigo, Halina hidden within the folds of her travel cloak. Returning to Tatlis never brought her joy. Sometimes it offered a mixed bag of pleasure and displeasure, but never happiness. Here, she'd fought too many battles as a young, freckled bastard child. Ignored too many insults until they couldn't be ignored anymore. Received too many beatings for beating the insulters. She'd succeeded in revenge too many times and had too many regrets afterward when the sweetness of revenge had soured too quickly. Vengeance never tasted as sweet in reality as it did in her dreams.

Dominated by the sprawling castle's long, crenelated walls and abundant towers, Ursinum's capital city draped over the rolling hills on the southern shore of Lake Tatlis, like cream-colored icing laid over a cake. Tatlis was the largest of Quoregna's cities and the castle occupied a fifth of its acreage, a village unto itself. A series of bridges led into the city, crossing massive ditches, the first set of fortifications to protect the Bear King's realm. The bottoms of the ditches held rows of upright iron stakes, the decaying remains and rusted armor that bespoke failed siege attempts, and the refuse of a teeming city.

A mishmash of cobblestone streets framed by tall, yellowish stone buildings, and dominated by the massive sandstone walls of the citadel, Tatlis seethed with residents, travelers, and merchants. The smells of thousands of bodies, dung, animals, and cook fires always turned Halina's stomach. The stench of the city vied with its noise. Feet and hooves and wagon wheels crunched across cobblestones. Thousands of voices echoed through the streets, arguing, crying, laughing. Noise tumbled down the narrow ways and bounced off the high walls. Sparrows sang from their perches in the trees or rose in clouds of flapping wings, leaving feathers and droppings behind. Dogs barked. Cats yowled. Horses snorted and stamped.

Halina and Vi entered the Iron Quarter where the clang of hammers on anvils, the whoosh of the bellows and the hiss of steam added to the clamor. They left their horses with Vi's brother Sevik then split up. Vi shadowed Halina as she made her way to the castle's postern door. Luck was on her side and one of the oldest night guards was still on duty.

She slid into the shadows of the small gate arch besides the man and raised her hood. "Hello, Cleaver." His eyes widened, but she pressed her fingers to his lips. "I want to see my brother but don't want attention drawn to my presence. Will you let me in?"

"Of course, Your Ladyship. You're a welcome sight and it's a great relief to see you healthy and free of that sorcerer's control."

Which sorcerer he meant she didn't want to contemplate, so she squeezed his forearm, smiled, and slipped past as he unlocked the postern door. "Let's keep this between the two of us. I don't want a fuss. I've been through a lot."

"I understand." He closed the gate and turned away, the dutiful soldier guarding his king's back door.

Tatlis was old and cold, its interior walls built from the same yellow sandstone as the defenses and with few thoughts to comfort. Halina's footsteps echoed in the empty arched halls as she made her way through the galleries. She turned up the less-traveled rear stairs to the fifth floor passage, her destination the royal apartments. Ilker would be taking his morning meal with his guest, with Waldram. A chill skittered up her spine at the thought of facing her second cousin again. The man should be dead. There was no way he could be alive. Yet, rumor said he was. She felt in her belt pouch for the pellet. Cold. Smooth. Deadly. Halina took a deep, steadying breath and climbed the last set of stairs.

The guards outside the double door entry to the apartment stiffened, stared, came to attention as she strode toward them. She tried to find some of her old swagger. It came off as more limp, her hips and back were still sore. She plastered confidence, a little arrogance, across her face. "Is Ilk in his room?"

"His Majesty is breaking his fast with King Waldram in the great hall, Your Ladyship," one of the soldiers replied.

Halina caught her tongue between her teeth, nodded, pointed to him. "Thank you, Bardos." He flushed, pleased she'd remembered his name. She eyed the other man, leaned close to study his face. "Do I know you? You look related to Captain Vanix."

He grinned. "His fifth son, Your Ladyship."

"Arthenox?" He nodded. Halina whistled. "You've grown a lot in six years." He shrugged, blushed. A year ago, she might have invited both men to her bed. "I'll wait for the king in his chambers. Don't tell anyone I'm here. You know I despise fussing and when the ladies of the court learn I've returned they'll flutter around like a flock of deranged chickens." She rolled her eyes, muttered, "I might have to break a nose or two to make it all stop."

They chuckled. Bardos nodded. "We understand, Your Ladyship." He opened the door.

Halina stepped through, paused. "Is my mother in her chamber?"

Arthenox shook his head. "His Majesty sent Countess Surquay home to Gwyncadarnlei with your new brother."

"I have a brother." She'd forgotten Ianthe's pregnancy and

Ilker hadn't bothered to mention the babe's birth. "What's his name?"

"Prince Vernard Halinos Persinna."

Halina winced. "Thank you."

They closed the doors behind her. She strode past her own royal apartment, long neglected. Passed Ilker's old chambers, recently abandoned. She came to the king's chambers, slipped into the apartment, and crossed the room to the hearth. A low fire smoldered, reddish-orange. A brazier sent flickering shadows to dance across the walls beside His Majesty's desk. The same ancient desk where generations of Persinna kings had sat. Three chairs were arrayed before the hearth, one large and made of black leather. King Vernard's chair. The others were smaller with red velvet fabric. She ran her fingers over the back of the king's chair but sat in one of the smaller ones. Tears stung her eyes. "I didn't think I'd miss you so much, you old pillock." She blinked. The tears slowly slipped down her cheeks. She swiped her palm over her eyes, wiped that on her trouzes, sniffed. "The world seems infinitely more unstable without you in it, Bear King." She closed her eyes, saw the knife tearing open this throat, opened her eyes, cursed. How could such a powerful man be so easily killed?

Halina fingered the pellet in her belt pouch. If she could get close to Waldram she could kill him, again, or expose Shemel. The wraith must've protected him somehow, transported him out of the collapsing cavern and kept him alive. Gethen had explained that Shemel was something between ambit and wraith — dependent on Waldram to exist and capable of killing.

Muffled voices carried through the door. Footfalls approached. The door creaked open. "I'll join you momentarily."

Halina wiped her eyes again. She stood, faced the door.

Ilker entered the room, muttering, and unbuckling his belt. He looked up, started, and stepped back. "Halina!"

"Hello, Ilker." He looked around the room, his hand going to his dagger, his body tense, eyes wary. She scowled and sat. "Gethen's not here. You can relax."

He came to her, sat in the black chair, took her hand. Taller than their father but just as powerfully built, Ilker fit the Bear King's chair well. He shared her auburn hair, her blue eyes. "Thank the One God, you escaped." But he didn't share her gods or, apparently, her belief in the Sun Mage.

"I escaped because Gethen helped me. You can thank *him*."

He shook his head, his brows knit together with worry. "He's twisted your mind."

"What? That's idiotic. Gethen saved my life. Again." She tugged her hand away and stood. She felt stifled by him. "Is Waldram really here?"

"Yes, King Waldram is here to help us move against that bloody necromancer. He told me everything that happened, Halina."

"So did Gethen. You got his letter?"

"His lies, yes. No one blames you for our father's death or the shrikers or the Boorsook murders."

Stifled became stunned. "Of course they don't. None of those things are my fault. Nor are they Gethen's." She stabbed her finger toward the door. "Waldram's lying to you. He's telling you what he wants you to hear. *And you're listening.* He paid the mercenaries to assassinate our father. He slaughtered his family *and* children from Drevya to Kharaton. He summoned the shrikers. He's a necromancer, Ilker, a powerful one, trained and still working with Shemel."

Ilker regarded her with calm control. "Halina, your mind's

been compromised by that damned mage. He's twisting you to his purpose. Everything you said has been firmly pinned on him. Arevik testified that the mercenaries were Beseran and were financed by Sun Mage Gethen. I wanted to take an army to his doorstep to free you, but Waldram counseled me to be patient, to draw you out. He was right. We'd have never broken through the Sun Mage's wards." He reached for her hands, but she refused his grasp. "But now you're here and I can help you, sister."

The conversation was heading in the wrong direction and Halina fought to gain control and steer it toward the truth. "Arevik said what the mercenaries wanted her to say. She only knows a fraction of what occurred." Halina thrust her scarred palms up to his face. "*Waldram* did this to me, Ilker. In Drevya Linna. He stole my blood and tried to kill me."

He folded her hands in his. "It pains me to see you like this. You've suffered so much; I can't imagine what the torture was like. I know it still haunts Arevik as much as our father's death does; it's why I sent her to wed Lord Essendra. She needed a new start. You do too." His blue eyes held sincerity, concern, pity for her. "I know you don't want to believe your lover would betray you this way, but think logically."

His pity pissed her off almost as much as his stupidity did. "How long do you intend to be this foolish, Ilker?"

"I will remain steadfast until this spell he has upon you is broken and you regain your senses."

She threw up her hands. "There's no spell."

"Of course there is." Ilker had the manner of a man taming an enraged animal. "I haven't forgotten the tale you told me of the night you met him. How he fooled your mind so thoroughly that you believed you were trapped in the snow-bound bailey of his citadel and thought you'd die."

Gods. Her father's paranoia had become her brother's and that first encounter was still being twisted and turned against her and Gethen. She shook herself. *Stay calm.* "That was a trick and lasted only moments. There's no trickery here."

"Besera was massing for war before you went to Ranith. The Sun Mage convinced them to ally with *you*, yet neither envoy nor letter has come to Tatlis from them in the six months since they aided Khara. The first time you were trapped in the mage's citadel, you condemned him to our father for colluding with King Zelal. Now you expect me to believe that's changed, despite Arevik's testimony that Beserans murdered the king, Beserans tortured you, Beserans held your castle and killed your soldiers and servants? Beserans killed Philippa, Halina. She loved you."

"I know what Waldram did to me, Ilker," she said through clenched teeth. "What he did to our father, my people, my lady-in-waiting. You. Weren't. There."

"Our second cousin has changed, Halina."

"For the worse!" She thrust her palms out again. "Are these wounds illusions?"

"You can't prove the mage didn't inflict them."

"And you can't prove he did," Halina snarled. "I suffered, not you. Waldram stole my blood, Ilker. He's using my strength to manipulate you, mine and the souls of his family, his children, Nalvika's children, Khara's children." She grabbed his wrists, yanked him forward, their faces mere inches apart. "And I can prove that."

"I was thinking, Ilker." The chamber door opened and Waldram strode in. "Why don't we—" He stopped mid-stride. A smile bloomed across his face. "Halina. What a relief to see you." Like Ilker, he looked around, searching, suspicious. "Where's your dangerous friend?"

"Not so easily led into your trap." *Unlike me.* She'd been so sure she could make Ilker see the truth. Her hand strayed to her belt pouch.

Waldram frowned. "Too bad. We could've put an end to your suffering and all your confusion. He needs to be stopped. He and Zelal." He shook his head. "I never imagined Besera would betray Ursinum this way."

Ilker nodded. "They're using you to get a toehold in Khara."

Waldram came further into the room. "The first step to an invasion, Halina, to war."

"Oh, no you don't," she said. "I know everything, Waldram. What dwells in your shadow; what you've done. You're the one who wants war. You and Shemel planned this for decades."

He looked confused. She didn't buy it. "Shemel? My *uncle*? He's dead. Killed by your mage."

She grabbed Ilker's wrist and pulled him with her as she edged around Waldram, her eyes on her enemy, the door her goal. If she could just get her brother out of the room, she could release the wraith.

"Halina," Ilker said. He stayed with her. His concern for her was evident in his voice. "Please relax."

Waldram turned with her, his hands loose at his sides. "I thought you understood that I've changed, Halina."

"I know how much you've changed. There's a lot of royal blood on your hands." She was almost to the door.

"I've come here for you, cousin." He raised his hands slowly, palms out, a man approaching a startled horse. "I've come to finish what was started in Kharaton."

She withdrew the pellet from the pouch. "Me, too. See you in the Void." She shoved Ilker through the door and popped the pellet into her mouth. Waldram shouted. She crunched, exhaled a black, inky, shrieking cloud of madness, stumbled through the doorway and yanked it shut.

"What have you done?" Ilker grabbed her, tried to pull her back. Something slammed against the door. "Damn it, Halina, what have you done? Open it!"

She spat out the pellet shell. "I've killed them, if we're lucky," she shouted over the shrieking, wailing, roaring racket coming from the room. "Where's the key?"

He grabbed her hands, tried to pry them off the door handle. "Let him out!" The door groaned, crashing, smashing, wailing rose behind it. The floor shook, the door hinges creaked, cracks appeared in the wood. Dust rained from the ceiling and rose from the floor. Soldiers crowded into the apartment, swords drawn, shields raised. Ilker commanded, "Pull her off the door. Get it open!"

Three men grabbed her. "No!" She tried to hold on. The door groaned, the split spread, following the wood's grain. "No!" Halina's hands ached, her fingers slipped, slipped. She was yanked free and landed in a heap with the soldiers.

Everything stopped. Eerie silence filled the room.

The door slowly opened, groaning.

Waldram crouched in the middle of the floor, arms over his head, clothes covered in soot and debris. The room was storm-tossed, windows shattered, desk overturned, curtains shredded, chairs gutted, splintered. Huge gouges scored the floor as if something massive had clawed it apart. Nalvika's new king looked up, around. "Is it gone?"

Ilker bared his teeth. "Lock Princess Halina in her apartment."

Princess. She hated being called that. It was entirely too prissy. She grabbed her brother's sleeve. "Come with me, Ilk. I can prove he's a monster." He jerked free of her, nodded to his soldiers, smoothed down his tunic. "You have to believe me!" she shouted. Bardos, Arthenox, and two other men pulled her into the hallway. "Ilker!" She was stripped of her sword and dagger. They shoved her into her old chamber. She grabbed the door, used all her weight and strength to keep it open. "The king is in danger. I'm not lying. Promise you won't leave him alone with King Waldram."

"His Majesty is safe in his castle, Your Ladyship," Bardos said and pulled the door closed. Halina yelped as it pinched her fingers.

"Idiots!" The apartment was cold and dim, its hearths and braziers long unlit. She kicked an empty coal scuttle some maid had left in the middle of the room. It clanked and clattered across the floor, ricocheted off a table leg, spun into a wall. Expecting Waldram to come sauntering through the door at any moment, she armed herself with the iron fire poker and dropped into a chair. She shivered from cold, from fear, from confusion, frustration. "Bollocks." She pulled her knees to her chest, rested her forehead against them, rocked her head from side to side.

"Why didn't it kill him?" she moaned.

Because Waldram is innocent. The thought slipped into her brain like Vi into camp. Another followed, this even more insidious. *He's telling the truth about Gethen manipulating my mind.* She felt on the brink of breaking, covered her mouth, swallowed a sob.

"He wants you to doubt."

Halina gasped, jerked upright.

"Sorry." Vi settled into the chair opposite hers. "Didn't mean to startle you." She jabbed her thumb toward the windows. "The chambermaid should always check the shutters. You never know who'll come crawling up the side of the castle."

Halina nodded. "I did start doubting Gethen and my own mind." She clasped her hands to stop their trembling and sat back. Her left hand found the black ring and twisted, twisted, twisted.

"I know. But you have Feddie and Elof." Something jingled in Vi's lap. "And King Ilker hasn't seen what I have."

"What's that?"

"The way Lord Rhyshis looks at you." She held something up, squinted at it, a dark shape in a dim room, then went back to sorting. "You can't fake that kind of love. Or doubt it."

Halina swallowed a lump. She whispered, "For a moment I did."

"No. You doubted yourself." Vi held up another item. "Here it is."

"What?"

"The key to your armory."

"My what?"

"Gown room, where Philippa kept your court armor. This afternoon there'll be a Moot of the Lords."

"I wasn't invited." Bitterness stuck the words to her tongue and the memory of her dead lady-in-waiting would've choked her if she could've swallowed.

"No, but you're the subject. You and Lord Rhyshis and King Zelal."

Halina stopped turning the ring, her gaze fixed on the key in Vi's hand. "Can you leave the castle and get back in before that moot?"

"Easily. What do you need?"

"My finest court armor."

Tegwen's gown. Vi had retrieved it from Halina's saddle bag. Gethen had suggested they bring it thinking, perhaps, the seamstresses in Tatlis could save it. In the afternoon light spilling through her chamber's narrow windows, Halina looked down at the ruined surcoat. Repair was utterly hopeless. The bloodstains were more obvious, the moss and slime stains more egregious, the water damage to the color absolutely hideous. Bits of dried muck twisted about and into the gold embroidery, the sleeves and hem were tattered, the sol avuus closure torn and hanging so that the front couldn't be properly fastened. The gown hung slack, dead, weightless. She wore a dark blue kirtle beneath. Vi plaited her hair, hung blue jewels around her throat and in the braids.

Halina considered her reflection. She didn't look beautiful or feel powerful. "I look terrifying."

"I know. Isn't it great?"

Halina sniffed then wished she hadn't. The dress stank faintly of shrikers, vomit, and urine. "I want you to return to your brother's house. Stay there and spy for me. I'll need ears and eyes in Tatlis until this battle ends."

"How long will that be?"

Halina offered her hands. "I don't know." Vi clasped them and pressed her forehead to Halina's scarred knuckles. Khara's margrave leaned forward and kissed her assassin's lowered head. Fealty offered and fealty accepted. "Be safe. Flee if you have to. I'll send Enor to you for messages." They straightened.

"Whatever you need, Red Blade."

Halina squeezed her hands. "Thank you." She set her shoulders and went to the door.

Vi proffered another key and two needles, their tips glistening with a fast-acting venom. "Sleepy time."

Halina unlocked the door, yanked it open. Vi popped out and pricked each surprised guard on the cheek. The men staggered, went limp. They were caught and dragged into the room.

Vi slipped into the hall and blended with the shadows. Halina straightened her shoulders, paused. Her sword and dagger were on the floor beside the door. "Thank you, gentlemen." She strapped the weapons at her waist.

Now she felt terrifying and dangerous. A glimmer of battle joy tingled her fingertips. The effect preceded her as she strode through the castle. Servants stared, shrank back as she cast a baleful eye upon them. The tingle turned into a thrum. The more crowded the halls became, the greater the unease rolled outward from her passage until, like a quake, it rumbled before her as she entered the great hall, sending the minor lords and ladies tottering from her path. It gained noise, mutters of recognition, shocked gasps at the sight of her in Tegwen's destroyed gown.

The king's small, dark meeting chamber was located through a door off the great hall. It was a dark room for dark decisions. The guards at its modest entrance stared, eyes widening, as Halina approached. "Your Ladyship," both murmured. They'd guarded this door since she was a girl.

"Belen. Ezio. Are you going to stop me?"

"We don't have orders to keep you out, Lady Khara." They bowed, stepped aside, and opened the door.

She arched a brow, surprised. Ilker knew she couldn't be so easily caged. That he hadn't warned his guards showed how much influence Waldram wielded over his judgment.

"Sorry I'm late." Her voice rang off the stone walls. "I had some difficulty with my dress." The quake shattered the calm of the meeting room, crushing some lords beneath their own astonishment, forcing others to grab hold as they stared from Halina to Ilker, wondering what was happening, wondering which Persinna really held power now. Several stood, drew their swords. She raised a finger. They stopped. "Sit. You don't need those."

The tables were arrayed face-to-face, with a shorter one at the end to form a horseshoe. She strode down the center of them toward her brother. Waldram sat at his right hand. She stopped midway.

"There was a time not long past when I sat on the king's right, but it seems strange times make strange alliances, Your Majesties."

On her left and half-risen from his seat, Margrave Etherias proclaimed, "You're not welcome here, Lady Khara,"

"And you're a coward with a limp dick, Lord Etherias," she snapped.

She pointed at Waldram. "Are all you idiots so thirsty for power that you'd willingly suck from the poisonous teat of Ursinum's enemy?" That brought a rumble of protests. She waited for it to settle. "I've come with a warning, Your Lordships."

Waldram and Ilker said nothing.

"Your threats don't scare us," Landgrave Valmer whined.

She eyed the shaggy northerner. "Warning, dolt. It's not the same as a threat. Read a book. Educate yourself and, maybe, bathe every once in a while." She turned back to her brother. "I told you the truth this morning, Ilker. You're sitting with the man responsible for the Bear King's death. He'll destroy you and Ursinum and all of Quoregna. I have that on the authority of his own tongue."

More protests. More threats. But there were those lords who stayed silent, watchful, holding back as the quake rattled everyone around them. Lords she'd strategized with on the battlefield. Lords she'd fought beside, bled with. They knew Militess Halina, the Red Blade of Or-Halee, was no fool.

"Enough!" Ilker stood. "Halina, return to your apartment. Your mind is compromised by a sorcerer's magic."

"I'm not the one fooled by a necromancer here, brother." She closed the space between them. "Please listen to me."

"No. You don't know what you're saying or doing." He straightened. His expression hardened. "Because your judgment has been so compromised, Princess Halina, and though it pains me greatly, I'm placing the governance and protection of Khara in the hands of your steward Eugen until your senses are restored."

Halina flinched and stepped back like she'd been slapped.

"No." She shook her head.

She'd lost Khara. Everything she'd fought for. Every sacrifice she'd made, every triumph she'd earned, stripped from her in an instant. Fiery hatred surged through her. She looked down, captured her fury, controlled it. Ilker and every lord in the room watched her, waiting to see if she'd fly into rage or hysteria, if she'd cry and beg for forgiveness. She felt all those gazes, Waldram's heaviest of all.

She made a fist of her right hand. She wouldn't draw her sword and run it through that ratsack, though the temptation was great. Shemel must be forced to reveal himself and destroyed by Gethen. She couldn't do it. Not even her lover's wraith had managed it. If she killed Waldram now Shemel would escape to spellbind someone else, someone like Ilker. It was agony to leave her brother subject to necromancy, but she needed allies. If she showed weakness or demonstrated anything but control now, the lords would believe the lie that her judgment was compromised.

Halina stepped to the table, rolled her tongue around her mouth, and spat in her second cousin's face. "Federika sends her regards, murderer." She smirked. *Let him wonder if he's vulnerable.* His silver eyes widened, shock flashed across his cool features, followed by doubt. Her spittle slid down his cheek.

She turned, murmured, "Ambit, take me to Gethen." The ambit cocooned her in cold and darkness.

"Halina!" someone shouted.

Her neck was painfully wrenched as the shadow yanked her into nothingness, hurled her across Quoregna, and dropped her on a marble floor in the middle of an elegant hall. She curled into a ball, groaning. Everything hurt. Astonished cries assaulted her ears. Afternoon sunlight assaulted her eyes. The loss of her home and her brother's trust assaulted her heart.

"Halina." Gethen's arms enfolded her. "Are you injured?" She shook her head, squeezed her eyes shut. He lifted her.

"Take her to my room."

Halina's eyes opened. She knew that sweet voice. "Arevik?" Her sister's face was a blessed sight, her cool elegant fingers a comfort. She wore pearls in her hair and silk the color of sea ice. She looked like a dream. "Wait, wait. Put me down. I'm not hurt."

Gethen ignored her. "Ambit travel is violent."

She growled. "So am I."

A deep laugh followed that. "Sounds like Lady Khara's well enough to walk."

"Magod?" Halina thumped Gethen's chest hard enough to

elicit a grunt. He tipped her onto her feet. She swayed, grabbed him, her knees like jelly.

"Welcome to Ostendra, Your Ladyship," Magod said.

She looked around. They stood at the entrance to an elegant great hall. It was festooned with flowers and filled with bejeweled guests, all seated around four long tables, all gawking at her. "I've interrupted a feast," she murmured, one more lump of horror to swallow.

"It's all right," Arevik said. She glanced at Magod, squeezed Halina's hand. "The most important part's over."

A white-haired man with large brown eyes approached. He was familiar. "It's been a long time since we've spoken, Lady Khara, I'm not sure you'll remember me."

"You're very memorable, Duke Ostendra. I recall our conversations. You taught me much about patience before a battle." She offered a wobbly curtsy.

"Are you unwell?" he asked.

Gethen answered. "She traveled by ambit. It leaves you feeling like you've been trampled by a herd of horses."

Halina tightened her grip on Gethen. "Where are the children?"

"Safe. In their room probably eating too much cake."

"Cake?" She was confused. But Elof and Feddie were safe. Thank the gods.

"Have interrupted an accession ceremony, Margrave Khara," Magod said.

Halina grimaced. "Don't call me that." She shook her head, squeezed her eyes tight. "You can't call me that, Magod." Her voice broke. "I've lost Khara."

Duke Ostendra scoffed. "What fool would remove you from Ursinum's first line of defense?"

"A fool being manipulated by a monster." She looked at Gethen then Arevik. "We can't go home."

Her sister caught Halina's hands, a new strength in her grip and gaze. "You'll tell me everything after you've rested and eaten."

Gethen wrapped his arm around Halina's shoulders and steered her toward a wide, dark wood staircase. He murmured, "What happened?"

"The wraith failed." Her hands dug into his. "Ilker believes Waldram's lies. He believes you're responsible for everything and I'm compromised by your sorcery. He believes you're scheming with King Zelal to attack Ursinum."

"Bollocks. Shemel's grown strong if that wraith had no effect." He kissed her temple. "I'm grateful to the gods that you escaped."

"So am I, but it sickens me to leave Ilker, Khara, and Ursinum in that monster's power. His lies spread faster than floodwaters."

"Only temporarily. We *will* defeat Shemel and Waldram. We're not about to give up. Right?"

Halina wanted to believe him. As they ascended the stairs, she looked out across the hall, down at the gathering. Lords and ladies, curious and concerned, turned slowly back to their companions. Conversation resumed. Forks, knives, spoons clicked and clattered, crystal rang, sounds to remind her of what could be lost if she stopped fighting. Thin strips of ribbon — red, gold, white — fluttered between the high rafters, some tied around fresh flowers, pungent and sweet. Along the large room's perimeter, gold baskets held red and white flowers. Red for Khotyr who bled to birth the world and everything in it, white for Skiron who ruled death, and

Semele's gold to remind everyone of the richness of their long lives.

Halina felt the weight of the gods' presence, their judgment, their expectations.

Or maybe that was her own and the gods were waiting to see what she would do with the riches she'd been given. Would she stop fighting? Run away? Give up on Khara, Ursinum, Quoregna? Would she disappoint her gods and her loved ones? Would she disappoint Gethen and herself?

She looked at her lover, touched his jaw, his lips. She kissed him. "You're right. We've never given up before. We won't do it now." She'd save Ilker. She'd save her kingdom, her people, and her lover. Or she'd die trying.

EPILOGUE

"Magod. Margrave of Essendra. The bastard son and heir of the duke." Halina shook her head, her expression bemused. She looked sidelong at Gethen. "You knew?"

He swallowed the bit of cheese he was eating. "That Lonan Osten was Magod's father? Of course. My parents agreed to shelter Noni and her baby when she was pregnant. She and my mother were very close." He arched a brow at Halina. "I told you some of my favorite people are bastards. It's your fault if you assumed I only meant you."

She wrinkled her nose. "But a margrave destined to become Ostendra's duke. That'll take some adjusting."

"Especially for him. But he has Arevik to help navigate court politics." He filled her glass with mead. "And he managed all my trade for a decade. Lonan's brother Kierz oversees Ostendra's defenses; I don't see that changing." He shrugged. "Only I'll be worse off. I've lost an excellent groundsman."

"Poor mage," she murmured. They sat on a balcony

breaking their fast. She looked down into the garden. "There's a much longer story behind Magod's accession."

"Yes, and I will tell it to you but not today." Gethen followed her gaze. Magod walked with Arevik, their heads close. They wore dark blue, aqua, and a soft sandy hue, the colors of Ostendra. Magod fidgeted with his cuff while he talked. Arevik laid her hand upon his to settle him.

Halina sighed. "Sad to hear of Kieran's death, though not surprising. He was reckless, on horseback, in battle, at sea." She shrugged. "I'm glad Arevik is happy with the change from him to Magod."

"They seem quite taken with each other."

"The shared ordeal at Kharaton forged a bond between them."

After King Vernard's death and at Ilker's behest, Arevik had agreed to marry the future Duke of Ostendra, thinking that man would be Kieran, Lonan's legitimate son. But Kieran had died in a fall from a horse during the time that the marriage contract was being finalized.

Gethen added, "It was fortuitous that she insisted Magod accompany her to Ostendra from Tatlis."

Halina sipped her wine, thoughtful. She lowered the glass. "He was very good to her. He protected her when I couldn't. He gave her a lot of strength that she continues to cultivate here."

Gethen glanced at the sandy-hued embroidery on the cuffs of his own borrowed dark blue surcoat. He considered Halina, her simple gown also borrowed, also the color of a white sandy beach. She wore pearls at her throat and in her loose, dark red hair. He looked at her hands, the left one with its two war-stunted fingers, the battle-scarred right one that bore the black enchanted band he'd given her. Brutal hands that dealt death.

Gentle hands that delivered pleasure. Hands of a woman, a warrior, soon a wife.

She sighed. "It's a shame we can't stay."

"I know. But we need help. Waldram's already recruiting Nalvika's scattered mages and witches to his cause."

"I think we should go east to Teleyansk and meet with their emperor." She sipped the honey-wine.

"Magod's suggestion? It's a good one; worth exploring. But it means crossing the Great Green. I have no experience sailing in open ocean. Do you?"

"We can hire an Ayestran ship and crew."

He made a dismissive "pfft" sound. "To sail for the militess and the mage who plotted to destroy Quoregna?"

Halina batted that away with her hand. "We have Lonan's support. He carries more weight than Ilker does among the islanders. Teleyansk has a large army and a larger navy. Magod and Arevik interacted with Emperor Lokshin while I was recovering at Ranith. It's said he's dangerous but not unreasonable." She tapped her fingers on the glass, squinting her eyes thoughtfully. "The East will fight for us for the right price."

"Which is?"

"Nalvik iron. Teleyansk has numbers and enthusiasm, but they lack good steel. The Boorsooks slapped them with a steep export tariff before the War of the Winds and have doubled it since. That created resentment we can use."

Gethen looked toward the distant dark-blue ocean. It was a cloudless day and seagulls rode the wind, dipping and slipping around each other, calling their joy to the sea and the sky. "There's power in the East, methods of magic I've read about, ways to harness the spirits. Ways to destroy Shemel." A knock at their chamber door interrupted their conversation.

"Yes?" she called.

"His Majesty is ready to see you," Jessavon replied from the hall.

"We'll hasten down." Halina pushed back her chair and stood. She started across the room, but Gethen caught her elbow and steered her toward the looking glass.

"Wait," he said. "I have something for you."

"Now? We shouldn't keep Ayestra's king waiting."

"It'll only take a moment." He opened a wooden chest and removed a small bundle of linen. He held it out to her.

She worried her lower lip between her teeth. "Well, it's too small to be a gown, which is probably good. We both know how hard I am on clothes."

He smirked. "It's not a dress, no." She hesitated. He prodded. "You're keeping King Danas waiting."

She stuck her tongue out at him, folded back the linen, and gasped. "How?" She lifted a long sash of blue Beseran silk. Gold embroidery glittered in the sunlight spilling through the castle's wide windows.

"I have no idea what magic the seamstresses and laundresses worked, but this was more than I expected. They cleaned as much as they could, took those pieces, repaired the embroidery, and created this." He took it, stepped behind her, and wrapped it around her waist, tying an elaborate knot at her back. The sash was long enough to trail past the hem of her borrowed dress. "I only expected to get back a ribbon to tie around your wrist."

Halina looked down at the sash. She bumped her fingers across the sol avuus at the center, the bees and liminth flowers surrounding it. She turned in his arms, grabbed him, kissed him, long, hard, deep. "Thank you," she murmured against his mouth.

Gethen pulled back, looked down at her, brushed tears

from her cheeks. "Now you look like a Beseran bride." He offered his arm.

She took it, kissed him again. "How fortunate that there's an Ayestran king in the great hall waiting to wed me to a Beseran man."

He pressed his lips to her hair. "How fortunate indeed."

ALSO BY MONICA ENDERLE PIERCE

Militess & Mage Series

The Shadow and the Sun

A Castle to Keep

To Give Her Heart (short story)

Glass and Iron Series

Girl Under Glass

The Mother Element

A Sad Jar of Atoms (short story)

Rust and Ruin (short story)

The Apocalyptics Series

Famine

Anthologies & Collections

The Dragon Chronicles

Prep For Doom

The Doomsday Chronicles

Once Upon a Time in Gravity City

ABOUT THE AUTHOR

Monica Enderle Pierce and her characters have been kicking the crap out of evil since 2012. Her first novel, *Girl Under Glass* was an Amazon Breakthrough Novel Award semi-finalist and a multi-category sci-fi bestseller. Of her dark fantasy novel, *Famine*, reviewers have said, "Jeez. Effing heck. I need more now!" And of her epic fantasy romance, *The Shadow & The Sun*, they've written, "One of the best fantasies I've read in quite some time." Her stories are filled with intrigue, love, adventure, powerful heroines, and intelligent heroes. Monica has an English literature degree from the University of California, Los Angeles. She lives in Seattle, Washington, USA, with her husband, their daughter, a neurotic dog, two crazy tomcats, and a one-eyed fish.

~

How to reach me:
monicaenderlepierce.com
monicaenderlepierce@gmail.com